THE FOREVER CRUISE

DEBORAH KLÉE

Print book ISBN: 978-1-8380804-5-7 First Printed 2022

Published by Sherman House

OTHER BOOKS BY THIS AUTHOR

The Borrowed Boy

Just Bea

For Mr Long Island

PROLOGUE

Half a day of media training had not prepared her for this. A camera flashed to the left. Then right. A bright light blinded her and she shielded her eyes. Words disjointed from sentences found their target, as questions were fired from every direction.

She cleared her throat. 'There's no cause for alarm. Halcyon Seas has temporarily lost engine power and this has affected communications.'

The level of noise rose significantly. 'Outrage.' 'Incompetence.' 'Disaster.' The reporters were after a sensational story.

'One question at a time,' the press liaison said with authority.

It was the relatives she felt sorry for. They weren't getting a chance to ask their questions.

'Carolyn Stanton. The Telegraph. Halcyon Seas is drifting in the Indian Ocean. What is her expected course? And what action has been taken to tow her to safety, given the danger of entering unsafe waters?'

'Halcyon Seas had left Seychelles and was headed for South

Africa when Captain Moore reported a loss of engine power. Sea conditions were moderate giving us no cause for concern. It's routine for tow boats to be sent from the nearest port to assist a ship with engine failure.'

'So, you don't know where she is, or where she's headed, since losing power more than twenty-four hours ago?'

The noise in the room grew. Anger. Distress. The roar of a wounded animal. She wanted to reassure the relatives to tell them everything was under control, but she couldn't. Not yet.

Let the relatives speak, she wrote in a note to the press liaison. He nodded.

'Fiona Hardy. Travel and Cruise. Halcyon Seas has been branded as an innovative concept in retirement living. What measures were taken to protect these vulnerable, older people from the risks associated with cruising?'

'The residents of Halcyon Seas are no more at risk than the guests of any cruise ship. If anything, they are better cared for as our staff have come to know them well and can anticipate and respond to individual needs.'

'Did you anticipate how they would survive on a ship without power, drifting for days in the Indian Ocean?'

Bursts of light around the room. Flash. Flash. It was hot with so many people crammed together. She held the desk for support.

'Adrian Buckley. Daily Mail. In 2021, a Turkish ship was hijacked by pirates just off the coast of Nigeria. The first thing the pirates did was disable most of the ship's systems. Have you considered that this ship of pensioners has been taken hostage by buccaneering pirates?'

The sensational headline had obviously been written already, with no evidence to support it. 'No, we have not, because that is highly unlikely.' Would it be inappropriate to laugh? To make light of it? Of course, it was preposterous.

'Let's take some questions from family and friends.' Press liaison came to the rescue.

'Kate Flynn. My brother and friend are on the ship.' The woman's voice warbled with nerves or emotion. 'I've been following social media… trying to find out. An announcement was made *Safe Haven*. I looked this up. It means pirate attack.'

The room fell silent.

1

TEN MONTHS BEFORE

Alice Wagstaff gasped for breath. Breathe. Deep breaths. But her body wasn't listening. Her fingers tingled and she felt as though her knees might give way. Less than twenty minutes to get on the connecting train to London. Or she could cross the platform and go back the way she had come. Back to her bungalow in Norfolk where there was nothing and nobody to disturb her.

Get a grip, Alice, you can do this. Kate, her old school friend, was having a surprise 70th birthday party in a hotel at Canary Wharf. How would she explain her absence? Worse – what would her daughter Rachel say if she admitted defeat? I told you so – that's what she would say. Her breath had slowed a little and although her heart was still racing, she felt a little steadier. Alice checked the printed travel route crumpled in her hand. Platform four. She still had fifteen minutes to get on the train to London.

. . .

'I've missed you,' Kate shouted above the music – a band of older musicians with a young female singer. 'If you lived in London we could meet for the occasional lunch.'

Alice sipped her Pornstar Martini. A pretty pink with a slice of passion fruit floating on top. It was nectar. Kate threw back her shot of Prosecco, reminding Alice that one had been served with the creamy cocktail. This is perfect, Alice thought, as she started to feel a little fuzzy around the edges and she remembered Rachel's first Barbie doll. Pretty in Pink. 'Rachel's trying to persuade me to move closer to her in Bethnal Green.'

'Good for her. I don't know why you moved out to the sticks in the first place.'

'It was right at the time. Tom loved living there.'

Kate put her hand over Alice's. 'We all miss him.'

'Maybe we should have made more of an effort to become part of the community – joined clubs or something. I didn't really think about life after Tom.'

Kate snorted. 'You could join the W.I.'

'Every time I visit the post office the woman behind the counter suggests I join. That or a knitting group. There's even a friendship group for no-mates like me.' Alice took a slug of her cocktail.

'In London, you would have the theatre, art galleries, a Freedom Pass to use on public transport.'

Alice knew that Kate was right. The quiet cul-de-sac of bungalows was perfect nine years ago but in the five years since Tom died, it had felt like God's waiting room.

'I was just telling Alice that she should move back to London,' Kate said to her brother Gideon when he joined their table.

'I don't think the East End's ready for the two of you.

Kate's bad enough on her own. Talking of which, I came to refill the birthday girl's glass. Another Pornstar, ladies?'

Kate waggled her eyebrows at Alice. 'I'm game if you are.'

'It seems a bit decadent. But this cocktail is heaven. I'm tempted to have another.'

'Go for it, Alice. It's a special occasion. I have plans to completely indulge myself. Cocktails at sundown, a different destination every day.'

'Are you going on a cruise?'

'He's signed up for this forever cruise package. You know - retirement living but on a cruise ship.'

Gideon rubbed his hands together. 'What a life. Everything that you need to live well. All of your meals provided. Staff tending to your every need and you get to see the world.'

'Isn't it expensive?'

'If you do the sums, it works out cheaper than a care home, not that any of us are anywhere near that stage of life, but a great way to live from – say … seventy, to the end of your days, whenever that might be. If you have a decent home to sell, it's affordable. Okay, nothing to leave as an inheritance but better to spend your money on living the good life than throwing it away on ludicrous care home fees. Let me get you another Pornstar.'

'That's adventurous of him.' Comparing herself to Gideon, Alice couldn't believe he was only five years younger than her. If only she had a little of his courage. 'Your baby brother is still a looker.' They watched Gideon's slow progress across the room as one woman after another intercepted him with a kiss or a hug. 'I remember you having status as Gideon Flynn's sister.'

'It was a nightmare. All of those lovelorn girls trying to befriend me, hoping to get an introduction to my rock star brother.'

'Did his fame ever extend beyond Bow?'

'Absolutely. Bow, Bethnal Green, Hackney. Do you remember that gig in Canning Town?'

'The one where we got talked into serving behind the bar?'

'Yes. How did that happen? I remember there were lots of gangster types. I don't think we got paid. I always felt responsible for my little brother. He got himself into some questionable situations. We were probably serving behind the bar that night to get him out of trouble.'

Alice laughed. 'I know what you mean. He may be sixty-four but to me he will always be your annoying little brother.'

'Believe me – he's still annoying. A great dad though.' Kate nodded to where Gideon was now sitting opposite a young woman, their heads bent together. 'That's his daughter Paige. She's having problems at work. His girls rely too heavily on him. To be honest, I think he's a bit of a soft touch where they are concerned. Paige has him around her little finger.'

'What about their mum?'

'The marriage didn't work out but they split amicably. His ex lives in Spain. They jointly own and manage a restaurant there. It doesn't look as though he's going to get our drinks.'

'I'll go.'

'No. Let's dance.' Kate pulled Alice to her feet.

'Brown Sugar,' Alice yelled as the band played the opening to their favourite Stones song. She kicked off her shoes and boogied with Kate to the dance floor. Dancers parted to welcome the birthday girl and her friend. Alice danced with abandon – throwing her arms wide, then above her head, twirling, jumping, laughing. They were ageless. Free spirits. Children of the sixties, born to rock. Alice's children, Rachel and David, were old beyond their years. They didn't know how to have fun.

Alice was taking a break from dancing to cool down when an announcement was made by the female singer.

'Sorry to interrupt. I have an announcement to make.'

The birthday speeches had finished some time ago, Alice wondered if there was another surprise for Kate. Everyone was waiting to see what it could be.

'Would Alice Wagstaff please make her way to the foyer where her daughter is waiting for her?'

There was a cheer from the crowd and then the singer introduced the next number. Alice felt like a teenager humiliated in front of her friends. It was only… oh dear, twelve-twenty. She had agreed to meet Rachel at twelve. Why couldn't the silly girl just come in and say hello to Kate?

'I'm sorry you have to leave so early,' Kate said, kissing her goodbye.

Alice, always in bed by nine-thirty, didn't consider it early but it looked as if the party was far from over. 'I just have to find my bag.'

'Do you want me to go and tell Rachel?'

'No, it's fine. I've probably left it at the table.'

Fifteen minutes later, someone found her bag in the ladies, where she must have abandoned it after reapplying her lipstick. Rachel was not amused.

2

Marianne Moore had finally got the summons. She was going to captain a cruise ship. It had taken six years of study, a master's degree in engineering, ten years' experience obtaining a license, and a further five working as a staff captain. If only her father was alive to hear the news. He always believed in her. From the day he told her she could be anything that she wanted to be. 'I want to sail around the world and be captain of the ship,' six-year-old Marianne had said. That was all she had ever wanted to do.

Marianne checked her appearance in the mirror – smart but glamorous. She had a penchant for very high stiletto heels. In the years that she worked as a ship's engineer, Marianne liked to indulge her femininity and the habit had stayed with her. She applied a vibrant lipstick and pouted at her reflection. Not just gorgeous – she was about to become a ship's captain. She waved her arms and swayed her hips. 'I've finally done it, Dad. Captain Marianne Moore.' She hoped that she would be allocated The Royal Ionian's biggest, newest ship but that was unlikely. Still, no harm in aiming for the moon. Wasn't that what she had always done?

Counting Crow's *American Girls* blasted from the speakers of her BMW sports car, as Marianne took the coast road. It was too early in the year to have the roof down but Marianne was bursting with energy and needed the open top or she might just combust. Her long blond hair caught in the breeze and she swept it off her face. *Captain Marianne Moore. Woo Hoo!* She pulled into the staff car park, changed trainers for stilettos, slung her discarded shoes onto the back seat, and tamed her windswept hair.

The glass-fronted building, home to the executive team of The Royal Ionian, was one that Marianne had visited on previous occasions, mostly for interviews. She checked her letter again just in case she had misread it. No, it definitely said that she was being offered the position of captain. A Libby Braithwaite, Chief Operating Officer, had signed the letter, a name unfamiliar to Marianne.

'If you wait over there, someone will come down to take you upstairs,' the receptionist said.

A captain Marianne recognised came out of a lift and was about to walk by when he caught sight of her, or rather her stilettos, and then his eyes slid up her uniform to her blonde mane. 'Marianne. Good to see you.'

She stood up so that she was looking down rather than up. This captain had once been her junior. 'Gary,' she nodded.

They were saved from an awkward exchange by a woman coming to claim her. 'Miss Moore?'

'We must catch up sometime,' Gary said, and Marianne followed her escort into the lift.

A woman in her forties and a heavy-set man with a florid face sat behind an enormous oak desk with a green inlay – Libby Braithwaite and Patrick Dunn. They were not forthcoming about their roles and were a bit evasive when Marianne asked outright.

'We'll come to that when we explain the setup. It's complicated. Tell us first about your experience.'

As Marianne talked through her resume, she felt Patrick's scrutiny. They had her CV in front of them, so she wasn't telling them anything new. Maybe they were interested in how she presented herself. Marianne delivered her CV as if she was auditioning for Hollywood. When she had finished, Patrick nodded enthusiastically. 'I think that you will be perfect.'

That was all they wanted from her? It was a bit different to the other five captain interviews she had endured. The thought *Why* had come into her head but she had batted it back, not wanting the thought goblins to rain on her parade.

Marianne beamed. 'Thank you. Can you tell me which ship I will be captaining and when we are due to set sail?'

'Halcyon Seas. She leaves Florida on 7th March. It's an exciting new venture for us all,' Libby said.

'I haven't heard of Halcyon Seas. Is she a new addition to The Royal Ionian?' Marianne couldn't believe her good fortune, a brand-new ship. They must hold her in much higher regard than she realised.

Patrick grinned at Libby. 'The first ship in a new fleet.'

Marianne was confused, she'd never heard of a new Jamboree cruise line. 'A new fleet?'

'Sorry, I should have explained from the outset. This is a completely new venture. Ground-breaking. It is, you understand, commercially sensitive. Patrick and I have got so used to talking in code, making sure no information gets out, that we didn't even tell you – the captain of our first ship. This is so exciting.' Libby paused to take a sip of water.

'I thought you represented The Royal Ionian.'

'We are part of the Jamboree group but Silver Seas is a new line, jointly owned by Jamboree and McIntyre Retirement Living USA. The first cruise ship to offer a retirement home for the over fifties. Halcyon Seas is a small ship, nothing like the size of The Royal Ionian cruise ships. Full capacity is 148 passengers but we are making all of the cabins single occupancy except for couples, so it is more likely to be sixty to seventy residents.'

A lump formed in Marianne's throat. She was being fobbed off with a freakin' retirement home. Of course, she was perfect – she was a woman! They were fucking well signing her up as a care home manager. She clenched her teeth.

'You would have all the usual captain duties,' Libby said, perhaps reading Marianne's face; she had never been good at hiding her emotions. 'It would be no different really.'

'Why did you think I was perfect for the job?'

Libby and Patrick shuffled their papers and studied their notes.

'You were recommended to us by the Chief Operating Officer of The Royal Ionian. He said that you were overdue for being appointed to captain through no fault of your own. Apparently, the right opportunity had not come up until now.' Libby had the grace to look apologetic.

So, she was being tossed from one cruise line to another. A castoff. 'Obviously, this isn't what I was expecting. I would have to think it over.'

'Marianne. *Captain Moore.* This is an opportunity for you to prove yourself as captain. It may be the first retirement cruise ship but the way this industry is going, it is likely to lead the way for many more. In a few years most cruise ships will be retirement homes. Let's face it, our demographic has always been the over fifties. It is the perfect solution for later life.'

Patrick chipped in. 'Retirement living complexes have not had the take up we anticipated, especially in the UK. This is a win-win for the cruise industry, for retirement living, and for older people. So many selling points. The families do not have to visit but will know their loved ones are being taken care of and have a good quality of life. It costs no more than living in a care home. And our existing retirement complexes can be sold off to a developer at a time when housing is in short supply.'

'The cruise industry is quite frankly in decline. The chief accounting officer and CEO of Jamboree have great expectations of this venture – another reason why you should seriously consider taking up our offer.'

Marianne knew that she would accept the job, although she let them sweat a bit longer. Eventually, when she had negotiated 10k more on the annual salary, Marianne signed a contract. Maybe she should have waited until they had discussed the set up some more but it seemed that Libby and Patrick were reluctant to share any details until she had not only signed the contract but a confidentiality clause, too.

'All of the communications are being carefully managed by Jamboree. You must not share any information on social media, unless approved by head office.'

'What kind of information?' Marianne had never been restricted in the past and enjoyed sharing information about each cruise with friends, family and her Instagram followers.

'The model of operation, costings, and certainly no bad press – at all. This cruise has to be a success. Jamboree and McIntyre have a lot invested – not just finances. We will corner the market for over fifties as a lifestyle choice.'

'You must have shared some information with the public, and what about the crew?'

Patrick answered that one. 'The marketing team has done a

good job; we already have forty residents signed up. The crew was carefully selected and trained long in advance.'

'The cruise industry is aware of this development. All eyes are on us. Communications have prepared press releases to go out in February. Now, we need to talk through your induction and preparation before Halcyon Seas sets sail,' Libby said.

She drove home with the roof on. No music. Maybe it wasn't all bad. Maybe this would be her opportunity to show Jamboree what she was capable of. Not just Jamboree. If this venture had stimulated as much interest in the industry as Libby claimed, then she would make her name. There would be the opportunity for media interviews once the world knew retirement cruising was the way of the future. Marianne was determined to make this cruise a success. In a year she would have her pick of jobs as captain. She just had to use this opportunity to showcase her unique combination of skills and attributes, gained over the past two decades as a captain in training. It was a small ship with a high profile. There was very little chance of anything untoward happening. It was going to be a walk in the park and next year she would have the job she had always dreamed of.

3

Olivia was dizzy from dancing – the balls of her feet blistered, and intoxicated with the sheer magnificence of her life. Raf caught her hand as she twirled and pulled her to him.

'You're leaving tomorrow.' His voice was plaintive. They had known from the beginning that their relationship couldn't last but that didn't make parting any easier. 'Let's get out of here. Spend the last few hours alone.'

Her flight to Madagascar was early the next morning and Olivia doubted that she would get any sleep. In the past six months she had made friends with people from all over the world. For a girl from a sparsely populated village on the southwest coast of Madagascar, Miami, with its audacious white buildings towering higher than any baobab tree, twenty-four-hour noise and bright lights, was like a film set. And she, Olivia Rose, the heroine. 'First, I must say goodbye to everyone.'

Raf screwed up his face. 'You'll be seeing most of them

again on Halcyon Seas but who knows when we will be together again.'

He was right. The six-month training programme was for scholarship students selected for a new venture, a retirement home cruise ship, Halcyon Seas. They would set sail in four weeks. 'I wish you were sailing with us.'

'I wish you could stay here with me until your ship leaves.' This was a discussion that had been repeated almost every day since Olivia announced that she was going home for the month before sailing.

'Let's make the most of our last night together,' she whispered and gently kissed the side of his mouth. She could feel the muscles on his face twitch as though between a smile and tears.

They strolled along the beach from Ocean Drive to South Beach holding hands. In the other hand, Olivia dangled a pair of strappy sandals and enjoyed the feeling of cool, soft sand massaging the soles of her feet. In the distance, the cruise ships lined up on Dodge Island resembled a city. Neither said a word. There was nothing else to say.

She had met Raf in her first week, when they had arrived together dragging suitcases and trepidation. Like college kids away from home for the first time, they had bonded. Just friends at first. Raf's accommodation was in a different block. If they hadn't met at the registration desk, it was unlikely that their paths would have crossed. Raf was training as a cocktail waiter and bar manager. He would work on regular cruise ships. No scholarship for Raf, he was smart and came from an affluent American family. A long baleful sound – the trumpet from a jazz band – haunted the night like the cry of an Indie lemur and Olivia shivered.

Raf put his arm around her. 'Stay with me tonight.'

She would have to leave in six hours to catch her flight. 'Won't that make it harder?'

'How could it be any harder than it already is? I love you, Olivia. I can't bear the thought of never seeing you again.' He held her in the circle of his arms and gazed into her eyes. 'There must be something we can do to stay together. To make this work.'

She loved him too. It was impossible not to love Raf. He was kind, funny, handsome, and had become her best friend. But they were from different worlds. She had to be strong, to protect him from his spontaneity, his generous spirit and romantic notions. Raf belonged with a rich American girl. He was destined to become a cruise director. She was lucky to get a job as a cleaner in what was really an old people's home. If Raf saw her village, he would be shocked at how her family lived. It was best just to keep the memory of him. A miraculous gift that was part of this incredible dream life with which she had been blessed. 'If we are meant to be together it will happen. Let's not make any plans. Just see where the tide takes us.'

'I don't want you to go.' Raf dropped kisses on and around her mouth like butterflies settling then taking flight.

'My bags are packed and so I could ...'

Raf didn't wait for her to finish the sentence. He grabbed her hand and ran along the sand whooping. He was too fast for Olivia. She let go and gasped for breath. Raf ran for a few seconds and then slowed to a stroll. Watching him, Olivia tried to imagine his life without her, to see him as separate as if she was already sailing away. *No,* she wanted to scream. Her head might talk sense but her heart would break when they had to say goodbye. She ran after him and flung her arms around his back. Raf hoisted her up into a piggy-back and they circled the beach, shrieking like children. Olivia started to slide down Raf's back. He threw himself onto the sand, taking her with him. They lay, legs entwined, looking up into the night sky.

'You see that constellation, there?' Raf pointed.

'The Little Bear?'

'Or Little Dipper. Anyway, just below that string of stars, there...'

'The North Star?'

'Yes, Miss Know-it-all, The North Star. When we are apart, that is where I'll meet you. Wherever we are in the world, that same star will be above us both. So, look for it and think of me and I'll do the same – I'll think of you.'

They kissed. At first, it was a sad kiss, full of longing and regret, but as his tongue flicked against hers, a passion stirred that had to be spent. She broke away, her heart racing, 'Your place or mine?'

They lay together on his bed watching the sunrise. 'Do you really, really, have to go?' he said again.

Olivia replied with a gentle kiss. 'I'm going to miss you as much as you will miss me.'

'That is not possible.' He kissed her again. 'I'll see you when you return to Miami to board your ship?'

'I think it's better we don't see each other again. It will only make this harder.'

'You can't stop me from waving at Halcyon Seas when she sets sail.'

'I will probably be busy and won't even see you but you're right, I can't stop you.' Secretly, Olivia was pleased. She knew that she would scan every face on the harbour until she found him.

'I know you think I will forget you but I promise I won't, Olivia. You are my one and only. My North Star.'

'You are full of crap.' Olivia laughed, proud of her American speak.

'It doesn't sound right when you say that,' Raf teased her. 'I might be full of crap most of the time but not when it comes to you.'

'I have to go. Now. Really. Let go of me, Raf.'

He rolled away from her and watched as she dressed. 'Can I see you off at the airport?'

'Best not. I'll remember you lying here in bed with your beautiful sleepy eyes.'

When she closed the door of his dorm Olivia felt as though she had shut down her heart. She could never have Raf but there would be no one else for her. Maybe a suitable match found by her parents but Raf would always be her true love.

4

Lying in bed with a hangover, Alice kept out of Greg's way as he prepared to leave for work. In the five and a half years that Rachel and Greg had been together, Alice had not formed a relationship with him. She had tried but he always seemed a little aloof, talking to her as though she were one of his insurance customers. His son Alfie was a good kid. Polite but shy. In fairness, Alice had only stayed in their Bethnal Green home three or four times and Greg never joined Rachel on her rare visits to Norfolk.

'I won't be back for dinner,' she heard Greg say.

'Why?' Rachel had left the kitchen to stand at the bottom of the stairs, calling up to Greg, who was now on the upstairs landing. Alice heard him mumble something under his breath.

'Playing squash.'

'I'll leave something out for you.'

Greg thumped down the stairs. 'Don't bother. I'll get something while I'm out.'

The front door slammed and they were alone. Alice waited until enough time had passed for it not to seem obvious that she was waiting for him to leave and then crept down the stairs, careful not to jolt her delicate head.

Rachel was sitting at the table working on a Sudoku. She jumped up when Alice walked in. 'What would you like for breakfast, Mummy? Bacon and eggs? An omelette? Home-made yogurt with berries and homemade granola?' Rachel beamed when she gave the last option, as though she were seven years old again, presenting her mum with breakfast in bed – then it had been tea made with cold water, and uncooked Pop Tarts.

'Just a strong coffee please, darling.' Rachel looked disappointed. 'Well, maybe just a spoonful of your homemade yoghurt.' The thought of it turned Alice's stomach but she could always tip it into the bin unobserved.

'I've added some linseed, blueberries and banana. You don't want to come over faint on your way home.'

Alice's heart started to palpitate and she felt a cold clamminess on her back and under her arms. She used Rachel's Sudoku to fan herself. 'Hot flush,' she lied.

'Here, have some water.' Rachel slid a glass across the table to her. 'Eat up.'

Alice toyed with the glob in her bowl. She would be on the loo all morning if she attempted to eat all of that fibre. 'What are you eating, darling?'

'I had breakfast with Greg.'

Alice could see no evidence of breakfast things, no scent of toast, just the clean smell of detergent. 'I'm sorry I missed him. I hope we didn't wake him when we got back last night.'

Rachel left the table to tidy and wipe over her already scrupulously clean worktops. 'No, he sleeps soundly. But he said hi.' Alice doubted that to be true.

While Rachel's back was turned, she pretended to study

yesterday's paper from a recycle pile and then tipped the contents of her bowl onto the centre pages.

'Really, Mummy, the state you were in when I collected you from Canary Wharf. Kate has always led you astray. Don't you think it a little unseemly at your age?'

Alice folded up the paper with more force than she intended. When yoghurt started to ooze from the sides, she bundled it into her bag. 'Interesting article. I'll read it on the way home.'

'Oh, about that. I'll drop you off at Liverpool Street. There's somewhere I want to take you first.'

Alice dreaded to think where that might be. A correction centre for delinquent pensioners. 'What makes you think Kate led me astray? I seem to remember that I was the ringleader of our misadventures at school.'

Rachel sighed. 'That's it. At school. Honestly, Mummy, you and Kate can be a little silly when you get together.'

'So where is it you want to take me?'

'Wait and see. Just keep an open mind.'

Wait and see was what Alice had said to the children when they were small and asked what was for dessert. It usually meant, I don't know but there's a tin of prunes and one of rice pudding in the back of the cupboard. Alice hoped that Rachel's surprise was more exciting than prunes and rice pudding but her gut was telling her otherwise – unless that was the after-effects of Pornstar Martinis and this morning's breakfast, which was probably now seeping through the contents of her bag.

Rachel checked her watch. 'There. It only took fifteen minutes to drive here from my house.'

Outside Chestnut Court, *Thoughtfully designed apartments*

with assisted living options for the over 60s, there were images of glamorous people in their prime, one relaxing with a book, a couple sipping wine and a group of friends laughing together. The advertising was more fitting to a cruise ship than what Alice guessed was behind the doors of the white building with its cheery flag. Gideon had made a good point last night about the cost of his forever cruise, compared to that of a care home. Rachel must really think she had lost it, to be suggesting this.

'I don't know why you've brought me here. I'm sixty-nine, not ninety.'

'You know why. Since Daddy died, you've stopped going out or seeing anyone. It's been five years, Mummy.'

'I know exactly how long it's been.' Alice felt the familiar stab to her heart. 'How do you know what I do with myself? I don't tell you everything when you phone me *once a week.*'

'And that's the other reason. You live too far away. What if you have a fall or become seriously ill?'

Alice harrumphed. She had tripped on a paving slab in the garden last summer. When did falling over become *having a fall*? 'It's not just people over fifty who fall over. You had a fall yourself a couple of years ago and as I recall broke your leg.'

'Skiing, Mummy, that's hardly the same thing.' Rachel was getting out of the car. The discussion was obviously over and Alice was expected to follow.

When she was satisfied that Alice had entered the building, Rachel darted off in search of Malcolm, a salesman she had apparently arranged to meet. There was no need, as Alice had absolutely no intention of being incarcerated within these floral walls.

'Sit down, love and I'll get you a nice cup of tea.'

Alice turned, expecting to see a dithery old lady, and then

she realised the young woman was talking to her. 'No thank you.' She straightened her back and gave what she hoped was a formidable stare. It had worked on the children when they were small. 'If you could just send me in the same direction as my daughter?'

As she tried to find Rachel, a woman with wild hair and a vacant stare ambled toward Alice. 'Bobby will be getting off the bus. I've got to meet him.'

Alice avoided eye contact and tried to pass by but the woman grabbed her arm. 'Where's the bus? I'm going to be late.'

'Don't worry, we've another thirty minutes. Plenty of time.'

The woman nodded and Alice was glad that she had lifted the woman's anxiety for at least a few seconds. Her aunt had dementia and Alice had learnt to go along with things. As she turned into another corridor, she could hear the woman's plaintive cry. 'Where's Bobby's bus? He'll think I've forgotten him.'

'Joanie, what are you doing down here? Let's get you back upstairs.'

Alice's heart went out to Joanie, lost in a world where nothing made sense. But it would drive her mad to live here. Where the hell was Rachel? She marched along the corridor and turned into another one. They all looked the same. A man and a woman with walkers were heading in her direction. A person in a wheelchair was coming from the other direction. She had to get out of there. It was too hot. Airless. She squeezed past the wheelchair, taking in the swollen purple feet that burst out of ill-fitting slippers, the catheter bag hung from the side of the chair. She didn't look at the person, didn't know whether it was a woman or a man – she just had to get out. Where was the reception area? Alice's heart raced as she took one turn and then another. It felt as though she were burrowing deeper and deeper into oblivion. A place with no sun. No joy. No hope.

'Steady, love. Hold on to the rail and I'll come and get you.' The woman's voice was kind but it made Alice more anxious. She didn't belong here.

A chair was pushed against the back of her knees and Alice collapsed into it. Cold sweat trickled down her spine.

'Deep breaths.'

'Mummy!'

Alice couldn't see past the carer who was watching over her. She struggled to her feet, ignoring her wobbly legs. 'I'm fine. Just having a rest after walking the length of this place trying to find you.'

The carer squeezed her arm and then slipped away, leaving Alice to face Rachel and a skinny man with a simpering smile.

'This must be Mum.'

'Mrs. Wagstaff,' Alice said through gritted teeth.

'This is what I mean, Malcolm,' Rachel said in a stage whisper. 'She gets these panic attacks. I don't like her being alone.'

'It's just a hot flush. It doesn't help that this place is like a sauna. I just need some fresh air.'

'Then you must come and see the show flat to access our lovely communal garden, Mum.' He took hold of Alice's elbow.

'Take your hands off me. I'm not your mother.'

'Mummy, don't be rude. I'm sorry Malcolm.'

'Don't worry. We have all sorts here. Mrs. Wagstaff, your daughter would like you to view the retirement flats for independent living. Aren't you lucky to have such a caring daughter, with an eye for a good deal? These flats are selling like hot cakes. I'm sure you won't be disappointed.'

Alice wanted to tell him where he could stick his hot cakes but she knew Rachel and there was no way they would leave until Alice had gone through the motions. She took a deep breath. 'Then lead the way.'

Rachel beamed. 'I know you will love it, Mummy.'

The show flat was beautifully presented. Small. A kitchenette, a sad-looking table for one with a solitary dining chair – this was positioned by the patio door which led into the communal garden – and a two-piece suite. A bedroom and a bathroom came off the main living space. Alice peeked into the bathroom. She was horrified to see a frame around the toilet and a plastic chair on wheels.

'Getting in and out of the bath is a challenge for most of our residents. We find a wet room is the perfect solution.'

'What do you think, Mummy?'

Rachel didn't wait for a response; she and Malcolm were cosying up, talking about the price of property. Alice opened her bag and tipped the yogurt-oozing newspaper into the bin. That's what she thought.

'It's all wonderful, darling, but we've taken up enough of Mr. Malcolm's time. I'll give it some thought.'

This seemed to do the trick, as Rachel and the slimy salesman walked to the door, holding it open for Alice. 'Lovely,' she said, hoping that would put an end to the nonsense.

Rachel made encouraging remarks as she drove Alice to the station. If she had the energy, Alice would have argued that she was too young and able to give up her independence and move into what was a care home – the show flat had not convinced her otherwise. But she needed all of her energy to calm herself for the journey home. So she concentrated on her breathing and blocked out the sound of Rachel's voice.

On the platform, Rachel said, 'Now, are you sure you're going to be alright getting home, Mummy? I've ordered your cab the other end. Just one change at Norwich. I've written it all down here.'

Rachel was a good daughter, despite being bossy. She just wanted to keep her mother safe and well. It was Alice's fault, giving her cause for concern.

'I'll be fine, darling. Thank you for looking after me.'

'So, you'll have a good look at the brochures? With Daddy's pension, and your investments, you may not need to sell the bungalow. But you heard what Malcolm said, they're selling fast.'

Alice nodded and kissed her goodbye.

The train pulled out of Liverpool Street Station and Alice relaxed into her seat. As the train rumbled and lurched, she closed her eyes and relived the party – dancing with Kate, sipping cocktails. She was *that* person, not a timid old lady in need of care. And yet, she was letting fear reduce her world in ever-decreasing circles – the bungalow and handkerchief garden might as well be her prison. It was self-inflicted but could she break free? Last week, the thought of travelling to London had terrified her but she had overcome that fear and was so glad that she had. If she didn't take control, then she couldn't complain if Rachel did what she thought best for her mother.

Outside, a woman was hurrying up the stairs dragging a folded pushchair, a baby under one arm. Alice willed her to reach the platform before the train pulled out. The guard was about to blow his whistle. He hadn't seen her. Then, she was on the platform – in a few seconds she would be on the train. She did it. Alice watched as she stored the pushchair and then collapsed into the seat opposite, a look of triumph on her flushed face. Alice had once managed two small children under five. Then, she had that same courage and determination. It was still there, she just had to dig deep to find it.

Alice wiped a glob of yogurt from her phone. There was no harm in asking for more information. She tapped in a message to Gideon and then sat back and closed her eyes. By the time he responded, she would have lost her nerve.

Ping. A message came by return. *Fantastic. Here's a link to find out more. Let me know what you decide. Gideon.*

Alice felt a flutter of excitement around her sternum. She pressed the link and her screen filled with the image of a majestic white ship. It was tempting. An impossible dream to see the world. For that beautiful ship to be her home – her forever home. A forever cruise. Could she? Dare she? The young woman opposite grinned at Alice, and she realised that she had been smiling. Why not? Life was too short to waste any more precious time.

5

Below, the ground resembled an elephant's hide – parched and cracked. But even then, it was beautiful from up there with its soft red glow, as though the land had been rubbed with henna. As the plane came to land, sprinkles of green became forests and baobab trees welcomed Olivia Rose home. Her eyes felt gritty, dried by artificial air and staying open for too long.

'Please fasten your seat belts as we are preparing to land.'

There was a collective murmur of anticipation and relief. It was a small plane; people from Malatanga rarely travelled by air and it wasn't a place for tourists. The other passengers were mostly male – businessmen, maybe a few students who had escaped like her into the big wide world and were doing a duty trip home. This one-hour flight from the capital, Antananarivo, Tana for short, completed what had been forty-eight hours of travel. The plane landed with a thud and juddered along the runway, which felt as though it were filled with potholes.

Her brother, Pascal, was one of a dozen people waiting to

greet passengers in arrivals. He was the only one not holding up a sign with a name. Olivia threw back her shoulders and tried to look cool but when Pascal grinned, she ran to him, pushing past the men in long trousers.

'Hey. Lookin' mean,' he said.

They hugged and Olivia smelt the island: baked earth and wood smoke. Nothing in Florida had smelt so good. She was home.

The truck bounced along the dirt road, leaving behind a scatter of shanty towns and a few terraces of rice that had survived the drought. Ahead of them children and women crammed together in the back of an open truck around a cage of chickens.

'How about the food in the States? Did you eat ice cream?'

'Ice-cream. Gateaux. Pancakes with bacon and maple syrup. There's so much food. You can eat anything, anytime. As much as you want. Our cruises have *Eat as much as you want* buffets with every kind of food. Things I'd never seen before.'

'Mamma is roasting anything in sight. Word must have got around because anyone who can use a spear or sling-shot has been visiting with an offering. Pappa has invited the whole village to welcome you home and celebrate your success.'

'I daren't imagine what delights have been offered up for roasting. So long as there are no rats.'

'I knew America would turn your head. Make you too high and mighty to enjoy barbequed rats.' Pascal laughed.

'I can't wait to see Mamma and Pappa. How are Gracie, Jay Jim, Samuel, and Kanto?'

Pascal was still chuckling at his joke. He slowed down behind an ox-driven cart piled high with bundles of fodder. 'I hope you've brought back some Western glamour for Gracie, your life in America is all she talks about. She thinks that you are living with Rachel and Phoebe from Friends. Jay Jim has been working on the fishing boat with me – early morning shifts, and then helping Pappa in the shop.'

'He ought to be in school. He's only ten.' Jay Jim had been working since he was seven, although Mamma insisted all of the children studied for an hour every day. Olivia and Pascal benefitted from the tutoring of their French grandmother, who was an intelligent woman. She would have been so proud of her Olive Oyl, as she called Olivia, after Popeye's girlfriend.

They overtook the cart and the driver waved.

'Kanto and Samuel are excited about the party.'

'Not about seeing me?'

Pascal laughed. 'I don't think they know what to make of you. You've been gone for what's a big proportion of their lives if you think about it. You've barely seen them in eighteen months and at six and seven that's a long time. Kanto asked me if you were a saint. I think she was confused because Mamma has your photo in her little shrine and mentions you in her prayers every day.'

'But she does know I'm her big sister?'

'Yeah – but I guess *you are* some kind of a saint.' Olivia thumped him.

It made her sad to think that she had missed so much of Kanto's and Samuel's lives. It wasn't as if they could keep in touch by Zoom. There was an old computer in Pappa's store which villagers occasionally paid to use, sometimes in exchange for a cassava or small bird, and Pascal had a smartphone, but despite the family's pride in having access to this technology, Olivia realised now it was outdated.

The further they drove from Malatanga, the quieter the road. No more trucks or carts carrying wares to and from the market. Even the trees had become scarce. In front, behind, and all around, there was nothing but parched earth. The road ahead was distorted by a heat haze. Olivia felt her eyes become heavy.

The truck hit a pothole and Olivia jolted awake. Ahead of them, a bridge crossed a dry river. Three skinny cows and a cluster of half-naked children seemed to have found some water. Pascal drove over the bridge and Olivia twisted in her seat willing them to succeed. The tallest, a boy, held aloft a tin can as though offering thanks, or maybe it was a plea. 'Has the drought been bad?'

'Yes. One of the worst in years. But it can't go on, we're bound to get rain soon.'

They were getting close to their village now and Olivia's heart was full to burst. A couple of men working in a field of red and gold sorghum – a cereal that could grow with little water – waved and Pascal tooted his horn. Baobab trees towered above them, like friendly giants welcoming her home.

'I'll take you to Pappa first as I've got to return the truck.'

Olivia couldn't get there quickly enough. She sat on the edge of her seat drinking in the sights, sounds, and smells of home: salty sea, rotting fish, and bonfires. Cattle lowing. Children laughed and shouted as they ran alongside the truck. Pascal turned off the main road and they bumped across a track between dwellings made from bamboo.

Pappa came out of his shop and stood in the centre of the road to greet them. He feigned a coolness, reprimanding Pascal for taking too long, but Olivia felt his love and as soon as her feet were on the ground, she threw herself into his arms.

'Our Olive Oyl has returned from the big city. Let me look at you.' He held her at arm's length and smiled approvingly. 'What would you like to drink? Sit down. I'll bring you a Pepsi Cola.' He indicated that she should sit in one of the two plastic chairs outside his shop.

'I'll come and sit here another day. First, I want to see Mammon and the children.' Olivia knew that her pappa wanted to show her off to his friends. To boast about her success.

'Sit anyway. I have to fetch some things from the store for Mammon. Every day there is something else that she wants for this big party.'

Olivia's heart sank. All she wanted to do was hug her family and then curl up on a mattress and sleep for a week. 'How big?'

Pascal laughed. 'The whole village. Maybe the neighbouring ones too.'

Later that evening, Olivia leant against her mamma, enjoying the patter of Malagasy and the flicker of flames from a fire. The villagers had brought all sorts of meat to share, quails, enrec, and a chameleon, which was proudly presented in honour of her homecoming.

'Your grand-mammon is so proud of you,' her mammon whispered into her hair.

'I know. I wish she had lived long enough to hear about my scholarship.'

'Our ancestors know the joy you have brought us. They are proud of our daughter.'

'I have missed you all. America is like a different world.'

'It is your destiny. We always knew that you would achieve great things. The money that you send back will be a great help – not just to our family but to the whole village. Our ancestors are celebrating with us tonight.'

Olivia yawned. She had managed to have a nap before the party but had been woken by Gracie bounding into her room, shrieking with excitement. She watched Gracie now, showing off the dress that Olivia had bought for her in Miami. The other girls crowded around her as though she were a celebrity.

'Do you think anyone would notice if I went to bed?'

'No, you must be exhausted. This could go on for hours. Have a good long sleep and tomorrow you can tell me everything about your life in America.'

Not everything, Olivia thought, remembering her last night in Miami. She allowed herself to relive each caress, his loving words, and their lovemaking, as she watched the flames dance and flicker. Because after tonight she would have to pretend that they had never met. To wrap up the memories and hide them away where they could not hurt her, or tempt her to act selfishly. Raf would forget her in time and find a woman more suited to his world. Olivia hoped that it wasn't too soon and then chastised herself. Raf had a big and open heart, he would soon fall in love again and that is how it should be. Tomorrow, there was something she must do to protect her future but now she was going to sleep.

21st March

Hi

Day 14. Halcyon Seas arrived in Southampton today after crossing the Atlantic from Miami. The UK residents joined the ship here. Captain Moore will be greeting the new arrivals at a formal dinner just as she did in Miami. An opportunity to dig for information that may be of interest to you.

I'm not addressing or signing this email. As we agreed, there is nothing that can trace it to me.

Over – for now.

6

A long loud siren interrupted Olivia's concentration as she checked and rechecked the stock on her cleaning trolley. Attention to detail was key to the success of a Silver Seas cabin maid. Olivia had written this down along with seven other rules committed to memory from the Exemplary Cabin Staff Guidelines. The alarm sounded again, *Please report to your muster stations,* and Olivia realised, in a panic, that to be late for muster practice was not exemplary.

The English lady with silvery blonde hair seemed to be waiting for someone. She was standing halfway down the corridor blocking Olivia's path.

'Excuse me, madame.'

The woman jumped when Olivia spoke, dropping her cabin key. Olivia picked up the key card, which was also a credit card for residents to pay for things on the ship, and tried to hand it to the woman.

'Thank you. I don't know what came over me.' Instead of

taking the key card, the woman clung to Olivia's arm. She was shaking.

'You are welcome.'

Being an exemplary cabin maid did not include socialising with guests. Only when the need arose in carrying out the duties of a cabin maid. Olivia was unsure what to do. The alarm was deafening now as though giving a final warning. The poor woman seemed terrified so Olivia kept hold of her arm and led her along the corridor to find their muster station on deck. If it was a real emergency, she would be expected to help anyone who was struggling.

'I was a bit nervous the first time I heard that alarm,' Olivia said. 'It's my second muster practice. The first, when we set sail from Miami, and now, as the last of our passengers have boarded the ship in England. All cruise ships have to carry out muster practice so that passengers and crew know what to do in an emergency. It is just for our safety. It doesn't mean that there is any real risk. Please do not be afraid.'

'How can I be afraid when I have a beautiful, gentle angel looking after me?'

Olivia looked around then realised the woman must have second sight like their village witch doctor. It was reassuring to know that there was an angel with them right now.

'I hope your angel will look after me too.'

'You are my angel.' The woman laughed and she looked twenty years younger. 'Alice Wagstaff.'

'Oh, I understand.' Olivia giggled. They had reached the floor where the outside deck for their muster station was situated. A few senior officers were patrolling the area around the stairwell and lifts ushering late arrivals to their posts.

'Olivia Rose. I'd better give you back your cabin key.'

It was at this moment that Hans Peters, the hotel director, stepped directly in front of Olivia, cutting her off from Alice.

Olivia's hand shook as the key card was now proffered to Mr Peters. He snatched it from her. 'Don't move.' Then, he turned to Mrs Wagstaff.

'Please keep your cabin key safe at all times. It is not just a key – you must think of it like a credit card. Never, under any circumstances, give it to a fellow passenger and certainly not to our hotel staff. All of your living expenses have been covered in your fee. Gratuities and gifts are not to be accepted by our staff. Now quickly, to your muster station.' He signalled to an officer in a white tunic. 'Please escort this lady.'

He turned to Olivia. 'I am disappointed in you…' he checked her name badge, 'Olivia Rose. I hope that you are not going to be a problem.'

Olivia couldn't speak. She was aware that her jaw had dropped. Grand Mammon would have said, 'Ferme la bouche.' Olivia closed her mouth. Unlike Grand Mammon, Hans Peter was not going to allow her to explain.

'Don't try ingratiating yourself with our guests in the hope of some extra money on the side. Let this be a warning. I'm going to be watching you.'

Olivia bit her lip, concentrating on the feel of sharp teeth drawing blood. The distraction was enough to stop her tears. Three weeks on the ship and already she was in trouble.

7

Marianne always enjoyed the first dinner at sea. In the past, she had mingled with cruisers at the captain's champagne party, attracting attention in her stilettos and white uniform with purple and gold stripes on the epaulettes. Tonight, she wore four stripes as captain of Halcyon Seas. Marianne waited until all her guests had full glasses and then, following an introduction by Hans, the hotel director, she began her welcoming speech.

'This is my first ship as captain. Don't look so nervous. I have been second in command for more years than I will admit because that might give away my age.' There was a ripple of laughter. Then a man called out, 'We're all forty on this cruise.'

Marianne moved so that she could see around the women in their finery who blocked her view. He was a good-looking man with a stylishly close-cropped beard of grey and white. 'I'll tell you a secret,' she said. 'This is, as you know, a forever cruise. It means that you will stay the same age as long as you are with us. None of us is going to age on Halcyon Seas.' There was a roar of approval and glasses clinked.

The guests on Halcyon Seas looked no different to those on any other cruise ship Marianne had worked on. The energy of expectation and excitement was the same. They had stepped out of their everyday lives and were off on an adventure. The only difference was – these were not her guests, they were residents. This was their new home. Marianne refused to call them residents, as they sounded like the occupants of a care home and despite Patrick Dunn, the CEO of McIntyre Retirement Living, saying, *In the end, they all need the same care. It's just a different setting,* Marianne was determined to make this retirement experience magical. They would be pampered and treated like VIPs because they were – every one of them. They deserved to live like kings after a lifetime of service to others. Besides, they had paid good money for this experience. And her future career as a captain depended upon the cruise being a success.

'We need to go through for dinner now,' Hans said when Marianne had finished her speech. 'I've put you on the top table after the last episode.'

'It was fine. Of course, some of our guests are going to be a bit emotional. Patty was just upset to be leaving behind her grandchildren. No, I will do as I did before – eat each course at a different table.'

Hans's eyebrows raised just enough for Marianne to see that he was trying not to roll his eyes. The absence of other senior officers was going to make her relationship with Hans challenging. It had been a shock to discover that there was no chief engineer or first officer. Libby had explained that, as it was a small ship with an expected capacity of seventy residents, there was no need for the organisational structure of a big ship. Marianne's experience as an engineer meant that she took on both the chief engineer and first officer roles. If a different candidate had been appointed, they might have taken on the role of hotel director instead. She did at least have a cruise director, although Patrick Dunn insisted on calling Gloria an activities organiser. The ship wasn't new either. It was only when she was ready to board that Marianne recognised the ship that had been sold off by a failing cruise line and renamed Halcyon Seas. None of that mattered. These guests were going to have the best retirement ever. Halcyon Seas would run efficiently under her leadership. Marianne could see herself being interviewed on Good Morning America. Her photo was already in the cruise industry magazine, Travel and Cruise.

Hans had kept the guests who boarded in Miami to tables of two to four so that the British arrivals could join them to make up tables of six. It was inevitable that the seating arrangements would get fixed through choice and Hans didn't want there to be a divide between the guests who joined on day one and those who boarded at Southampton. Marianne couldn't sit at all eleven tables but she would try and visit each one to say hello. The man with a close-cropped beard caught her eye as she decided where to sit so she headed for his table.

An elegant-looking woman with white shoulder-length hair sat to the man's right. Then there was another newcomer, a man with thick-rimmed glasses who was intently studying his menu, seemingly oblivious to her arrival. She knew Patty and the Connecticut couple, Richard and Barbara Lopez.

Each table had an extra place setting so that guests could visit other tables and accommodate VIPs such as the captain or an entertainer. The vacant seat happened to be next to the man with a beard. His eyes seemed to follow her across the room, igniting energy within Marianne that she found unsettling. She dipped her head on the pretence of checking the cutlery arrangement. Then, when her emotions were in check, she greeted them all with a smile.

'May I join you?'

'Captain Moore always sits with each table on the first night,' Patty informed the UK newcomers.

'I try to get to know all of our guests. Of course, I have the luxury on this cruise of spending many months with you all, so we can take our time. Before the first course arrives perhaps you could tell me a little about yourselves?'

'Well, you know all about me.' Patty didn't need any encouragement to talk and Marianne hoped that she would not monopolise the conversation. Tonight, she wanted to welcome the British guests. 'I'm from Kansas, although born in Kentucky. Mother. Grandmother. Three grand-kiddies. Divorced many years ago. Worked in retail.'

'Thank you, Patty.'

Richard and Barbara Lopez were discussing the menu as they had heard all of this before. Marianne addressed the elegant woman with white hair. 'Welcome to Halcyon Seas, I hope that you are settling into your new home.'

'Thank you. I expect it will feel like home eventually. Right now, it feels as though I'm on a luxury holiday. I'm Alice Wagstaff.' Alice smiled and tilted her head. 'This is my travelling companion Gideon Flynn.' She indicated the man with a beard whose eyes were still fixed on Marianne. 'It was Gideon who persuaded me to take this adventure.'

Gideon laughed. 'It was a no-brainer, Alice. Although the Pornstars may have played a part in the seduction too.'

Alice's face turned crimson. Richard and Barbara stared across the table wide-eyed. Patty giggled. The man with thick-rimmed glasses looked up from his menu with a questioning look, he had missed the exchange.

'It was Gideon's sister's birthday party. We were drinking a cocktail called a Pornstar Martini and Gideon told me about the forever cruise.' The Gideon/Alice act broke the ice and conversation started to flow freely, along with the wine.

The first course, a duet of tuna with watermelon and ginger cucumber, had been served, eaten and cleared. Marianne thought she should move to another table but she was relaxed and enjoying the company. 'I am assuming you have retired, Gideon?'

'That's hard to say. I've never had a proper job so it's not a concept that fits. I've always done what I loved. First, it was music – a rock band, then I managed bands. Later in life, I bought a restaurant in Spain.' He shrugged. 'I guess I'm a bit of an entrepreneur. I have money in different projects and now and again I dabble. My business associates are probably relieved I'm on this cruise so that they can get on without any interference. I saw on your resumé that you are an engineer.'

Marianne was impressed that he had done his research. 'That's correct. I was chief engineer on three of the Ionian cruise ships.'

'It must have been tough for you as a woman in a male-dominated profession.'

They paused as a waiter topped up their wine. Marianne was used to these observations. She had been interviewed many times in her career and her gender was usually the focus of discussion. 'All the men I have worked alongside have been fine but you're right, it's harder for a woman to climb the career ladder.'

'I admire your tenacity; I believe for a woman to succeed in a man's world she has to be twice as good. Here's to our captain.' Gideon spoke the last sentence loud enough for all to hear and they joined him in the toast.

The second course arrived, grilled scallops with green asparagus spears and Kashmir curry. It was time to move on but Marianne was aware of the man with thick-rimmed spectacles; he had hardly spoken and her role this evening as hostess was to make all of the new arrivals feel welcome. He sat between Alice and Patty but it was difficult to get his attention without knowing his name. It was as though he existed within a little bubble, unaware of those around him. 'Would you both mind shuffling along one seat so that I could sit the other side of Alice?' she said.

The man sat up straight when she landed in the seat next to him. She wanted to say, *at ease,* he looked so uncomfortable. 'Please don't let me interrupt your meal. I just came by to say hello.'

His eyes were magnified by thick lenses and despite her reassurance, he continued to stare as though caught in the headlights of a car. 'William Fellows.' He wiped his hands on his thighs before extending one in a handshake. His grip was limp and clammy.

'The scallops look good,' she said trying to divert his attention back to the food to ease his discomfort.

'Indeed. Indeed.'

Marianne took a forkful of succulent scallop and swirled it in the curry. She might have a scaled-down crew but her chefs were second to none. Poor cuisine might have been the real deal breaker, she smiled at the thought. 'So, William. Which ports are you most looking forward to visiting?'

He put down his fork and wiped his mouth on the linen napkin. 'I am most looking forward to Reunion Island as I'm particularly interested in wildlife – flora and fauna.' He picked up his fork and returned his attention to the scallops.

'Good choice. How about you Patty?' Marianne could not subject William to more questions; he looked as though the stress of having to talk to her might give him indigestion.

Patty did not need any encouragement; she filled the silence as they all concentrated on eating.

If anyone could coax William out of his shell, it was Patty. Marianne stood up when the second course was cleared away. 'Enjoy the rest of your meal everyone. I will look forward to seeing you around the ship. In three days, we will be docking in Gibraltar. I hope that you have booked an excursion. I recommend getting a cable car up the Rock to see the monkeys. But if you don't want to go on shore this time, remember we will be returning in the future. The world is now your playground. The ship your home.'

Just one year. She could do this. Maybe Patrick Dunn and Libby Braithwaite were right – this was the future for retirement living – but would all cruise ships become retirement homes? Marianne hoped not. Her guests were wonderful but a cruise that never ended? The same passengers – month after month, year after year? Wouldn't they get bored of it? You could have too much of a good thing.

25th March

Hi

Day 18 We sailed from Southampton to Gibraltar where we are docking for the day. There is going to be a staff training session when the passengers are on shore. I'll use the opportunity to snoop.

Over for now.

8

Where was her eternity ring? Alice threw the pillows from her bed and looked underneath it, on the bedside table and behind that. Oh, Tom, how could I lose that ring? It was his gift to her on their twenty-fifth wedding anniversary.

They had docked in Gibraltar and Alice was anxious that if she made herself late searching for her ring then she would miss the excursion. Gideon was staying on board as he had visited Gibraltar many times in the past, so Alice was going alone – alone with twenty-five other passengers who had signed up for a tour of the island and a cable car to see the monkeys. She didn't know if it was excitement or trepidation making her so jittery. Now that she had started to settle into her new home, Alice marvelled at her audaciousness in signing up for the forever cruise. Rachel, of course, had been outraged. But then, she had been a coward, only telling Rachel when it was a fait accompli.

'What do you mean?' Rachel had shouted down the phone.

'That's impossible. We've exchanged contracts on your bungalow, you can't back out now.'

'I don't intend to.'

'What do you mean?'

'I'm going ahead with the sale.'

'Then where are you planning to live?'

'I was hoping I could stay with you,' Alice used a little girl pleading voice. 'Just for a couple of weeks.'

'And then what? No, I'm sorry Mummy, you can't live with us. There just isn't the room. It wouldn't work.'

Her suggestion had at least taken the wind out of Rachel's sails – set her off course. The truth might be less of a shock. Maybe even a relief. 'It's okay, darling. I don't want to live with you. No offence, but I think it would drive me crazy. Losing my independence, that is.' Alice heard Rachel let out her breath. 'I do have plans, darling. Rather exciting ones, actually. I've signed up for a forever cruise. It's a cruise ship for retirement living.' Her voice went up an octave the way it had when she was cajoling her children to swallow a spoonful of Calpol. 'I'm joining the ship in Southampton on 21st March. Gideon Flynn, Kate's brother, is going too, so Kate's driving us from London. That's why I would like to stay with you for a couple of weeks if you don't mind?'

There was a stunned silence. Then, 'Does Dave know what you've planned?'

'No. I wanted to tell you first as you've been so helpful with selling the bungalow.'

'But... you won't have any property – no capital. It's a lot of money. We'll have to invest it wisely. Greg can help.'

'I'll need the money from the sale to contribute to the weekly fee on Halcyon Seas. I'm gifting you and David a little something from the proceeds of the house.'

'Mummy. You're not thinking straight. If you move to Chestnut Court, you will still have a property to sell when you – well, leave.'

'Die?'

'Well, yes. Daddy wouldn't want you to throw away our inheritance.'

'I think I know what your father would want better than you, darling. Tom would have wanted me to be happy.' Alice was disappointed in Rachel but not surprised. Had they raised their children to be greedy and materialistic? 'As I said, I've made some provision for you and David. But if staying with you is going to be a problem, I can book into a hotel.'

'Of course, you can stay with us. I'm sorry Mummy, it's just a shock. I never expected this. I just don't know what to say.'

'I'm sorry I surprised you. But my mind is made up, darling. This will be a great new adventure for me. A new beginning.' As she said it, Alice realised just what this meant. She was getting a second chance at life. Her life had not ended with Tom, it was just the ending of a chapter. 'I think it is what I need.'

'But what about me? It's not just the money. Although I was relying on that for my pension.' Rachel sighed and Alice felt a pang of guilt. 'It's just that I'll miss you. When will I get to see you?'

They had barely seen each other in the past few years but Alice did not remind Rachel. 'You can visit me anywhere in the world that you choose, and we will have regular stops in the UK.'

Gideon's daughter Paige had helped Alice to sort out her visas and paperwork and now here she was, four days into her new life and about to discover Gibraltar – that's if she didn't miss the excursion bus.

'Please let me find my ring,' she said to any deity who might be listening and tipped everything out of her bag. But it wasn't there. 'Blast.'

Olivia, the cabin maid, popped her head around the open door. 'Mrs Wagstaff. I am sorry. I will come back later.'

'No, it's okay. Come in. I've lost my diamond eternity ring.'

'Your ring?' Her brow furrowed. 'Maybe I will find it for you.'

'Would you look help me look for it? I would be most grateful.'

'Of course.' The girl smiled, revealing dimples on both cheeks. She had a beautiful curvaceous figure and smooth skin, like a ripened plum.

'Thank you, Olivia. I hope that I did not get you into trouble with that stern-looking man.'

Olivia covered her mouth as she giggled. 'He is just doing his job. Hans Peters is the hotel director. He is a very important man.'

'So long as he is kind to you. Maybe I should stay here and search for my ring. I would hate to lose it.'

'No. No. You must go, Mrs Wagstaff, and enjoy your visit to Gibraltar. I will find your ring and leave it on your dresser. You see – it will be here waiting for you when you return. Espérons.'

'Espérons! Vous êtes trés gentil, merci.'

'You speak Français? My grand-mammon was French. You remind me of her.' Olivia clamped a hand over her mouth as though she had said too much.

'We must speak again, so I can practise my French. Now, I'd better get going or I'll miss the excursion.'

It was the upset of losing her ring that had unsettled her. She wished Gideon was going with her. Maybe she should just stay on board; they would visit Gibraltar again. *Come on Alice, you didn't join this cruise to hide away in your cabin. You are strong. You are courageous. You can do this.* There was no way she would prove Rachel right. 'Gibraltar, here I come.'

9

Olivia had barely made a start on Alice Wagstaff's cabin when she was summoned to the theatre for staff training.

'How many of you have worked on a cruise ship before joining Halcyon Seas?' Captain Moore said addressing her crew and staff from the stage. A few hands went up, mostly officers. 'It is unusual to have so many staff that are new to cruising. We must use this opportunity to create the most efficient, caring and accomplished crew of any cruise ship. Our passengers deserve the very best.'

The hotel director, Hans Peters, said a few words about keeping passengers and crew safe by washing hands and reporting any signs and symptoms of a virus immediately. 'There is a heightened sensitivity concerning cruise ships where there has been an outbreak of a virus. We must detect any signs early and manage the situation effectively.'

A man at the back raised his hand. 'Most of us are on self-employed contracts. What arrangements are there if one of us becomes unwell?'

'That is correct. Silver Seas have taken a progressive approach to recruitment, generously providing you with training and a certificate that will give you access to jobs across the leisure industry. However, that does mean that you will not get paid for days when you are absent from work. If a member of staff is unable to work for a period longer than one or two weeks, we will make arrangements for them to leave the ship at the first available port. We cannot afford to have unfilled posts. It is fortunate for us that there are plenty of hopefuls waiting for the opportunity to join our ship. The woman at the back.'

'I've heard that our training certificate isn't recognised on any of the other cruise lines.'

'Give it time. Silver Seas are leaders in the field. I can take just two more questions and then I must hand over to Captain Moore to introduce the emergency practice.'

Anxiety bunched in Olivia's stomach. On her last day in Madagascar, she had visited Disney, the village witch doctor. In his cool, dark cabin she had drunk a bitter potion. Dazed, she had imagined the medicine like a river of black ink seeping through her veins, rewriting her story.

Disney filled a cow's horn with hair and dung. 'I did not have a scorpion's tail or a crocodile's tooth.'

'Will it still work?'

Disney murmured over the talisman, rocking on his heels. Then, he wound a string of sikidy beads from his pocket. 'Let us see.'

Olivia had held her breath. She asked Grand-mammon for mercy, to protect her and forgive her. Disney was deep in a trance, rocking and mumbling. Had she imagined the chill creeping across her arms? Maybe it was an effect of the potion.

Disney had thrown back his head and laughed.

'What did you see?'

'Our golden child. You are going to bring prosperity to this village.'

'Does that mean the potion and magic have worked?'

Disney shrugged. 'I have done all that I can. You have a bright future ahead of you. All will be well.'

That is what he had said. All will be well. Olivia tried to put aside her anxiety and focus on the present.

Captain Moore was back on the stage. 'I am going to outline the scenario for today's emergency practice and then Gloria Busby, our cruise director, will tell you where to meet for the safety role briefing. As you may know, Halcyon Seas will be sailing across the Indian Ocean as we visit Asia. We only sail in safe waters but for the purpose of today's practice, we are going to imagine pirates are threatening to board the ship. It has happened to cruise ships in the past, although it is a rare occurrence. However, it doesn't hurt to be prepared and it is something a little different.'

There was a babble of excitement and apprehension as each person turned to their neighbour to comment.

'Do we have weapons on board?' An officer asked.

'No. It is more dangerous to hold weapons as they could be used against us. It is recommended that we sound the ship's horn loudly. There are other devices on board for creating loud noises as a deterrent and high-powered hoses. Your briefing will explain all of this.'

'What if a passenger tries to play the hero? How do we keep them away from the pirates?'

'At the first sign, all passengers will be asked to go to their cabins and turn off their lights. The code Safe Haven will alert the crew and staff. I know you all have lots of questions but we need to get on with the practice. Gloria will tell you where to go to get the briefing on what will be required of you in your safety role and then you will go back to your duties until I announce Safe Haven.'

Olivia returned to Alice Wagstaff's cabin to continue cleaning. She wiped hand lotion from the bathroom sink and then flipped open the wastepaper bin to remove the contents. There were just a few crumpled tissues. As she tipped the contents into her refuse sack, Olivia noticed they glistened with hand cream and it gave her an idea. She sank to her knees and retrieved all three tissues. Yes. One of them was heavier than the others. Olivia teased open the tissue to find Alice's ring. Her ancestors were protecting her; this was a sign. She wiped the ring clean with fresh tissue.

'Safe Haven. Safe Haven. All staff proceed to your designated positions.'

Olivia was still smiling when Hans Peters poked his head around the door. 'Why are you still here, Olivia Rose? Out! Out! To your designated position. What's that in your hand?'

Olivia tried to speak but could not find her voice. She unfurled her fingers.

'Give that to me.'

'It's. It's...'

He plucked the tissue from her open palm. 'Just as I thought. What's inside this?'

'Mrs Wagstaff--'

'—I don't want to hear. I'll deal with this later.'

Olivia walked in a daze to the lift, burning with anger, resentment and humiliation. She could feel his eyes on her back.

Bopha, Olivia's cabin mate, intercepted her at the end of the corridor. 'We're together outside the restaurant.'

Olivia nodded, afraid to speak in case she cried. Outside the restaurant, Olivia waited for imaginary passengers to emerge so that she could ask them politely and calmly to go straight to their cabin and turn off the lights. Most of Halcyon Seas' guests were on shore visiting Gibraltar, like Alice Wagstaff. Alice. Would she believe Hans Peters? Olivia hoped not. Grand-mammon had once told her, 'Nobody can make you feel less than you are unless you allow them to.' Olivia had been a child then, her tormentors the village boys.

'Does everyone know what they are doing?' Gloria Busby called from inside the restaurant.

Olivia felt like an outsider, as though she were no longer part of the team.

Mr William Fellows strolled out of the restaurant and Bopha said, 'Please would you return to your cabin and turn off your lights?'

'Why?' He looked confused and upset.

Olivia forgot her worries and intervened. 'It is just an emergency drill, Mr Fellows. You don't have to go to your cabin. This is just a practice for the staff.'

It was the first time she had spoken since Hans Peters had reprimanded her. It was easier standing up for others than it was defending herself. Life in the village had been hard in many ways, the lack of food and water, the daily toil, but she had always been seen and respected. This was harder. Being good was not enough, she had to stand up to people like Hans Peters – people who had the power to change her life. She didn't know if she could do that.

27th March

Hi

Day 21.

We left Gibraltar on 25th March and tomorrow will dock in Barcelona. I picked up a lot of useful information from the staff training session and have done a bit of investigating since.

Jamboree cruises are cutting costs on the Silver Seas project with inadequate staffing. The captain is also the chief engineer. 90% of the hotel staff have no previous experience working on a cruise ship. They have been employed from third-world countries and it seems they have been conned into accepting a self-employed contract in exchange for a free training programme and a worthless certificate. It's outrageous.

I hope that's the sort of information you wanted. I'll be in touch again when I have more to report.

Over – for now.

10

Alice watched the sun go down from her seat by the window, delighting in the shimmer of light on water.

'Mind if I join you?' Gideon slipped into the chair opposite.

Alice enjoyed Gideon's company; he was a link to Kate and memories of her youth. 'Be my guest.'

'Will you be signing up for an excursion in Barcelona or doing your own thing?'

'Is there one you recommend? You are more familiar with Spain than me. I loved Gibraltar. To be honest I haven't been anywhere out of the UK apart from France. Tom and I had a favourite campsite in Normandy we visited when the children were small.'

'Don't bother with an excursion. It's easy to get around Barcelona from the cruise terminal. Trust me.'

Alice didn't know whether he was inviting her to explore Barcelona with him. She had been careful not to cramp his style. Gideon got on with everyone and was popular with the single women, of which there were plenty. Whilst Gideon was a social butterfly, Alice had tried not to encourage any friendships until she had got the measure of her fellow cruisers. It was like the first day at a new school. Friendships made on day one would probably be lasting and already the passengers were starting to pair off or form groups. Alice was content to watch from the sidelines.

'What will you be doing in Barcelona, Gideon?'

'Visit La Rambla. There's an incredible market. Maybe order paella and sangria in one of the little restaurants. Then there are the Gaudi attractions: La Sagrada Familia and Parc Güell. It's a beautiful city.'

Alice sipped her G&T. She arched her back and wiggled her toes. This was the life. To think she might have ended up in bloody Chestnut Court. She decided to be brave. 'Do you want company?'

'Not any company but I would be delighted to show you my favourite city.' Gideon grinned.

'Excuse me, madam. May I have a private word?' It was the man who had reprimanded poor Olivia the day she helped Alice.

'I'll see you at dinner.' Gideon winked and left Alice with the serious-looking man who, it seemed, was about to cast a shadow over her idyllic evening. She wondered if he was going to tell her that she had no business being on board this marvellous ship. That there had been a mistake and she was expected at Chestnut Court. Maybe there wasn't enough in her bank account to cover the fees. Could Rachel have interfered? Alice went to take another slug of gin but her glass was empty.

'I am sorry to interrupt your conversation. May I sit?' Heads turned to watch them. 'Hans. Hans Peters.'

Alice nodded.

'Let me get you another drink.' He clicked his fingers and a waiter jumped to attention. 'A gin and tonic?'

She nodded again. If he was about to tell her that this was where her voyage would end then he would not be buying her a drink. Unless his news was so dreadful, he thought she needed one. What if something had happened to Rachel?

'I am sorry to inform you…' Alice received his words with dread. '…that your cabin maid was found in possession of a ring which I believe belongs to you.' He opened his hand to reveal her diamond eternity ring.

'Oh, bless her. She found it. Thank you.'

Hans Peters looked as if he had received a blow to his solar plexus. At that moment a G&T was placed in front of her and Alice was tempted to offer it to Mr Peters, as the colour had drained from his face.

'If Miss Rose or any of our staff have been asking favours of you then you must tell us. We take financial abuse very seriously. It is a dismissible offence, as is stealing.'

Alice had taken a dislike to this man from the moment she met him. Then, he had been bullying Olivia Rose.

'Olivia Rose has behaved professionally at all times. If it wasn't for Olivia then I would have left the ship on my first day. I was having a panic attack when she kindly reassured me and assisted me to the muster station. I asked Olivia to look for my missing ring. If it was in her possession, then I believe without a doubt that she intended to return it to me. I appreciate your concern, Mr Peters, but there is no need. I am perfectly capable of managing my affairs and know who I can and cannot trust.' Alice gave him a steely look.

The bar emptied as fellow cruisers made their way to the dining room. Alice knew that her table would wait for her arrival before ordering. They had only dined together for six days, the Americans had of course had longer to bond, but friendships were being forged and Alice felt comfortable in their company.

'Everything okay?' Gideon said as soon as she sat down. All eyes were upon her.

'Yes. A silly misunderstanding. The good news is my eternity ring was found.'

'I never remove my rings,' Barbara said.

Patty displayed the many rings adorning her plump hands. 'I'm like a magpie, anything that glitters I can't resist. But my fingers have swollen up and so it's probably foolish of me. But rings are my weakness.'

'I had swollen fingers and ankles,' Barbara lowered her voice and leaned across Richard to discuss this with Patty.

Richard was chatting with Gideon about the Suez Canal. 'Why don't we change seats?'

So, with the two men and two women in conversation, Alice found herself alone with William for company. 'You stayed on the ship in Gibraltar, will you be visiting Barcelona?' she said.

William was writing in a notebook. His handwriting neat, the words and lines close together. He did not look up until he had finished his sentence or line of thought, and when he did, he closed the notebook and turned his attention to Alice. 'I will be visiting the Parc Güell designed by Gaudi. The architecture and planting are of interest to me.'

Alice thought about her garden in Norfolk. The daffodils would be making a good show. 'That is one thing I will miss – my garden.'

William's face seemed to melt a little, the taut lines of concentration softening. 'I nearly cancelled the cruise when I realised, I might never see my magnolia again.'

'Where did you live before here?'

'Surrey.'

'Did you have a big garden?'

'It was full but always room to squeeze in something else.'

'I had a small garden. Just a square of lawn when we bought the bungalow but over time, I created a little haven. Lots of filled pots. A bird feeder.'

'Why are you on this ship?' The directness of his question floored Alice. She was aware of Barbara and Gideon pinning back their ears. It would have been easy to give a pat response but Alice felt the question press gently on her heart. It was the same thing she had asked herself every day since boarding.

'Honestly?' She paused, searching for the reason. 'Because I thought that there had to be more to life than the one I was living. How about you?'

'So, I could breathe.'

Gideon interrupted. 'Alice, Barbara and Richard have recommended a restaurant in Barcelona. We should have paella for lunch.'

'Aren't you taking the excursion, Alice?' Patty looked crest-fallen, as though Alice's decision to spend the day with Gideon was a personal affront.

'No. Gideon is going to be my tour guide.'

'You do know that the ship won't wait for you if you are late boarding?'

Gideon laughed. 'Alice will be safe with me Patty. I promise to return her on time and in one piece.'

Alice was a little discomforted by Patty's remark. It would be dreadful if the ship left without them. But then she reprimanded herself. Anxiety was not going to hold her back. Besides, Gideon would be with her. There was nothing to fear.

11

Marianne had been hoping to spend a couple of hours on shore in Barcelona. Most of the passengers had disembarked, three excursion coaches filled with men in short-sleeved shirts and shorts, women in straw hats and sunglasses – loaded up with drinking water, sun cream and anything else they could fit into their bulging bags. She loved to watch them all as they queued with their sea passes, buzzing with chatter and expectation, then down the gangplank onto the shore – heading for tour buses or clutching maps and setting off like explorers.

'A call came through for you, Captain. Libby Braithwaite at Silver Seas HQ.' It was her second officer. Marianne thanked him but when she made no sign of moving, he added, 'Ms Braithwaite said it was urgent, Captain.'

Marianne couldn't imagine what could be urgent; as captain of Halcyon Seas, she was confident everything was in order. She hoped Libby Braithwaite was not going to interfere in the running of the ship. As Marianne strode to the bridge, she rehearsed how she would communicate to Libby the boundaries of their working relationship. It was Libby's first job as a chief operating officer and therefore she might have the wrong idea about her role regarding the ship. They both needed to be clear from the start.

The message had been sealed in an envelope. Libby Braithwaite and Patrick Dunn wanted a face-to-face with her that morning. She sent an email suggesting a video call in thirty minutes. They had been at sea for barely more than three weeks. What could be so important and why did they both want to meet with her? It could be good news. Maybe she had already made an impact – unlikely. A media interview? She would take the call in her cabin, but first a strong coffee. She stopped at the café where the staff were enjoying a quiet morning. A few of the passengers were sitting in the lounge, a couple poring over tourist information while sipping hot drinks and a woman engrossed in a word search puzzle.

'Hello, Captain,' the young barista greeted her. 'Cappuccino?'

'Yes, please.'

Fredric, the pastry chef, bagged an assortment of pastries and handed them to Marianne. She took them with a smile. 'You are spoiling me.'

'You deserve to be spoiled. They are freshly baked. Tell me what you think of the Mocha Heaven. It is a new creation.'

Marianne enjoyed this part of her job. A captain, after all, should take an interest in every function of the ship. 'I am looking forward to indulging. Thank you, Frederic. Halcyon Seas has the finest pastries I have ever tasted.' They would help to sweeten the conversation she was about to have with Libby and Patrick.

When Marianne joined the meeting, Libby and Patrick had already signed in, each from a different location.

'Captain Moore, thank you for joining us.'

At first, Marianne wondered whether this was a barb at her not being immediately available and bristled but Libby looked sincere. She took a deep breath and tried to relax. 'It is a pleasure but I was a little surprised you felt the need to meet with me so early on in the voyage.'

'Then you have not seen this week's issue of Travel and Cruise?'

A tingle down her spine. They were making news already. Marianne beamed. 'No. Hold on I'll make a call and get one delivered.' She sent a text with her request to Gloria. 'Okay, I will have a copy in a few minutes. Is there a big news story on Halcyon Seas?'

Libby frowned. 'You could say that. A news story that we did not want published. One of the most important responsibilities assigned to you is to keep the business model of Silver Seas Retirement Living confidential.'

'I thought the safe navigation of the ship was my most important responsibility and then the welfare of passengers and crew.' She was the captain of the ship, not a fucking public relations manager.

There was a knock on the door. A junior officer passed Marianne the Travel and Cruise, still in its cellophane wrapper.

'Page five,' Libby said.

Page five was hardly headlining news. Marianne was getting a bit impatient. There were a hundred far more important things she ought to be doing than discussing a magazine. There was a meeting with her directors, and those reporting to her, that should have started by now. She thumbed past the contents page, a double-page advert for on-board repairs, an article on The Expedition Boom, and then page five, The Retirement Market. As far as Marianne knew Silver Seas was the first line to branch solely into this market although scanning the article, she could see other cruise lines were starting to offer a handful of retirement deals on some of their ships.

'Third column, from the second paragraph.'

The retirement living package offered by Jamboree's Silver Seas line has profit at the centre of its business ethos. A business model which employs inexperienced staff on a minimum wage has a significantly reduced senior management team, with the captain taking on the additional roles of chief engineer and first officer, is short-sighted and could be costly in the long term. There has been much discussion in the cruise industry and retirement living about the suitability of this lifestyle choice for elders. Time will tell if forever cruises are to become a popular retirement option or a passing gimmick.

Blood rushed to Marianne's cheeks. Her throat was dry. 'I don't know how they got this information. The only time reporters might have come into contact with passengers or crew was when we set sail from Miami and Southampton and I understood from you that all of the communication was carefully managed by Jamboree. A reporter could have found out about the business model and organisational structure from someone in your offices. I don't know why you have pulled me away from my duties as captain to discuss this.'

Libby threw her copy of Cruise and Travel across the desk. 'I know exactly what goes on in the offices of Silver Seas. If there was a leak it would not escape my notice. This information has come from your ship. We were very clear from the outset that due to the commercial sensitivity of this voyage, absolute confidentiality is vital. You need to find the source and take appropriate action. Do I make myself clear?'

Marianne's heart beat a tattoo high on her chest. 'I have a meeting with my senior officers – in fact, I should have been having it now. I will discuss this breach of confidence and we will of course investigate.'

Marianne hesitated before asking her next question. It could piss them off – but if she was going to do her job properly, she had to stand tall and not be intimidated. 'I was surprised myself to discover ninety per cent of Halcyon Seas staff had no experience of working on a ship. This is not normal practice for Jamboree.'

'All of the hotel staff have had extensive training. They were selected for their experience and skills in caring for older people. This is after all a retirement home on sea. They may all seem healthy and hearty now but when you consider the age demographic it's only a few years until they become more dependent and in need of personal care. Trust me, I've years of experience in this field.' Patrick Dunn's speech was depressing and patronising. Marianne was glad she didn't have to work too closely with him.

'I have no complaints about the quality of service provided by the hotel staff team. They will learn all they need to know from Hans Peters and the supervisors. Is there a reason that the majority of staff are from Asia and Africa?'

'Silver Seas takes equal opportunities very seriously. We encourage a diverse workforce. Do you have a problem working with people of colour, Captain Moore?'

Now Marianne was furious. She abhorred discrimination of any kind and was incensed at this suggestion. 'Absolutely not. We've recruited kids from countries where there's a poor socio-demographic and got them working on a contract that doesn't pay when they're sick or take leave.' It was a statement, not a question, but her accusation was clear.

Patrick Dunn's eyes flashed. She noticed his fists clench. 'We are rescuing these people from poverty. Giving them a qualification, which will open doors – maybe not immediately, but in time, when Silver Seas have more ships and the rest of the cruise industry follows.' He smiled at his munificence. 'With respect, Captain Moore, you know very little about the care industry. Westerners do not want to work with older people. We recruit staff who come from countries where their elders are respected. They earn good money. It's a win-win.'

Marianne checked her watch. She could not waste any more time listening to this shit. Most of the men cruising on Halcyon Seas were fitter and appeared more youthful than him. An image of Gideon Flynn came to mind. 'If that's all, I have a meeting to chair.'

She had kept her team waiting for fifteen minutes but Marianne needed to cool her temper before presenting herself. Two pains au chocolat later, she freshened herself up and hurried to join them in the library. Patrick Dunn was the least of her worries. His career in the care sector was about making money; he was the least caring person she had the misfortune to meet. Jamboree had partnered with McIntyre Retirement Living for the Silver Seas project for financial reasons and that was fine – so long as they didn't take any risks with the staffing of her ship. So far, she had no complaints, but, if she had the slightest concern, she would take the matter up as commanding officer and captain. No, it wasn't Patrick Dunn that troubled her, it was the leaking of information. If it had come from her ship, her future career could be at stake.

12

BARCELONA

'Hotel staff, please make your way to the theatre for an emergency meeting.' It was the staff tannoy.

'I thought there was no emergency drill today.' Bopha was right. They had been told that all staff could take their off-duty time on shore.

'I hope it is a quick meeting,' Olivia said, as they joined their colleagues who were emerging from the neighbouring cabins in casual attire. 'We won't get another on-shore break for a few weeks.'

Hans Peters paced up and down the stage as team managers and supervisors ushered in their staff, ticking off names. He didn't look happy. For a fleeting moment, Olivia thought it was something she had done and then she pulled back her shoulders. She had nothing to hide. Alice had shared the conversation with Hans the Horrible, as Alice had named him, and reassured Olivia that she was not in any trouble. As Mr Peters had not asked to see her since the incident, she had decided to let it go and look forward. Today, they were going to explore Barcelona. She and Bopha had planned their day.

There was a rumble of dissatisfaction, as the hotel staff, impatient to escape the ship, waited to hear what was so important that it should cut into their free time. Satisfied that all were present, Hans Peters cleared his throat.

'This should not take very long. This morning, Captain Moore informed me that there has been a leak of confidential information from this ship. You are all aware of your responsibilities in keeping the operations of Halcyon Seas absolutely confidential, from your personal contracts through to the day-to-day management. You all signed an agreement to this effect. We are investigating the source of this breach and will take immediate action to terminate the contract of any staff member involved. If you have any information that might help with our investigation, please inform me or your supervisor immediately.' Why did it feel as though he was looking directly at Olivia? 'That is all. Thank you for your time.'

'What kind of information do you think he is talking about?' Bopha said as they waited in line to exit the theatre. 'The number of salt cellars we use in the dining hall?'

'Fredric's secret recipe for pain au chocolat,' Olivia giggled.

'How many shoes the captain owns?' one of the kitchen porters quipped from behind.

'I'm surprised anyone is interested in the day-to-day running of this ship. Why would anyone bother to leak such information?' Olivia said. 'Never mind. We are minutes away from freedom. Have you got everything you need?'

Bopha checked her bag. 'Yup. You?'

Olivia grinned. 'I do. Let's go.'

When they disembarked from Halcyon Seas, Olivia was filled with wonder. She knew that they were sailing around the world, each port a different country, but it did not prepare her for the buzz of this city. The wide sweeping port, all blue sea, sky and white ships. The statues, fountains and streets lined with palm trees. Bopha walked quickly with purpose but Olivia wanted to take her time. To enjoy the warm, rounded sound of the language.

'What are they?' she said drawn to the kiosk by the scent of warm butter and sugar. 'It says churros. I've heard of them. Shall we buy some to share?'

Olivia nodded. Her wages had to stretch but it would be a shame to visit another country and not sample the food. A cone of fried dough, drizzled with melted chocolate, was handed over in exchange for a couple of euros. Now, holding the warm, greasy paper, the scent turned her stomach.

She handed it to Bopha. 'You first.'

Bopha shrugged and got stuck in. When she handed the cone back, Olivia picked at the sugary treat, hoping Bopha would not notice. She need not have worried as Bopha was charging ahead, excited to see Las Ramblas.

The street was lined with what looked like statues. Olivia had seen one or two human statues before but nothing like the living works of art posing on Las Ramblas: an angel woman with a crinoline skirt painted gold, a Roman emperor that looked so exactly like a marble statue, Olivia reached out a hand to touch and he moved a fraction, making her jump and shriek in delight. Their progress along the wide pedestrianised street was slow because with each step there was something new to marvel at. An incredible circus of performers lined up as though waiting to greet the girls. Bopha had linked arms with Olivia; now and again one of them would squeeze the other's arm unable to contain their excitement.

The market was an explosion of colour, scents and sounds. It bore no resemblance to the markets in Malatanga or Tana, where a few rusty tools or a cage of live chickens would be offered for sale from a threadbare rug on the ground. Here, feathered birds hung from hooks, their plumage still glossy –

flashes of petrol blue and tawny brown. Brown and white eggs were piled amidst straw as though freshly laid. There was fruit everywhere, and every kind. Pineapples and bananas swung above them, plastic glasses stuffed with grapes, cherries, or kiwi fruit, creating a kaleidoscope of colour. Strings of bright red dried chillies hung like garlands. And silver fish glinted from crates filled with ice. Olivia covered her nose and mouth. She should have been used to the briny, ammonia scent of fresh fish but today it caught in her throat. They moved on between the stalls. Olivia averted her eyes from the sides of ham hanging overhead, the pink flesh indecent. She started to heave and distanced herself from Bopha until she had it under control. What was the matter with her today?

Bopha was standing by a stall that was serving bowls of paella, saffron rice loaded with muscles, king prawns, and calamari. 'Are you hungry?'

Even if she could face food, Olivia was reluctant to spend money on something that was plentiful on the ship. Every penny that she saved would be sent home to feed her family. The paella cost six euros, more than her dad earned in the shop in one day. 'No. I ate a good breakfast. Maybe our chef will make some of this Spanish food.'

It was a relief to Olivia when they moved away from the pungent smell of garlic. She steered Bopha towards a group of craft stalls just outside the food market. As they got closer, Olivia recognised Alice Wagstaff's head of white hair. It didn't feel right to greet her as though they were friends but Olivia was curious to see what she was examining so intently. She edged her way over to the stall, while Bopha was buying some spices to send home. Fans, wooden sticks and combs were displayed on a gold cloth. A girl behind the stall was demonstrating how a two-pronged stick could be used to pin her hair up in a messy bun. Mrs Wagstaff had a go herself and the girl held up a mirror for her to admire the effect.

Bopha returned with her spices. 'I know it's probably not real saffron because that is so expensive but I bought some to send home. Maybe I could learn to make paella.'

'Hey! Stop!' A man shouted in English and the girls turned to see a boy running through the crowd, chased by a man who Olivia recognised to be one of their passengers.

The crowd parted but the boy was quick and the man giving chase had to stop to catch his breath.

'Let him go. The police or security guards will catch him.' It was Mrs Wagstaff, close enough now for Olivia to hear her. She ducked her head, embarrassed to have witnessed the scene. It felt wrong – as though she was intruding.

'Keep hold of your bag,' Bopha said.

The male passenger had taken off again and now Mrs Wagstaff was running after him, her progress slow as she fought through the crowd. There were bound to be pickpockets. In Malatanga, the city closest to her village, you had to be on guard all the time.

'They should have left him to the policia,' Bopha shook her head.

'I doubt they'll catch him.' Olivia hoped that was the case. She felt a bit protective towards the English lady. 'Let's have a look at that stall.'

They wandered over to where Alice Wagstaff had been admiring hair combs. 'How much?' Olivia asked, holding up the one that she thought Mrs Wagstaff had tried in her hair.

'Twelve euro.'

Olivia put it down. It was too much to spend. But Mrs Wagstaff had been kind and without her support, she might have lost her job. What else could she give to show her gratitude? 'Eight euro?'

'Ten.'

Olivia handed over ten euros. It gave her a warm feeling. Maybe this small act of kindness would please her ancestors and tip the scale in her favour because Olivia was beginning to doubt the witch doctor's assurance that all would be well.

13

Afraid of being alone in a foreign city, Alice had little choice but to follow Gideon. She could have stayed to comfort the Spanish woman who was shouting and waving her hands, attracting a crowd of curious tourists and a few locals who were offering what Alice assumed was support but chasing after Gideon seemed the easiest option; if only he would slow down and admit defeat. The figure that darted out of the market clutching the woman's purse had a slight build. It could have been a woman or a boy.

She could no longer see Gideon but something was going on further down the street. People were stopping to stare and now a policeman ran past wearing a yellow vest with Policia. Thank goodness, Alice thought. Gideon was putting himself in danger attempting to tackle a thief. What if they carried a knife?

A young man had been handcuffed by a plain clothes policeman, who told Gideon not to go anywhere.

Alice sat beside Gideon on a low wall that surrounded a

tree. 'Will they return the purse to its owner or at least let her know?'

Gideon shrugged. 'I guess. Apparently, the pickpockets operate in gangs and they want to bring in more than the one I was chasing.'

'Well done you,' Alice said. She thought of Kate and wished she were there to share her exasperation – this was typical Gideon.

'Thanks, but I think they would have caught him anyway. The plainclothes cop stopped him before I got there.'

'I'm relieved you didn't get hurt. Shall we take a look at the marina, maybe have a jug of sangria?'

'I can't but you go on if you want to. I've got to wait here.'

Immediately, her breath quickened and she felt light-headed. It was as though she were already alone. 'No. I'll stay with you. I don't expect we'll have to wait long.'

Fifteen minutes passed and then the plainclothes policemen said, 'You must attend Carrer Nou de La Rambla station to complete an incident report.'

Alice's skin prickled. 'We have to be on board the ship by three.'

'We've plenty of time.' Gideon sounded calm and confident.

'How do we get there? Are they going to take us?'

'Hold on.' Gideon left Alice whilst he chatted with a police officer. He was behaving as if they had all the time in the world but it was just after two. They ought to explain that they couldn't stay and make their way back to the ship. Alice wrung her hands together. If only she could see Richard and Barbara or someone else from the ship, she would leave Gideon and return with them.

'It's just a few minutes walk. A street off this one.'

'Okay, but we have to be quick, Gideon.'

They asked for directions and after walking a few metres saw a street sign that looked like the one they wanted. Alice sighed with relief.

Fifteen minutes later, they realised it was a street with a similar name. The turning they wanted was on the opposite side of La Ramblas.

'We have to go, Gideon. If we are not on the ship by three It will go without us.'

'Come on, it's down here.'

They were asked to wait, just as Alice had feared. All the while Gideon kept telling her not to stress, that there was plenty of time.

'You do realise that if we miss the ship, we'll have to find our own way to Lisbon? I don't have my passport on me, do you?'

Gideon checked his watch. 'It's 1.45 Chill.'

'What?' Alice grabbed his wrist. 'That's UK time! It's 2.45. We have fifteen minutes to get back.' Her adrenalin fired up; Alice took control.

What are you doing?' Gideon jumped to his feet.

'Phoning the emergency number on the card they gave us. Yes, hello? Hello, this is Alice Wagstaff, a passenger on Halcyon Seas. Gideon Flynn and I were asked to attend a police station. We're leaving now. I'm so sorry. Please wait for us. No, we're on our way. I understand. Okay. Thank you.'

She grabbed Gideon's arm and propelled him out of the station before he had a chance to start explaining their dilemma to an officer. Outside there was a police car. Alice explained that they had to get to the cruise ship in ten minutes or they would need assistance getting to an airport, as they were senior citizens and had no passport or money on them.

By some miracle, the policeman understood and told them to get in.

Ten minutes later Alice and Gideon rushed up the boarding slope of Halcyon Seas with zero minutes to spare. As soon as they were on board, the ship prepared to sail.

Their dining companions were amongst the cluster of people waiting to greet them as they were checked in through security. Apparently, their near miss had aroused concern and a bit of excitement.

'Thank the Lord, you made it,' Patty exclaimed, hugging a bewildered Alice.

Her bewilderment was not the terror of almost missing the ship, it was astonishment at the way she had taken control. If not for her decisive action and the tactics she had used to get a flashing light lift from the policia, they would be watching Halcyon Seas sail away without them.

'What's this I hear about you being detained by the policia, Gideon?' Richard said.

'Gideon chased a pickpocket in Las Ramblas,' someone said. News travelled fast.

Gideon grinned. He had not seemed at all perturbed by his part in making them late.

'This guy needs a drink. A strong one. Come on Gideon buddy, you can tell us all about it in the bar.'

Alice waved Gideon away. She too would have a drink but needed to be alone.

Later, as she sipped a gin and tonic and watched Barcelona diminish in size, Alice felt the fear she had been carrying since Tom's death get smaller too, until they were both a dot on the horizon. She closed her eyes and savoured the sharp, sweet taste in her mouth. The coolness in her throat. The layers of protection she had been building since Tom's illness were dissolving too – no longer needed. Beneath that hard, dark shell of fug was the fearless Alice of her youth. It had been a surprise to discover her today, making an appearance as though she had been there all along. Alice smiled and hugged herself. She didn't want to experience that kind of drama again but it was good to know that she was more than capable of coping in an emergency.

3rd April

Hi

Day 28 Since leaving Barcelona on 28th March we have stopped at Lisbon, and then Cadiz where several passengers travelled independently into Seville. This might be considered high risk given what happened in Barcelona when two passengers were late boarding the ship. Given the age demographic this is a serious concern. What happens when passengers get confused – forgetting the time or getting lost when independently visiting a port? Are vulnerable older people going to be left to fend for themselves or will the ship be delayed leaving, incurring additional fees? How will this impact on other cruise ships? Another factor that has not been thought through. Fortunately, there have been no similar incidents since Barcelona. Tomorrow, we dock in Livorno and many passengers are making plans to travel independently from the port into Florence. I'll observe what preventative action is taken to minimise risk but I suspect there will be none.

Over for now

14

Marianne had not reported the delayed departure of the ship from Barcelona to Libby Braithwaite, despite Hans Peters's insistence that this was required.

'Why is this incident different to any other cruise ship? The delay was less than thirty minutes and no fines were incurred. We've made up the time. No other captain is expected to report such things.'

'With respect, Captain Moore, this is not any cruise ship. We are pioneering a new model of retirement living and this voyage is expected to identify and minimise any potential risks.'

'What risk?' Marianne tried not to raise her voice but her jaw was tense with irritation.

'If we had set sail without two of our residents then we would have left them in a vulnerable situation.'

Marianne tapped the desk with her pen. She was coming to despise the word vulnerable. The guests concerned were Gideon Flynn and Alice Wagstaff, who were capable, intelligent adults. 'We had already arranged for passports to be handed over to the onshore cruise agent. The lifetime cruise fee includes a provision for untoward incidents – transporting residents on to the next port or a hospital if required.'

In the end, they had agreed that Marianne would talk to Gideon Flynn and Hans would log the issue for a future discussion with McIntyre Care. The retirement living aspect of this cruise was having a greater impact than she had anticipated. It was the interference of McIntyre Care, and she suspected Hans was closely aligned to Patrick Dunn, as they seemed to speak the same language. Just one year, she reminded herself. I'll prove myself to be an efficient captain and then I'll then get transferred to captain a Royal Ionian cruise ship. She had come this far, her goal within reach. Let Hans fuss over the bureaucracy of care and she would focus on giving all of their guests the best possible cruising experience.

Marianne had rehearsed her conversation with Gideon Flynn regarding the need to board the ship in plenty of time for departure. She was going to explain the consequences of not doing so and ask him to be more diligent in the future. It was not a conversation she would have had with a passenger on any other cruise ship but, as Hans had reminded her, this wasn't any other cruise ship. Tea, coffee, and a plate of pastries had been delivered to the private meeting room. Gideon was ten minutes late.

'Mr Flynn. Late again.' She wanted to kick herself for sounding like a schoolmistress. It had been intended as a light-hearted quip but Marianne was on edge. This was going to be awkward.

'Captain Moore.' He stood with his feet apart looking straight at her and Marianne felt as though she was the one being held to account.

'Please sit. There's tea or coffee.'

'I don't think you invited me for a tea party. Was there something specific you wanted to discuss?' His eyes darkened and Marianne's stomach lurched.

She tried to sound upbeat. 'You're right. I wanted a bit of a debrief following the incident at Barcelona.' Why had she said debrief? It sounded too formal, as if they were colleagues. A handsome man less than ten years older than her, and looking a lot less than that, was standing before her and she was expected to remind him that he was a vulnerable adult in what was a care home at sea and there were rules to be followed. It was ridiculous. Embarrassing.

'Oh, that.' He seemed relieved and sank into the chair opposite her. Marianne wondered what he had imagined to be the purpose of their meeting. 'I'm sorry we nearly missed the ship. Good job Alice had the emergency phone number on her. What would you have done if we went AWOL? I guess that's something that might happen given the age demographic.' He checked each of the thermos jugs and then poured himself a coffee. She noticed that he didn't offer to pour one for her but neither had he expected her to serve him.

'Well, you didn't. As you say, your partner, Alice, had the good sense to let us know the situation and we were able to wait on this occasion. However, if you had been any later then we would have had no choice but to leave without you.'

'What makes you think Alice is my partner? We're just friends.'

Was he flirting with her? Probably used to women swooning over him. Not this woman. She was his captain and any relations between passengers and crew were strictly prohibited – even if she was interested, and she wasn't.

'Suppose the pickpocket I tackled had put a knife in me? What if Alice did not have the emergency phone number?

Surely allowances must be made for a later departure when circumstances require it?'

Now, Marianne felt wrong-footed, as though he was questioning her decision-making, challenging her authority when he should have been apologising. Hans had told her about the pickpocket and she had to admit to being a little impressed at his bravery. 'I applaud your heroic act, although you might have thought through the consequences before putting yourself in danger. However, I don't think you understand the implications of a delayed departure. The ship has an itinerary to follow...' Gideon rolled his eyes. '...as do other cruise ships waiting for our place at the port. And --'

'-- tea or coffee?' His mouth twitched in a smile. He was playing with her – winding her up and then flirting.

It's not going to work with me, Marianne thought. 'Coffee. Thank you. And we would have had a considerable fine. The point is, Mr Flynn, if passengers of cruise ships thought it did not matter what time they returned from their day on shore, then the ships would always be late departing. The age demographic and nature of this lifetime cruise means that some of our guests are vulnerable.' His eyes narrowed and Marianne cursed herself for using that word. Freakin' Hans and Patrick Dunn were getting into her head.

Gideon drew a deep breath and let it out slowly. 'Vulnerable? Is that how you see me?'

She could smell his aftershave – a musky scent. A tiny scar on his left cheek drew a fine line in the close-cropped beard. 'Of course not. You didn't let me finish. I just meant ... I just wanted to make you aware of the implications. I respect all of our guests. I did not mean to offend.'

He held her gaze until Marianne blushed and had to look away. Gideon sighed. 'As I said, I'm sorry and I'll make sure it doesn't happen again. Unless of course being a vulnerable old geezer, I have a heart attack but I'll try not to have one when on shore.'

'That's very good of you Mr Flynn.'

He stood up and so did she. In her heels, she was a little taller than him. There was a triangle of sunburn beneath his throat. 'If that's all, I'll leave you to get on with the more important jobs of captaining.'

'This was important too.' Her voice came out hoarse.

'Was it?'

'The safety of this ship, the passengers and crew are paramount to me as captain of Halcyon Seas.'

Marianne was afraid that he would hear her heart thumping. It was anger – nothing else. The man was infuriating and the whole situation demeaning. A captain should not be required to have such conversations with their guests. When he left the room, Marianne collapsed into a chair and poured herself another coffee. The sooner she was transferred to a regular cruise ship the better and if she could avoid Gideon Flynn until that time, it would be a bonus.

Marianne was not yet ready to review the financial accounts provided by the ship's purser, there was the ship's log too. Halcyon Seas was too small. Claustrophobic. Her encounter with Gideon Flynn reinforced her need to work on a ship that was properly staffed with three or four chief officers and to escape the boorish, patronising scrutiny of Patrick Dunn. Instead of logging on to the accounts, Marianne checked the Jamboree intranet. A new ship had been added to The Royal Ionian fleet – Mermaid of the Seas. She was a beauty. Twenty-four decks, fourteen restaurants, a theatre and an ice rink. The maiden voyage was early next year and the crew had yet to be appointed. She knew from the way her heart soared that she had to captain that ship. It was what she had dreamed of and it might just be her last chance. It wasn't the guests, they were lovely – except for Gideon Flynn – it was the lack of chief officers and the micromanagement of McIntyre Care. Marianne was pretty sure Hans Peters was reporting to Patrick Dunn. An old friend Jonny– well, ex-boyfriend – was working in HR at The Royal Ionian. She no longer kept his personal number so tried the office.

'Marianne! You've brightened my day. Please tell me you've phoned to invite me to lunch.' He never gave up.

Marianne smiled, warmed by his adoration. 'That would be tricky unless you are in Italy or more specifically the Tyrrhenian Sea. I'm captain of the first Silver Seas lifetime cruise for retirement living.'

'Of course! I did hear something about that. Congratulations. There's a lot of interest in that line of cruising.'

'Yes. It's a great venture. What I'm phoning about, apart from the pleasure of talking to you, of course, is Mermaid of the Seas. I will be looking for a new ship to captain in a year's time and so I would like to be considered. What's the selection process? Is it internal?'

'The Royal Ionian always try to use staff within the group. I'll put you in touch with the recruiting team. So, it's going well, the Halcyon Seas voyage?'

'Yes, it's been a huge success. The future of the cruise industry. I am so glad I got this opportunity – to be at the leading edge. Riding the wave of change.' Marianne wondered whether she had gone a bit too far.

There was a silence and then, 'Ah here it is. I'll send you over the details and put a word in for you, if you would like me to. Maybe next time you are in Miami we could meet for a drink so you can thank me?' He said this with a laugh, as though nervous of misinterpretation or Marianne reading it exactly as it was meant.

'I will look forward to that,' she said. She had no intention of meeting him for a drink but needed to use any influence she could to get that job. If she was successful, it meant she only had to put up with thirteen more months on Halcyon Seas.

15

Day 33 Heraklion, Crete. Alice read the daily news sheet with information about that day's excursions and activities on the ship. Patty had taken the cultural tour with a visit to the Cave of Zeus, historical Heraklion, and traditional villages. It was the first time Alice had chosen to remain on the ship but she was exhausted. In the past twelve days, she had visited Lisbon, Seville, Florence, and Rome – all of the excursions had been wonderful but the Duomo Cathedral in Florence had left a lasting impression. She had gazed up at the spectacular façade, trying to commit to memory the intricate carvings and the majestic statues looking down at her, until her neck ached, but still, she could not tear her eyes away. Her first sight of Rome was breathtaking, too, with its magnificent ancient buildings and wide streets. If only Tom had been with her to sip a Campari and watch the world go by. Life was too short. She was trying to make the most of each day but her body was telling her that it was time to rest. Today she would take her battered copy of The House on the Strand up to the top deck to doze in the shade with an iced tea. But first, she needed to check her emails and see if David could meet her when they toured Australia in May and June. There were nine destinations in Australia and, although it was a big country, Alice was sure that one of them would be close enough for her son to meet her. Just thinking of their reunion squeezed Alice's heart and she placed a hand on her chest. Seeing David again would be more precious than any sight on this cruise. She would give a thousand Sistine Chapels to see his beautiful face again. To hug him and check that he was well – all in one piece and surviving. When he moved to Australia, she had experienced a physical pain, as though her baby had been torn from her womb – never mind that baby was a grown man, to her he would always be her precious babe – her first born. The last time she had seen David was the year after Tom died. A mother should not be parted from her son for so long.

Alice ignored Rachel's email waiting in her inbox; she would enjoy reading it once she had sent off an email to David with the ship's itinerary. Rachel's objection that her mother was travelling too far from home was outweighed by the benefit of sailing across the world so that she could keep in touch with both children.

Satisfied that her email was upbeat and not sounding too needy, Alice signed off with three kisses. David lived in the territory of New South Wales and she suspected he might choose to meet her in Sydney. It would be a day to remember.

Alice made herself comfortable in her armchair, tucking her feet beneath her, and opened Rachel's email. So far from home, it was good to have this solid communication. It made her feel rooted and loved.

Dear Mummy. I hope you have settled into your new home on Halcyon Seas. I would have liked to see you off from Southampton. You left so suddenly we didn't say goodbye properly. It wouldn't be so bad if you were just going on holiday but this is, as you said, a forever cruise. I don't even know when I am going to see you again.

Alice covered her mouth. 'Oh, Rachel darling. I didn't mean to abandon you.' Was she being selfish? Alice sighed and read on.

I had such plans for you and me, once you had settled in Chestnut Court. We could have gone out for the day shopping in John Lewis and lunch at Carlucci's. You know I would have seen more of you if you and Dad had not moved out of London.

Alice cupped her face in her hand. It was true – they had moved away from the area where Rachel and David had grown up. Maybe it was she who had deserted Rachel and not the other way around. When Tom was alive, they would have been happy to celebrate Christmas alone, tucked up in their cosy cottage – a real fire, lots of goodies to eat, a pile of books to read, and films marked out in the Radio Times. And now she had done it again, only this time she was travelling across the world further and further away from Rachel. Was she a bad mother?

I have done a lot of thinking since you left. I can understand why a cruise was attractive, you deserve a good holiday. But once you get over the novelty, I am sure you will become tired of constantly being on the move. You have always been a homebody Mummy. The problem is – the longer you are at sea the less capital you will have left from the sale of your bungalow. The money going out each month is ludicrous. I have spoken to Greg and with some persuasion, he has agreed to my proposal. Here it is.

Alice wondered what this proposal could be. Rachel seemed determined to rescue her, to fix things. Since Tom died, she had been trying to organise Alice as though she were a loose end that needed tying in. Maybe she had been a little rash, caught up in the moment. Alice decided to keep an open mind and was intrigued as to what Rachel might suggest. It would be good to have somewhere to return to once she had seen the world.

I have done the sums and after paying the forfeit for coming out of the retirement package early there would still be enough left over for you to buy something like this property (see link).

Without reading further Alice opened the link. A three-storey Georgian house in Hackney priced at £1,700,000. Rachel must have made a mistake because her bungalow had sold at less than £500,000, and even with her pensions and investments it was nowhere near enough. It was a beautiful house with four bedrooms, the master bedroom on the second floor and three smaller ones above. Alice returned to the email. Rachel was trying to find her somewhere she could afford in London and although it seemed unlikely it was a kind thought. Her daughter really did want her mum living close by.

We would have to sell our property first and I'm not sure what we would get for it. If we could afford the Hackney house between us then you could have two of the bedrooms on the top floor and use of the upstairs bathroom. Alfie, Greg's son, would use the third bedroom when he comes to stay, as well as any guests. We could make one of the bedrooms into a little bedsit for you with a kitchenette and living room. I know your contribution would be minimal but I have persuaded Greg that when we come to sell, the profit should more than make up for any inconvenience and the moving expenses. David might take a bit more persuading but I have explained to him that he would not have received an inheritance anyway, and at least this way we would get to see you and know that you are safe.

Why did her daughter always disappoint her? There she was thinking Rachel cared and all she wanted was to snatch back her inheritance by buying a bigger house. 'If I moved in you would wait until I couldn't manage the stairs and then get social services to fund a care home claiming that you owned the house, not me.'

Her cabin door opened. 'Oh, I am sorry, Mrs Wagstaff. I thought you had gone out for the day. I'll come back later.'

'It's fine, Olivia. I'm about to take myself up on the deck with a book. Just checking my emails whilst we are in port.'

Alice suddenly felt very weary, and a little sad. The excitement that she had felt in seeing David again was clouded by Rachel's thoughtless message. However hard they tried, she and Rachel just seemed to clash. If only she could believe that Rachel was acting out of love and concern for her mother.

'Please wait there. I have something I would like to give to you.' Olivia dimpled and then slipped back out of the door.

Olivia had stored the hair comb in a drawer in the room where her cleaning equipment was kept. She had wanted to hand it to Alice rather than leave it in her cabin but the opportunity had not arisen until now. Since her day in Barcelona, Olivia had not felt sick. The day off must have done her good as her energy seemed to have returned and everyone said how well she looked. Her periods were always irregular, and the nausea she felt that day understandable – she was in an unfamiliar country, subjected to new sights, sounds, and smells. Her body was just adapting to life at sea. Standing outside Mrs Wagstaff's room, Olivia suddenly felt shy.

'Come on in, Olivia. I've got everything I need so I'll get out of your hair.'

That was a strange expression. Olivia wasn't sure exactly what it meant but Mrs Wagstaff had a bag over her shoulder and sunglasses pushed above her hairline so she could guess.

'I bought this gift for you to say thank you.' Olivia passed

Alice the package and watched in delight as Alice folded back the tissue paper and exclaimed over the gift.

'I was admiring these at Las Ramblas market. How clever of you. It's perfect, but you did not need to buy me anything. You do so much for me. It is me who should be buying you a thank you gift.'

'Would you like me to put your hair up?'

Alice sat at her dressing table. 'Yes please.'

Olivia wound Alice Wagstaff's soft hair into a coil and secured it with the comb. 'You look very pretty.'

Alice smiled at Olivia's reflection in the mirror. 'And so do you. Maybe now you could start calling me Alice rather than Mrs Wagstaff? I consider you a friend and if you were my daughter, I would be very proud of you.'

So far from home, Alice's words warmed Olivia. 'And you too are my friend, Alice.'

6th June

Hi

Day 92. Sydney, Australia. It has been some time since my last communication for which I apologise. I have been suffering from a flu-like virus. A few of the passengers and staff have come down with the same. The doctor on board is pretty ancient and as much use as a glass hammer. He recommends paracetamol, plenty of fluid, and rest but seems unconcerned about testing us to identify the virus. The captain sensibly made sure we self-isolated and is playing it down. I'll keep you informed if things develop. Meanwhile, we have crossed the Suez Canal and visited ports in the United Arab Emirates, Sri Lanka, Thailand, Malaysia, Singapore, Vietnam, and Hong Kong. This is the third port stop in Australia and another five after that. The passengers seem to be getting weary after so long at sea.

Over for now.

16

It was Olivia's first day on shore since Singapore and she was looking forward to feeling solid ground beneath her feet.

'Are you ready?' Bopha said. 'We only have three hours but most things are within easy reach, according to this map.

'You go on ahead. I won't be ready to leave for a while yet.'

Bopha tutted. 'What have you got to do that is so important?'

'I want to send an email to my family.'

'It's cheaper to do it from your cell phone at a café with internet. You know they charge us way more than it costs.'

'I have to pop into one of my passenger's cabins too.'

This seemed to satisfy Bopha and she finally left Olivia to explore Sydney on her own. Olivia would have loved a care-free day enjoying the city but there was something that she had to do and she couldn't confide in Bopha. It had been five months since her last period and Olivia could no longer deny the possibility that she was pregnant. Her full figure disguised an expanding waistline, although she would need to request the next size up in uniform. It could be her diet. She hadn't eaten so well her whole life. The lack of a period just one of those things. Who knew how a dramatic change of lifestyle could affect your body? Disney's mantra that all would be well had become meaningless. The only way to quieten her mind was to do a pregnancy test. She had heard about them while doing her training in Miami. It seemed so long ago now – her final night with Raf. As if it were a different world. That's what made the idea of a pregnancy so hard to believe.

A joyous rhythmical sound greeted Olivia as she disembarked, the hot dry air more pleasant than the humidity of Singapore. It reminded her of home. Their passengers had stopped to watch a performance and that was where the sound was coming from. There had been local dancers, and people in traditional dress at most of the main ports but up until now Olivia had only spied them from a deck on the ship. Alice Wagstaff was amongst the crowd. Today, she was meeting her son, David. Olivia had delivered Alice's best day dress from the cleaners and had helped her to pin her hair up, a style that suited her long neck and fine bone structure.

Concerned that she would meet Bopha in the crowd, Olivia edged past, only glancing at the three Aboriginal men who dressed in thongs and headbands, their bodies plastered in white paint, reminded her of Disney doing what he called a traditional dance on Independence Day – although she suspected it was only traditional to Disney. The men were blowing long wind instruments and beating sticks together as they pounded the ground with bare feet.

Alice stepped away from the crowd when she saw Olivia. 'It's good to see you away from the ship for a change and out of uniform.'

Olivia pressed an elbow against the safety pin which was

holding together the gaping zip of her skirt. Alice frowned and Olivia sensed her unspoken question.

'The food on this ship is too good.' She patted her stomach and smiled. 'Is your son meeting you here?'

Alice bit her lower lip and looked into the distance. 'That's what we arranged but he's late.'

'Maybe he got held up in traffic.'

'Yes. That will be it. Tell me all about your day when you get back, Olivia.'

Alice watched Olivia hurry away. She had noticed the girl's increasing weight but it was only today, seeing her dressed in ordinary clothes that it had occurred to Alice that Olivia might be pregnant. She obviously didn't want to share the news. It was a shame, as she had become fond of Olivia and would have liked to celebrate with her. No wonder she looked so tired.

David was forty minutes late. Alice checked her phone but there was no message. They had planned to drink cocktails in the Sky Tower and admire the view. Alice wasn't bothered about having a cocktail but to sit with David and talk face to face would be the best day of this cruise. It had been hard waiting six weeks for his reply. The Far East had been amazing but nothing compared to seeing her boy. What was keeping him? Maybe she was waiting in the wrong place.

William Fellows greeted her when he got off the ship. 'Gooday, Alice.' His Australian vernacular made Alice smile. 'Where are you planning to visit?'

'I'm meeting my son, David. He should be here by now.'

'Maybe he's waiting at the other port, White Bay.'

'Oh, that will be it.' Alice felt both relieved and panicked.

She didn't want to keep David waiting. If only he would answer her texts. 'Do you know how far away it is?'

No, but it can't be far by taxi. If you weren't otherwise occupied, I was going to suggest that you visit the botanical gardens with me, being a fellow gardener. Like me,' he added with emphasis.

'Oh yes – Fellow gardener, very good. That would have been lovely. Take lots of photos and tell me all about it at dinner. I'd better get going so I don't miss my son. Thank you!'

William patted his bag. 'Photos and lots of notes.'

Alice dithered a little. Should she stay or go to the other port. It was over an hour from their meeting time. What if she went to White Bay while David, realising his mistake, was making his way to Circular Quay? Alice stabbed another text into her phone. She felt so helpless, and foolish, standing there in her Joseph Ribkoff navy shift and heels. At least she could sit in the shade. But Alice was afraid to move; standing where she was David would see her straightaway. Besides, her breath had become rapid and shallow. Her knees shaky. She didn't want to stray too far from the safety of the ship.

Another cruise ship was berthed alongside Halcyon Seas and so hundreds of tourists bled into the area around Circular Quay and beyond, instantly recognisable by their lanyards and disorientation. Olivia stood behind a couple who were consulting their map.

'This here is The Rocks. Ooh, there's a market, speciality stores, boutiques, and galleries.'

Other tourists were following a path from the quay and Olivia joined them, hoping that one of the stores in The Rocks would be a pharmacist. There were stalls displaying crafts which had been made by Aboriginal people – wood carvings, paintings, and coasters. Olivia recognised a distinctive style of dotted patterns in earthy hues. She could no longer hear the performance on the quay but now and again there was the sound of a percussion instrument, as tourists turned a tube called a rain stick or blew on a long wooden horn. Olivia imagined how the same tourists would react to the wonders of her village in Madagascar; they too produced local crafts and had their traditions.

There were several expensive-looking stores selling dresses similar to those worn by their passengers. Barbara and Richard Lopez were looking in the window of one. Olivia hurried past unnoticed. Although there were plenty of stores, stalls, and restaurants, Olivia couldn't see a pharmacist. She was going to ask someone who looked local, maybe a stall holder, when the girls from the beauty spa on Halcyon Seas came towards her en masse, wearing tiny shorts and vests, they were causing a few heads to turn. Olivia ducked into an alleyway. It was called Suez Canal. Their ship had sailed through the Suez Canal. Olivia wondered why this lane had the same name. At least here it was quiet and shady. She followed the paved lane downhill, passing a jeweller. It gave her hope that she might find a pharmacy here off the beaten track. She turned into another lane; this one was narrower. The walls on either side seemed to press against her, taunting her, *You have shamed your family. You can no longer hide.* The silhouette of a man was pinned to the wall, a kind of plaque. Olivia paused to read the inscription, a poem about the Laneways where many had died and how their ghosts still haunted the area. She shivered. Another plaque had the words whores and prostitutes. Had her ancestors led her to this maze of narrow alleyways to give her a lesson, a message – that she was no better than the prostitutes who had once inhabited this part of the city? Why was she the only one down here? Olivia turned from one lane into another, desperate now to escape their cool, dank confines. At last, the sun penetrated the end of a lane and Olivia followed it into a wider one where there was a babble of noise – glasses clinking and laughter. The Rocks Café and alongside it a pharmacy. Thank the Lord.

She sat in the café with a Sprite, the pregnancy test in her bag. In her heart, she knew that she was pregnant but so long as she didn't see the test result, she could still believe that, all would be well. But, away from home, Olivia was beginning to see the local beliefs and traditions for what they were – superstition. Disney had deceived her – how could he possibly know what the future held? Unless the test showed negative. Maybe her ancestors were testing her faith. A busboy cleared her table, taking away her empty glass. She couldn't put it off any longer.

As Olivia waited for the line that would determine her future, she closed her eyes and prayed. Whatever the result, she would accept it with grace.

She opened her eyes and tried to still her breath before looking down at the stick clasped between her fingers. It was positive. She was carrying Raf's baby. Olivia put her hands on her belly. I knew you were there, little one. You've been in my heart and head even when I denied you were in my womb. Raf must never know. He would do the right thing by her but Olivia didn't want that. If they had a future together, she wanted it to be through choice. Raf had not been at the quayside to wave her off. He was young, handsome, and carefree. He would have moved on and that was as it should be – they came from very different worlds. But I will love and cherish you, little one. She stroked the swell of her stomach. Telling Mammon and Pappa that she would be coming home to give birth to their grandchild would be hard. They would be disappointed not to receive the extra income but, hopefully, a first grandchild might soften the blow. She had a certificate so maybe she could find work on another ship when she was ready to return to work.

Olivia strolled back to the ship, this time using the main thoroughfare. When Halcyon Seas and a much larger cruise ship came into view, she wondered how her feet had found their way, as she remembered little of the journey. Bopha ran up to greet her at the gangplank.

'There's been a delivery of mail.'

'Could you all wait outside until the mail is ready for distribution?' The officer sorting mail looked a bit harassed, as eager staff pressed in around him searching for their names.

Olivia saw an envelope with her name written in green ink. It was from Mammon. 'Please can I take it?' Her hand hovered over the envelope.

The officer jerked his head a fraction and Olivia interpreting this as yes, grabbed the envelope and fled before he could stop her. She found a quiet corner in the staff computer room, knowing that it was unlikely anyone would be using the internet. Olivia kissed the envelope and then tore it open.

Dear Olivia

We are all so proud of our little Olive Oyl. Whenever there is a ship on the horizon one of the children says, that is Olivia's ship. Thank you for the money you transferred from the bank in Indonesia. Your grand-mammon is surely looking after us as your job will save this family from starvation. With the shop low in stock and villagers without money or produce to barter we are all relying on the daily catch. The fishing boat Pascal, and some of the other villagers, use has sprung a leak – a big one. It could not be repaired.

We put down the money you sent as a deposit on a new boat. Everyone knows that you have a good job and so, thankfully, we have been trusted to take possession of it immediately and pay monthly instalments. So, you see, your ancestors knew what they were doing when they blessed you with a job on a cruise ship.

Olivia couldn't read anymore. She put her head in her hands. Leaving the ship was no longer an option but neither was staying. The baby would arrive in four months. Even if she did find work after giving birth, it would take months. Halcyon Seas was Silver Seas' first retirement cruise ship and as far as she knew her certificate was not yet recognised by any other cruise line. If she told Hans Peters that she was pregnant as she had planned to, he would find a replacement for her immediately. For now, she had to work as long as she could without being discovered and hope for a miracle.

17

Marianne hadn't visited Sydney for a few years and would have enjoyed spending the day exploring the shops around The Rocks and the Botanical Gardens but the ship's engine light was signalling a concern and, with the decreased gas mileage, Marianne suspected that the engine needed some attention. Time to put on her boiler suit and take up the role of chief engineer. Before getting to work she checked her emails. At the top was an email from her friend Jonny in HR with the reference Mermaid of the Seas. Marianne's heart beat a little faster as she opened it.

I am introducing Captain Marianne Moore as promised. I have attached her CV and application for the role of Captain of Mermaid of the Seas. Captain Moore comes highly recommended and meets all of the job specifications.

The email had been sent to the recruiting officer of The Mermaid with her copied in by way of introduction. There was another email from Jonny telling her that he thought it would just be a formality and the job was as good as hers.

'Wow.' Marianne let out her breath. At last, the job she had worked for all of her adult life. She wanted to celebrate with someone – share the news, but apart from Gloria Busby there was nobody, and Gloria was doing a tour of the Sydney Opera House. Instead, she went in search of a pastry to enjoy with her coffee. The engine room could wait.

Frederic greeted her. 'Captain Moore. What a pleasure to see you. Are you here to sample my Pistachio Cannoli? Freshly baked – for you.' He kissed his fingers.

'Frederic! I didn't expect to see you back at work. I hear you've been sick with this flu virus.'

'I am well, thank you, Captain.'

'It's a nasty virus but thank the Lord it's not Covid.'

Frederic frowned. He continued packaging her pastries. When he handed them over, he inclined his head, signalling that there was something he wanted to say in private. Marianne walked with him away from the counter.

'How do we know it was not Covid?'

'Dr Miles assured me it was the common cold and nothing to be concerned about.'

'But we do not know that. I didn't do a test. The doctor just told me to rest and take paracetamol. I self-isolated as you instructed us to but I was surprised nobody was tested.'

Marianne's jaw dropped. 'Maybe Dr Miles just forgot to test you?'

'Nobody has been tested, as far as I know.'

'Thank you for telling me, Frederic.' Marianne handed back the pastries. 'Another time.' She made an apologetic face.

Dr Miles was alone in his consulting room. He jumped up when Marianne entered, having knocked and received no reply. She heard a draw slide shut beneath the desk. 'Captain Moore. How can I help you?' His face was flushed.

'You told me that everyone with symptoms had been tested for Covid.'

'I do not believe I said that, Captain Moore. What I said was, nobody had Covid. It was – *is*, my medical opinion.'

Marianne wanted to haul him out from behind his desk and slap him. 'I don't give a damn about your opinion. You were ordered to test everyone with symptoms.'

'It seemed a waste of resources to use the tests when it is clear to me that this is nothing more than a bad cold.'

Marianne put her hands on his desk and leaned in so that her face was close to his. She could smell alcohol on his breath. 'Test every person who has or has had a cold or any other symptom. That is an order. I will be taking this further, Dr Miles.'

As she stormed out of his office, she saw William Fellows sitting in the row of seats outside the consulting room. He would have heard every word. Marianne took a deep breath to try and calm herself.

'Hello, Mr Fellows. I hope you do not have this virus.'

'No, I've already had it. Dr Miles said it was just a cold. I'm fully recovered now but it was a bad one.'

'Good. Pleased to hear you are better now.'

If they had Covid on the ship and she hadn't followed policy and procedure then her transfer to Mermaid of the Seas would be jeopardised. How she handled this was critical. At least there hadn't been any more leaks of information. There had been one unfortunate article in Care Matters, a journal for care home providers, which Hans had brought to her attention. *What happens when a resident with failing memory gets left behind? The lifetime cruise model of retirement living needs to consider how to keep residents safe without compromising the ship's itinerary.* They had responded by putting in place risk assessments of each passenger's capacity to determine if anyone should be encouraged to stick to supervised excursions. Since then, it had been quiet and Marianne hoped that whoever had been passing on information had given up, following Hans's warning to the staff.

Four days later, Marianne contacted HQ asking for Dr Miles to be transferred from her ship. They couldn't risk the health of passengers being compromised due to the incompetence of a doctor who Marianne strongly suspected had a drink problem. It wasn't her concern, let personnel at HQ sort it out; she just needed him to be replaced. The poor condition of the ship's engines was also worrying her. Halcyon Seas may look shiny and new after its refurb but the mechanics were old and needed serious attention or they risked engine failure.

The only good news – apart from the promise that she would be captain of Mermaid of the Seas, in the new year – was that nobody had tested positive for Covid. There was some sort of virus doing the rounds but Dr Miles had been right, it was most probably the common cold.

5th July

Hi

Day 121, Santa Cruz, Tenerife

The virus that I had a few weeks ago spread quickly as viruses do on cruise ships. Nobody has tested positive for Covid but the ship's doctor suggested the test might not pick up all strains. If that is the case then this presents a serious concern. I bought the doctor a few Jack Daniels to get this information. From what he said, it sounds as though he's being kicked off the ship when we reach Southampton. The doctor likes his drink and I suspect this is why he is being dismissed.

Staffing is getting stretched with so many of them sick. As they are self-employed they will be losing pay so many trying to struggle on. All things considered – a recipe for disaster.

Over for now.

18

'I cannot move,' Alice said, her limbs liquid as she melted into the sun lounger. 'I had no idea a massage could unknot every muscle. Honestly, I don't think anything is holding me together now.'

'I told you,' Patty said. She sat up with a towel wrapped around her. 'I went early on in the cruise and then I had to keep going back.'

'Isn't it expensive to make it a regular thing?' Alice said, and then regretted sounding mean. 'I just wondered.'

Patty pulled her chair closer to Alice's lounger. 'I don't mind paying if it goes to Charanya. She has a four-year-old girl at home in Thailand. The poor darling, she misses that baby girl. After the first few massages, she relaxed with me and I encouraged her to talk. Now, I look forward to our chats and I think she does too.'

Alice knew what it was like to miss family. David never did arrive in Sydney. She had returned to her cabin with a headache from standing so long in the sun. Fortunately, there was nobody there to witness her humiliation. She kicked off her heels and stepped out of her dress not bothering to hang it, before slipping between her cool sheets. Cocktail hour and then dinner came and went before Alice crawled out of bed. Before setting sail, she checked her emails to see if David had offered any explanation. His email had been sent the evening before. An unexpected work meeting meant that he could not spend the day in Sydney with her as planned. Her head was still pounding when she reached for her phone. A text. *Sorry, I left my phone at home. Just saw your messages. Hope you didn't wait around too long and had a good day in Sydney.*

The time apart from her eldest son would have been longer than the time Charanya might spend away from her infant, Alice thought, and then felt mean. She had enjoyed David and Rachel's childhoods.

'Did Charanya get to see her family when we were in Thailand?'

'No, and that must have been so hard. Her parents couldn't afford to travel to Phuket and we didn't stop long enough for Charanya to visit them.'

'Hello, ladies.' Barbara joined them in the astro-turfed solarium. She waggled her manicured nails. 'What do you think? Stars and stripes.'

'Very patriotic,' Patty said.

'I would order a coffee but I hate to ask. The staff are so stretched and to be honest, I'm getting a bit tired of being waited on.'

Alice sat up. 'So am I! Olivia, my cabin maid, looks dreadfully pale and tired. I can't bear to watch her cleaning my room when I know she's dead on her feet.'

'You haven't been off the ship since Sydney,' Barbara said arching an eyebrow.

'I think I just needed a rest,' Alice said. 'I've loved every port but the point of a holiday is to refresh you so you can return to normal life. Nothing about this feels normal.'

'I told Richard that we would get tired of living like this. At home, I kept busy volunteering at the community library, Pilates class, and book club. I've always loved travelling but there's something wonderful about getting home. Sleeping in your own bed. Seeing what's grown in the yard in your absence. Catching up with neighbours and friends.'

'Sugar, you are sleeping in your own bed and like it or not we are your neighbours and friends,' Patty said.

'If you feel like that, why did you agree to this lifetime cruise?' Alice swung her legs round to sit on the side of her lounger.

'Richard has been miserable since retiring from work. I tried to get him interested in something – *anything* – but I was wasting my breath. The only time he seemed happy was when we were travelling. Then, on our last cruise, he said, "We should sell up and live on a cruise ship." We were on holiday – it was easy to go along with the fantasy. I mean, wherever we have visited on our travels we've talked about what it would be like to live there – it's what you do.' She looked to the two women for confirmation.

'Tom and I discussed moving to France every summer when we visited. As soon as we were home, he would forget all about it. I wouldn't have minded.'

'France isn't far from you in England. It would be like moving to another state for us. But you know what I mean. Anyway, when the Silver Seas advert was featured in the Sunday supplement, that was it. He interpreted my mild interest when we were on holiday as my approval and went ahead planning it – as a surprise. Of course, he didn't sign anything or put down a deposit until he had spoken to me but by then he was emotionally committed to the idea. I have to admit he was transformed. Then, seeing him so happy and excited I felt as though I was being selfish insisting that we stayed put. He had been the main provider all of our married life and it seemed wrong to stand in the way of him doing something that he really wanted.'

'So, you gave up everything for Richard to follow his dream?' Patty said.

'I'm not complaining. Not really. How could I when we are living like this?' With a flash of stars and stripes, Barbara gestured at the blue sky, the sea, and the sun loungers. 'It seems so ungrateful.'

'What brought you here, Alice?' Patty said.

'It was this or an old peoples' home.'

Barbara and Patty laughed.

'I'm not joking. My daughter had written me off. It's my fault. Since my husband died, I had retreated a bit. Well, a lot now I look back on it. When you stop doing things it's easy to lose your confidence. Tom did all of the driving, for example, and so when I sat behind a wheel again, I was scared. I gave the car away. Rachel, my daughter, was worried about me living alone and wanted me to move closer to her.'

'You could have moved into an apartment, why a care home? We are nowhere near ready to be written off,' Barbara raised her voice in indignation.

'I'm not sure I could have afforded a flat in London. I'm exaggerating because Chestnut Court did have apartment living but it was within a complex to meet the needs of older people as they deteriorated.'

Patty shrieked with laughter and Barbara joined in, holding her stomach. Alice giggled and then she laughed too, letting go of any hurt. Saying it out loud as she sat on a sun lounger feeling as though she were thirty years old, it did seem hilarious.

Barbara wiped the tears from her eyes. 'Honey, you look a million dollars and can still set the world alight if you have a mind to. Sometimes, I'm glad I don't have any kids to remind me that I'm ageing. I can just stay at my favourite age – fifty.'

'Did you choose not to have any children?' Patty said, diving in as usual.

'We couldn't have children but Richard and I accepted that fact. It has never caused me any sadness. Until now, I have enjoyed a very full and rewarding life.'

They sat in silence. It sounded ungrateful to complain when, to the outside world, they would appear to have everything, but Barbara was right – life seemed to lack purpose.

'Would you consider leaving the ship?' Patty directed this question at Alice.

'I honestly don't know. I don't think so. Where would I go? Here, I have friends and I do love seeing the world. I never dreamt I would visit Asia, Africa, and Australia, and now we are headed back to Europe before we do it all again.'

'And again. And again,' Barbara said, her tone weary.

'I guess we can't have everything.' Patty sighed, as she arranged herself on the sun lounger, reclining.

'You haven't told us why you are on this cruise, Patty,' Alice said.

Patty put on her sunglasses and turned her face to the sun. 'Because my daughter, Beth, refuses to speak to me and has denied me access to my grandchildren. My sister sends me the photos because she does see them. It's as if I do not exist in my daughter's life. We only had one child and wanted to give her the world. I don't know what we did wrong. She rebelled as a teenager and looking back maybe I was a bit hard on her. I didn't like the crowd she was mixing with and as it turned out I was right. Beth left home at seventeen to move in with a man who abused drugs and alcohol. Still, we tried to support her.

When we realised that he was beating her up we got the welfare involved. That was it. She was furious and stopped speaking to us. We paid for her rehabilitation – because she was an addict by then – and kept in touch through the staff working with her. Now, she has three children and lives near my sister. No partner but my sister helps with childcare. I kept hoping that one day we might be reconciled but when you want something so much and keep being disappointed it gets so that you can bear it no longer. All I can hope is that one day, when they are young adults, my grandchildren might ask to meet me. So, I came away to try and make a new life before it's too late.'

Alice lay a hand on Patty's arm and then she stroked it as if soothing away the pain. She knew all about disappointment. 'You are a good mother and grandmother. They are lucky to have you. And so are we.'

Patty removed her shades. Her eyes were red. 'Please don't leave the ship, Alice, or you, Barbara. You're the best friends a girl could wish for.'

Barbara extended her arms and they all held hands.

'I'm thinking that we need a toast. Have you tried a Pornstar Martini?' Alice said.

'It's only just after three,' Patty gasped, widening her eyes.

'*I know*. What are you thinking Alice Wagstaff? Trying to lead us astray. We'd better humour the poor girl, Patty, what with her failing memory and disorientation of time.' Her two friends shook their heads, and then they laughed. 'I can't believe your daughter tried to get you into a home for seniors.'

As the three friends rocked back and forth clutching their stomachs and howling, Alice wondered at their tears of laughter so close to those of grief.

19

'You look tired,' Alice said to Olivia when she stepped into the cabin with a pile of clean towels.

Olivia closed the door behind her. She wasn't meant to clean when a resident was in the room but they had fallen into this habit and Olivia looked forward to their chats. 'Some of the hotel staff are sick and so I have had to cover extra shifts.'

'What time did you start this morning?'

'It's okay. I had a couple of naps during the night. I do not need much sleep.'

'You mean you've been working since last night?'

Olivia yawned; she couldn't help it. So long as she didn't think about sleep and kept going, she might fool her body into believing she didn't need any. 'Oh!' She wrapped an arm across her belly as the baby kicked. 'Oh, I forgot to fetch more tea bags,' she improvised.

'There's no need. Why don't you have a little lie down on my bed?'

'I cannot Alice. I must clean your cabin and the others in this corridor.'

'Just a few minutes. You will feel better for it. Is there any other reason you might be feeling tired, Olivia?'

'No. Just busy.' She hated lying to Alice but if anyone found out her secret, she would be sent home and her job immediately filled. By keeping quiet she hoped to work right up until the ninth month. A couple more months' wages would make a huge difference to her family and, if she was lucky, she would be able to give birth and return quickly to work before a replacement was found. It wasn't a great plan but it was the best one she had.

Alice smiled. 'Go on. I won't let you get into trouble with Hans the Horrible. Trust me.'

'I've made you a cup of tea.' The mattress shifted as Alice sat on the edge of the bed, waking Olivia.

'What's the time? How long have I been asleep?'

'You've had a lovely nap. Here, drink your tea before it gets cold.'

Olivia checked her watch. 'Oh no! I have been asleep for 90 minutes.' She sat up but Alice put a hand on her shoulder.

'Patty, Barbara and I have cleaned our own cabins and most of the other ones in this corridor. We've seen you do it enough times and all of us are experienced in doing housework. To be honest it made a change.'

'Thank you, but what will the other passengers think?'

'Between us, we know them all and they had no objections. Fortunately, no one is sick on our deck. You must take good care of yourself, Olivia.'

Was it her imagination or was Alice looking pointedly at her belly? Alice was so kind, her face inviting a confidence, but Olivia couldn't tell her the truth. She just had to get through a couple more months.

'Please thank your friends. If Mr Peters hears about this – '

'—He won't. We've enjoyed ourselves and you are better for a sleep.'

Olivia did feel much better but she was afraid that if she continued working long shifts that she might harm her baby. Flying home when she was close to her due date was going to be risky but she had to earn every penny that she could. There was nothing that she could say to her family – she was a coward. But despite the shame of bringing misfortune to her family, Olivia couldn't regret the babe in her womb. It was Raf's child. The baby would be a reminder of him – a little Raf. Maybe her ancestors had blessed her. Losing her job and failing her family was the price she had to pay.

14th July

Hi

Day 130 Copenhagen, Denmark. I don't know if it's the after-effects of the cold/flu but there seems to be a general feeling of malaise on board the ship. When Halcyon Seas arrives at new ports and when she sets sail there is no longer the excitement. This is what we thought would happen. You can have too much of a good thing and it seems that passengers may have become weary with travelling.

Very few people are sick. Whatever was doing the rounds seems to have died off.

We are visiting the Baltic cities, then UK and back through Europe.

The staff seem very tired after working double shifts. This is the result of working with an underfunded staff establishment there is no slack to cover sickness.

Over for now.

20

Marianne decided it was time to treat herself to Frederic's pastries as she had intended before Milesgate – the alcoholic doctor who had failed to test passengers and staff with Covid symptoms, almost costing Marianne her job and any hopes of promotion. Thankfully, a serious incident had been averted by her quick action. Although the right noises had been made about removing Dr Miles from the ship and providing a replacement doctor, Marianne was still waiting to hear when that would be. In the meantime, Dr Miles was being closely monitored and they were relying on his able team of support staff to provide day-to-day medical care.

Marianne loaded a pastry fork with a mouthful of deliciousness. Frederic had delivered a Religieuse cream puff to her room. Two choux buns, one filled with mocha and the other creme pâtissier, both covered in a dark ganache. Decadent, indulgent, and friggin' gorgeous. Oh, she so deserved this. There was a knock on her door.

'Captain?'

'Come in, Gloria,' Marianne wiped the corner of her mouth and sighed in contentment.

Gloria stood at her cabin door for a couple of seconds before her eyes alighted on Marianne's treat. 'I didn't mean to interrupt your private time. I could come back later.'

'No, come and join me. I'll call for more coffee. You *could* share this with me.'

Gloria laughed. 'I wouldn't come between a captain and her chocolate. Get me a Portuguese tart?'

'So, what gives?' Marianne said once they had sorted refreshments.

'I'm sensing a mood shift in our guests. Most of them are now in reasonable health but there's a general feeling of despondence. I wondered if you would join them for dinner this evening. It's been some time since you made an appearance and I really think it could lift the mood.'

Marianne had routinely mixed with guests but had avoided meeting with them en-masse. The confrontation with Gideon Flynn still embarrassed her, if she was honest with herself. Meeting guests in small clusters had allowed her to be selective but Gloria was right it had been too long since the last formal dinner.

'Sure. That's a good idea. Is it formal dress?'

'No, just smart casual. I'll make an announcement as soon as I leave you. One other thing, Captain. I told you that our staff checks didn't show up anything to help identify the leak.'

Marianne pushed a chocolate-smeared plate away from her. Damn it, she had chocolate on the sleeve of her jacket.

'Here.' Gloria seemed to produce a wet wipe from nowhere and passed it to her. 'Nothing on any of the staff but we've looked at the passenger files again. Rosemary Diamond is a freelance writer.'

'The source? It has to be. Good job, Gloria.' Marianne

satisfied that her jacket was presentable, discarded the wipe. 'I'll be joining Rosemary Diamond's table first, this evening.'

'Excellent. The entertainer who joined us in Cittavecchia is a big hit with the guests, and…' Gloria leant across the table a smile flickering, 'with Hans.'

'Really? I did notice that Hans seemed more relaxed. Are they involved?'

'Don't know but a mega crush for sure.'

'If they are involved let's hope it lasts until Antonio has to leave the ship.'

'He's with us until Naples. Sixteen days. Hopefully not long enough to break any hearts.'

Gideon looked directly at Marianne the second she entered the dining room and she was cross with herself for noticing. Marianne turned away and sought out Rosemary Diamond. She remembered her now, an English woman who wore cat-eye spectacles. As Marianne approached her table Rosemary was swapping her spectacles for the reading glasses worn on a chain around her neck.

Rosemary, 'Call me Rosie,' wrote romantic fiction – short stories for women's magazines. 'I must confess Captain Moore you are the inspiration for my current heroine. *Love at Sea*. It started out as a short story but might become a novella. You lead such a glamorous life.'

Marianne did not like to disillusion Rosie. Her life was far from glamorous. As if a captain would have time for romance. Apart from a few dates with colleagues and one longer-term relationship years ago, she had avoided any involvement. It didn't work. She was at sea for long periods and had decided in her early thirties that being a ship's captain was more important to her than having a partner or a family. What she hadn't expected was for it to take so long. Satisfied that Rosemary was not hiding anything, Marianne chatted with some of the other guests.

'Where would you like your dessert served?' Gloria asked Marianne.

'Table fifteen.' Gideon was standing behind Gloria and answered on Marianne's behalf. Except he didn't because she had no intention of joining his table. Gloria looked from one to the other.

'I was going to skip dessert and get back to the bridge.'

'Please come and join us. I've been waiting for the opportunity to put things right since... well...' He looked uncertain, his defences down.

Marianne nodded to Gloria and followed Gideon across the dining room to his table. Patty greeted her enthusiastically and then they all started speaking to her at once. All except for William Fellows who was writing with great concentration in a notebook.

Patty caught Marianne watching him; she must have been frowning. 'Don't mind William, he always writes up his ship's log at dinner. You'd be surprised at the things he notices.'

Marianne's scalp tingled. 'We should share notes, Mr Fellows. Maybe I will learn something from your log.'

William looked up as if noticing the captain for the first time. He blushed and closed his book, tucking it into the inner pocket of his jacket. 'My ramblings are of no interest to anyone but myself.' Marianne hoped that was the case.

'Don't think we haven't tried to sneak a peek?' Patty laughed.

'I think William is a secret author,' Barbara joined in.

Their desserts arrived and William, who now looked extremely uncomfortable, focused on the careful pairing of cheese and cracker.

'I've been wanting to talk to you alone since we last met,' Gideon began in a low voice. 'This is hardly alone but I could not miss this opportunity to explain myself and ask for your forgiveness. I behaved appallingly.'

The pistachio ice cream in Marianne's dish was beginning to melt but she sat very still, afraid of saying or doing the wrong thing. She wished that she had slipped away before Gideon intercepted her. She would not look at him. Let him finish what he had to say. Give herself time to think.

'I should not have been late boarding the ship in the first place. I know that has had repercussions and resulted in a new policy on independent travel.' Opposite them, William had started writing in his notebook again. 'I made your job harder than it needed to be. For that I am sorry. Then, when you spoke to me as the captain of Halcyon Seas, I was disrespectful. I did not mean to be but I'm finding it hard – this ageing thing.'

Now Marianne did look up and saw the anguish in his eyes. She wanted to take hold of his hand to be his friend, not his captain. 'You're not old. I told you that everyone who boards this ship stays fifty forever.'

Gideon's mouth lifted one side in a half smile. 'When you said I was vulnerable. Well, it was my stupid male pride. A beautiful young woman looking at me as though I was a pathetic old geezer. Maybe I am but…'

Marianne's hand covered his before she could stop herself. 'I didn't think that. I don't. I'm old enough to qualify for this cruise as a passenger too. I'm sorry I made you feel that way.'

Gideon turned his hand over and squeezed hers before letting go. 'Your ice cream's melting.'

. . .

The next day, Halcyon Seas passed under the Oresund Bridge to the sound of cheers. Most of the guests had gathered on deck to watch, as the ship crept under appearing to have only millimetres clearance. It was a navigation Marianne had achieved many times but it was great theatre and she enjoyed increasing the tension with a commentary from the bridge. The next stop was Helsinki. They had just completed the navigation when a senior officer signalled for her attention. Marianne was still smiling, as she always got a buzz from the passengers' reaction when he delivered the news.

'What do you mean the port's closed to us?' It was ridiculous. The itinerary had been scheduled and docking fees paid in advance by Silver Seas.

'Apparently, a communication has been passed to Silver Seas restricting the debarkation of passengers in Sweden.'

Marianne radioed the harbour pilot, demanding an explanation.

'We cannot risk contamination. Helsinki is closed to the crew and passengers of Halcyon Seas.'

A call came through from Libby Braithwaite as Marianne was trying to make sense of this statement.

'It's not just Sweden.' Libby's ashen face filled the screen of Marianne's phone. 'Norway has sent the same message. Somehow, they have heard about the virus.'

'But everyone, passengers and crew, has tested negative. There was a cold doing the rounds but even that has passed. I don't understand.'

'Word has got out that there's a strain of virus that isn't picked up by the tests we have. The world has got super sensitive. Could you take the ship around the British Isles for a couple of weeks, let this blow over?'

'Yes, that's no problem. It's not as though we won't visit those ports again. I expect our guests will be glad for a little break from shore visits. How did Sweden and Norway find out about the flu outbreak?'

'We don't know. Leave us to handle the communication; we don't want other countries overreacting. Did you check your staff records?'

'Yes, we did and reviewed the profiles of guests. It must have been Dr Miles. He's been spreading false rumours. We have to get him off this ship. When am I getting a replacement?'

'We're trying to find a doctor willing to work on a retirement cruise ship – it's not a popular option with medics in the industry.'

Too right, Marianne thought. Her patience was wearing thin. 'Then we need to check all of his communications. If he's responsible for the leaks he has to be dismissed.'

'I agree. In the meantime, we'll try and sort out this mess. If Dr Miles was being properly managed in the first place, then this whole situation could have been averted.' Libby Braithwaite hung up.

Marianne checked no one was watching and then gave the communications deck a good kick, stubbing her toe.

15th October

Hi

Day 224. Somewhere on the Indian Ocean.

Sorry for the delay since my last communication. The signal at sea is not good. You would have heard on the national news that Halcyon Seas has been permitted to stop at designated ports to pick up supplies but so far passengers have not been allowed to disembark. There are apparently ongoing discussions about ending the cruise and isolating residents before repatriating them. It is complete nonsense as there is no virus on the ship. If you could use any influence in getting the truth out there it would make my life easier. I'm ready to come home, having achieved what you asked of me. Besides, the Captain has started to monitor communications. The passengers aren't aware but it is obvious to me. The ship's doctor was accused of leaking information and he willingly passed over his phone and laptop to be checked. Of course, he is in the clear but it is only a matter of time before my cover is blown.

A lot has happened on board in the three months since Copenhagen. Three months without putting feet on terra firma – it's driving us all crazy.

The hotel director, Hans Peters, left the ship on a helicopter. It was sent to pick up a singer Antonio Caruso but Hans managed to sneak on board with him. Nobody was sorry to see him go, Hans wasn't popular, but it has left the ship with few senior officers. The cruise director has doubled as hotel director but there is very little order or supervision of staff. The captain's priority seems to be convincing the world that there is no virus. So, absolute chaos on board.

Over and out.

21

'What will you do if you have to go home?' Patty asked Alice, as they sat in the dining room polishing cutlery.

'I don't know. Rachel's made herself the leading light of this Facebook group demanding the return of residents and a generous refund. Nobody's asked us if we want to go home.'

'And do you?'

'There's nothing to go home to. Home is here with you, Barbara, Richard. William too. You've become my family. I'd like to get off this damn ship. It's discrimination. We're healthier than some of the passengers on a regular cruise ship, for God's sake.'

Rajesh, the young waiter who usually served their table, came up behind Alice. 'You do not need to polish the silver, that is my job. But thank you. I will put these away. If you need something else to do...'

'Whatever's needed.' Patty bestowed a warm smile.

'Would you mind laying the table-cloths?'

The transition from being waited on to assisting hotel staff happened gradually, starting with the day they helped Olivia by cleaning cabins. At first, it had been under the radar but now that Hans Peters had left the ship, leaving Gloria in charge, they didn't bother to hide their activity. Gloria was too busy with the ship's choir and dance troupe – Barbara had joined both – to involve herself in the hotel management side of things.

'Gideon says that Captain Moore is fighting for our rights. She's been on national TV speaking from the ship. If Gideon's to be believed, she's winning and all restrictions will soon be lifted.'

'Mrs Alice! Mrs Alice. Please, come quickly.' Bopha ran into the dining room waving her hands. 'Quickly! Come now.'

Alice looked to Patty, unsure what to do. She wasn't good in an emergency. Patty shrugged her shoulders; she seemed unfazed. Maybe Bopha was over-reacting – she had spilt bleach on the carpet or run out of cleaning fluid. Filling the vacated role of hotel director, or at least the occasional supervision of staff, seemed to have fallen to Alice. 'I'll catch up with you at dinner,' she said and followed Bopha at a pace resembling a jog.

Olivia was clinging to the posts of the bunk bed and digging her heels into the mattress. She let out a long wail.

'We have to get her to the medical centre,' Alice said. Why hadn't she acted on her instincts? She had guessed Olivia might be pregnant but the girl had vehemently denied it. 'Alright, Olivia. I'm here. It's going to be okay.'

Olivia breathed heavily, now the contraction had passed. 'I am sorry, Alice. I was going to tell someone but it came so quickly. Argh.' She cried out again.

'Okay. Try and take slow deep breaths and we'll get you to the medical centre.'

The contractions were close together and by the time they

were in the lift, Alice started to lose confidence that they could do this. 'We'll get out on my floor. There's a wheelchair in the empty cabin at the end of that corridor. Once Olivia is in the chair, we'll whizz her upstairs.'

Bopha nodded and rushed off to find a wheelchair.

'I have to lay down, or sit,' Olivia wailed as they waited outside the lift. There was no sign of Bopha and so Alice helped her the few yards to her own cabin. 'Argh!'

'Okay. Deep breaths. Bopha will be here in a minute. I'll ask her to bring the doctor to us.'

'Argh.'

The contractions were too close together. There wasn't enough time. Alice scrubbed her hands and fetched clean towels. Giving birth was a natural process. A natural process. If she repeated this enough times, she might convince herself. Alice regretted watching so many episodes of Call the Midwife. There was too much that could go wrong. The contractions were very close together now.

'Push, Olivia.'

The girl's face was wet with perspiration. Alice wished that there was another person to help – to hold Olivia's hand and wipe her brow.

'Again. Push with all your might.'

Olivia let out a long wail loud enough to summon the whole ship. The babe's black hair became visible and Alice's heart almost stopped as she realised the enormity of what she was attempting to do. Now was not the time for a panic attack. She took a deep breath. Focus.

'The baby's head has engaged. We're nearly there. You're doing really well. Ready? Push.'

With one last push, Olivia's baby arrived in the world and Alice could not have felt prouder. It was a miracle.

'A boy. A perfect little boy.'

Within seconds he tested his lungs and Olivia laughed. 'Hello, baby boy.'

Alice removed the placenta, detached the umbilical cord, and wiped the baby clean. Then she wrapped him in a towel and nestled the bundle in Olivia's arms.

Bopha crept into the room. 'The wheelchair wasn't there,' she said, as if in a daze.

Alice and Bopha sat on the bed on either side of Olivia, transfixed by the miracle before them. Eventually, Alice said, 'We'd better let someone know. The doctor will want to examine you.'

'Do we have to?' Olivia's eyes pleaded with Alice. 'My family do not know. They need my wages and I will lose my job. If that happens, they will have to return the fishing boat. No fishing – no food. All of the village will suffer and I will bring shame to my family.'

Olivia seemed so distressed Alice thought it best to wait until she had settled down. 'We don't have to do anything for now. I'll look after you. Maybe just let the doctor check that the baby is okay?'

'No,' Olivia exclaimed. 'I do not trust that doctor. He drinks too much of the spirits. My baby is well. Please do not tell, Alice.'

Alice didn't know what to do but she had to respect Olivia's request for secrecy. 'He's hungry.' Alice smiled as she watched the baby nuzzling against Olivia as though seeking out her milk. 'Here let me show you how to encourage him to latch on.'

Later, when Olivia and the baby were asleep Alice crept out of her cabin. Although she had made herself a rule not to drink during the day, she needed something stronger than a cup of tea. Patty caught her as she was coming out of the lift.

'What was it this time? An argument between the girls?'

Alice shook her head slowly – she hardly knew how to convey the news. It wasn't something that she could keep entirely to herself, she needed help to manage this impossible situation. 'I was going to the bar. I've got some news but first, let's order our drinks.'

They found a secluded corner of the lounge and while Patty was ordering their gin and tonics Alice gazed out of the window. The late afternoon sun was descending and she felt as though its golden light was filling her up. She sighed, not wanting to return her attention to the world but Patty was waiting.

'You can't keep me in suspense any longer. Is it a man? Frederic? I've seen the way he gives you extra cake.'

Alice talked Patty through the events of that afternoon, to exclamations from Patty that she hushed. 'We have to keep Olivia's secret until we've figured out what to do.'

'Can I see him?' Patty clasped her hands together.

Olivia was feeding when they crept into the cabin. She looked questioningly at Alice.

'It's okay. Patty is sworn to secrecy. You mastered breast-feeding quickly.'

Olivia smiled down at her baby. 'He is an angel. A perfect little angel.'

Patty was hugging herself. 'What are you going to call him?'

'For now, I am calling him Hal. That can be a name? For Halcyon. Maybe later I will change it. Find a name that means something to my family.' Hal turned away from her breast.

'You need to wind him. Let me show you.' Patty put out her arms to receive Hal. 'Oh, you are a darling. A gorgeous, beautiful boy.' She rested Hal on her shoulder and rubbed his back with a circular motion. 'That's right. You need to let that air up, don't you?'

'We need a plan, Olivia. For a start, you must see one of the medical team, if not the doctor. We can't hide the baby forever. I know you're afraid of losing your job but I'm sure if we spoke to someone – Gloria or Captain Moore they would understand. You can't lose your job for having a baby,' Alice said.

'No! No. That is not possible. You do not understand. If I don't work, I won't get paid. I will have to leave the ship and somebody else will take my place. If I lose this job my family will starve and I will not be able to show my face in my village. My mammon did not have a doctor or a nurse when she gave birth to my brothers and sister. I am fine. But maybe you want your bed back. Do not worry I will get up now.' Olivia heaved herself up the bed and threw back the duvet.

Alice re-covered Olivia tucking her in. 'You need to stay in bed at least until tomorrow. We know your duties and will cover them between us. To be honest, nobody is going to complain if their cabin isn't cleaned every day.'

'Where will you sleep?'

'Alice can sleep in my room. The double is two twins pushed together so we can separate them. We'll look after you sugar don't you worry. Now, what about the baby's father? Or your mom? Could one of them look after Hal?'

'The father does not know and I am not going to see him again. How can I get Hal to my mammon without telling the captain? If I tell the captain, I lose my job.'

'I have an idea,' Alice said. 'Turn on the TV channel that shows the ship's voyage.' Patty found the channel. It showed the ship as a dot on the Indian ocean.

'Seychelles, Reunion, and then look.'

'I was so looking forward to Seychelles, maybe we'll be able to get off the ship by then as it's in a week.'

'Concentrate, Patty. The ship comes close to the Southern tip of Madagascar as we sail towards South Africa.'

'Are you suggesting we ask the captain to detour?'

'Please don't. I promise you, if I get off the ship, I will never be permitted to return.'

'This fishing boat your family purchased. Is it powerful?' Alice said.

'It has a motor. It was expensive, so maybe it will have power enough.'

'Do you think your brother could come alongside the ship and take Hal?'

'That's crazy. How many gins did you have Alice? It's dangerous and darn well impossible.'

Patty was right. They would have to come clean. Maybe Captain Moore would take pity on Olivia and allow her to return after some maternity leave.

'We could do it. I know we could. If I can get a message to Pascal.' Olivia's face lit up and Alice regretted giving her false hope. There was no way. It was pure fantasy. How could a fishing boat get that close to the ship undetected? Unless it was in the early hours of the morning.

22

It had to work. It was Olivia's only hope. Mammon and Pappa would be shocked at first but when they met their grandson Hal, they would fall in love with him. His little trusting face with those huge brown eyes, the way his tiny mouth worked as though silently practising his vowels. Saying goodbye to him would break her heart. He was still so small and needed her milk. What if there wasn't milk on the island? Mammon said the drought was one of the worst they had experienced. She remembered the children trying to catch a dribble of water from the cracked river bed. That was months ago. If things had got no better her darling Hal could risk malnutrition on the island but when he was discovered on board, they would both be sent home and she would not be able to earn the money so badly needed by her family.

Hal was being cared for by Alice and Patty. Olivia was back to working shifts but she slipped out at feeding time. That morning Alice had arranged for Olivia to send an email to Pascal from her computer. As Olivia approached Alice's cabin her breasts filled with milk. The tissue paper stuffed in her bra felt soggy. It was as though warm milk seeped from her constantly. If only she could bottle it and send it home with Hal.

Someone was walking briskly behind her. Captain Moore. The captain never visited guests' cabins or ventured below deck nine. Olivia dived into her storeroom just past the door to Alice's cabin. She kept the door open as she loaded a cleaning trolley, waiting for Captain Moore to swish past in her heels. But she did not. Olivia heard a loud rap. She leaned out of the cupboard to see Alice opening her door to the captain. Hal was inside.

The thought of her baby released more milk. She imagined Captain Moore standing over Hal, demanding an explanation. Alice would get into trouble. She had to confess – tell the captain it was all her fault. That she had left her baby in the cabin whilst cleaning and as he was fast asleep forgot to take him with her. She would be dismissed immediately, and her wages stopped. Disney's prediction was wrong she would not be bringing prosperity to the village – just shame to her family.

Olivia grabbed a couple of towels and stood outside the cabin door, mustering the courage to knock. She strained to hear Hal's cries but heard only the captain's voice.

She knocked and the door was opened by Captain Moore. Alice was sitting at her desk firing up the computer. Olivia's eyes darted around the cabin, searching for Hal. He was out of sight – maybe in the bathroom. Would he smell her milk and cry for her? The captain was staring at the damp patches on Olivia's tunic. She crossed her arms high trying to cover the stains. 'I bought you fresh towels, Mrs Wagstaff.'

'Thank you, Olivia. Would you mind taking some to Patty too? We seem to have been missed this morning.'

'That is not the service we expect,' the captain said

addressing Olivia. She didn't know Olivia's name yet but that would change as soon as she discovered Hal. 'I hope that things are not slacking now that Officer Peters has left the ship. The good news is, we will be docking at Seychelles. A chance for everyone to get off the ship. The past few weeks have been difficult but we now have an agreement that the World Health Organisation guidance will be applied in the same way to our ship as it would be to any other country. Unless we are experiencing a pandemic and are at risk of spreading a life-threatening disease, we will be welcomed at all of the ports on our itinerary.'

'Bravo Captain. We know it's down to your efforts. Does that mean we'll be able to leave the port to explore Seychelles?' Alice said.

'Yes, and then onto Reunion. Your friend William will be pleased. I seem to recall he was looking forward to that stop. I think we will all be glad to feel land under our feet. Now, you wanted internet access to send an urgent message to your family. I could arrange for you to send your message from a computer on the bridge where we have a good connection, or you could wait until we dock.'

Olivia was still standing there holding the towels. If she managed to contact Pascal from Seychelles would there be enough time for him to put a plan into action? The captain was looking at her and Olivia realised that she had been openly eavesdropping.

'I'll just put these in the bathroom.'

'No need.' Alice sounded firm. She widened her eyes at Olivia as though trying to convey a message. Of course, if Hal was asleep in the bathroom and she woke him he would cry. 'Don't forget to drop some towels into Patty.'

The captain was edging her way towards the door and Olivia prayed that this would be an end to her visit. She slipped out of the door ahead of the captain and collected a couple more towels to deliver to Patty's cabin. She hoped the captain was not going to make a habit of visiting below deck.

Patty opened the door as soon as she knocked. 'I'm sorry I meant to get him back to Alice but the little darlin' dropped off to sleep and he looked so peaceful.'

Olivia sank onto the bed. 'Andriamanitra ô!' She unbuttoned her tunic; milk was spurting like a fountain. On cue, Hal made a plaintive cry and Olivia swept him into her arms.

Patty poured her a glass of water. 'You need to keep hydrated when feeding. Look at him guzzling away.'

Olivia told Patty about the captain's visit. 'I was so scared that Hal would start crying and it would all be over.'

'If I had returned him at the agreed time then we would have been found out. But this is good news – about the Seychelles and Reunion. Will your brother be able to meet the ship with just five days' notice?'

'I don't know. I will send a message to his phone and an email to Pappa's shop. I didn't want my parents to find out this way but I don't have a choice.'

'If they are not trading, will they check their emails?'

'I don't know. I hope so. The computer in our shop is used by the whole village.'

They sat in silence watching Hal feed. Then, Olivia burped him and moved him to her other breast. 'You and Alice have been so kind to us. I don't know how I will ever thank you.'

'Trusting me with your precious babe is thanks enough. I did not get to hold my grandchildren as babies. You have no idea the joy you bestow by letting me help care for this little one.'

The door flew open and Alice tumbled in. 'Oh, thank God. That was close. I can't keep this up for much longer. I'm sure the others are getting suspicious. Gideon and Barbara have started cross-questioning me about where I have been and who I have been with.'

Patty laughed. 'That might be my fault. I may have given them the impression that you were having an affair with Frederic.'

'Did Olivia tell you the plan?'

'She did and I still think it crazy.'

'Okay, then game on. We mustn't tell another soul – not even Gideon or Barbara.'

The two women grinned like a couple of school girls. Hal murmured in his sleep and they all gazed at him. Olivia wished she could curl up and join him. Now that the day when she would hand him off the ship was getting close, her heart folded in on itself – if she could somehow return him to her womb where she could keep him safe and hidden, she would. She kissed the soft curls of his head and breathed in his delicious scent. He was a miniature Raf and if he grew up to be like his father, he would make her very proud. Mammon and Pappa were going to adore him. So long as she could get him home safely.

23

Marianne loved this time of the night, standing on deck at the bow. Halcyon Seas cutting through the midnight blue ocean, small crests of white illuminated by the moon, and the stars. So many stars.

'Your interview in Seychelles went well.' His voice came from the shadows and Marianne felt goosebumps tingle her arms. They had met here before, in the early hours of the morning. It was not an arrangement – just a coincidence that they had both been enjoying the quiet night sky.

'It was down to head office really – getting media attention for the interviews. I was surprised at how big a story our voyage has become.'

Waves hushed against the hull and the moon lit their way like the torch of a cinema usher. Gideon leant on the rail and looked out to sea. 'A cynical part of me wondered whether sending older people out to sea and forgetting about them was starting to sound like an attractive solution. Cut us off from the rest of the world with the pretence of keeping us safe and containing disease.'

'That is very cynical. We can put all of that behind us now. In future, no port will be closed unless a deadly virus is detected on the ship. I can't believe it took so long to fight that battle.'

'We have you to thank for that, Marianne. You were amazing the way you stood up to critics and got legal representation.'

It was the first time Gideon had used her first name and although she should have corrected him, standing together in the dead of night it felt as though they were just a man and a woman. She liked the sound of her name on his lips. 'Thank you for your vote of confidence but I didn't do it alone. Maybe now we will return to some normality. Don't think I haven't noticed the goings on since Hans Peters jumped ship. We'll be picking up a new hotel director in Durban.'

'What goings-on? I have no idea what you're talking about.'

Marianne laughed. 'Sure. You didn't notice our passengers trying to run the ship and my cruise director setting herself up as the producer and star of passenger and crew productions? I turned a blind eye because everyone seemed to be having a blast and with months at sea they needed the diversion, but Alice's daughter is right – it's not what you've paid for.'

'Yes, Alice told me about this Facebook group. Her daughter's a bit of a bully, I hear. I hope she's not causing any problems for you?'

'Heck no. The friends and relatives of passengers are bound to be concerned, especially with the media attention we've received. Hopefully, we can now move on and enjoy the cruise.'

. . .

Olivia sat alone on Alice's bed giving Hal one last feed before handing him over to Pascal. Her father's email to Alice's address had been short and formal. Pascal will be in a motorboat with Luc. Keep a lookout for them and be ready. Do not put yourself or the baby in any danger. Pappa. Olivia felt like a child waiting for her father's reprimand. He wasn't accustomed to writing emails and would have been uncomfortable writing to alicewag197 but Olivia could feel his disapproval. Hal lifted his head from her breast, his huge eyes fixed on hers. 'How am I going to give you away ma petite? Mon ange.' She kissed his soft forehead and ran her fingers through the downy curls of his head. 'Mammon and Pappa will adore you. Gracie and Jay Jim will look after you.' She kissed him again and buried her face in the nape of his neck breathing in his milky scent. 'I'll be home soon. I promise.'

Alice crept into the room. 'Have you packed everything? Bottles of water, our makeshift nappies?' They had cut nappies from towels when Hal was first born.

'What about my milk? He will be hungry and cry for me.'

'The ship doesn't have formula milk. Hal will have to wait until he's on the island. You said that there will be other nursing mums who might feed him?'

Olivia nodded, she couldn't bear the thought of another woman suckling her babe, but there was no choice – without milk, he would starve. She sent up a prayer to her ancestors for Hal to be blessed with nourishment and love. 'Should we come out now?'

'Not yet. Patty is keeping watch. I'll go back and as soon as we see the boat approach I'll come and get you. Here, wrap my shawl around him too.'

'Am I doing the right thing?'

'Only you can answer that.'

It had seemed the best solution but now the thought of

sending her beautiful son out to sea not knowing if he would survive the journey or Malatanga's drought and famine she had doubts. 'If I stop sending money home my whole family and the village may starve. At least this way Hal will benefit from my family's fishing business and in time the shop will pick up again. It is hard for me now but God willing Hal will soon be safely home with Mammon and Pappa. It is the right thing.'

Alice put her arms around Olivia and Hal. 'We will miss him too. Okay, I'd better get back on deck. Pascal should be approaching soon.'

Olivia changed Hal's nappy and tried to commit to memory every fold of his skin, and dimpled flesh. His soft pink lips and cute nose.

'He's pulling alongside. Quickly and quietly now.' Alice took the holdall from Olivia and together they crept out of the cabin. Hal was hidden in a large shawl wrapped around Olivia that served as a baby carrier.

They headed for deck five on the aft starboard side. So far, so good. Nobody else were around. It was the quietest time on the ship, the late shift finished and the early morning one about to start. Maybe this was a sign that her ancestors were with her and all would be well. Pascal's friend Luc was helping him to throw a big hook on a rope. It banged against the side of the ship and the sea splashed as the boat tossed on the waves.

'They won't be able to climb aboard,' Olivia said. Mingled with her disappointment was a joy – she would not have to part with Hal.

'Stand back,' Pascal shouted. He threw the rope again and this time the hook caught on the aft railing. Then, he started to climb, one hand over the other, his feet swinging until he gained purchase against the ship's side.

Olivia held her breath. If he lost his grip Pascal would fall into the sea. She need not have worried; Pascal was as quick-footed as a monkey. Patty and Alice helped him over the railing. Seeing him there on her ship was like a dream.

'You came,' she said. Her heart was bursting with love and gratitude that her brother had risked his life to respond to her cry for help.

Pascal put a finger to his lips and then removed a rope ladder from his rucksack. He secured this to the rail and motioned for Olivia to climb down with Hal.

'No, you take him,' she hissed.

Pascal shook his head and opened his rucksack wide. 'Where are the kitchen stores? We need water and food.'

'You can't steal from the ship.' Olivia's voice carried in the still night and Pascal glared at her.

'We need water.'

'I'll show you,' Alice said. 'You get Hal safely onto the boat, Olivia. Patty will help you.'

They had to act quickly. The captain may have been alerted by now, they had made too much noise. Luc steered the boat closer to the ship so that the ladder was straight. He signalled for Olivia to descend.

'Leave the holdall here and concentrate on getting Hal down safely.' Patty tightened the shawl around Olivia and Hal. 'He should be secure.' She kissed Olivia. 'Go.'

Hal was between Olivia and the side of the ship as she slowly descended. Every time her foot or hand let go of the ladder, she panicked that she would not find the next secure hold. If she looked down or thought about what she was doing, then she would surely freeze with fear. With each step Olivia repeated in her head, I am doing this for Hal. At last, she felt Luc's hands on her waist and she was swung aboard the boat.

Patty leaned over the rail dangling the bag. Luc put out his arms to catch it but Patty must have had a change of heart because she tested the rope ladder and then started to descend herself, the holdall secured by its handles across her back. Olivia was surprised at the older woman's confidence but she wasn't carrying a precious baby. When Patty landed in the boat, they had to raise their voices to be heard above the engine.

'Let's make a little bed for him in this bag.' Patty arranged the towelling nappies into a little cocoon.

Marianne and Gideon were at the bow of the ship discussing Reunion Island when the call came through, 'Safe Haven. This is a Safe Haven. Repeat Save Haven.'

Marianne's heart thumped as if it had shifted from first to fifth gear. 'I've got to go.'

'What does that mean?' Gideon started to follow her but Marianne was back in captain mode. This was an emergency.

Her second officer must have it wrong. She checked port and starboard as she made her way to the bridge. If pirates had been spotted, she couldn't see them. Would there never be a moment's peace on this friggin' ship? She threw open the door to the bridge and was greeted by an ashen-faced officer.

'Starboard. Stern. A motorboat.'

Marianne checked the ECDIS monitor. 'I see it. Careful, it might just be a fishing boat we are sailing close to Madagascar.'

Her second officer took control of the ship whilst Marianne went to check that operation Safe Haven was being implemented. Most of the guests would be sound asleep, so no need to alert them just yet. Everywhere was quiet. It was going to be a false alarm but good practice for her crew. She met a sleepy-eyed Gloria by the stairwell, her silk leopard print pyjama bottoms visible beneath her coat and life vest.

'I don't think there's any need for a life-vest, Gloria. Can you make sure that any guests who appear are directed back to their cabins?' As Marianne finished speaking the ship's lights went out. 'Where is the staff? We should have staff stationed on every gangway and stairwell guiding people to safety.'

What if this was for real? Shit. They didn't stand a chance if pirates boarded the ship. The bad publicity about Halcyon Seas would have broadcast the lack of experienced senior officers. Why hadn't she thought of that before they sailed across the Indian Ocean? This was known pirate territory. She had allowed herself to get distracted and now it was too late. The passengers and crew of Halcyon Seas were in serious danger; their captain had led them into unsafe waters and failed to protect them.

'Safe Haven. Safe Haven. All passengers must remain in their cabins until they are told that it is safe to leave. Captain to galley 19.'

Why was she being called to one of the kitchens? Was it a trick? Had her officer been told to make this announcement at gunpoint? Would she be shot or stabbed? They should have had a code to alert one another to false information. As these thoughts went through her head Marianne was already running towards the galley. She was aware of two male officers following fast behind and was grateful for their backup. A loud bang sounded from the galley and the three of them froze.

'Shall I investigate, Captain?'

Marianne nodded. As captain, she had to keep herself safe so that she could lead her passengers and crew to safety. Before the officer had a chance to enter the galley, a black teenage boy ran out with a rucksack on his back. Gideon followed brandishing a long kitchen knife. Marianne was horrified. What the hell was he doing?

'Stop. I command you to stop the chase and return to your cabin.' Her words were useless, Gideon was almost upon the boy. 'The hose. Set the hose on them.'

It took a while for the hose to be rolled out into position and turned on. If they had been following the Safe Haven drill, manning the hose would have been one of the first tasks. Now, it was blasting Gideon and the boy as they tussled on the deck alongside the motor boat. Except it wasn't the boy. Alice was clinging to Gideon's back, there was no sign of the boy.

'Turn it off,' Marianne shouted. But it was too late. Alice and Gideon were swept overboard in a jet of water.

24

'Where's Pascal?' He was taking too long. What if he had been discovered?

'Argh.' A long, loud shout that sounded like a tribal cry was followed by the pounding of feet and then shadowy figures above them. They had been discovered. Olivia wasn't sure exactly what happened next. Hal started to wail and she bent her head to attend to him. Then, a powerful hose was turned on them rocking the boat. Above, she heard Alice scream. Pascal was climbing down the side of the ship. On Halcyon Seas, a man was brandishing a knife. Someone tackled him and there was a tussle. Then, a jet of water threw them both overboard. Olivia shrieked. Two people from her ship were in the sea; they could drown.

'Help them,' she cried, but her voice was lost as Luc powered the engine and as soon as Pascal's feet hit the deck he pulled away.

'Alice and Gideon. Over there!' Patty stood up in the boat pointing into the black waves. 'We've got to rescue them.'

Luc steered close to the two bobbing heads and then cut

the engine. Gideon had Alice under her arms and was treading water. Pascal dived in. Olivia and Patty clung to each other as they watched Pascal swim out to their friends. For a terrifying second, Alice's head disappeared underwater. Olivia shut her eyes and prayed.

'He's got her.' Patty squeezed her arm.

Alice was floating on her back, supported under each arm by Gideon and Pascal as they swam towards the boat. Patty, Luc, and Olivia pulled Alice on board, and then Luc helped the two men out of the water.

'Is she going to be alright?' Olivia bent over Alice, who had been positioned on her side.

Alice coughed up water and Patty rubbed her back. 'Is there a blanket? Anything?'

There was not. Olivia eased a few towelling nappies from beneath Hal and he started to cry. They were of little help in drying or warming Alice but Patty and Olivia sat close to her on either side, hoping that they would transmit some heat.

There was now some distance between their boat and the ship. Halcyon Seas seemed to be drifting from them. 'Pascal, you have to take these people back. The ship's leaving without us.'

'It's not possible. They will have to come with us now.'

'But I didn't want to leave the ship! You were meant to collect Hal so that I didn't lose my job.'

Alice could not have understood what Olivia said but she picked up on her frustration and yelled at Gideon. 'Why did you have to act like a bloody hero? I thought you had learnt your lesson in Barcelona.'

Hal was wailing now. Alice and Gideon would be cold and wet. 'How long will it take for us to get home?'

'We are taking this boat back to Toliara, then using our fishing boat for the rest of the journey. By midday. Maybe.'

Olivia worried about Alice, who was shivering. The boat rocked on the waves, tipping one way and then the other, whilst her passengers sat in stunned silence.

'Hush,' Olivia cooed to Hal. His huge brown eyes gazed at her and Olivia felt Raf's presence. Meet me at the North Star, he had said, on their last night together. Up until now, Olivia had banished such thoughts but tonight she needed him and so she searched the velvet black sky, where stars shone like diamonds and found the Little Bear. At first, she could not see the North Star but as if in answer to her call it twinkled. Olivia smiled. I'm sorry that you will never meet your beautiful boy, she thought. Forgive me but it is for the best.

'Is that a whale?' Alice's cry interrupted Olivia's meditation. Hal had at least stopped crying.

'It is.' Malagasies were used to seeing whales but Olivia knew from the cruise ship that Westerners got excited when they saw them, so she pointed out a school of whales and was pleased to see that this enchanted her friends.

Despite her discomfort, Alice was delighted to see a school of whales so close to their boat. It was a gift. 'Look Patty.' She pointed to a whale that had launched itself out of the water and was twisting onto its back. When a few whales had followed Halcyon Seas, the captain had informed them over the speaker that this was called breaching. They had all been excited then but it was nothing compared to the close up display they were being treated to that morning. And then the sun rose. A golden globe of light, seeping yellow into the indigo sky.

Beautiful but surreal. In the past hour she had been thrown overboard, nearly drowned, and was now in a motorboat with a couple of lads who could have been pirates had she not known otherwise, sailing away from their cruise ship with no money, passport, emergency contact, or phone. Maybe she would wake up to find herself in a warm bed. So long as that bed wasn't in Chestnut Court, the attic of Rachel's new home, or alone again in Norfolk because if that was the case, she preferred this nightmare. But there was the most glorious sunrise. Orange and crimson reflected off the sea. They were sailing in a bowl of molten gold. Hal was miraculously asleep, oblivious to this adventure. But if Olivia chewed her lip anymore, she would bite it right off.

'It's okay,' Alice lay her hand on Olivia's arm. 'We are all in one piece and soon we will be visiting your village. Hal will meet his grandparents.'

'I am so sorry,' Olivia sounded close to tears.

'It's not your fault.' Alice looked pointedly at Gideon.

'Don't look at me like that. If you had told me about your crazy scheme, I might have been able to help. Of course, it looked as though we were being hijacked by pirates. What did you think would happen?'

Pascal responded to Gideon's raised voice by appearing at the cabin entrance with a stern look on his face. He said something in Malagasy to Olivia and she responded in a reassuring tone.

'It's no good arguing over whose fault it is. How are we going to get back on the ship?' Patty said.

'Marianne will feel responsible for us falling overboard. I wish we could get a message to her to say that we're safe.'

'Never mind feeling sorry for her. I don't see any rescue boats coming to our aid. If you and Alice hadn't been picked up by Pascal and Luc you might have drowned. Did anyone throw you lifejackets?'

'I don't know, it all happened so quickly. I'm just grateful that they did rescue us.'

'Mozambique.' Pascal bent into the cabin and pointed at the land mass on their right, as though they were on a guided excursion.

When Alice and Patty nodded enthusiastically, he left them to assist Luc at the wheel. They huddled together in silence each with their thoughts. Maybe she dozed a little because Alice was aware of Hal crying and then Olivia feeding him. She was glad that Hal had his mother with him. If the plan had worked then he would have gone hungry with only his uncle Pascal to comfort him.

Madagascar came into view and soon they were following the shoreline. The sun must have seeped into the earth because the island looked red – red, bronze, and rusty. Forests of green towered above swaths of wasteland; now and again Alice would spy a scattering of dwellings, cattle being herded, and children– some of them gathering driftwood. She joined Gideon on the deck. He had made his peace with Pascal and Luc and they seemed to have found a way to communicate.

'Is this your fishing boat?' Alice spoke loudly to be heard above the motor.

'No. I borrow. We stop at Toliara to eat and from there we go in my boat.'

'Maybe we should wait for the ship at Toliara,' Gideon said to Alice.

What he said made sense but Alice wanted to meet Olivia's family and make sure Hal was going to be properly fed. Having brought him into the world, she couldn't help feeling responsible for his well-being.

'What's in Toliara?' Gideon asked Pascal.

'It is a small shipping port, used for cargo. No cruise ships.'

'We will wait there for our ship.'

Pascal shook his head. 'It is not safe for you. The ship will not be able to dock there. You come with us to our village.'

'He's right, Gideon. We're best staying close to our Malagasy friends. If he leaves us here with no money, passport or identity and we can't speak the language – who knows what might happen?'

'The captain will be following using the ship's radar. I think we should wait at the port.'

Patty joined them as they sailed into Toliara. 'Olivia says it's not safe for us to wait at the port on our own.'

'It's not as if we have anything that can be stolen and I'm perfectly able to protect myself and both of you.' Gideon pulled back his shoulders.

'Of course, you are.' Alice hoped that she sounded convincing. 'But let's not take a risk. We don't know this island and if Olivia is warning us against waiting here maybe we should take her advice.'

'We need to get back on the ship. Marianne is going to be frantic. We have to let her know we're safe.'

Patty broke off what was becoming a heated exchange between Alice and Gideon. She turned to Pascal. 'Could we wait in Toliara for a little while and if Halcyon Seas doesn't show, go with you?'

'No. Sorry. I cannot risk. If captain of ship catch us then we go to prison. We must hurry.'

25

Oscar. Oscar. Mr Mob. Oscar Mr Mob. Marianne watched in horror as the emergency call for man overboard went out. She needed to be on the bridge, not staring into the black sea feeling as though her insides had been ripped out. Why couldn't Gideon have done as she asked? If she could just get a sight of him and Alice.

'There. Over there.' One of her officers pointed to a couple of specks that could have been Gideon and Alice bobbing in the waves. At the same time, the pirate boat turned around and headed for them.

'Cut the engine,' Marianne radioed to the bridge. If they approached the pirate boat, they would create a surge. Best wait and see if the pirates were going to rescue them. She might have to negotiate for their release but at least they would be alive.

'They've got them,' someone shouted.

'Keep watch from here,' she commanded an officer. 'I'm going back to the bridge.'

It seemed as though all of her staff and crew had congregated on deck five to watch the action and now they impeded her progress as she tried to rush back to the bridge.

'Should we start preparing breakfast?' The head chef.

'Do the passengers have to remain in their cabins?' Gloria.

'Is that South Africa, Captain?' Rosie Diamond, dressed in a flouncy nightgown and robe.

'Are we following the pirate drill or man overboard?' An indiscreet junior officer who would be getting a dressing down once things returned to normal.

But for now, things were far from normal and if she didn't act swiftly, they could get ten times worse. 'Gloria Busby, please ask all of the passengers to remain in their cabins for now, where they will be served their breakfast.'

'We do not have time to collect the orders,' one of the catering staff said.

'Where's Head Chef? Please provide a continental breakfast to everyone this morning with a Bucks Fizz. Just say it's a special treat. Now, please clear the way.'

When Marianne reached the bridge her second officer pointed to the radar. 'The pirates are taking the Mozambique Channel. Should we follow?'

'We can't let them disappear from view. Have you made contact by radio?'

'I've tried but not getting through.'

'Okay, let's follow them.'

'Isn't the Mozambique Channel high risk for piracy?'

He was right. It was a huge risk but she had put Gideon and Alice in serious danger. Silver Seas and Jamboree had already been alerted to the pirate attack. Hopefully, the boat would soon be in sight and they could negotiate for Gideon and Alice's safe return. The pirates were a couple of boys, amateurs. They were probably just chancing their luck, working alone. Gideon's safety was all she could think of – and Alice's of course.

'They aren't far ahead. Follow them.'

If she got out of this situation alive and still had a job, she would insist on recruiting a first officer, and chief engineer. If Silver Seas had not cut costs, they might never be in this situation. She had been a fool to agree to their terms.

They had been following the fishing boat for a couple of hours when there was a thud. The lights flickered and then the ship slowed down until it was barely moving.

'What's happened, Captain?'

'It feels like we've lost power in one of the engines.' She made a call to her second engineer.

'I'm checking now, Captain.' A few minutes later he radioed back. 'Three of the engines have died. It's the cooling system. I'll see what I can do.'

They could limp along with the one remaining engine but progress would be very slow and a strong tidal wave could set them off course. 'Start up the emergency generator. We can't risk losing the navigation system.'

'It looks as though the pirates docked at Port Toliara,' the second officer said, later that morning. Halcyon Seas was still thirty miles away from the port.

'We need to stop them before we lose contact. Try again.'

'Nothing. Sorry, Captain.'

There was another thud. They had lost all power. 'Contact the port and ask for assistance. I'll talk to them.'

'They're telling us that we can't berth. It's a container port.'

Marianne took over. 'This is Captain Moore of Halcyon Seas.' She gave the ship's position. 'We have engine failure.

Please send emergency tugs to tow us into port. There are sixty-nine elderly passengers on board.'

Satisfied that assistance was coming, Marianne updated Libby at HQ.

'Relatives are being informed now. We are planning a press conference to try and contain the situation. Keep your phone on and provide regular progress reports. Jamboree is in communication with Madagascar officials regarding the hijack and is negotiating the release of hostages,' Libby said.

Marianne agreed. Her next job was to inform the passengers.

'This is your captain speaking. We have lost power in all four engines. There is no need for alarm. Rescue tugs are being sent to our aid as I speak. They will tow us into Port Toliara, Madagascar. Please remain on board and listen for any instructions. The emergency generator will provide essential electricity until repairs have been made but please help to conserve energy. I hope that you enjoyed our celebratory breakfast and the incredible sunrise. I will update you when I have more information.'

Gloria met Marianne on deck. 'Captain, one of the hotel staff, Olivia Rose, and another guest, Patty Gray, is missing. Neither of them has been seen since late last night.'Four hostages. It was getting worse. 'We had better get everyone to muster stations to do a proper count.'

The muster drill was taking place as Halcyon Seas was towed into port. The entertainment of putting on life jackets and watching the emergency tugs seemed to keep the passengers happy. Rumours were circulating about the events of the night and Marianne knew that she would have to make an announcement but first she wanted to get the ship safely to shore and find out what had happened to Gideon and the other hostages.

It was a small port and Marianne could see that by berthing there, Halcyon Seas would interfere with the transport of goods, as there would be little room for container ships.

'We've been told to remain on the ship. The port captain wants to talk to you.' Her second officer handed over the radio.

'Captain Moore. It is not possible for you to berth at Toliara. Stay there. I will come to you.'

Captain Lambert boarded the ship an hour later. A broad man with a high forehead and an air of superiority. Marianne greeted him wearing her full uniform, complete with stiletto heels. They felt incongruous given the situation but they gave her height and his attire of a sports jacket teamed with flip-flops was equally questionable.

Marianne thanked Captain Lambert for towing them to safety. She understood his reasoning that Halcyon Seas could not take up a berth and would discuss that but first she needed to find her missing passengers. 'We were in pursuit of a fishing boat. Two men boarded our ship in the Indian Ocean without authority. There was a scuffle that resulted in a couple of our passengers falling overboard. They were picked up by the fishing boat and we believe they docked here earlier this morning. I would be grateful if you could locate these missing passengers and two others that we have since found missing.'

'Ah, so you are the ship that was hijacked by pirates?'

It must be headline news by now. Marianne dreaded to think how relatives would react. A retirement cruise ship hijacked by pirates with elderly passengers being held hostage. They could not cover this one up. 'I'm afraid so. Maybe you have information that can lead us to the boat?'

Captain Lambert took a cigar from the inner pocket of his

sports jacket and lit up. He made himself comfortable in a seat and looked around him. 'This is a fine ship. You will need to pay port dues.' He gave a salacious leer and Marianne cringed.

'Of course. I'll ask an officer to make arrangements. The fishing boat, Captain? This is the information that we have on it.'

Was that a wink? Marianne tugged the bottom of her jacket to try and hide the curve of her breasts which seemed to be the focus of Captain Lambert's attention.

'I will tell you what I can do. When you have paid your port dues, I will arrange for you to be taken to your pirates.'

This wasn't the response that Marianne had expected. 'If you could just put us in contact with them. Maybe you could ask them to release the hostages?'

Captain Lambert gave a big round laugh as he rocked backwards. 'You are very funny. Captain Moore, pay the port dues and I will see what I can do.' He stretched out his legs and rested them on a low table.

When Marianne realised that he wasn't going anywhere until she had paid what was owed, she summoned the admin officer. Uncomfortable under Captain Lambert's scrutiny, Marianne found a quiet place on the ship where she could get a signal and then updated Libby.

'Do not enter into any negotiations regarding the hostages. Jamboree is seeking advice from the FBI. Your responsibility is to keep the remaining passengers and crew safe and assess damage to the ship. We are handling communications. Do not leave the port under any circumstances.'

'But we may not have a choice.' Marianne tried to explain but Libby wasn't listening. It sounded as though Jamboree and Silver Seas were blaming her for the incident.

Cigar smoke smarted her eyes when she returned to the bridge. Captain Lambert was drinking coffee, his sports jacket discarded to reveal a Ralph Lauren polo shirt. The kind that Marianne had seen in markets all over Europe specialising in fake designer gear. 'I hope that you have been well looked after, Captain Lambert?'

'There will be paperwork to complete and additional fees but for now, everything is satisfactory.'

'As soon as the ship has been repaired, we will be on our way.' Marianne gave her most gracious smile.

'Be ready to move. We will reposition you. And you said that you wanted to meet with your pirates?' He chuckled. 'I will see what can be arranged.'

Marianne didn't bother correcting him. It looked as though he was going to leave the ship and she didn't want to give him any reason to stay. He stood up and looked expectantly at her. A tip. She hated lining pockets, but from the look on his face, he was hoping for payment of another kind. She thrust ten dollars into his palm. 'Thank you for your assistance, Captain Lambert.'

When they felt the tugs re-engage and the ship start to shift, Marianne and her second officer assumed they were going to be towed to another area of the port but they headed north along the Mozambique Channel. She made a call to the port, demanding to speak to the captain but was told that they were acting on Captain Lambert's orders.

'I am the Captain of Halcyon Seas. You have no right to move this ship without my authority.' Her words were having no effect. 'I command you to release this ship. If you fail to do so then I will report a hijacking.'

As her words fell on deaf ears, Marianne had no choice but to report to Libby that the ship was no longer under her control.

26

The fishing boat engine silenced. They were drifting along a shoreline of dark golden sand edged with scrubland in shades of green, russet, and red. Palm trees swayed in winds that came from both shore and land. These winds seemed to take hold of their boat guiding it along the shore. They were heading for a little bamboo jetty around which children and adults squatted or bent over crates of glittering fish. As the boat drew closer, people abandoned their work to watch their arrival. A couple of young men helped Luc to tie the boat up then Alice and her companions stepped onto the rickety jetty.

'This is my home,' Olivia said with pride in her voice. My village. And this...' she spread her arms wide, 'is Madagascar. We call her izao rehetra izao. It means: This is all.'

Olivia was glad to be home. Hal slept peacefully in the holdall. She just hoped that the joy of welcoming their grandchild would suffuse any anger at her for leaving the ship. If Gideon,

Alice, and Patty were returning to Halcyon Seas then maybe she could go with them. They could say the pirates had taken her and Patty as hostages.

'It's a beautiful island, Olivia. We are glad to be able to meet your family before re-joining the ship.' Alice and Gideon exchanged a look. Olivia thought they may still be worrying about how they would get home. She didn't know either but for now, they could rest in her village.

She led the three Westerners along a path that cut through palm trees and cacti before meandering through the scrubland that led to the village. A few children abandoned their fishing duties to follow them and as they progressed, other interested villagers joined the procession. Olivia knew all of them but they were too shy to ask her what she was doing back in the village in front of strangers. Maybe Mammon and Pappa had already told them. As they approached the path that led to Disney's hut, Olivia saw the witch doctor sitting on a fallen tree trunk. Olivia bent her head in shame.

'You have come back.'

Olivia nodded. 'I am sorry for bringing misfortune to the village.'

'That is his name? Misfortune?' Disney laughed. He took Hal from the holdall and inspected him. He handed him back to Olivia. 'Disney is never wrong.'

Olivia frowned. Disney had either forgotten his prophecy or was going to change it to match the reality. He was grinning broadly at Alice and Patty. Olivia was concerned that he would alarm them with his dreadlocks, beads, and bare torso but Alice extended her hand. Instead of shaking it, he kissed it and made a small bow. 'Welcome to our island,' he said in English. Olivia had forgotten that Disney studied abroad before she was born.

Her friends stopped to ask about life on the island. Meanwhile, their followers hung back waiting for the procession to recommence. Becca, a middle-aged woman in a pink straw hat, stepped forward to find Olivia. 'Your Mamma and Pappa know about him?' She nodded at Hal.

'Yes, Becca. They know about Hal.'

'Shame girl. Shame.' Becca shook her head in disapproval and Olivia's stomach dipped.

How could she feel shame for the little miracle in her arms? He was her compensation for living without Raf. But Becca was right, her family would be disappointed. Her friends traipsed out of Disney's cabin having completed their tour and Olivia prepared herself to meet her family. She wanted to throw her arms around them. To cry and beg forgiveness but it would have to wait until they were alone. Neither would they meet Hal properly until they had first shown some hospitality to their unexpected guests.

News had reached them and so they were standing outside their hut waiting. Olivia formally greeted her parents and introduced them to Hal by opening the holdall wide, inviting them to take a look. Mammon peeked first and she gave such a broad smile, Olivia could feel her love. Then, Pappa took a look and nodded his approval. His expression did not change but Olivia knew that he too was proud of his first grandson. She sent up a prayer of gratitude for her loving and forgiving parents. Somehow, she would repay them.

'Your friends must eat,' Mammon said.

Olivia knew that her mammon would give away the food intended for her family that day. 'There is no need. We ate in Toliara and Pascal took some food from the ship.'

'He should not have taken from the ship. What will your friends think? We are not thieves.'

'It's fine, Mammon. A warm drink and dry clothes would

be good. And then, they perhaps need to rest.' She was unable to stifle a yawn.

'Gracie,' Mammon shouted. Olivia knew that her sister and brothers would be watching everything from inside their hut. 'Get lamba for lady and man.'

Gracie appeared at Mammon's side. She stared wide-eyed at the strangers. 'Yes. Mammon.' Olivia winked at her.

'Jay ...' He darted out of the hut before Mammon had finished saying his name, '…Jim, boil water and herb for our guest.'

Alice stepped forward and offered her hand. She spoke in French. 'Mrs Rose. We are sorry to arrive at your home uninvited. We are very happy to meet Olivia and Hal's family but we do not want to trouble you.'

Mammon seemed delighted that Alice had spoken to her in the language she had known as a child. 'It is no trouble, you are our guest. Now, you must have our home. Please make yourself comfortable.'

They all shook Mammon and Pappa's hands. Kanto and Samuel crept out of the hut and cowered behind their mother. Jay Jim got a fire going and Gideon sat with him, warming himself on the embers as a pot of water boiled.

'Ici,' Gracie giggled.

'Shall we follow you?' Alice said in English. Olivia nodded on Gracie's behalf. Alice and Patty followed Gracie inside the hut.

With their guests occupied, Olivia sidled up to her father. 'I am sorry, Pappa.'

'Why are you sorry? You have blessed us with a fine grandson. And I am glad to have our Olive Oyl home. We will stay in the shop so that your friends can have our home. Will you stay here with them?'

'I'd rather be with you, Mammon and the children.'

'Someone will need to stay with them to keep them safe. You rest here and when you are refreshed, we will make a plan. Can we take Hal with us?'

'You can but how will you feed him?'

'The same way we would have done if you had sent him here alone.'

Olivia frowned. Had they already found a nursing mother to replace her?

'Your mammon has found a baby's bottle and there is the milk of the goat.'

'I'll feed him now and then he should be fine for four hours.'

Alice and Patty came out of the hut dressed like Malagasies, with colourful lambas wrapped around their bodies. They looked elegant, as the lambas Gracie had chosen were Olivia's and Mammon's best robes. The ones they wore for celebrations. They both put their hands together and bowed to her parents.

'Jay Jim has made you a hot drink. I am going to feed Hal and then my family will leave you in peace to rest in our home.'

'That is very kind of them but we can relax on the beach. When we've had a little sleep, we will try and make a plan to get back on board the ship. Will you return with us or stay here?'

It was the question that had been going round and round Olivia's head. If they could explain away her absence from the ship maybe she could return as though nothing had happened. She would be able to send money home and pay off the instalments on the fishing boat. Hal would be cared for by her parents and with the money she sent home, he would hopefully receive nourishment and thrive. But how could she part with him? It would be like losing Raf all over again – except worse. If she did the right thing then she would die inside. Olivia squeezed Hal to her. Her precious babe. 'I don't know.'

'You have time to think.' Alice touched Olivia's arm. It was as if Alice could read her mind.

'Please accept my parents' hospitality. It is important to us that we make you welcome.'

'Then, thank you. But we will not stay for long. Hopefully, we will soon be back on board the ship.'

Olivia hoped that day would not come too quickly.

27

Alice awoke to the sound of children laughing and she wondered where she was. The woven mat beneath her and a blanket that smelt of woodsmoke brought her back to the present. She opened her eyes and was surprised to find that she was alone in the hut. Patty's mat had been rolled up. If Olivia had slept, she was now up, and Alice did not know what had happened to Gideon. She had left him at the campfire, where he was bonding with Pascal over beers stolen from the ship – although, as Gideon was a paying guest of Halcyon Seas, it was not strictly theft. Her watch had stopped working since she was pulled out of the sea but Alice guessed it was late afternoon. She ought not to have slept so long. Olivia's family had vacated their home and she felt indulgent sleeping when she should be paying back their hospitality by helping out. Her own clothes had been taken away and so Alice shook out the pink and green cloth she had worn earlier that day and wrapped it around her. She looked for a comb or something to untangle her hair and was drawn to what looked like a collage above a low table. There were clippings from magazines: Madonna, Beckham, The Beatles, and one of Halcyon Seas. Old photographs, yellow and faded, of smiling faces. Verses in what must have been Malagasy. Strings of beads hung over the images, a rosary, and a garland of dried flowers. Arrangements of shells, feathers, and candles littered the table as though it was an altar.

'I think my photograph came down when Mammon and Pappa received my email.' Olivia had crept in behind her. 'That is my grand-mammon. Grand-papa. And they are my pappa's parents, his brothers.' She traced a finger over the photographs as though caressing them. We keep our ancestors close. Mammon lights candles every day.' She did not explain why Madonna, Beckham and The Beatles had a place on the wall and Alice was not going to ask.

'It was kind of your family to let us stay in your home but now we have rested we must leave.'

'How will you leave? Is the ship coming to collect you?'

'I don't know but I'm going to talk to Gideon. We must make a plan. Have you decided what you will do, Olivia?'

'I am waiting for my ancestors to tell me what is for the best. If I do not work on the ship, the fishing boat will have to be returned because we cannot make the payments. But if I go...' she shrugged. 'I will have to leave mon ange, Hal.' Despite the agony Olivia must be feeling at this impossible decision, she stated it with a beatific smile. 'They will know what is right.'

Outside the hut, children were laughing. It was a joyful sound and Alice smiled, feeling a warmth within. She could not imagine living in this sparsely furnished hut with its two rooms and outside latrine. Olivia and her family managed with so little. There was a small television in a corner of the room that looked like one Alice once had in her student bedsit, a fridge, a washing-up bowl, and a shelf with pots and pans but little else. A chicken squawked and ran through the hut flapping its wings. Olivia opened the door to let it out and Alice spied Patty sitting cross-legged surrounded by children.

It was funny but Alice felt more at home and at peace than she had staying in Rachel's house in Bethnal Green. She ran her fingers through her matted hair to detangle it. Like Olivia, she would manage with what she had.

'Good afternoon.' Patty greeted Alice as she stepped out of the hut. 'You needed that sleep. I hope we didn't wake you.'

The two youngest, Kanto and Samuel, were playing a game of catch, where Patty threw a deflated football and they both ran after it shrieking with laughter. They wrestled like pups to get the ball and be the one to return it. Meanwhile, Gracie was braiding Patty's hair with a look of concentration on her face.

'They will not let you go unless you are firm,' Olivia said.

'I don't mind. I would be happy to play with them all day. They're little darlings.'

'Well, so long as they are looking after our guests, they are saved from their work so they won't be leaving your side.'

'I don't want to keep them from their lessons.'

I don't know how much school they have had this season. Work in the fields and fetching water are more important, although Mammon insists the children do their reading and sums before going to bed.'

Patty exchanged a look with Alice. They both knew better than to let their feelings be known. The Malagasy people seemed to be proud and put a brave face on their hardship but a comparison between the luxurious life on board Halcyon Seas, where they had actually complained about being pampered too much, and life on this island was stark and Alice felt a little ashamed, remembering past conversations with Olivia.

. . .

Gideon, Jay Jim, and some other boys were working on the shore. As Alice drew closer, she saw that they were spreading silvery fish upon a mat. Crates of them glittered in the sun like shards of glass. Gideon had tied a sarong around his middle and was bare-chested as were the boys who mostly wore shorts.

'Did you get any sleep?' Alice asked, standing over him.

'Nah. Pascal lost a couple of days' work collecting Hal and so I wanted to make it up to him. But I do have some good news…' Gideon scrambled up to take an empty crate from Jay Jim.

'Now we have to salt the fish and pack them. See, like this.' Jay Jim demonstrated. Alice copied him and he laughed. 'You help?'

She nodded, glad to be doing something useful at last.

When Jay Jim left for the pier, Gideon continued. 'Yes. Good news. We heard that Halcyon Seas is being towed to a berthing spot on the Maloogy River. Apparently, she's lost all power. Engine failure.'

'Does Captain Moore know where to find us? Where is the Maloogy River? We must reach her before she sets sail again.' Alice was both relieved and a little disappointed. Madagascar was peaceful, the people kind and light of heart.

'It's not far. Luc, the guy who picked us up with Pascal, was still in Toliara when Halcyon Seas arrived. You saw the size of the port? She would have stopped container ships loading and unloading and so the port captain arranged to have her towed. Luc told him that we were here and needed to get back on the ship. I can't see her going anywhere else in a hurry if the engines have failed. I tried calling Marianne but her phone must be switched off or no signal. Let's finish off here and then go and find her.'

They worked in silence. Alice's hands found a rhythm as

she packed and salted the dried fish. Little boys with catapults chased away the raucous black and white gulls. The melodic sound of the boys' voices, the cries of gulls and the gentle lapping of waves provided a soundtrack and Alice felt her mind empty. Their work was almost complete when the sun began to set, a dazzling display of crimson and purple before it dipped down into the sea. They finished up and when Jay Jim was satisfied, stretched their aching backs, before strolling back to the village.

'I don't think we should let Olivia's family feed us or give up their beds for the night. If our ship's close let's see if we can board.' Alice was already thinking ahead. She would donate her clothes to be sold in the shop, and anything else that might sell.

'Agree. It can't be far. I'll ask Olivia's dad for directions.'

'Okay. I'll find Patty.'

At first, Alice could not see Patty. The small gathering of children had multiplied and Patty was hidden in their midst. They were playing a singing game in Malagasy. Patty repeated a verse and they giggled at her pronunciation. Then, she would sing a line in English which they tried to copy. As Alice stood on the periphery marvelling at the joyous energy, the smiling faces and easy laughter, a girl started to sing something new. It was Kanto. Her voice was beautiful and what started as a whisper grew in volume until she seemed to lose herself in the song. Another voice joined hers. Then a harmony. And another. It was a heavenly choir – pitch perfect. Alice wiped a tear from her eye. They sang like angels. When the song came to an end there was complete silence.

Alice clapped and fifteen or more little faces turned to her. 'That was amazing.'

Patty stood up. 'Can you believe that? Jeez. I've got goose pimples.'

The children scattered, running and shouting as they darted between the huts.

Alice felt the same way and rubbed her arms. 'Wow.' She couldn't find the words to express her awe. Then, Alice remembered why she was there. 'The ship. Apparently, she's lost power and has been towed to the Maloogy River. Gideon's finding out how to get there. We should go now, so we don't impose on Olivia's family any longer than necessary.

'When we've left the village, those children will be sent to work in the fields. Gracie told me she has to fetch water every day, walking four kilometres uphill.'

They shook their heads at the injustice of the world.

28

Halcyon Seas had been towed and then moored on a bank of the Maloogy. It was a wide river and so did not obstruct the fishing boats, of which there were a number: motorised skiffs which resembled rowing boats, and some double sailed ones which Marianne knew to be ketches. Halcyon Seas was moored close to a dense thicket of trees at a bend in the river. Although positioned close to the river's mouth, Halcyon Seas was not visible from the Mozambique Channel where one of the tugs remained. Marianne had eventually got through to Captain Lambert on the ship's radio.

'I am sorry we had to move your ship,' the captain said, although Marianne did not detect the slightest remorse in his tone. 'It is safer for you and us. The position of Halcyon Seas will not interfere with our container ships and with one of our tugs guarding access to your ship from the channel you have some protection.'

'Protection from what? You said you would take me to meet the pirates who captured our passengers.' The last thing

Marianne wanted to do was come face to face with a knife-wielding pirate but she needed to know if they were in the vicinity.

Captain Lambert laughed. 'Ah, those pirates. The men who took your passengers are close by. I'm sure that they will make themselves known to you.'

Marianne's stomach lurched. Had the captain made them a sitting target? 'If anything happens to this ship, our passengers, or crew, I will hold you personally responsible, Captain.'

'I hope that you enjoy your stay in Madagascar. You will need to sign some papers and settle your fees before leaving.'

When Captain Lambert signed off, Marianne beat her forehead with a closed fist. They had no electricity and were stranded in what looked to be the middle of nowhere. Pirates were close by and would be seeking her out. The absence of a first officer and chief engineer had never been more keenly felt. The crew would be looking to her for leadership and guidance but she was way out of her depth.

'Should we lower the gangplank?' her second officer said.

'Not yet. I need to talk to senior officers and staff.' Marianne was afraid of lowering the gangplank in case pirates were lying in wait.

Everyone was in a sombre mood, their thoughts with the missing passengers and Olivia Rose.

'How long will the emergency generator last?' the head chef asked.

'Three days but there's a back-up. So, four to six if we're lucky,' the second engineer replied.

'There should be enough electricity for the storage and preparation of food but anything that you can do to conserve energy will help. Generators will power the toilet systems and elevators but guests who can use the stairs should do so.'

'What about communications, Captain?' It was her second officer. He looked concerned and she understood why.

'Again, we will have some power for up to six days but after that…' she didn't know what to say to reassure them. 'Hopefully, we can get the engines going by then. How are we on supplies?'

'We've enough food and water to last up to eight weeks but we will have to ration it.'

'Good. Then we have a plan. There's no need to alarm our guests.'

'What about the missing passengers?' Gloria said.

Marianne sighed. This was her greatest concern. She felt helpless. 'The FBI is negotiating for their release. All we can do is pray.'

'We ought to check that the immediate area is safe,' the senior security guard said.

'Of course. Lower the gangplank but only security guards are to leave the ship until further notice and at least one must stay on board at all times.'

'The guests are asking questions. What should I say?' Gloria bit her lower lip.

Marianne was afraid that if she didn't inform her passengers of the hijack then they would find out from worried relatives. 'If we can serve dinner as normal – well, as normal as possible, I will update them then. Hopefully, we will be able to repair the engines and get out of here in a few days.'

Although she had managed to sound confident, Marianne was terrified. Everyone was relying on her. She ought to contact Libby Braithwaite but with nothing positive to report, she was reluctant to do so.

'I'll accompany you when you leave the ship,' Marianne

said to her security officer. 'I need to get a sense of where we are.' She could tell from the look that crossed his face; he thought this a bad idea but he knew better than to question her judgement.

The gangplank was unsteady. If the guests were going to leave the ship, then a makeshift pier would need to be erected. She was discussing this with the second engineer who had joined the exploration party when a group of people silhouetted by the sun came towards them.

A burly security guard stepped in front of her, his back blocking her view. 'Three locals. I suggest you slowly board the ship, Captain, and leave this to us.'

Marianne peeked around his great build. Three people in traditional dress. One of them male – his torso bare. There was something about the way he moved. Marianne stepped around the security guard to get a better look.

'Gideon! Alice. Patty. Our missing guests.'

'Careful Captain. It could be a trap.'

Marianne wanted to run to them. To hug them. To behave in a very un-captain-like way but he was right. 'Understood. I'll board the ship. Let me know when I can interview them.'

Alice washed herself down at the sink in her bathroom, careful not to waste any precious water. Then, she used the same water to wash the lamba she had borrowed from Olivia. She tugged a brush through her salt-encrusted hair. It was good to put on clean, fresh clothes but not the evening attire she would have worn to dinner pre-Madagascar. It was as though she had returned to the ship a different person from the one that had fallen into the sea that morning. The thought of sitting down to a four-course meal did not sit well with her. Olivia's family would be sharing a few cups of rice and fish from today's catch and would consider that a feast. They were to meet with Captain Moore in half an hour but first Alice took her time, selecting and folding garments from her wardrobe, including the Joseph Ribkoff dress that she had worn the day she thought she was meeting her son in Sydney. She only needed three or four changes of clothes. The rest would fetch a good price in a nearby town. Money that could buy food or help pay for the fishing boat. Jewellery too. Tomorrow, she would hand over these things to Olivia's father.

Patty and Gideon were seated at a table with Captain Moore and a security guard when Alice joined them in a meeting room. With her hair braided and still wearing a lamba Patty looked like a local. Gideon had changed into a clean shirt and chinos but he had a glow about him as though he had absorbed a wholesomeness with the sun's rays.

'Thank you for joining us, Alice. I was just saying to Gideon and Patty that we would appreciate a debrief on what happened the night you left the ship right up until now.'

Gideon and Patty seemed to be looking to her to tell their story and so Alice took a deep breath and started at the beginning, leaving nothing out. It meant exposing Olivia for her deceit in hiding her pregnancy and for summoning Pascal to take Hal from her.

'I'm shocked to hear that one of our staff was driven to take such drastic action because she feared for her job. I'll be taking this up with Silver Seas. However, I'm relieved to hear that we weren't hijacked by pirates. We may have to stay here for a few days, so following a risk assessment, we may invite guests to visit the island. Perhaps you and Olivia Rose could assist our cruise director Gloria Busby by suggesting possible excursions?'

Alice looked to Gideon and Patty hoping to find inspiration. There was the village, forest, and wasteland. It was a beautiful island but without guides and transportation, there was nothing to entertain seventy mature travellers. 'We'll give it some thought,' she said.

'Thank you. I guess you're all exhausted after your ordeal. We're serving dinner this evening as usual. I'll be updating everyone on the current situation, if you've recovered by then I'd be grateful if you could say something about your experience of the island and reassure your fellow passengers that you're safe and well.'

'It's the least we can do after all the trouble we've caused,' Gideon said. Alice noticed a softening of Captain Moore's face under the warmth of Gideon's gaze. Something was going on between those two, the electricity between them was palpable.

Now that she had good news to report, Marianne was ready to update Libby Braithwaite. She used her mobile, as the battery had now charged a little. The signal was weak but she only needed a short call to reassure HQ that all was well. Before she could explain anything, Libby barked at her.

'Halcyon Seas is front page news in all of the tabloids: "Pirates hijack retirement cruise ship." "Halcyon Seas missing in the Indian Ocean believed to have been hijacked by pirates." "Elderly residents of the retirement cruise ship Halcyon Seas have been kidnapped by pirates and are now being held hostage on a remote part of the island." A group of relatives are talking to the press accusing us of negligence.'

'That's ridiculous. How have things escalated so quickly? There were no pirates. We are safe. As soon as we've assessed the damage to our engines, I'll know what's needed to get us back on course.'

'What did you expect Captain Moore? You reported a

serious incident, one that threatened national security. The FBI was informed. We'll take advice on damage limitation. Do not under any circumstances talk to the press.' Libby gave an exaggerated sigh.

Tomorrow Marianne would take on the role of chief engineer. Hopefully, the engine failure would be easily fixed. She needed to get the cruise back on track before her reputation was completely destroyed. Since Jonny had assured Marianne that the captaincy of Mermaid of the Seas was as good as hers a lot had happened.

After dinner, Alice, Patty, and Gideon found a quiet corner of the bar. They had a lot to discuss but it was difficult because everyone on the ship wanted to stop and talk about their ordeal. When Captain Moore addressed the room at dinner, there was more excitement than distress. After months at sea being pampered, their peers seemed to welcome the uncertainty of their situation and the prospect of adventure.

'I have no idea what we can suggest for an excursion,' Alice said, as she swirled the ice in her gin and tonic.

'Seventy aged Westerners descending on the village is going to cause mayhem.' Gideon rolled his eyes. 'Although I do see Marianne, I mean Captain Moore's point. It's not fair to keep everyone cooped up on the ship. Pascal and Luc say Westerners are at risk of being robbed. It could be dangerous for folks to wander off on their own.'

'So, what do you suggest? I can't see villagers taking time out from the daily chores to entertain us.'

'That's it.' Patty slammed her palms down on the table. 'The villagers need help with chores like farming and collecting water. The excursions could be the opportunity to take part in village life.'

Alice could see where Patty was going with this idea. 'An experience of village life: working on the land with locals, a walk up the hillside to enjoy breath-taking views and to experience how water is carried down to the village.'

'There must be some local crafts. An excursion to view and buy!' Patty clapped her hands together.

'Are you sure the villagers will welcome this intrusion?' Gideon said.

'We can ask them through Olivia. Maybe there will be a budget.' Alice was relieved that they could offer some practical help and possible remuneration. If the villagers weren't comfortable with this suggestion, they could always say no.

29

'These clothes are too good to sell in our shop. We'll get more for them in Malatanga,' Olivia's father said.

When Alice had arrived with her arms full of evening gowns and pretty dresses the day before, Olivia hadn't wanted to accept but she had been insistent.

'Why can't I try them on? Ooh, let me keep this blouse.' Gracie tugged a glittery top from the pile.

Olivia slapped her sister's hand away. 'These clothes are not for us. You heard Pappa.'

'Are you sure your friends will be interested in looking at our crops? It seems a strange kind of entertainment,' her mother said.

'They want to help for the day. Experience village life.'

'We can't ask them to carry water from the spring.' Mammon took Hal from Olivia's arms.

Olivia fastened her blouse. 'We didn't ask them to do any of this. Alice asked us if we would be willing to show them. If they want to help out...' She shrugged.

Gracie laughed. 'They wouldn't find it entertaining if they had to climb that hill twice a day, every day.'

'These are old people. They should not have to work.' Mammon cradled Hal, rubbing his back. 'Good boy.'

'They want to. I'm going to meet them off the ship. Disney is taking a few people on a tour of the forest, and I've asked some other villagers to join us so that they can lead small parties.' Olivia was delighted to be welcoming the guests to her island. The villagers did not need any encouragement to greet the ship; it was the most exciting thing that had happened since a blue whale beached on the shore when she was eight.

Olivia led Disney, and seven other locals along the path that led down to the Maloogy River where Halcyon Seas was moored. As soon as the ship came into view, they stopped walking and gazed in wonder.

'So big. She will bring us great fortune,' Disney said, making Olivia nervous.

'Can we go on board?' A man said, and Olivia guessed what he was thinking. There would be a great bounty.

'No. You cannot board the ship. There is very tight security.' She would have to warn them to keep a close guard.

Alice and Patty were already organising people into groups of ten. Olivia felt as shy as the villagers who clustered behind her.

'Olivia!' Patty waved, beckoning her over.

There were groups for the fields and others for the hill climb. Olivia had briefed the villagers on what was required of them. Gideon headed off with three groups of ten, each of these groups had a local guide. Patty led another twenty people with two local guides to find water carriers and then up the hill.

The remaining tourists were chatting with the locals, using

gestures. Olivia recognised Richard and Barbara amongst the group. A woman Olivia knew well from the village was telling Barbara about the handicrafts they made for the market but Barbara obviously had no idea what she was talking about. 'I will ask if you can take a group to your hut to show them what you make,' Olivia said. They might buy souvenirs.

Alice agreed that this was a good idea. 'Let me just check with Gloria.'

Olivia noticed for the first time that Gloria Busby and Captain Moore were standing together at the top of the gang-plank. She didn't want the captain to see her, despite Alice's reassurance that the captain did not blame her, Olivia knew that she was responsible. It was too late; Alice had signalled to Gloria and now the two of them were coming down the gangplank.

Fortunately, the captain was more interested in meeting the remaining villagers. Barbara, Richard and some other tourists left with her friend to admire the handicrafts. Disney was partnered with William, who seemed to be the only one interested in venturing into the forest.

'What are you planning to do, Alice?' the captain asked.

'I was just going to go where I was needed, once everyone else had found a group.'

'Why don't you join William? I'm sure he would welcome your company.'

So, Alice, William, and Disney left for a forest adventure. When the last of the groups had set off along the path, Olivia prepared to leave. She ought to speak to Captain Moore, apol-ogise for everything, but she didn't have the courage. The captain couldn't have recognised her because she was returning to the ship. But Gloria did.

'Well done for organising the excursions, Olivia. I think they'll be a hit.'

'We are grateful for the help. It means that my brothers and sisters can go to school for the first time in months.'

'Where is the school?'

'It is on the edge of our village. I am going there now to help.'

'May I join you?'

'You would be most welcome.'

They walked together, and as they did so, Olivia apologised for the grief she had brought to the ship. Gloria agreed that Olivia's actions were outrageous and reprimanded her as acting hotel director, but she didn't sound angry. If anything, she seemed dismayed that she had not noticed Olivia's pregnancy or the baby that they had successfully hidden for the first two weeks of his life. By the time they reached the school, Olivia was consoling Gloria on her lack of observation, reminding her of how busy she had been managing two director jobs. The truth was, Gloria's mind had been on producing a show but Olivia kept that thought to herself.

'It's up there,' Olivia pointed to a long building. As they climbed the path, she saw that the wind had taken off half of the roof and some of the side panels. 'Nobody has been up here for a while.'

They once had a full-time teacher, but he had moved to Malatanga when children stopped turning up for lessons. Olivia was one of the most educated in their village and so she, her mother, and a couple of other women took turns teaching lessons. Gracie, Jay Jim, Kanto, and Samuel were sitting at one of two bench tables with their friends.

'This table is for the youngest children, and this the older ones,' Olivia explained to Gloria.

'Where are the teachers?'

That is what Olivia wanted to know too. She couldn't teach all of them at once. Where were the other women?

Maybe she should have rallied them first. Olivia had barely recovered from giving birth; she would have to feed Hal in a couple of hours. 'I teach but I need help. Maybe we should let one of the groups go. The oldest ones could go back to work.'

'Absolutely not. I am here to help you. What are today's lessons?'

'I was going to teach English and French to the older children. I don't know about the younger ones. They like to sing, especially Kanto.'

'Perfect. We'll have a singing lesson. Shall I take them outside so I don't disturb your class?'

When it was time for lunch, Olivia went home to feed Hal and find the other teachers. Gloria seemed content to stay at the school eating a packed lunch she had brought with her. The children had brought rice wrapped in palm leaves, dried fish, or nuts and berries. Gracie and Jay Jim had fetched buckets of spring water so the children could take sips from a shared cup.

At the end of the day, Olivia walked back to the ship with Gloria. 'Those children sing like a choir of angels and the little girl…' Gloria threw up her hands to express her wonder. 'She could train professionally.'

Olivia guessed that Gloria was referring to Kanto. Sometimes it seemed as though she had started to sing before she spoke. There were no such thing as professional singers in Malatanga but Olivia didn't want to correct Gloria, as she meant well. 'Kanto loves to sing.'

Olivia arrived home to find a group of villagers crowded around their hut. Hal cried from within and her breasts ached as they filled with milk.

'Let me see.' A woman tried to push past Olivia to get a better view.

'What are you all doing here?'

'We want to see what else is in the stash.'

The crowd parted when they saw it was Olivia. All of them bursting with news of the tourists. She listened to their stories and laughed with them. Then she noticed what had attracted the crowd. The entrance to her hut was blocked with bags of clothes and other donations.

A truck pulled up. It was Pappa. 'You go inside Olivia and see to Hal. I'm locking these away until I can take them to market.'

One of the women had put on a fascinator and was dancing around bobbing her head to shrieks of laughter. 'Let me have that, Becca. The money that we raise from the sale of these donations will benefit the whole village.'

Alice's generosity in donating her clothes had started something and now it seemed everyone wanted to make donations of clothing and other valuables. So much had happened that day, Olivia was finding it hard to take in. The coming together of her two worlds was unsettling. She was afraid that she might be responsible for something catastrophic. What if they regretted giving away their clothes, or accused her family of stealing? What if her friends came to harm? The island was a dangerous place for people who were not used to their ways. News of the ship would attract thieves. She had to keep her friends safe until the ship was repaired and ready to set sail. Olivia guessed, that if she asked, Gloria would allow her to return to work. Her family all assumed that was what was going to happen. Although common sense told Olivia it was the only way, it still broke her heart.

30

Alice felt as though she were standing in a magnificent cathedral, the ceiling more exquisite than any she had visited. Trees towered above creating a canopy of green, shot with golden light from the sun. High up, tawny lemurs wrapped their limbs around branches. Motionless, they resembled soft toys. Then, one darted up the tree and Alice shifted her gaze, rubbing the back of her neck.

'Yes. We have many lemur in Madagascar.'

William was taking photographs and Alice regretted not bringing her camera. 'Are they protected living in this forest?'

'Nobody harms the lemurs. Not even on Independence Day. Well maybe we will roast one or two but it is an honour for them to be the celebratory meal.' Disney laughed from deep in his belly and Alice wondered whether or not he was joking.

'I guess if you have plenty of them then it is no different from us having roast lamb for dinner.'

'You roast a lamb? Savages.' Disney laughed again. It was a

warm, rich sound. Alice felt cocooned in the most beautiful place imaginable and Disney's calm, gentle explanations soothed her soul. William, too, seemed to be in his element. Here in the forest, he appeared to be more relaxed and spoke easily. But none of them felt the need to talk as they meandered through the forest path, high above the sea.

'Shh, follow me.' They crept behind Disney until he raised an arm and they stopped. 'There,' he whispered. Big amber eyes stared out of the foliage. A creature resembling a gremlin, his eyes huge in a small face with pointed ears. 'An aye-aye lemur. Watch.'

The little gremlin revealed a long ET-like finger and poked it into the bark, extracting a morsel which was met with its quick tongue. As William stepped closer to take a shot, the snap of a twig startled the lemur and he disappeared into the foliage.

'It is rare to see an aye-aye in the daytime. They are nocturnal.'

They continued through the forest with Disney pointing out edible mushrooms and berries. They spotted a giraffe-necked weevil, and a chameleon whose exquisite turquoise and green colouring made it appear like a jewelled brooch bedecking the foliage in a perfect match. The scent of sea salt blended with earthy tones and sharp sap. A faint lapping of waves. There was a clearing in the trees and beyond that an expanse of blue. Sun danced on the sea, making it shimmer with diamonds.

'I don't ever want to go home,' Alice said, sighing with contentment.

'I could live here,' William agreed.

Disney squatted on the stump of a tree facing the horizon and William wandered closer to the edge of the cliff. Alice made herself comfortable on the burnished gorse close to

Disney, content to listen to the waves and bask in the beauty of the island. Behind her, Disney was rustling around in his woven tote bag. She wondered if he had a packed lunch and maybe they should have brought one too. A few minutes later, the pungent smell of marijuana took her back to her student days. Disney was puffing on a thin roll-up. He offered it to her and Alice thought, why not?

It was strong stuff, neat grass, no tobacco. The scent filled her nostrils and the smoke her lungs. She was breathing in the forest, becoming one with it. 'Oh, that's good.' Alice passed the joint back, then she laid down to gaze at the sky. Blue. Nothing but blue. She could fall into it, as though diving into the sea. Below, the waves crashed against the cliff edge.

'Alice in Wonderland.' Disney's voice was deep and honeyed.

'That is exactly how I feel. I don't know how I ended up here but I'm glad I did.' Alice laughed at her huge understatement.

'I saw you coming.'

'On the boat? We came from Toliara.'

'No, before that. I told Olivia that she would bring prosperity to the village. She brought you here.'

Alice rolled onto her stomach and looked up at him. He grinned at her through half-closed eyes. 'Good huh?' He took another long inhale and handed it back to her.

She felt as though she were liquid and resolved that would be her last inhale of the joint. 'What else did you see?'

'Ah,' Disney gave a knowing smile. 'I see much.'

'What?' She gave a playful kick of his ankle and he exploded with a laugh letting go of the breath he was holding down with the smoke.

William joined them. 'Oh, you're getting high.'

Disney handed him the joint. 'We saved some for you.'

William took the joint without hesitation and took a toke as though it were second nature. He was a dark horse, definitely more at home out here in the wild than in a social gathering.

'There's a Cynorkis orchid growing out of the cliff.' William bounced from one foot to the other.

'There are many species on this island. You know about orchids?'

'A little. I was editor of a horticultural magazine and became interested when reading about the discovery of a rare orchid.'

Alice's attention was piqued. 'I love orchids. Do you know where we can find more, Disney?'

Disney extinguished the joint and slipped the butt end into his bag. 'They are all about. I'll point out the places you might find them on our walk back down.'

'Come and have a look at the Cynorkis,' William said. He offered his hand to help Alice up.

Disney closed his eyes as if lost in an inner world whilst they went to look at the orchid.

'Just beyond that rock, there,' William said, his head close to Alice's.

Little white flowers with a scattering of tiny, purple spots within each petal. The orchid seemed to grow from the shelter of rock just below them on the cliff face.

'It's perfect,' Alice said.

'Incredible. If only I could take a cutting.'

'Let's go on an orchid hunt. See what other species we can find. Maybe we could take some cuttings.' Alice felt an unfamiliar surge of excitement.

'That would be amazing.' William's face lit up, his eyes

bright and cheeks flushed. 'Maybe we'll find a rare species. If it hasn't been catalogued then we could name it. Wouldn't that be something?'

Alice didn't know whether the grin that was now making her face ache was a result of the joint or the sheer joy of discovering a whole new world – one filled with magnificent orchids growing in the wild. William seemed as excited as her, if not more so.

'Let's start tomorrow. We don't know how many days we have – best not waste any.'

William held out his palms and Alice high-fived them.

At the end of their tour with Disney, Alice and William had a good idea of where to find orchids. Disney seemed amused by their enthusiasm. Although he foraged for herbs and medicines, searching far and wide for some of the rarer plants, orchids were to him commonplace. Marijuana was, Disney explained, one of his potions used to relieve pain.

'I need to find a computer with an internet signal,' William said when Disney left them.

'There's one in the village shop but I don't know if there's a good signal. I'll take you there, I need to speak to Olivia's father anyway.'

Olivia's father was in the shop, sorting through the bags of donations, when Alice and William stepped in through the open plan front. At night, boarding would be pulled across and a padlock fitted but with flimsy walls and roof this offered little security.

'You have all been so generous. Thank you. Thank you.' He greeted them with open arms.

'You are welcome, Mr Rose. Would it be possible to use your computer? That's if you are connected to the internet.'

'Of course. Of course.' He ushered them into the back office where there was a desktop computer similar to one

Tom had used many years ago. The computer component was a heavy box, unlike Rachel's modern one, which was built into a flat monitor screen.

Alice hoped that it would suffice for William's needs and left him to it while she discussed with Mr Rose what would sell best at market. Everyone had been asking her what they should donate and Alice needed some direction.

Thirty minutes later, William joined them in the shop. 'Thank you, Mr Rose.'

'Did you get a connection?' Alice asked.

'I did thanks. So, tomorrow– and if not, as soon as we can get away.' William grinned.

'Definitely. I can't wait.' It was true. The thought of an orchid hunt in this beautiful setting was something to look forward to.

William was an entirely different man from the one she had perceived him to be. The fusty bachelor was a disguise. Alice had glimpsed the bubbling energy and excitement of a younger man. She watched him leave, consulting that notebook again. It wouldn't surprise her to find out that he was a famous author. William had hidden depths. While she was in the shop, Alice thought she had better check her emails and asked Mr Rose for permission.

'You do not have to ask. My home is your home, Mrs Wagstaff.'

The password was 1234. It took a few minutes but then Alice was connected and looking at her inbox. The usual spam offering her funeral plans, equity release on a home she no longer owned, retirement home adverts, and then one from Rachel.

Dear Mummy,

If by a miracle this email reaches you then know that we are all thinking of you and praying for your release from captivity. I was devastated to find out you were pushed overboard and then kidnapped by pirates. The first we heard was on the evening news. You can imagine my horror. Dave and I have been in constant communication with the authorities here and in the USA. Nobody is giving us a straight answer. It seems they are now denying it. I don't know what to believe. I should never have let you embark on this ridiculous voyage. It is a scam. A way of fleecing old people and their families of their wealth and inheritance. If only you had taken my advice and moved into Chestnut Court. I bet you are regretting it now. I won't tell you I told you so. I'll make sure you are home safely by Christmas.

Alice thumped her chest. Poor Rachel. She would have been beside herself with grief and anxiety. The press blew things out of all proportion. At least she could now reassure her that all was well. Alice remembered her last Christmas alone in Norfolk and wanted to run for the hills. She typed a loving reply to Rachel reassuring her.

It is all a misunderstanding. Once the ship has been repaired, we will be back on course. In the meantime, we are all enjoying our stay in Madagascar. You would love it here. Do not fret about me darling and please don't worry about getting me home safely – there is no need. Think instead about your own Christmas. I'm sure we will be at another exotic port by then, celebrating in style. She asked about Greg and Alfie, sending her love, and then signed off.

5th November

Hi

We are stranded in Madagascar, as you have no doubt heard. Attached are some photos and video which will be of interest. More to follow. I will try and keep you posted.

Over and out.

31

While the passengers and crew had been enjoying a day experiencing village life, Marianne had donned a boiler suit and inspected the engine room with her second engineer. A large school of krill fish had blocked the cooling water intakes and there was damage to the plates where the ship had hit a reef. It would take at least three weeks to repair the damage and that depended upon them having the parts. When Marianne contacted HQ to report the damage and request a replacement ship, she was shocked to discover that the refurbished ship was in fact forty-two years old.

'Jamboree didn't want to make a big investment until they were confident that the Silver Seas initiative was a success,' Libby had explained.

So far it had been anything but and they both knew it. Marianne sighed. 'If Halcyon Seas isn't sea-worthy we'll need a replacement ship.'

'I'll discuss it with Jamboree – see if there's an available cruise ship. In the meantime, you had better do what you can to repair the damage.'

'How long until a ship is sent to relieve us? The emergency generator will only last a few more days. We can't keep our guests trapped on this island.'

'I'm sorry, Captain Moore. We will do everything that we can. Are you able to source a generator locally? It would be wise to plan for a longer stay just in case.'

Marianne was furious. Jamboree had put her passengers and crew at risk using a ship that was no longer fit for purpose. Now she had to safeguard seventy pensioners from the risks of staying on an island that was experiencing a drought, a limited supply of food and water, and no power supply, unless she could source a generator. Libby Braithwaite had instructed her to make a plan. The best Marianne could do was find hotel accommodation for their guests. When a ship came to relieve them, they could return.

Gloria did her research and reported back to Marianne that hotel accommodation in Madagascar was not an option. There was not a hotel big enough to take all of their guests and it was preferable to keep them together under the supervision of cruise staff. In the end, Gloria found a hotel in Durban close to the port. It would be easy to pick up their passengers as soon as a replacement ship arrived.

At dinner that evening Marianne explained the situation to their guests. 'The good news is, we have discovered the reason for our engine failure and while we will be working to restore power there is no guarantee that we will be successful. Silver Seas are making arrangements for a ship to replace Halcyon Seas.'

Noise built as every table started a whispered conversation. Gloria called out for silence so that Marianne could continue.

'Unfortunately, our emergency generator will not last much longer. You can't stay on this ship if we are without power. Having considered all of the options we have decided that the safest one is to fly you all to Durban, where you will be accommodated in a hotel close to the port. As soon as a replacement ship arrives, we will pick you up and continue the cruise as planned.'

There was an uproar. Everyone shouting to be heard. 'One at a time.' Gloria projected her voice like a true professional.

'When are we leaving? Should we pack our bags and leave them outside the room tonight?' Rosie Diamond was the first one to ask a question.

'In two days' time. We have yet to arrange transfers and flights.'

Alice raised her hand. 'Why can't we stay here? The locals manage okay. We just have to think like the locals. Let me go and talk to Mr Rose. He has a computer with internet access. William and I just used it. I'm sure he could make it available to you. Maybe there's a generator for the village. Olivia's family had an outside latrine, just a hole in the ground, but if we have to live like Malagasies, it won't kill us.'

Marianne wasn't so sure. She couldn't imagine their well-heeled guests accepting the indignity of third-world sanitation. They would have to fly them home and accept that this voyage had been a disaster from beginning to end. She was just thinking this through and imagining the damning account of Halcyon Seas in the trade magazines when Alice's words hit home. William had used the computer. She had asked Alice to accompany him on his tour as an unofficial spy. Of course, Alice had no idea but Marianne made a note to talk to her later. The suggestion that they stay on the island was out of the question.

'I understand what you are saying, Alice, but Silver Seas is responsible for the health and safety of our residents. It sounds as though you all enjoyed your day on the island but staying here, given present conditions, is not an option. I'm sorry.'

Marianne did not dine with her guests that evening there was too much to organise. She was leaving the dining room with Gloria discussing next steps when Alice, who had followed them out, cleared her throat.

'I'm sorry to interrupt, Captain Moore. May I speak to Mr Rose about finding a generator? I'm sure he will be able to help. Mr Rose is considered a village elder and according to Olivia has business contacts in Malatanga.'

'Go ahead, Gloria, I'll join you in a moment.' Marianne then gave Alice her full attention. 'I would appreciate that, thank you.'

'Then can we stay? If we have the use of a generator?'

'It really isn't an option, Alice. I'm sorry. Did you enjoy exploring the forest with the village witch doctor? He's an expert on the wildlife and fauna.'

'Disney's very knowledgeable. William took loads of notes and photographs.'

Marianne thought he might. 'What did he photograph?'

'Our friends working in the fields, a couple of them carrying water on their heads like the locals, the Baobab trees, lemurs, a chameleon, ocean views. I'm impressed with the way he captures everything – notes, photographs.'

Marianne could guess what he was up to. William Fellows had been outside Dr Miles's consulting room when she had confronted the doctor about his incompetence. When she discovered Dr Miles was not the leak it became obvious to her who was. An in-depth search revealed that William Fellows was listed on a database of journalists. She could imagine the caption under his photo: *Fee-paying passengers of Halcyon Seas sent to toil under a hot sun, unpaid labour, exploitation.*

'I understand that Mr Fellows was a reporter. Maybe he still is?'

'Yes, William did mention that.'

Confirmation that William Fellows was the leak and it sounded as though he was still up to his games. Well, not for long because Marianne would be sending him and the other guests to Durban. Her reputation was not completely ruined. If she got them back on course without further incident then she might just salvage her career.

32

Alice sat on the deck sipping her coffee. It was only seven-thirty but already the river was busy: two young women stood at the water's edge washing clothes. They worked, slowly turning their heads every couple of minutes to watch activity on the ship. A dug-out boat sailed by with a goat on board. She didn't want to leave in two days' time. When she had made plans with William to go on an orchid hunt, it had been with the expectation that they would be staying for at least a week.

'Gloria has asked us to organise excursions for guests who want to visit the island today. Do you want to help with the harvest this morning? Barbara and Richard are joining the hill walk to collect water.' Patty sat down next to her.

'Yes, of course. I need to talk to Mr Rose first about a generator. I don't want to leave here, Patty.'

'I'm not going to.'

'I know. If we could just have a couple of weeks in one place other than on the ship. It's beautiful here. So peaceful.'

'I mean it. I'm not going to Durban. If I can't stay on the

Halcyon then I'll ask Olivia to find me somewhere on the island.'

William joined them as Patty made this declaration. 'That's what I've decided too. I'm going to look around today to try and find an alternative in case we can't stay on the ship but I'm not going to Durban.'

'We can't just...' Alice was having trouble processing what felt like a radical proposal. 'I mean is it safe? Surely the captain wouldn't have suggested we leave the island unless it's in our best interests?'

'You must do what is right for you, sugar. I know that staying here, helping the kiddies, is what I need to do.'

'I can't leave here until I've seen the orchids. There must be hundreds of species. No, I'm definitely staying.'

Alice felt butterflies in her stomach. 'Maybe we can persuade Captain Moore to let us stay on the ship. If I can help source the generator, I might have some bargaining power.'

'It looks as though we have more volunteers.' Patty nodded towards the river bank where a group of twenty or more had gathered awaiting direction. They were being entertained by a couple of villagers who were selling woven baskets and embroidered table cloths.

It took more time than Captain Moore had estimated when she first announced her plan to fly passengers to Durban. In those three days, Alice and her friends had worked hard collecting water, harvesting crops, and assisting in the school.

Alice's arms and back ached but it felt good. As she scraped dry earth and mulch to expose the cassava roots and eased them from the plant, her mind had relaxed – absorbed with the task, noticing the heat of the sun, the strength of the roots holding the plant firm, and the sounds of laughter, and birdsong. She felt at peace. A sense of belonging. Of purpose. Patty and William were adamant that they were going to stay, could she be so bold? Rachel would be outraged but that wasn't reason enough to rebel. Most of her life she had been swept along a path determined by the needs and wishes of others. It was her own fault; she had never really considered what she wanted – what would make her happy. Alice didn't know what she wanted beyond staying where she was– for now. It felt right. Now, four days on, Captain Moore was explaining the arrangements for their transfer to Durban.

'What arrangements will be made for those of us who choose not to leave the ship?' William asked.

A murmur rippled throughout the room. A splash of pink bloomed on the captain's throat; her jaw tightened. 'It's not something we've considered. Staying here is not an option. There's limited electricity and poor facilities.'

'I thought this was our home,' William said.

Emboldened by his courage, she raised her hand. 'As you know, Mr Rose has been able to source a generator for the ship. If we stay here at our own risk, prepared to accept the limited facilities and live like the Malagasies – well almost, could you then consider it a viable option?' Her heart was racing. Gideon looked at her in surprise and then nodded his head in approval.

'If one or two of you were adamant that you wanted to stay, we could come to some arrangement but it would be very uncomfortable for you.'

'I'm up for staying,' Richard said. 'We might as well make good use of our time here. There's a source of spring water, four kilometres up. I reckon we could dig a trench and with some pipes and a storage tank get fresh water to the village.'

Several people laughed. 'In a couple of weeks?' someone shouted. There was more laughter.

'We may not achieve much in a couple of weeks but Richard's right, we can make good use of our time here,' Patty said.

'If you are prepared to sign a waiver and accept the poor living conditions of remaining here, please raise your hand.'

Several hands shot up straight away. Conversations went on at each table and then one by one other hands were raised. Alice gripped Patty's hand under the table. It sounded as though they were going to stay.

Marianne once again left the dining room with Gloria at her side but this time she was at a loss for words. It was crazy. Thirty-one passengers wanted to remain on the ship despite having limited power, little food, and questionable sanitation. It would mean changing the flight and hotel bookings. She daren't tell HQ. Marianne blamed William Fellows. That man was determined to ruin her career.

'Do you want me to change the bookings?' Gloria said.

'They can't mean it. Our guests signed up for a life of luxury not this. Talk to them, Gloria. Tell them they can't live like this.'

'I'm afraid I agree with them, Captain. Life on the ship is way better than the life experienced by Olivia's family and other villagers. I can't help feeling guilty for how we have contributed to this drought through climate change.'

Marianne threw up her hands – she didn't need her cruise director getting principled when they were trying to save Silver Seas' reputation – and her own. 'What difference can thirty elders make in two or three weeks? I'm hoping we can be out of here in less than that.'

'I've been thinking about that, Captain. To show our thanks for the use of a generator we could offer the use of Halcyon Seas as a temporary school. The school they use now has no electricity, and, with a wall and half the roof missing, it's a lot less hospitable than the ship's lounge, for example. A goat and some chickens roamed into the classroom when I was there and there was little protection from the sun. I know it would only be for a couple of weeks but with our guests' help it would free up the children to study.'

Marianne thought Gloria had completely lost her mind. 'No. It's out of the question. Two weeks of education is not going to make a scrap of difference.'

'If I had two weeks as a singing coach, I could work wonders. Please let me try. Have you heard those children sing?'

Marianne wasn't surprised to discover Gloria's true motive. 'I don't approve but if this project is properly managed, I guess you could give it a go. It might even help our global reputation but let's keep quiet until we're confident it's news we want to share.'

33

In just two weeks Halcyon Seas had transformed into the village hub. A corner of Frederic's café was used by Olivia and some other mothers as a creche. Patty was in charge and took her role seriously, supporting the mothers to breastfeed, providing nourishment for those babies on solids, and caring for the mothers.

Olivia had never felt more content. 'I don't want this to end,' she sighed, gazing at Hal who was asleep in a catering-size bread basket.

'I wish it didn't have to.' Patty sat down next to her. 'We're all better off living like this. I can't bear the thought of going back to the cruise. Have you decided what you will do? I know you can return to work if that is what you choose.'

'I can't leave Hal. Not now. It is a risk. This drought is longer than any we have known before. So far, we have managed by growing crops that need little water, with that, and the fish, the village can eat. It's a real help having you all here but when the ship leaves, we're on our own.'

'I know, darlin', but we only have enough rations on the

ship to last us a few more weeks. I don't know the solution. I wish I did. Saying goodbye to you, Hal and these other darlins are going to break my heart.'

'Do you know how long we have?' Olivia said.

'The captain is still waiting for a replacement ship to be allocated but she's hopeful repairs might be complete in a week. Let's hope not. Christmas is in six weeks. It would be the best Christmas ever if we could spend it together. You've all become my family.'

Olivia felt a weight upon her shoulders. The villagers did not understand the way a cruise ship worked and the captain and crew of Halcyon Seas did not understand village life and the reality of drought. 'Everyone is happy now but I am afraid for the future. Do you mind taking Hal? There's something I need to do?'

Olivia just needed time out to think. Things were moving too fast. What had started as a kind gesture to offer the ship as a temporary school in exchange for the use of a generator had escalated and now it seemed the villagers were treating the ship as an extension of the village. In one week, it would all come to an end and where would that leave them? Olivia was most concerned for her siblings who were buoyed up with ambitions put into their heads by well-meaning Westerners who did not understand the harsh reality of their lives. They had always been content accepting life for what it was. How would they feel when the ship left and with it all hope for a better future?

Olivia did a tour of the ship. First, she visited the classrooms. These were not all traditional teaching sessions; several students were receiving apprenticeships by learning from cruise staff. Jay Jim loved working in the ship's kitchen under the tutelage of the head chef; some of the other teenagers worked with Frederic in the bakery. It seemed that they had taught him a few things too, as sorghum flour was often used in the pastries. Olivia worried about their expectations being raised. Whatever they all learned in three weeks would soon be forgotten. Few, if any, of them would get the opportunity to work on a ship, or even in the restaurants of Tana.

She sat in on the choir rehearsal. Kanto's voice was amazing. With Gloria's coaching, her voice had developed. As Kanto's solo came to an end, Olivia wiped a tear from her eye. Nobody had seen her and so she crept out. Kanto deserved to have her voice heard far and wide. She had been blessed with an incredible gift; surely their ancestors would find a way for Kanto to follow her dream.

Gracie was not in the English class or singing with the choir. A couple of students were working with the maintenance staff learning how to paint and repair but Gracie was not among them.

'You could try deck eight,' a man in overalls said.

'But there's no electricity up there.'

'The beauticians and hairdressers are using their facilities without power. It's light during the day but hot with no air-con.'

How had Gracie sneaked off to the beauty salon? She was meant to be using these weeks to further her education, not hang out with the glamorous girls. Typical of Gracie. Olivia sighed and went in search of her errant sister.

In the salon, Gracie was braiding a girl's hair. She was the only student up there and Olivia wondered how she had found them. It would be rude to interrupt and Olivia would never chastise a person in public. Instead, she sent a piercing look but Gracie seemed oblivious.

'Would you like me to paint your nails?' A Thai girl asked Olivia.

Olivia could not see the point in painted nails. The paint would come off as soon as she scrubbed their clothes in the river or collected driftwood to burn. Then she noticed a photograph of a toddler pinned to the wall. 'Is that your little boy?'

The girl took down the photo. 'My Anurak. He is not so little now.'

Olivia checked the girl's name badge 'How old is he now, Charanya?'

'Four. Congratulations on your baby boy.'

Everyone on the ship now knew about Olivia's pregnancy. Before the supposed hijack she was of no importance, now she was something of a celebrity. Maybe that was how Gracie had talked her way into an area that should have been out of bounds to the students.

'If you have time then I would love to have my nails painted,' Olivia said. It would give her the opportunity to find out about Charanya's experience working on a cruise ship away from Anurak.

'It breaks my heart every single day,' Charanya replied, in answer to Olivia's question.

'But you budget to take leave. Maybe a few weeks?'

'I do not know when I will get leave now – since this happened. I don't even know if we will get full pay whilst in Madagascar. I expect we will be told that this was a paid holiday. All the while I am away, my son is growing up without me. He will not know me when we meet again. If I could go to him now, I would, even if it meant losing my job.'

'What about the money?'

Charanya shrugged. 'You are right. My family tell me that I do not have a choice. If I want to keep my baby then I must find a western man who will support me and our children.'

Olivia was aware of Gracie's eavesdropping. She did not

want her sister to get any ideas. 'Have you finished braiding, Gracie?'

Gracie scowled at her. 'I'm going to learn how to manicure.'

'That's wonderful but maybe not right now. Gloria Busby would like you to practice with the choir. I think they're rehearsing for a show.' It wasn't a lie. If Gloria had seen Olivia, then she might well have asked about her sister's whereabouts – she was after all a member of the choir.

When Gracie had left with the promise of a return visit, Olivia asked Charanya about Anurak's father.

'He works in the rice paddies. His family look after Anurak. I ought to be grateful. We have plenty of food and Anurak is well cared for. Women like us do not have a choice, Olivia. What about your baby's father? The guy you were dancing with at the party. Raf?'

Olivia had told her family and anyone who asked that Hal was the result of a one-night stand – a stupid, careless night of recklessness following the graduation party but she couldn't hide the truth from her co-workers. They had seen them together and news travelled fast in their world.

'Raf comes from a wealthy family and has a great future as the bar manager of a cruise ship.'

'Then you're okay. He will support you both. Clever you.' Charanya finished the last of Olivia's nails with a top coat and then screwed shut the pot of varnish.

Olivia took in her bright green nails and wanted to scrape off the paint. She would never trick a man into supporting her or making a business deal. Olivia forced a smile and pretended to admire her manicure. 'Thank you. No, not clever. Stupid. I fell in love. Raf must never know about Hal. We will manage. Somehow.'

Charanya did not voice her opinion but Olivia suspected

that she thought her naive. She thanked Charanya and the other girls, who she found sipping Fantas as they listened to a radio in the waiting lounge, then went in search of Pascal to find out about progress with the trench.

The hill climb was hard for Olivia. She had not regained her strength since giving birth and had to keep resting. 'Why don't you wait here and I'll go ahead,' Pascal said.

'No. Just give me a few seconds.'

They sat on a grassy hummock. Below them, the day's catch was being salted and dried by some of the ship's volunteers.

'When do we have to return the new fishing boat?' Olivia said.

'So far, we've managed to hang onto it. You've seen how much more we can catch with a proper boat. Anyway, the old one is past repair. You'll be going back to work soon so we can carry on with the repayments.' Olivia didn't correct him. She was still weighing up what was for the best.

'Ready?' When Olivia nodded, Pascal pulled her to her feet. 'Not much further.'

They didn't have to walk as far as they expected because almost a kilometre from the source of the spring, they saw the men and women at work. Richard came down the hill to greet them.

'An inspection party? Come on, I'll show you.' He looked younger and more alive than the restless, complaining man she had observed while cleaning his cabin. He had a bounce in his step and looked bronzed from too much exposure to the sun.

His wife, Barbara and another lady wove their way down the hill between the hillocks which they seemed to have learnt, just as Olivia had as a young girl. They balanced pots of water on their heads, supporting them with one hand. In their lambas they looked Malagasy.

'One kilometre in two weeks,' Barbara called out as they passed by. 'Can't stop or I'll lose momentum.'

'Don't work too hard,' Olivia called after them.

'Better than a Pilates class,' Barbara shouted, but Olivia didn't know what she meant.

'You've done a great job brother,' Pascal put his arm around Richard. 'Six more weeks and it will reach the village.'

Richard did not point out that they would be leaving in a week. The village would be left with a half-dug trench and no hope of ever finishing it. Even if they had the manpower, they could not afford the cement, piping and storage tank. There were aid programmes but their village did not qualify, as a four-kilometre climb for water was not considered a problem compared to other villages.

Pascal had joined the other men so Olivia made her way back down the hill. Everyone seemed happier – the villagers and the cruise passengers who had opted to stay. But half of the passengers were waiting in Durban to join the cruise ship next week. Then there was the staff. Olivia had experience of Silver Seas and agreed with Charanya that the staff might well get reduced pay for the Madagascar stay. If they stayed much longer than a week then the food supply would run out.

But when the ship left Madagascar, the village would miss the support of their new friends. The children and young people would return to work with dreams of a different future crushed. There would be no fresh water supply to the village. If the drought continued there would be more loss of lives. Hal and the other babies would suffer from malnutrition. If she left with the ship then she could at least send money home but she would worry every day for Hal, her family, and the rest of the village. They all tried to stay positive, to be thankful for what they had but the villagers had experienced droughts before and knew the reality.

Her friends would be sad to leave too. Patty loved caring for the mothers and babies, Alice and William spent every day hunting for orchids convinced they would find a rare unnamed species. Richard and Barbara were like different people to the ones on the ship who had bickered like children whenever she had observed them in private.

Olivia felt as though she were the only grown-up. One who was about to tell the enchanted children that it was time to pack up their toys and get ready for bed. If they could all have their dreams come true then she would be united with Raf and live happily ever after with him and Hal but life was not a storybook.

34

William and Alice had slipped into a routine. At sunrise, they went hunting for orchids. Alice carried a sharp knife, moss, and an assortment of recycled containers to hold the specimens. They had discovered five species and taken two or three cuttings from each. William was more knowledgeable than he first revealed. They tended the orchids, writing notes and taking photographs in the evening. The rest of the day, they joined the other workers: William digging the trench and Alice working in the fields. Alice wound her way up the path to an abandoned cabin that she and William had commandeered for the orchid project. It had been ingeniously made from flattened oil drums and, according to Disney, unoccupied for many years.

As she approached, Alice breathed in the woodsmoke and the sweet scent of herbs from Disney's cabin. It had become part of her routine to pop in and say hello to him as she passed. Dream catchers and strings of shells hung by the front door.

'Disney, are you there?' Alice spoke softly, in case Disney was consulting with a patient.

'Come in, Alice in Wonderland.' He laughed as he always did when he greeted her in this way. Alice loved to hear him chuckle, it was like drinking a mug of hot chocolate – warm and comforting.

'I have something for you.' Alice lowered the basket she had been carrying on her head. 'Tuna steak and some sorghum cakes made by Frederic and his band of helpers.'

'Come and join me. We can cook the fish on my fire.'

'I would love to but William is waiting for me. We need to work fast before the sun goes down. Our collection of specimens is modest but we have such plans. We spied a real beauty this morning. Halcyon Seas could set sail any day and there are so many more we want to find.'

'Then you must not keep William Tell waiting. I also have a gift for you. Come. Come.' Disney led Alice through his consulting area where stone pots and woven baskets filled with dried herbs, tinctures, barks and berries lined the shelves, along with other oddities such as cattle horns, coconut shells, assorted animal skulls and hoofs. At first, this room had spooked Alice but when Disney explained the properties of each and how the medicines, together with his gift for seeing into the future, benefitted the villagers, she accepted that this was just the Malagasy way of life.

At the back of the room, Disney reached into a cupboard. 'Here it is. A kerosene lamp and some fuel to light it. Now you can work past sunset.'

Alice wanted to hug him but knew that he would feel uncomfortable with such a show of emotion. Instead, she put her hands together and gave a small bow. 'Thank you. This will really make a difference. Now, I must go before William wonders where I am.'

. . .

William had lit a fire in the backyard of their cabin. He was crouched next to it, feeding twigs and bracken into the crackling flames. His face glowed and Alice imagined how he must have looked at twelve years old. His open, gentle face, the joy he found in simple pleasures, had been disguised in the man she met on the ship. William didn't do small talk or social artifice – he hid behind his awkwardness. Here, on the island, it was as if his spirit had been set free.

'What a shame we don't have any marshmallows to toast,' Alice said, settling herself on a log close to the fire. 'Look what Disney has loaned us.' She held up the lamp.

William leapt to his feet. 'Fantastic. We can work at least a couple more hours in the evening, although it may strain your eyes.'

'I don't mind. I would work all night if we had enough light. Did you find out about that unusual orchid we spotted?'

'I have a feeling about it, Alice. It could be an unidentified species. You know what that means?'

He had told her several times but Alice loved to watch the animation of his face, it was like watching a child experience Christmas for the first time. 'Tell me.'

'It could be named after us. What would we call it, Fellows and Wagstaff? Alice and William?'

'I would be delighted if it were named Fellows – after you. My children are my legacy.'

'You are the kindest and most generous woman I have ever met.'

Alice was about to make a quip but William removed his glasses and she saw that his eyes had filled with tears. He used a handkerchief to wipe his glasses and surreptitiously dried his eyes.

'Have you any tuna in that basket?' he said.

As the tuna cooked, Alice asked him about his life before joining the cruise. She had heard snippets, that his family were the Fellows who produced throat lozenges, and that he had not joined the family business. The old advert played in her head: *A fellow needs a Fellows when his whistle starts to wheeze.*

'Did you ever consider horticulture as a career?'

'I considered a lot of things but never had the gumption to follow through. If I had to work for a living maybe it would have forced me to take a risk, to put myself out there. But I had a generous allowance and so it was easier not to bother.'

'I can see how it might make a person complacent but surely it was an opportunity to follow your dreams?'

'Yes, you would have thought so. The truth is...' William paused as he turned over the tuna steaks, 'I guess I had my confidence beaten out of me. Not literally, although my father was a bully. When I showed no aptitude or interest in the business, I was considered a failure by my family.'

'That's so unfair. Why do parents do that to their children?'

'I have three siblings who were only too glad to take over the business from my parents. I was given the use of a house in Surrey and an income. In return for that, I kept out of their way. We kind of lost touch until last year when my brother contacted me to say that my house – well the house I had been living in, was being sold and I had to vacate. I'd saved a decent amount of money and so when I saw this cruise it seemed like the solution.'

'I did a similar thing. Saw it as a way out. A way of having my future solved without having to think too much about it.'

'But you are a strong, independent woman. I think you're just being kind.'

Alice laughed and shook her head. 'I kind of lost myself or lost sight of who I was. Thinking back, the real Alice first started to disappear when I had David, and then Rachel. I became a mum and although that was wonderful, it meant losing part of my identity. I loved being a wife and mother but my purpose was focused on those roles. When Tom, my husband, died and the children no longer needed me, I felt as though I had ceased to exist. It was as though I were drifting in a huge ocean without any power – a bit like our ship before we were rescued.'

William served them both tuna steaks on palm leaves. They ate watching the fire each lost in their thoughts.

'Shame Disney didn't give you any weed. It would be good to have some right now.'

Alice grinned. 'I know what you mean. I hadn't smoked cannabis since I was in my early twenties. Disney insists it's for medicinal purposes only. We don't need any substance to make us high, we have this.' Alice threw her arms out wide. 'This amazing place. Our adventure. Everything.'

'It's more than I could have hoped for when I signed up for this cruise.'

'I don't think Captain Moore would agree but being stranded on this island is the best thing that could have happened.'

They abandoned their work that evening to watch the fire and reflect on their lives. Alice felt a closeness to William that she had not experienced since her early years with Tom. She wanted him to discover a new species of orchid so that he was remembered for all that he brought into the world. Damn his family for making him feel inadequate.

35

Marianne felt as though they had been forgotten by HQ. The promised replacement ship had not been identified and Libby was vague about when they could expect to be rescued. In the meantime, Marianne and her second engineer had been working to repair the damage to Halcyon Seas. There was a replacement part needed to strengthen the plates. Marianne had made enquiries and was hopeful that one might be available in Toliara. This was her mission for the day but first, she stopped in the lounge to listen to the choir.

The lounge, once a retreat for guests reading a book or dozing in the reflected warmth from the sun, was now alive with the noisy chatter of children. Marianne tucked herself from view close to the door so that she could observe the happy scene.

'Kanto, you stand here in the front. Now the youngest boys and girls behind.' Gloria waved a hand summoning the children. 'Gracie, Samuel. Over here. That's right. Now, where are our Halcyon Seas singers?' A few of the guests stepped forward and positioned themselves to one side of the Malagasy choir. 'Ready? One, two, three.' Gloria tapped her music stand.

The clear, angelic voice of the youngest girl, Kanto, started softly and then built in volume. Then, the other children joined in creating harmonies. It was a Malagasy song. Soulful and beautiful. The Halcyon Seas singers picked up different backing harmonies. It was incredible. If they were hiring an act for the ship, Marianne wouldn't hesitate in offering them a contract.

'Amazing, eh?' Gideon was filming the choir on his phone.

'It sure is.' Marianne wiped a tear from her eye. 'Incredible.'

He kept his phone poised until the end of the song. 'Day off?'

'When do I ever take a day off? No, I'm just doing my rounds checking all is well. What are you up to?'

'Me? I'm delivering these to the kitchen.' Gideon pointed to a sack at his feet. 'Barracuda and tuna.'

'How is that working? The sharing of fridges and produce.'

'Pretty good. We're all eating a lot less which isn't a bad thing and the Malagasies are eating more. So, I think that's a result. We are sampling the best fish from the catch, as you can see from this offering, in exchange for fresh meat. It's a win-win. I'm not keen on the sorghum flour Frederic is using but it won't hurt me to forgo the cakes. The kids love them.'

'If you're visiting the kitchen, I'll join you.'

The kitchen was always a busy place and today was no exception, although many of the usual staff had been replaced by teenage apprentices. Marianne recognised Olivia's brother Jay Jim. He was filleting a seabass under the watchful eye of head chef.

'I was just checking in before I take leave to sort out a problem.'

The head chef waited until Jay Jim had eased bone from flesh and laid down his knife before giving Marianne his full attention. 'Yes. All is good here. If you gave me a few months more with these kids, I think we would have at least four competent chefs.'

Jay Jim seemed to have understood and looked questioningly at Chef. 'Yes. You will make a fine chef.' He patted the boy's back.

Marianne took Chef to one side. 'Be careful not to raise their expectations. We will be leaving soon and then life will be very different for them.'

He nodded. 'I know Captain. Ah, is that my tuna?'

Gideon swung the sack up onto the counter. 'Yep, and some barracuda today. Have you got the lamb?'

'Where are you taking that?' Marianne followed Gideon out of the kitchen.

'To the shop. It's the only place in this village that has a decent fridge.'

'Of course. Mr Rose's generator. I need to use his computer. May I walk with you?'

The generator that had been loaned to the ship had helped to keep some things going but communication systems were not one of them. She had managed to charge her phone but the signal was poor. The cranky old computer in the back-room of Mr Rose's shop had been their lifeline to the rest of the world. The villagers they passed greeted Gideon but seemed shy of her, the women and girls giggling behind their hands, the men dropping their gaze. She wore her captain's jacket despite the heat but followed Captain Lambert's example and wore flip-flops instead of her usual heels. Maybe she did look a little strange.

Whilst Gideon was filling the freezer with meat, Marianne sent an email to Captain Lambert following up on his helpful suggestion that she might source the parts she needed from the port in Toliara. Hoping to receive an immediate reply, Marianne spent a few minutes surfing the net to check the news. Halcyon Seas was no longer a top story, thank goodness, although the trade magazines still seemed obsessed with the retirement cruise concept. Sadly, there were few favourable stories, as a result of the leaks. Marianne braced herself for the images of elderly cruise passengers toiling under a hot sun but William's photos could not have reached the media. And then Marianne flipped over to see a double-page spread of Mermaid of the Seas, introducing her new captain. A fortyish white man with a square jaw and a Hollywood smile. The last communication from Jonny in HR had indicated that the job was hers. She had naively hoped that this business would be behind her by the new year, maybe even strengthen her profile – how she had shown leadership during this challenging time. Marianne closed the window and tried to wish him well but it hurt. At forty, she had been more than qualified for a similar position and here she was at fifty-five still bottom of the heap. *I'm sorry Dad. I know you said I could be anything I wanted – but not this time.*

'I'm heading back to the shore. Are you coming?' Gideon said.

Marianne sighed and flicked back to her emails. 'I just need a few more minutes.' Gideon stood to one side, respecting her privacy.

'I was hoping for a response from the port in Toliara. Ah, hold on I've got a reply.' Captain Lambert suggested Marianne visit in person to collect the equipment, settle outstanding fees and sign some papers in preparation for the departure of Halcyon Seas. Why couldn't he just send over the equipment? She sent back an email with effusive thanks and asked if he could perhaps send one of his staff over by boat. Captain

Lambert's response came straight back. He wanted Marianne to visit him in person. She sighed. The captain was a lech and she didn't trust him.

'I've got to go into Toliara. Do you think we could hire a motor boat?'

'Let's ask Mr Rose.'

Mr Rose was sitting outside with a couple of other men drinking beer from a bottle. They all wanted to contribute to the discussion about the loan of a boat and how best to travel to Toliara. Mr Rose's English was good but Marianne had trouble understanding his friends. There was much laughter and she tried to be patient as she waited for an answer.

'It will take four or five hours by road,' Mr Rose said.

Gideon frowned. 'It only took a couple by boat.'

Mr Rose shrugged. 'By sea, it is easier.'

'Good. In that case, do you know where we might hire a boat?' Marion said.

Mr Rose rubbed his chin and then threw out a question to his friends in Malagasy. There was more talk. A lot of pointing. Marianne's hopes were raised but then Mr Rose said, 'No. Sorry. I would lend you our boat but it is needed for fishing.'

'Could we borrow your truck?' Gideon said.

'Of course. You are most welcome. Would you like me to drive you? It is difficult terrain.'

Marianne shook her head just enough for Gideon to pick up on her preference. She didn't want to offend anyone and Gideon seemed to have a good rapport with Olivia's father.

'No thank you. It would take you away from your work and you have already been more than generous. If we could borrow your truck for the day, I will drive Captain Moore.'

Marianne hadn't expected Gideon to accompany her. She would have asked one of her officers. She still could but the idea of spending the day with Gideon away from the ship was too inviting to refuse.

A couple of hours later, they were bouncing across country on their way to Toliara. As they were leaving, Pascal had warned them to be on their guard at all times, especially in Toliara, where they would attract thieves. Marianne had changed into a light summer dress. Her uniform and some toiletries were in a bag so that she could change before meeting Lambert. The sun warmed her shoulder. A light breeze ruffled her hair. The red, rust road unfolded before them, an occasional cactus or baobab tree punctuating the sparse landscape. Gradually her troubles fell away and she pretended that she was just a tourist enjoying a day out with… she slid her gaze over to Gideon, aware of his bare arm resting on the window edge… a pretty gorgeous guy. He caught her look and grinned.

'It's kind of wild, huh?'

'This whole adventure has been that. To think I once considered a retirement cruise to be tame.' She shook her head.

'Well, you didn't expect to have a troublemaker confronting pirates and then falling overboard.'

'No. You're more than I bargained for, that's for sure.' She laughed, enjoying the flirtation.

'I have to tell you,' Gideon slowed down, changing gear as a zebu wandered into their path. 'I'll be sorry to leave this island.' A herdsman followed the zebu and chased him off the road. They picked up speed. 'And I'm not the only one. You may not get the jubilation you expect when we set sail.'

'I don't know what to expect. I gave up trying to second guess some time ago. I'm sure everyone will take a while to get back into the cruising life but this stay has shown how adaptable we all are.'

'Maybe. You might have one or two mutineers.'

Marianne frowned. 'Mutineers?'

'Apparently, William Fellows intends to stay here in Madagascar.'

What was Fellows up to now? Trying to demonstrate the consequences of allowing their elders' free will. 'Mr Fellows has the freedom to choose.' She sighed. It would mean more paperwork and bureaucracy to approve his departure from the cruise.

'I didn't mean to wind you up.'

'You didn't. It's just that man – William Fellows. He comes over as an innocent but he has single-handedly destroyed my career and the future of Silver Seas.'

'Whoa. That's some accusation.'

Marianne couldn't keep quiet any longer. She unburdened herself, sharing with Gideon how each of the leaks had impacted her. 'We've had bad publicity from the outset. This voyage was my opportunity to prove myself a competent captain. All I had to do was keep the passengers and crew safe and avoid any negative publicity. And you know how that panned out.'

'But you're a brilliant captain. You've kept a cool head despite everything that's been thrown at you. Nobody else could have adapted to these extreme circumstances. You've shown courage, leadership, and resourcefulness.'

'Maybe you should write a reference for me.' Marianne tried to lighten the mood.

Gideon gave her a look, that had the effect of a warm knife on butter. 'If I could do anything to make your dreams come true I would. I promise.'

She believed him. They rested back into silence and Marianne let herself be soothed by the changing landscape. Tiny villages similar to Olivia's were dotted in the hills. They drove through a valley where eucalyptus hung like a heavy curtain. Then, a village of ochre and thatched houses. A group of men and women squatted outside a building weaving baskets. A skinny man with a toothless grin waved to them and they waved back.

'Do you want to stop or keep driving?' Gideon said.

'Let's stop so that we can stretch our legs. I don't mind driving for a while.'

They sat in the truck drinking from bottles of water and gnawing on roasted birds that Mrs Rose had packed for their journey. Marianne had no idea what the bird was but it was not much bigger than a sparrow.

'Where are we headed after Madagascar?'

'Durban, Port Elizabeth, Cape Town. We'll pick up the cruise where we left off.'

'Really?'

They both knew that the retirement cruise may not have a future. Halcyon Seas, like Marianne, was on her last legs. The delay in sending a replacement ship spoke volumes. Discussions were probably going on as they spoke about the future of Silver Seas.

'Let's see.'

'That wasn't a very long forever. The forever cruise.'

'Nothing is forever,' Marianne sighed.

'Nothing?' Gideon dampened a bandana with water and wiped the grease from her mouth. She had noticed him wearing it earlier and thought he looked like Bruce Springsteen.

He paused; his face close to hers. She could see the flecks of amber in his eyes. Smell the sun on his skin. Then he pulled away, slipping the bandana into his back pocket.

'You played in a band?' Marianne said and was surprised by the hoarseness of her voice. She drank from the bottle. Water spilt trickling down her neck. He watched through half-closed eyes.

'Several. None of them came to much.'

'What did you play?'

'Lead guitar and singer.'

Marianne guessed he was popular with the female fans. 'What will you do if this cruise comes to an end?'

'Go home. I didn't sell up, just let my London place on Airbnb. It was never going to be forever for me. I should have suggested Alice do the same. It didn't occur to me that anyone would invest all of their capital in this cruise.'

'I'm afraid that's what most of the residents have done. If this venture fails, we'd have let them down big time.'

'It's not your fault, Marianne.'

'I'm tired of blaming everyone else.'

He silenced her with a kiss. It was long and tender. His hand rested lightly on her thigh. Marianne kissed him back, losing herself in the moment.

'I'm sorry. I shouldn't have.' The veins in his neck pulsed in time with the rapid beating of her heart. He was flushed and dishevelled, as though they had acted out what was in her head.

'It's okay.' Her body had responded as a woman but until this cruise was over, she was still the captain. 'I mean…' she sighed. 'That was pretty wonderful, but I can't. There are rules.'

Gideon gave a long lazy smile that made her want to kiss him again. 'I get it. Maybe when the cruise is over?'

Marianne nodded, not trusting herself to say anything more. She was one breath away from casting caution to the wind. He was too damn sexy – there should be a health warning.

'So, Toliara?' Gideon said in a voice that could have been suggesting they go to bed, and then, with one last lingering look, he started the engine.

36

Halcyon Seas' horn sounded long and loud. In two hours' time, they would be leaving the island.

'It is time for you to go, mon coeur.' Olivia's mother reached for Hal. He writhed and wriggled in Olivia's arms, as though he knew she was about to abandon him. Olivia wrapped her arms tighter around her precious babe and kissed the curls on his head. She couldn't do it.

'Mammon?' Olivia pleaded with her eyes. They had discussed her options repeatedly, either Olivia took up her employment on the ship and sent money home so that Hal and the rest of her family could survive the drought, or she stay and they all starve. There was no choice, she had to leave her bebe.

'I'm sorry, mon petit. We will take good care of him.' Mammon took Hal from Olivia. He mewed his objection and Olivia's heart constricted as though he had wrapped his fingers around it.

'Have you got everything that you need?'

'No,' Olivia said. She was leaving behind her heart, for the second time that year. First Raf and now Hal. 'But I guess I will survive.'

'Our ancestors are with you. They will give you strength and courage. Soon you will return home to a healthy boy. Go now. You must not keep the captain waiting.'

Olivia had already said goodbye to her pappa, Pasca, and the children. Life was returning to normal on the island: Pascal and Jay Jim had gone out for the early morning fish, Pappa was in the shop, Gracie, Samuel, and Kanto had chores to do, collecting water – the trench would not get finished now, drying the fish, and gathering driftwood, but they hung around the hut with long faces. When Olivia stepped out holding her grand mammon's carpet bag, Kanto clung to her legs.

'Don't go, Livvy. Tell the captain not to sail away.'

Olivia bent down to the same level as Kanto. 'We have already stayed too long. There won't be enough food on the ship if we stay any longer and the staff want to go home to visit their families too. You must keep on singing. Practice the scales Mrs Gloria taught you. Promise?'

Kanto nodded.

'I'm coming with you,' Gracie swung a carrier bag of belongings. 'I will work with Charanya. I can paint nails and braid hair.'

'All of you. Get back to your work and let your sister go to hers. You have had too much freedom. You are forgetting your responsibilities,' Mammon said, her hands on her hips.

Gracie stomped inside with her bag and came back out with a pot for water. Olivia's siblings trailed after her as she followed the path down to the ship. On previous days the children would have run ahead, excited to start the day's lessons; today it felt like a funeral procession. Disney was sitting on the fallen tree trunk.

'Why the hurry?' he said, as they passed.

'The horn was our summons. Captain Moore told us at yesterday's briefing that we all had to be on board at least an hour before setting sail.'

Disney chuckled. 'You have plenty of time. More than plenty.' Olivia wondered if Disney had any idea of the time; he often seemed as though he were in another world.

At the ship, Kanto pulled hard on Olivia's arm, trying to stop her progress.

'Let me come with you,' Gracie said. 'Sneak me on board.'

'I can sing to the passengers like Mrs Gloria,' Kanto's lower lip trembled. 'Please ,Livvy.'

'I need you both to take care of Hal. If I could stay I would. Please promise me that you will love your little nephew?'

Gracie made one final plea. Tears rolled down Kanto's cheeks. Olivia kissed them both and then walked up the gang-plank back to a world she had almost forgotten.

Captain Moore had briefed them all the day before. There was to be more discipline and order on Halcyon Seas. The first stop was Durban, where a new hotel director and doctor would be joining the ship, along with the passengers who had been staying in a hotel. They had been reminded of their code of practice – passengers' cabins were not to be visited unless on official business. Olivia could not imagine ignoring Alice and Patty. They had become family to her.

Once everyone was on board, they had muster practice. Bopha and Olivia were assigned the same station as before and stood chatting as the other staff and guests arrived.

'Charanya told me about Hal's father,' Bopha said, without any preamble.

'I told her in confidence.' Olivia was angry and felt

betrayed. She should not have let her defences down.

'It's okay, I had already guessed. That American guy you were with at the graduation party?'

'He's training for a management job in hospitality. Raf's family would not approve of me. It's okay. Raf gave me Hal and for that I am grateful, but he must never know.'

'Why? Surely, he has a right to know that he is a father and what about Hal? One day he will ask questions. Besides, the father should pay. It's not right that you have to support your son without his help.'

'No.' Olivia's voice was harsher than she intended. Bopha meant well but she could be a bit bossy and opinionated. 'It's okay, Bopha. Raf is an honourable man. Of course, he would support me and Hal if he knew but that's why he must not. I don't want to destroy his future, to have him resent me.' Olivia remembered how Raf had not been at the quayside on Dodge Island when Halcyon Seas set sail. She had told him not to wave her off or say goodbye but part of her had hoped he would ignore her instructions. It proved that she was right. Raf would have forgotten about her by now.

'You are wrong, Olivia. It should be Raf's decision, not yours.'

'And have him throw away all that he has worked for? To feel sorry for me? No, I do not want that, Bopha. You mustn't say a word about this to anyone. Do you hear me?'

Bopha scowled. 'You are a stubborn mule. Okay. Okay.' She pretended to pull a zip across her lips. 'But you are wrong.'

The passengers had all assembled and Frederic was demonstrating how to put on a life jacket. Patty, Alice and William, Barbara and Richard looked as though they had been sentenced to life imprisonment rather than reconvening what should have been the cruise of a lifetime.

. . .

'We only needed a few more weeks; we could have dug that trench by Christmas,' Richard said. 'Fresh running water from a tap in the village. Surely, we could have done that for them before leaving.'

'What about the children? Kanto's only six. She should be playing and singing, learning her lessons, not working. They need me. I'm getting off. I'm not leaving Madagascar.' Patty tried to struggle out of her life jacket.

'Do you need assistance?' Frederic asked.

Alice put an arm around her friend. 'It's okay, I'll help her.' Frederic left them and Alice took Patty's hands in hers. 'William and I feel the same way. I had to force him to leave behind our orchid cuttings. There's an orchid we think might be a new species, can you imagine how hard it was for him to give up that opportunity?'

'So, why didn't he stay?'

Alice glanced over at William, who stood away from the other passengers. As soon as they had set foot on the ship he seemed to shrink in stature, to retreat back into himself. He had tried to persuade Alice to stay on the island, to make the abandoned cabin into a home. She had been tempted but knew that it was unrealistic. If she left the cruise then she wanted to do it properly. 'I don't know.' But Alice did know – deep down. He didn't want to leave her and, in a way, she felt the same. The time that they had spent together discovering, and cataloguing orchids had been the happiest in years.

The ship sounded her horn and tug boats drew near. Had she made a terrible mistake? Thrown away something special because she was too cautious? What if her future was back there on the island with William? Now, she would never know.

. . .

'Captain, a pilot wants to board the ship to guide us out,' Marianne's second officer said. She was relieved to finally be heading back out to sea.

'Good idea. We need to avoid shallow water and reefs.'

They had been on the island for just three weeks but so much had changed. Her reputation for one – although that had been a gradual process, thanks to William Fellows. She noted that he had not opted to stay on the island and, although it was a relief not to oversee the process of his leaving, it meant that she would have to be vigilant to avoid further leaks; although it was hard to imagine how Halcyon Seas could be presented in a more negative light. The retirement cruise concept had taken a nosedive and she suspected that Jamboree was trying to buy off McIntyre – good riddance to Patrick Dunn– but it left a question over her future. Jonny in HR had gone quiet, not even apologising about the Mermaid of the Seas job. She looked out from the bridge as the tugs drew close, and spied Gideon leaning against the ship's rail. It was the place where they had met late at night before everything changed. Even then, he had made her heart skip a beat. Infuriating. Reckless. Brave. Kind. And gorgeous. She wanted him – more than she wanted to be the captain of a cruise ship. This realisation hit her like a physical blow. Marianne wanted to abandon her post, to run to him and tell him how she felt. Life passed by too quickly and she had wasted decades chasing a dream at the expense of everything else. She had handed over the power for her happiness to the cruise industry – the captain posts she had been passed over for, and now the threat of going right back to where she was before becoming captain of Halcyon Seas. At one time this would have slain her but now, she watched Gideon look up at the bridge knowing that he was thinking of her, now, she felt a warm glow within and realised that it didn't matter quite as much.

'It's Captain Lambert.' The second officer interrupted her thoughts. 'He's boarding the ship now.' Marianne smiled to herself. She might have guessed that Captain Lambert would put in an appearance. She had managed to keep him at a distance when they met in Toliara. Having Gideon wait outside may have been a disincentive but the captain's intentions had been clear from his lusting face.

'How gracious of you to personally pilot us out to sea,' Marianne greeted him.

'I'm afraid you are not going anywhere.' Captain Lambert did not sit down. Today he wore leather shoes and an air of authority. 'To leave Madagascar you need permission and the local politicians have refused to grant this.'

'Why? I travelled miles to sign your papers and have paid the outstanding fee. On what grounds has permission been denied?'

'It is not in the interests of our people. Do not complain to me, it is the government of Malatanga.' He handed her a sheaf of papers. 'It's all in here.'

'You can't. They can't. It's not possible.'

'I'm sorry but it is. Hopefully, you will be able to leave in a few weeks' time.'

Marianne was furious and made her feelings known, shouting at the captain. It was outrageous. Corrupt. They couldn't do this to her. The American government would have something to say about this. It was then Marianne realised that if the American government had not gotten involved in the first place, then this might never have happened. The nonsense about being detained when they first arrived – the huge overreaction, had raised their profile and given the local politicians ideas.

37

'When will Pappa be back from Malatanga?' Olivia's arms were folded as she glowered at her mother, who was wiping the table outside their shop.

It had taken Olivia a few days to guess why Halcyon Seas had been detained. Disney's comment that she had plenty of time before the ship left Madagascar should have given her a clue but it wasn't until she heard of Pappa's trip into Malatanga to meet the councillor who had sourced the generator that Olivia strung all of the beads together.

Her mother put down the cloth and wiped her brow. 'He left early, but you know what Pappa is like when he meets with his associates.'

Associates? Drinking buddies, more like. They would be celebrating how they had tricked Captain Moore into staying longer on the island. Long enough to finish digging the trench. 'Did you know about this?'

'About what?' Her mother's face gave nothing away.

'If you knew that we weren't going to leave immediately,

why did you let me go through all of that heartache saying goodbye to my baby boy?'

'Sit down. Have a Fanta.'

Olivia's face did not change. She waited for a response to her question.

'I do not know your pappa's business. It is not for me to know. How could he stop your ship from sailing? It is not possible.'

'Mammon, it isn't fair. There aren't enough food supplies. The staff probably won't get paid and these are old people. They're not used to hard manual work in a hot climate. Have Pappa and his associates even thought this through? The USA will be up in arms. This could start a war!'

This thought had only just occurred to Olivia. It seemed that events had a way of escalating out of control. To think that she had started the whole thing by trying to smuggle Hal back home. It had begun before that. It had started that last evening she spent with Raf. Olivia regretted telling Charanya; she and Bopha meant well but they didn't understand. Raf had a glittering future ahead of him. In a few years' time, he would marry an American girl from a similar background to his. If he wasn't a cruise director, then he would be managing a fancy hotel in LA or New York. They would have beautiful children and a full-time nanny.

Her mother had gone into the shop and now returned with a glass of Fanta, which she set down in front of Olivia. 'I do not know if your pappa is involved in any way, or the reason why your ship is being held. But I do know that it is a blessing. Our ancestors have led your ship to our village. We will carry on as we did before. Kanto will go to singing classes; Gracie will train to be a beautician, and Jay Jim a chef. It is a miracle! You get to stay here with Hal. Everybody is happy.'

Olivia put her head in her hands. No good could come of

this. If Captain Moore found out that her father and the village elders had played a part in blocking Halcyon Seas' departure then she could forget her job. There would be more serious consequences, too. It was all her fault. She had guessed there would be trouble when her two worlds collided.

Alice was as relieved as the rest of the passengers when they heard that they would be staying a while longer. Richard called a meeting to organise their efforts on the freshwater project.

'We nearly lost our opportunity to change these people's lives. If we work smarter --short sharp bursts with relay teams, we might finish this job before the US navy come to our rescue.'

'We'll need pipes, cement, and a water storage unit,' Gideon said.

'We can buy those things. Maybe Mr Rose could pull a few strings, he seems to be well connected with officials in Malatanga.'

'Do you really think we could get running water into the village?' Patty clasped her hands together.

'I don't see why not – if we get another four to six weeks.'

'That would take us into the new year. I can't see Britain or the States accepting the detainment of Halcyon Seas,' Alice said.

'Then let's not waste any time. I've prepared some rotas. Take a look. If anyone thinks it's too much for them, say so. There's no shame in admitting our limitations.'

There was a buzz of excited chatter as the cruisers rose to the challenge. This, Alice thought, is more regenerating than living a life of luxury. Having purpose. Making a difference. Richard looked years younger, fired up with determination and vigour. He was a leader and a project manager, without anything to manage he had been as restless as a racehorse confined to the paddock.

They all agreed to take a shift each day digging the trench. Patty would fit it around her work with the creche and Alice would find time for work in the fields as well as the orchid project. Life was full on. They all had more to do than they could fit into one day but nobody complained.

Marianne found them all in the lounge making plans. It had been her intention to apologise for the delay in leaving and to explain that Jamboree had been informed and was taking immediate action but when she overheard Gideon and Richard making an inventory of the equipment that they needed to bring water into the village she pressed her lips together and remained silent.

Gideon saw her and smiled. She felt like a besotted teenager. It was going to be hard resisting him. How could she distance herself and maintain a professional role when her duties as captain were almost non-existent? Instructions from Jamboree's CEO were to keep a low profile and leave all negotiations and media management to them. Marianne had no idea whether they were going to be detained for a few days or weeks. Arrangements had at least been made for food supplies to be delivered.

She slipped out of the lounge, unnoticed by anyone other than Gideon, and made her way to the kitchen to check on supplies. The boy, Jay Jim, had already resumed his place in the kitchen alongside the head chef and was listening intently as Chef instructed him on the perfect seasoning of a stew. They both beamed at Marianne when she interrupted them.

'Captain. We have a proposition for you.' Head chef

winked at Jay Jim and, taking the hint, he removed himself to the far end of the kitchen, where he kept busy cleaning work surfaces. 'It's Thanksgiving this week. We thought it would be a nice gesture to host a Thanksgiving party for the cruisers and villagers – to give thanks for all that we have and to share the produce which needs to be eaten. The temporary refrigeration arrangement served a purpose but some meats and vegetables are coming to the end of their sell-by date. We are expecting new supplies tomorrow, something else to be thankful for.'

Marianne could sense Jay Jim following their tone of voice, waiting to hear if she approved. 'It would be a good distraction for our guests. Okay, why not? Have you spoken to Gloria?'

'It was Gloria's idea,' Chef said. 'She's already planning a concert.'

Gloria appeared in the doorway, she looked questioningly at Chef. When he gave the thumbs up, she whooped. 'Way to go, Captain. This is going to be some party!'

'Steady,' Marianne said. 'I don't want this to get out of control. I suspect that Halcyon Seas is now major news. The whole world will be watching us. Let's make sure that any publicity is positive.'

38

'Would you have stayed on the island, if not for me?' Alice asked William, as they packed moss around the roots of a keikis, a baby orchid they had cut from the stem of a mother plant.

William did not reply at first. He concentrated on the task, with the care of a father tucking up his newborn. 'We found these orchids together. It would be unfair of me to claim ownership of our collection.'

Alice smiled. She knew that his decision to board had little to do with the orchid collection. 'I'm glad that we didn't leave as planned. I'm not ready, and I would hate to be responsible for holding you back. You've said all along that you would stay on this island. I can see why. You are like a different person here – as if this is your natural habitat.'

William took off his glasses to wipe away the condensation. Alice was struck, not for the first time, by his eyes. She had assumed it was his lens magnifying them but they really were that big – his irises a clear hazel that reminded Alice of the marbles her son David would hold to the light to marvel at their colour.

'To be honest Alice, I have never felt at home anywhere. Not in my family home, nor boarding school.'

'What about the home you left to come on this cruise?'

William settled the potted keikis on a shelf alongside the other specimens. 'The cottage in Surrey? It was comfortable enough; within its walls and those of my garden, I lived a reasonable life.'

Alice thought back to her bungalow in Norfolk. She existed – neither happy nor unhappy but it was as though she had been resting in the sidings, whilst life passed her by. 'Was it in a town or village?'

'A small parochial village. Everyone knew each other but I didn't fit in there any more than I did at boarding school. It's not that I don't like people, I just don't know how to make conversation. It's easy with you. Being here, on this island, I feel as though I don't have to try. I can just be myself.'

A chameleon strutted in from the backyard. They both watched in awe as this vibrant, majestic creature made himself at home. He came close to the potting table before stopping. Alice held her breath. The colours close up were unbelievable: emerald, lime green, turquoise, and lemon. His bulbous eyes were surrounded by swirls of colour, like a beaded mat. He stood very still. Then, his tongue whipped out and snared a cockroach. He munched away, his eyes rotating, seeking the next morsel.

'He's beautiful,' Alice whispered.

William used a cupped hand to stop another cockroach in its tracks. He scooped it off the table and then offered it to the chameleon. The swirly eyes rotated and then swoosh the cockroach was gone. A squashed body just visible between the chameleon's jaws.

They returned to work, potting the next keiki and the chameleon basked in a rectangle of sunlight on the wooden floor.

'We had a tabby cat, Iva,' Alice said. 'She was bought for the children but it was me who fed her and she knew it. When Tom was at work and the children at school, I would talk to her. It's comforting to have a pet. Someone to come home to. Not that I left my bungalow very much in the past five years.'

'I've always lived alone. Well, since leaving the family home.'

'Did you ever consider marrying?'

'I don't think anyone would have had me.'

Alice was dismayed that he could not see himself the way that she did, a kind, sensitive man – intelligent, knowledgeable and fun. 'You do yourself an injustice. Any woman would have been lucky to.'

'I fell in love twice. Once when I was eighteen, and again when I was twenty-three. It hurt so much, breaking up. It wasn't worth putting myself out there again. I didn't mind. It's easier to live alone. You only have yourself to please.'

Alice felt great compassion for this man. She loved being with him but was wary. Maybe she was reading too much into his kindness but it was possible that William was letting down his defences. What if he fell in love with her and then she broke his heart? She needed some space to think things through.

'If you are happy to finish up here, I'll pop back down to the village to find something we can barbeque for supper.'

'Good idea. I'll get a fire going.'

Disney was sitting outside his cabin when Alice strolled by. 'Have you figured it out yet?' he said.

Alice had no idea what he was talking about. He was either stoned and talking nonsense or picking up on something she had said the last time they met but Alice had no recollection. She thought it best to humour him. 'No, but I'm working on it.'

Disney chuckled. 'You will, Alice in Wonderland.'

Alice followed the path back down to the village, enjoying the dappled sunlight and the sound of birds calling to one another. Sometimes she didn't even hear the katydids, the constant clicking of their legs had become her silence. Tonight, she took in everything – the scent of woodsmoke, and vanilla, the cry of a lemur, children laughing and shouting. The red earth, and bronze bracken. To think that she might have left all of this behind to live on a cruise ship. William was right. They should stay here, where he … they belonged. Alice pondered the *they.* It did feel as though she belonged here– on this island, in this particular place. But how could she live here alone? It wasn't fair to William to imagine a future with him. And yet, the simplicity of their life – the honesty between them– it felt natural. Right. No, she thought, I have not figured it out. At least the ship's detainment gave her a bit longer to make a decision.

Alice stopped by the shop to buy some fish. Gracie was sitting outside at a table listening to a transistor radio. She jumped up when Alice approached.

'Hello, Mrs Alice. Are you coming to the party?' The thanksgiving celebration was in two days' time. *Everyone* was going to the party. It had caused great excitement amongst the villagers and cruise passengers.

'I am, Gracie. Will you be singing?'

Gracie beamed. 'Yes. And I will dance too. Would you like me to paint your nails, Mrs Alice?'

'That's very kind of you but I don't think so. I do a lot of digging,' Alice mimed this and Gracie laughed. 'Is your papa in the shop?'

'Yes. Did you want to send an email?'

Alice was not planning to but now that Gracie mentioned it, she thought that maybe she had better check to see if there was a message from Rachel. There was a poor signal in the village and so she had not bothered to keep her phone charged. William was waiting to see if the photographs he had sent to an orchid expert had resulted in the identification of their mystery orchid and that was when Alice had intended to check her mail – but now that she was there.

'Go on through,' Mr Rose said. 'I'll make you a nice parcel of fish. Fresh caught today.'

Before reading her emails, Alice googled Halcyon Seas, to find out what was being reported. She wasn't surprised to see that they had made the headlines in most of the tabloids. There was outrage that Madagascar could prevent a USA-owned ship from leaving the island. The headline of one newspaper read *Elderly cruisers held hostage by pirates following hijack in Mozambique Channel.* Captain Moore thought that rumour had been quashed but evidently not, and Alice suspected, it would continue so long as it sold news stories. There was a photograph of Olivia in her work uniform, a head and shoulder shot that must have been supplied by Silver Seas. Her attempts to hide her pregnancy and then arrange for pirates to board the ship, in exchange for taking her baby, made a sensational story. All of it untrue, or at least, spun into something far from the truth. If Olivia saw this story, she would be mortified, so Alice resolved not to tell her. One thing was certain, with headlines like these, the US and British navy would not waste any time coming to their rescue.

Rachel had sent an email – just one, the same day that news had hit the UK of the ship's detainment. Alice could guess Rachel's response. She would, no doubt, be the voice of angry relatives demanding immediate action and reimbursement of fees. With a sinking feeling, Alice opened her email and read…

Dear Mummy,

I was horrified to learn that your ship has been prevented from leaving Madagascar. I knew that this was going to happen, despite your reassurances that all was well. Now, it seems, things have got completely out of control. We can't trust Silver Seas or the captain of your ship to make decisions that are in your best interests. I have taken legal advice and will be taking action to free you from your contract and have you return to England asap. Hang on in there. You can depend on me.

With love from Rachel.

Alice knew one hundred per cent that she could rely on Rachel. She would have her off the island faster than the navy. But Alice didn't want to leave. She couldn't, but neither could she stay.

39

Everyone seemed to be in a holiday mood except for Olivia. Mammon sat outside their hut plucking birds to roast on the barbeque. Becca, in her pink straw hat, did a little mamba and then, laughing, shouted something about seeing them later and sashayed off.

'Why do you look so glum?' her mother said.

'Because all hell is going to break loose. Do you realise that the US army is probably on their way here now?'

'You speak like an American. Live for the day. Have I taught you nothing?'

Olivia sighed. It seemed that the whole village was oblivious to the disaster they had brought upon themselves. 'Papa has to put a stop to this before it's too late.'

'I do not know what you mean. Everything is good. Your sisters are going to sing in a choir. Why can't you be happy?'

It was pointless trying to reason with Mammon, and Pappa would not discuss business with her. Maybe she should talk to Captain Moore. There was no evidence that the village elders were working with politicians to stop Halcyon Seas from leaving before the trench was finished, but Olivia knew how things worked. The captain would be furious and Olivia would risk losing her job. She didn't want to leave Hal but working on the ship was the only way she could keep her family from starvation. There was another way. Raf. Maybe Bopha was right, that Hal should not grow up without a father. With these thoughts battling in her head, Olivia made her way to the ship, to assist with preparations for the party that evening.

In the creche, some of the mothers were cutting bunting from sheets of coloured paper, and the children were splattering paint with chubby hands, supervised by Patty. Hal was asleep in a basket at her feet. It was a scene of peaceful contentment. These same mothers would have been working in the fields with babies strapped to their backs, if not for Halcyon Seas. The babies hungry. Olivia understood why her mammon and the other villagers preferred to ignore the reality but it wasn't right. They couldn't hold the ship hostage. She had to speak to the captain.

'Will this be your first Thanksgiving?' Patty asked Olivia.

'It will. We celebrate our Independence Day with a party like this. This year we have a lot to be thankful for.'

'Isn't that the truth?' Patty said. 'I feel so blessed. All of these little ones to care for. My cup runneth over. I thank the Lord that we did not leave. I think I might have jumped overboard and swum right back. I believe we have your ancestors to thank for this miracle.'

Patty was beginning to sound Malagasy. But maybe she was right. If her ancestors had intervened to keep them on the island together, who was she to interfere? Hal opened his eyes and gazed up at Olivia. Her own little cherub with his soft round face and black curls, a perfect angel. She scooped him up and sat him on her knee. He gurgled and seemed to smile.

Although the other mothers said it was too early for a real smile, Olivia could feel his joy.

'I'm going to change Hal and feed him,' Olivia said. She loved the quiet moments that she spent with her baby.

In a corner of the lounge, Olivia fastened Hal's nappy. She could not have imagined being so open in the care of her baby, a few weeks ago, when his existence was a secret.

'Ah, there you are,' Bopha said, sitting down next to her.

Olivia didn't want company. She was about to feed Hal and wanted to enjoy every moment that she had with him.

'I know that you said not to say anything,' Bopha said and Olivia's heart stumbled. 'But it kind of came up.'

Olivia knew that this was about Raf. In a way, it was a relief. If Bopha had got a message to him about Hal then maybe he would find them. She imagined him as he was when they said goodbye. Raf had said that he loved her. Maybe she hadn't been fair to him. To be together, the three of them. It would make her the happiest girl on the island. She waited for Bopha to continue, trying hard not to let her imagination run away with her.

'Have you seen the copy of Jamboree News in the beauty salon?'

Olivia shook her head, afraid now of what was to follow.

'Your American boy, Raf, is bar manager on the New World.'

'I told you that he was destined for great things. Raf is a clever man.' She clasped Hal around his middle, dangling his feet so that they brushed her lap. 'Hal is like his pappa. You are both very handsome,' she cooed.

Bopha wasn't smiling. 'Charanya knows a couple of the beauty therapists on his ship. She kind of contacted her friend to ask about him.'

Olivia didn't want to hear anymore. 'I asked you both not to interfere.'

'I know. We are sorry. But we thought you ought to know. Raf is involved with someone on New World and it's serious.'

'Did you say anything about me or Hal?'

'No. Of course not. I'm sorry Olivia. I guess you were right. Raf has moved on.'

She could feel the tears building behind her eyes and buried her face in the fold of Hal's neck, taking comfort in his scent. Although she had reasoned that Raf would forget her she had hoped that she was wrong. It wasn't until her dreams were completely crushed that she realised how much she had been hanging on to that dream.

'Told you.' It was all that she could say without giving away her utter misery.

'There's no reason he shouldn't pay you an allowance.'

'Absolutely not! Raf must not know about Hal. Please, please Bopha.'

Bopha put an arm around Olivia. 'I promise. If that's what you really want but with a management job he can afford to pay.'

'I don't want his money. We can manage without him.'

Why couldn't Bopha and Charanya have minded their own business? Now, they had taken away her dream. She knew it could never happen, that Raf would find a rich American girl, but when she looked up at the North star each night, she could have pretended things might be different. Now she knew without a doubt that they would not. She had more than most Malagasy girls, a job – if her pappa and his associates did not mess things up – and her beautiful boy. It was enough. She should be thankful, like Patty. This American Thanksgiving, Olivia would show her gratitude to their ancestors. If she did not, then maybe her son would be taken away from her. A thought occurred to Olivia as if it were a message whispered in her ear. A warning.

'If Raf finds out he has a son he might take him away from me. He could give Hal a better life in America. You must make sure he doesn't find out, Bopha.'

40

It would be a Thanksgiving party unlike any Marianne had experienced on previous cruises. It was taking place on the shore close to the ship. The villagers had built a fire earlier in the day and a barbeque had been set up by the kitchen team

'Are you coming, Captain?' Gloria found Marianne on the bridge. 'You don't want to miss the choir.'

'You don't need me. I think I intimidate the villagers. I don't want to spoil your party.'

'Don't come as the captain. Wear your civvies. There are so many people they may not even notice you if you want to stay hidden.'

'Maybe.' When Gloria waited, obviously reluctant to leave her, Marianne added, 'I'll change and then come out to listen to the choir.'

Sparks of light from the bonfire lit the sky. A crackle of flames and the smell of roasted meat greeted Marianne when she joined the party, wearing a summer dress. In the dark, it was hard to tell the cruise guests and villagers apart. The ship's passengers had taken to wearing lambas, and some of the villagers were dressed in the finery donated by her guests. They were all rocking their hips, dancing and laughing. A trumpet strained into the night, accompanied by a steady beat of drums. Gideon was standing by the bonfire, half of his face illuminated. He seemed to sense her presence and turned to look her way. It was as though there were a magnet, its pull activated as soon as they were within the same space. She walked around the periphery of the gathering avoiding him. Nobody else seemed to notice her. Disney, the witch doctor, sat alongside William, puffing on a pipe. A pungent scent of herbs– it reminded her of Patchouli oil and listening to A Stairway to Heaven. Of course, cannabis. William would be taking photos. She could imagine his next missive – Pot Party hosted by Halcyon Seas. What did she care? He couldn't do any more damage than he already had.

'Ladies, gentlemen, and children. I have great pleasure in introducing our Choir of Angels.'

Marianne edged into the crowd to get a better view. The children were centre stage, the youngest in the front and the older ones behind. A few adults from the ship stood on either side, a little back from the children. There was complete silence. Then one lone voice. The little girl, Kanto. Her voice broke into the night. Pure. Simple. Its beauty reached in and touched Marianne's heart. Then some other voices joined her, a cappella with harmonies. They sang in Malagasy. The adults formed a backing choir. When they finished their first song Marianne wiped tears from her eyes.

'Do you know what they were singing about?'

Marianne turned to see Gideon. He was holding his phone up to record the concert.

'No.'

'They were giving thanks for their lives. Can you believe

it? This is one of the poorest countries on earth, those children have nothing, and yet they are giving thanks.'

It made their song even more poignant. Marianne couldn't speak, she was so moved. They stopped talking as the choir began their next song. All the time, Gideon stood behind her capturing it on his phone. When the adults took centre stage to sing some songs from the musicals, the concert that they had performed at sea, Gideon stopped recording and came to stand alongside Marianne. When it had finished, she turned to go but Gideon caught her hand. The magnetic field was stronger now, shooting up her arm, and tingling her fingers.

'Fancy some mulled wine?'

Marianne nodded, incapable of coherent speech.

'Wait for me, over there.' Gideon indicated a sandy bank flanked by trees.

She could have come over haughty and reminded him that she was the captain but Marianne no longer had the energy or inclination to preserve her position.

Gideon returned with the mulled wine. 'I figured you wanted to keep a low profile.' He handed her a steaming cup. The scent of cinnamon and nutmeg reminded her of Christmases and Thanksgivings from her childhood.

'I wasn't going to come.'

'I'm glad you did. Here, sit on this.' Gideon untied the cloth from around his waist and spread it across the dry, flattened, grass. 'I wear one over my shorts to protect me from mozzies, but for you...'

'I'm honoured.' Marianne sank onto the cushioning of bracken her back supported by the bank. 'It's pretty comfortable.'

'And, I have additional supplies if needed,' Gideon pulled out a hip flask. 'Best malt whiskey from the ship's bar.'

Marianne laughed. 'I'm sorry this isn't the cruise experience that you signed up for.'

'Are you kidding? This is the best thing that has happened to me– ever.'

Marianne turned, her face close to his. She had a lump in her throat. Bittersweet.

'You are the best thing that has happened to me,' he said.

Marianne was afraid to speak, in case she cried. He kissed her. She slid a hand under his shirt and traced it over his pecs, his clavicle, the triangle of sunburn she had spied that day in her office. Gideon rolled over and gazed down at her. 'It's been torture seeing you every day and not being able to touch you.'

Marianne didn't want to talk. She pulled him to her, kissing him with passion. Gideon caressed her throat with butterfly kisses. His hands clasped her thighs beneath the flimsy dress. She arched her back and groaned. Hungry for all that she had been denied, Marianne would have made love there and then on that scorched island beneath the moon. But Gideon was sensible for both of them. He straightened her dress and took a moment to calm himself, taking short breaths.

'I'm sorry. I shouldn't have. If you need more time?'

Marianne had already wasted too much time, but he was right – not here like kids at a high school beach party. 'Let's go back to my cabin.'

They made love slowly, with the finesse of fine diners – taking time to delight one another. Then, they lay in each other's arms. The balcony door was open and a light breeze carried in sounds of music and laughter. For the first time, in as long as she could remember, Marianne felt completely at peace. She was happy. Not because of work but something deeper, more solid.

'You're the most amazing woman I've ever met.'

'I get the impression you've "met" a few.'

'It is all untrue. Whatever you've heard,' he laughed. 'Seriously, you take my breath away. I didn't think I would ever feel like this again.'

It felt right, lying there in his arms, as though it was where she belonged. 'This is new to me,' she whispered.

'Sleeping with one of the guests?'

'No. Although, yes. I've broken a big rule there. All of this. I'm not a nun. I enjoy sex but I've always put my career first. It seemed a no-brainer. I wanted to captain a cruise ship so much that I didn't want any distraction. It was best to stay single, avoid any emotional involvement.'

'And now?'

Marianne stretched, luxuriating in the warmth of his love. 'Now? Are you fishing for compliments, Gideon Flynn?' She kissed him, and in that kiss said it all. She didn't want to be apart from him. This was better than getting a promotion.

Gideon gave a dreamy smile. He stroked the outline of her body from her neck to the curve of her hip as though imprinting her shape in his mind. 'I don't want to get you into trouble. I know how important your career is to you – you don't have to choose, Marianne.'

'I think that ship has sailed – excuse the pun.' She tried to laugh but it wasn't funny and despite feeling absolute contentment in that moment the memory of how she had been wronged still hurt.

Gideon looked confused.

'It doesn't matter anymore. I failed. I had this one chance to prove myself as a captain. I told you about the leaks to the press? I'm pretty sure it was William Fellows; he has a background in journalism. That notebook he carries around – all of those photos that he takes. Anyway, if it wasn't for him, I might have stood a chance. Like I said, the one thing I had to do was avoid any bad publicity. We are now the hottest news in the USA, UK, the world! I can say goodbye to ever becoming a captain.'

'I'm really sorry.'

'Hey, don't look so sad. It's not your fault. Anyway, this – you, it's better than getting my dream job.'

'You deserve to be the captain of any cruise ship you choose and I believe you will one day but not if I'm discovered in your cabin. It pains me to say it but I'd better go before we're found out. We'll find a way to make this work.'

She didn't want Gideon to leave but knew he was right. There would be plenty of time for them to be together. For the first time in her life, Marianne could imagine sharing it with another. He had opened her heart and shown her another world. One that Marianne never wanted to leave.

1st December

Hi,

I promised more film. This was taken at a Thanksgiving Party hosted by Captain Moore, for passengers of the ship and villagers. You have to get this out there so that the world can see what is going on in this village. There's a big story here. Make as much noise as you can.

More photos will follow. Will be in touch again soon.

41

William was late joining Alice in their cabin that morning as he wanted to use the shop's computer. The party had gone on until the early hours and Alice knew that some of the villagers had started their day's work without going to bed. The chameleon, which William had named Sid, was basking in the rectangle of sunlight that started in one corner and slowly made its way across the room, marking time. They had been on the island for almost a month, but it felt like home. Alice had not mustered the courage to tell William about Rachel's email. Rachel meant business and would have Alice off the island within a few days – safely locked away in North London where she could come to no harm. She meant well but Alice couldn't go back. What was there to go back to? William had to stay in this village. She had seen him blossom like their precious orchids. If she said that she was leaving, Alice was afraid William would follow her as he had last time. Had Halcyon Seas picked up the cruise again they would now be sailing towards Oman, or Sri Lanka – countries that they had already visited, drinking cocktails at sundown, eating lavish meals, being waited on by Olivia and the other staff. It was wonderful as a holiday but not as a lifestyle, at least not for Alice. When Tom died, she had lost her sense of purpose. The cruise had helped her to view her life from a different perspective – renewed her spirit. But being here, in Madagascar, she had found that purpose. What they did mattered. She was learning new things. When she left Norfolk, Alice had been searching for the girl she once was; here, she had discovered the woman that she had become – was becoming. She didn't know her final shape – just that she was being moulded by the landscape, by experience and by love – a love for the Malagasies and maybe someone else. William would never declare his love for her; she knew that he was afraid of rejection but he didn't have to – she could feel it in the way he looked at her, and his gentle care. Alice couldn't bear to hurt him. She cared deeply but could she love another man after Tom? If they had time, things would resolve naturally, unfold as nature intended but Rachel's email was forcing her to make a decision and she didn't know what to do.

'Oh, you're here already.' William puffed, catching his breath after the climb.

'Did you get any news?' Alice asked, proffering a bottle of water.

William wiped his brow and took the open bottle. 'Thank you. News?'

'About the orchid. I thought that's what you were checking.'

'Oh. No. It's probably just a lesser-known variety. If it was something special then we would have heard by return. Would you mind if I leave you to it this morning?'

Alice was perplexed. They always met first thing to go hunting for orchids; it was her favourite time of the day. 'No, of course not. But if you're not going to join me, I might make myself useful back down in the village.'

'Good idea.' William seemed to be waiting for her to leave.

'What did you say you were planning to do this morning?'

'A bit of work I need to catch up on.'

'Work?' It was news to her that William had any work apart from what he chose to do on the island.

'You know, my editorial role.'

'I thought you gave that up.'

'Yes, but there are still some ongoing responsibilities. The occasional editorial. I'm planning to send an article on our orchid project. So, if you really don't mind.'

'No, of course not.' She was disappointed and felt excluded. Maybe William was preparing himself for the day that Halcyon Seas left the island. It would not be long now. If he was going to stay on alone then he would need to distance himself from her. It was self-preservation. 'Will I see you back here later this afternoon?'

'Yes, please. But if we could make it an hour later than usual?'

With her daily routine disrupted, Alice wasn't sure what to do with her time. She could start work in the fields early, or help out in any number of places, there was plenty to do. A longing to talk with a female friend led her back to the ship. There, she found Patty and Olivia enjoying a coffee before the mothers and babies arrived. Despite the scarce rations they had managed to preserve the luxury of good coffee as well as a reasonable bar supply – that's if the Thanksgiving party had not depleted their stock.

'May I join you?' Alice said, sitting at a table where they had once met regularly for mid-morning coffee and pastries. It seemed so long ago now.

Olivia jumped to her feet.

'Olivia, please sit down. I just wanted to chat with two of my favourite people.'

'I must not. Captain Moore said that when we return to work, we must abide by the rules and that means not socialising with guests.'

Alice laughed and then seeing the concerned look on Olivia's face, gently touched her arm. 'Sweetheart, I don't care what the rules are, you are like a daughter to me. Besides, I may not be a guest much longer.' They looked at her as though she had said she was going to turn into a unicorn.

'I do not understand,' Olivia said, sitting back down.

'My daughter wants me to leave the cruise and return to London. When Rachel gets the bit between her teeth...' Olivia's brow furrowed, and so Alice explained, 'When Rachel wants to make something happen then nothing can stop her. She's a force to be reckoned with.'

'But if you don't want to leave then she can't make you,' Patty said.

'I know, but this time I think Rachel is right. To be honest, I don't want to pick up the cruise where we left off as though nothing has happened. Olivia just said it – how can we treat her differently? We've been through so much together.'

'Yes, but what's the alternative? Please don't tell me you're going to move into a care home.' Patty looked horrified.

'No. I don't know. I'll have to see how much money I can get back. Maybe rent somewhere. Maybe stay with Rachel and her partner for a while.'

'Is that what you want?' Patty looked into Alice's eyes as if trying to read her.

'Not really, but I don't have much choice.'

Patty did not suggest staying on the island. Maybe, like Alice, she had considered this option and discounted it. The weeks that they had spent here had been amazing, an experience Alice never expected to have. It had transformed her – but not enough to do something as radical as retire to Madagascar and live in an impoverished village experiencing drought. She was seventy years old. Her birthday in July celebrated on the ship. Seventy-year-old women did not drop out to live in the jungle in a cabin made from oil drums with a pet chameleon. Rachel would have a fit. It was a wonderful dream but that's all it was – fantasy. William was different. He would be more at home here than anywhere else.

'How about you?' Alice asked Patty.

'I don't want to leave my babies and I don't want to leave you sugar. Either of you.'

'You won't be leaving me. I am going to stay on the ship. It means leaving Hal but as Alice said, sometimes we do not have a choice.'

Alice was surprised to find William waiting in their cabin that evening. He sat cross legged, whilst Sid crawled up his arm. 'This chameleon seems to have forgotten he's a thing of the wild.'

'With you feeding him live weevils, and cicadas he knows he's onto a good thing. Look what I found!' She held aloft a plastic bag filled with pink and white marshmallows. 'Frederic said we could have them.'

'Good, because I don't fancy roasting the cicadas.'

'That's what some Malagasies have to live on in the drought.'

With this sobering thought they prepared their supper of fish and rice. Working in harmony as though they had lived together for years. Alice couldn't bring herself to say that she was going to miss this – their life on the island. It was an unexpected piece of heaven – an experience that she would treasure. They were like children playing house. Soon she would be leaving. Knowing this unavoidable truth, Alice lived in the moment – making memories. She didn't tell William about Rachel's email or that she had been Googling places to rent in the East End of London.

William didn't say anything about his activity that morning, the work that he excused himself to do. Alice asked but his response was vague. She decided that she had made too much of his wanting to be alone and accepted it was work but then as they packed up to walk back to the ship he said, 'I won't be able to go hunting with you tomorrow morning, sorry. Things I've got to do.'

42

Halcyon Seas wasn't going anywhere and Marianne had been told firmly not to interfere in discussions. The story of the ship's detainment had captured global interest in the lead up to Christmas, although the plight of pensioners being held against their will in an inhospitable country could not be further from the truth. Marianne knew that she was going to have trouble corralling them back on board when the time came for Halcyon Seas to finally leave the island. William Fellows had made himself comfortable in a cabin that just happened to be available for his use. She suspected that he had people on the ground helping him, reporters working from Madagascar. Before the night of the party, this would have infuriated her – the way he acted all innocent, conning the lovely Alice Wagstaff, but today, nothing could mar her mood. The day after the party, she and Gideon had snatched moments to be together: standing on the shore, the deck below the bridge, and by Frederic's coffee bar, but they could not touch one another or speak freely. To be so close, to breathe in the scent of him, remembering his kisses on her throat and breasts, his lips, the feel of his beard brushing her thigh and not pull him to her, was agony.

His eyes said it all, a sleepy, sexy longing. 'Tomorrow,' he whispered, when they lingered together in the lounge pretending to be passing the time of day. 'I've persuaded Luc to let me borrow his motorboat. We can find a secluded beach.'

'I didn't know you were a sailor. There are some tricky reefs along this coastline."

Gideon grinned. 'I'm not but I know a woman who is. Oh, that's if you want to spend the day with me. I mean if you can.'

It took every bit of willpower not to reassure him with a kiss. 'I'll ask Frederic to pack a hamper. But don't tell anyone about our excursion or we'll have a boatful of tourists wanting to join us.'

'Won't he be suspicious?'

'No. I'll tell him I'm going out alone. It's fine. I've done it before. Captains are allowed free time. It's not as if the ship is going anywhere. Jump on board before I arrive and keep out of sight until we've left the shore.'

It was good to be at sea again, in control. Marianne steered the boat enjoying the cool wind on her face, the buffeting of the waves. It was exhilarating.

Gideon shouted over the roar of the engine, 'I think you'd prefer to spend the day in this boat.'

Marianne grinned. 'It's fun. Want to steer for a while?'

Gideon took over. The boat veered left and was then rocked hard by a wave. Marianne steadied the wheel and kept her hands lightly over his as he regained control. 'That's it. Just hold her there. A bit more power.'

'Do you know where we're headed?' Gideon kept his eyes fixed ahead as if afraid to relax or lose focus.

'Is that any question to ask a captain. Of course, I know where we are headed.' She knew where she planned to moor the boat, the rest – where their relationship was headed, she didn't want to dwell on. All she knew was this – she was happier than any other time she could remember. Marianne opened her arms and tilted her head to the sky to embrace that moment: the sea, the sun, the man by her side. Nothing else mattered – her job, the disaster of Halcyon Seas.

'Over there,' she pointed to a sandy cove studded with palm trees. 'Here, I'll steer us in.'

The beach was deserted. Just Marianne, Gideon, and the gulls. They waded from the boat to shore, the sea skimming the legs of her shorts. Gideon held the hamper on his head Malagasy style.

Frederic had packed a tartan throw, cold roasted meats, sorghum bread, and cakes, mango, and pineapple, and bottles of cold water. Gideon unrolled the throw in the shade of a palm tree. They had all day together. She had chosen this cove as the nearest village was twelve kilometres away.

'Swim?' She unbuttoned her shorts.

Gideon was on his knees. He pulled her hips to him and kissed her navel. 'Now? Really?'

She tugged down her zip. 'Yes. Swim first.'

They both stripped off and ran naked into the waves. Marianne floated on her back gazing up at a flawlessly blue sky. Sun glittered on water, a myriad of turquoise and aqua jewels.

'Your hair is like a mermaid's' Gideon lay his hand beneath a sheet of her hair as it drifted like seaweed on the waves.

She hooked her legs around his waist and they kissed. He tasted of the sea, his tongue warm, lips cool. Laughing she broke away to swim. Gideon followed, then overtook her with strong, confident strokes. A year ago, she could never have imagined this. Her world had completely changed. This was something that she hadn't searched for, didn't even know that she wanted.

Laying on the throw, the remains of the picnic packed away, Marianne asked Gideon how long he planned to stay on Halcyon Seas. If the cruise continued and he was a guest then they could not have a relationship. She did not remind him of this.

'I told you I have a flat in London. It's lonely living there – alone, but if a beautiful captain wanted to join me between cruises, then she would be very welcome.'

'Any beautiful captain?' Marianne tried to keep the conversation light but from the tone of Gideon's voice and the questioning in his eyes she knew he was offering more than an occasional place to stay.

'You know how I feel about you, Marianne. I'll do whatever works for you, just so long as we can be together. I don't want you to give up your dream of captaining a cruise ship.'

'I would, if that was the only way we could be together. Being with you means more to me than any job. Maybe it's just too late – I've waited so long to be promoted, been disappointed too many times. I really thought I would be the captain of Mermaid of the Seas in the new year. It would have made my dad so proud. William Fellows ruined that for me, leaking information to the press. I don't want to put myself through it all again. Maybe it's time I retired.'

Gideon stroked her hair from her face. 'No. You're a brilliant captain and should be recognised. I don't want you to give that up for me. I can wait. You don't know that it was William Fellows.'

'Who else could it be? I know that it wasn't one of the crew.'

'Have you had any leaks since the passengers left for Durban?'

'No.'

Gideon shrugged. 'Maybe that's the last you'll hear of it. I still believe you'll come out of this with your head held high. You did an amazing job keeping your cool despite everything that's happened. Keeping up the moral of your guests and crew.'

'Let's hope so.' She didn't want to think about it now. Why spoil a perfect day?

They sailed back as the sun set turning everything a reddish gold. When they approached the stretch of beach with the jetty, Gideon said, 'Let's try and get away again soon. It drives me mad seeing you every day and not being able to do this.' He kissed her in a way that aroused her passion – again.

'Don't! It's hard enough without you reminding me of what I'm going to miss. What are you doing?'

He had taken off his shirt. 'I'll swim back from here.' Before she could say anything, he dived off the boat and swam to shore.

Olivia's brother Pascal and his friend were at the jetty when Marianne steered the boat in. She folded Gideon's shirt to slip inside the hamper and found his phone in the top pocket. At least it hadn't got wet. He was hopeless, forgetting it was in there. She tucked it into the back pocket of her shorts and lifted the hamper. Luc jumped on board to help her.

'I'll get Jay Jim to deliver this to the ship, Captain.'

'Thank you. He can leave it in the kitchen, for Frederic. It was kind of you to let us ...', she corrected herself, 'let me use your boat.'

Luc winked. 'No worries, Captain. About what I said to your officer...' he trailed off watching her face for a reaction, his expression anxious. Whatever he had said, she hadn't been informed.

'It's fine. As you said – no worries.' He looked relieved and Marianne wondered what it could have been, maybe they had had words – two young men showing off in front of the girls. If she hadn't been informed it couldn't be important and she didn't want to know.

The sun had almost sunk into the sea and the light was fading. To celebrate her day off she would see if the bar tender could shake up a Long Island Iced Tea. They were hanging on to the last remnants of a cruising life, much like the ladies in Tea with Mussolini who had English tea parties whilst the war raged all around them.

The phone in her back pocket vibrated. Marianne instinctively pulled it out, forgetting for a second that it was Gideon's. A message showed as a banner notification: *Great coverage in The Guardian. Thanks for the film and photos.* Then it disappeared. Marianne's hand shook as she tried to find where this message had been posted: text, email, messenger, WhatsApp. Her fingers clumsy, unable to navigate the keys. It couldn't be what she thought. Gideon wouldn't. She shivered, cold to the bone. The only notification was against mail – three messages unopened. If she looked and she was right then it was the end of everything. *Please let me be wrong.* Marianne was tempted to close her eyes as she placed a finger over the mail icon.

The email she had seen was in response to one from Gideon. She read:

1st December

Hi,

I promised more film. This was taken at a Thanksgiving Party hosted by Captain Moore, for passengers of the ship and villagers. You have to get this out there so that the world can see what is going on in this village. There's a big story here. Make as much noise as you can.

More photos will follow. Will be in touch again soon.

There was a long string of emails, the dates coinciding with the leaks. Gideon was the leak. He was responsible for ruining her career. How could he have said all of those things *knowing*? She wanted to scrub herself clean of him. If only she could wipe away every trace – the memory of his kisses, his touch. It made her sick to think of him using her like that. How could she have let him? From the day that she met Gideon Flynn she knew that he was a womaniser, deceitful, and playing her. Why hadn't she trusted her instincts and given him a wide berth? It was too late now but he would not get another chance. They were going to get off this friggin' island and then she would find a way to get him off her ship.

Marianne handed Gideon's phone to a security guard when she boarded Halcyon Seas. Her second officer pounced on her as she strode to the bridge.

'Captain, I've been looking for you. At the party, I found out why we've been detained. It's local politicians trying it on. I'll brief you when you're ready. It sounds as if we could blow this thing apart right now and set sail.'

Marianne took a deep breath. That must be what Pascal's friend was talking about. 'Let's do it. We're ready to go.' It was time to let everyone know who was in charge.

43

Pascal was by the jetty, hauling the morning's catch out of his boat. Luc worked alongside him. Olivia sat on the jetty swinging her feet as she waited for them to complete the task.

'Hey, Sis. What's up?' Pascal loved trying to sound like an American movie star. To Olivia he sounded more Bugs Bunny.

Luc landed next to her. 'I didn't see you at the party.'

Olivia didn't even know Luc was back in the village. 'I was there. Had to leave early to feed Hal and settle him. I thought you were in Toliara.'

'Work there has finished for a while. Helping my man Pascal.' He thumped her brother on the back. 'It was some jol, eh bro? Some fine women on that ship of yours.'

Olivia dreaded to think what Luc had been up to – pestering Charanya and the other pretty girls most likely. 'Who did you talk to at the party?'

'Don't you worry. I only have eyes for you,' Luc clicked his tongue and winked. Olivia had known him since he was a boy. He was a nuisance then as now. 'The guys from the tug boats hung out with us. I know them from Toliara. They had no idea the ship was being detained just so the trench could get dug.'

Pascal was making a cutting throat action to Luc. He stopped when Olivia glared at him.

'I knew it! Are you crazy, Pascal? If Captain Moore finds out I could lose my job and *you* will have to send this boat back.'

'Hey, sister, chill.' Luc put a hand on her knee. 'It's all cool. The guy from your ship wasn't surprised.'

Olivia went cold. 'What guy?'

'Tall, skinny, shaved head.'

Luc had just described the second officer. 'American?'

'That's the guy.'

'In that case Captain Moore already knows, and if not then she will soon find out.'

The two men looked at one another. Luc shrugged. 'Sorry Liv.'

Pascal sighed. 'She won't fire you. It's not your fault.'

Olivia wanted to believe him. If Pappa apologised, made some recompense maybe they would be forgiven– and not a live chicken or a goat.

Jay Jim sauntered across the sand, waving a hand in greeting. He would be returning to the ship's kitchen after dropping something off at the shop. Olivia knew that he much preferred training as a chef than working as a fisherman. Until now, none of them had ever considered what they would choose to do for work, they just did what was required of them. Cleaning cabins certainly wasn't her choice.

'Olivia,' he called when he was a few yards away. 'You're wanted at home.'

Olivia slid off the jetty to land on the sand. 'Why?'

'A visitor arrived by cab. Very fine clothes. You speak English. Mammon said to get you quick.'

Olivia's heart lifted. 'Where is he waiting?'

Jay Jim was play fighting with Pascal and Luc. Pascal got him in a headlock whilst Luc tickled him.

'Never mind.' She took off across the beach, her heels sinking in the sand slowing her progress. Jay Jim shouted something after her but his words were lost on the breeze.

She tried to stay calm but it was impossible. Charanya must have told him where to find her. When she reached the path that led to the village, Olivia stopped to catch her breath and her thoughts. She was desperate to see Raf. In the months that they had spent apart her feelings had not subsided, if anything they were stronger. She loved him. He was Hal's father. If he had come of his own volition, she would have been overjoyed but there was only one way he could have found out she was here and that was through Charanya. Raf had found her because it was the honourable thing to do. He had a girlfriend and was only here as a result of Charanya's interference. By now, Raf would have seen how she lived; he would think it unfit for his son. She would deny Hal's existence. So long as her mammon did not give anything away.

Alice had plenty she could do to occupy herself that morning but she was irritated that William was being so secretive and that he was denying her the opportunity to go orchid hunting. It was an activity that brought her so much pleasure: creeping through the jungle watching and listening for lemurs, tenrecs, and chameleons; marvelling at the brightly coloured birds like flags in the trees; and then spotting a new orchid. Each one different. Precious gifts of nature. They had cuttings from several species but there were so many more to discover. There was no reason that she couldn't go alone.

It felt daring, exciting. Venturing into the jungle was less scary to Alice than getting on a London Tube. She flapped her loose shirt to stir a little breeze. It was nine-thirty and already 33 degrees. The forest would be cooler, with the shade of trees. She headed in the direction that Disney had first taken them, towards the cliff edge. It was a great look-out giving panoramic views of the sea, and an easy path to remember. She didn't want to get lost. Alice was wandering along the cliff top peering over the edge to spy any orchids clinging to its face when she saw what looked like a heap of clothes on the gorse path ahead. Alice stopped in her tracks, what if someone was waiting to ambush her? She could have been followed – there was nobody who would hear her cries for help. The stupidity of her venture struck home. She hadn't told anyone where she was going. If the clothes were a person, then they weren't moving. It could be a traveller's belongings. Then she heard a cry, 'Help!'

A large rucksack and a suitcase on wheels sat outside the hut when Olivia arrived home in response to Jay Jim's message. A friend of Samuel's and another boy were inspecting the luggage, wheeling the case back and forth, and investigating the pockets of the rucksack.

'Hey. Leave them alone,' Olivia said.

'We just keeping guard for the lady,' Samuel's friend said.

'The lady? You mean my mammon?'

'No. The English lady.'

Had Raf brought his new girlfriend with him? She couldn't meet them together. It would be humiliating.

'Olivia. Is that you? Come now. Quickly.' Mammon's voice came from inside. She had no choice but to go in.

A sturdy-looking woman dressed in khaki shorts, a vest and a bucket hat stood in the middle of the room. She spoke rapidly, waving a folded map. Mammon and Kanto stared at the woman as though she had landed from outer space.

'Who is she?' Olivia said.

'We do not know. She seems angry. Can you get her to go away?'

'Can I help you?' Olivia spoke in English and the woman threw up her hands in relief.

'At last! I am hot, tired, and exasperated. I've been travelling for what feels like days. Nobody can speak any bloody English. I had no idea that I was going to be taken into the back of beyond. Just tell me where I can find a hotel. Once I've had a cool shower, a change of clothes, and cup of tea I might just be able to function. Oh, and I need some paracetamol or ibuprofen. I put my back out carrying this lot from the airport to the cab.'

'I will try and help you. Can you tell me who you are and why you are here?'

'What did she say?' Olivia's mother asked. 'I told you she was an angry lady.'

Olivia shook her head at Mammon. 'Wait.'

'Rachel Wagstaff. I'm here to take my mother home.'

'Oh.' Olivia could not find any other words. This woman was so unlike Alice in build, and demeanour. 'I'm afraid she is not here, but I can take you to her.'

'I demand to know where you have taken her. If my mother has been hurt in any way then you will be paying for it for the rest of your lives. And so will Silver Seas. You don't want to mess with me.'

'She thinks that we are holding her mother, Alice Wagstaff ,against her will. I'll take her to Alice,' Olivia said to her mammon.

'Your mother is well and happy. If you would like to leave

your luggage here, we will take care of it and I will show you where to find Alice.'

'And a hotel?'

'I am sorry but the ship is the closest you will find to a hotel. Would you like me to take you to Captain Moore?'

Rachel sighed heavily. 'Now I have come this far I might as well continue until I find my mother. Perhaps one of the boys could take my luggage down to the ship?'

Olivia was about to object to the last request when Rachel extracted some Malagasy notes from her pocket. 'Does Alice know you are here?'

'No. I wanted to surprise her.'

They had to push their way out of the hut as inquisitive villagers had gathered at their door to look at the red-faced English woman. There was a scramble as four or five boys fought for the job of carrying Rachel's luggage, knowing that they would be generously rewarded. Olivia picked the two eldest and shooed the others away.

'It is a bit of a climb.' Olivia glanced down at Rachel's shoes and was pleased to see that she wore flat sandals. 'Alice will be in her shack with William. They've usually finished hunting by now. We may even meet them on their way back down to the village.'

Rachel stopped walking and gasped for breath. 'Slower. It's the heat. I thought you said hunting. You mean eating?'

'No. Hunting. They are hunting flowers.'

'Don't be ridiculous. Oh, you mean picking flowers. Have you got a bottle of water? I meant to buy one when I arrived in the village but there was only an old hovel and I didn't want to buy anything from there.' Rachel pulled a face to show her disgust.

'Maybe you should wait on Halcyon Seas. There you can get water and maybe have a shower if Mrs Gloria agrees.'

'I recognise you now. Aren't you the cleaner who smuggled her baby off the ship and caused this disaster?'

Olivia's skin prickled. 'How do you know what happened?'

'Oh, it was in all of the papers. Not a very flattering photo of you. It was a relief to find out that there were no pirates involved, just your brother and the baby's father I understand?'

'Can I see the newspaper story?'

Rachel pulled a phone from her pocket. 'No signal. Hold on, I saved it as a photo. Here. You can make it bigger like this.'

Olivia took the phone. It was the photo that had been used for her ship's ID card. Beneath it a story about how she had kept her pregnancy a secret and attempted to send her baby back to Madagascar. There was nothing about the baby's father, just mention of two Malagasy men, stating that one of them was her brother. 'I did not know that this was in the newspaper.'

'You do seem a bit cut off here. Very little information comes out of Madagascar. Mummy is completely unaware of the furore your situation has caused. I'll be glad when she's safely home. Is it much further?'

Rachel would not be persuaded to wait on the ship and so they continued stopping every few minutes for Rachel to rest. By now, Raf would definitely know about their baby. It would be easy for him to work out that he was the father. For a few minutes back there, she had allowed herself to imagine a romantic reunion. It was a fantasy and one that she could not indulge in. Raf would see her home in the same way that Rachel did, Pappa's shop, a disgusting hovel not fit to sell a bottle of water. At the training camp and on the ship, she *brushed up well,* as the Americans' said – Raf had been fooled into thinking she was in his league, and if not, then he was just having fun, using her as a distraction. If Raf's parents heard that he had a son, they would take Hal from her to give him a better home. She knew it would be in Hal's best interests but the thought of losing Hal and Raf tore at her heart. She couldn't give away her baby boy.

'Are you sure you know where you're going? We're heading into the forest. There must be tons of mosquitoes I don't have my spray with me.' Rachel's face was even redder. Sweat trickled from her brow, and her vest clung to her body as though a bucket of water had been tipped over her head.

'Not much further, I promise.'

They rounded a clump of trees and Olivia pointed ahead. 'There.'

'Where? By that pile of rubbish?'

'I do not see the rubbish?'

'Those discarded cans of oil. Terrible the way people dispose of stuff.'

'Oh no. That is Alice and William's shack. It has been made from oil drums.'

Rachel did not reply, but Olivia could tell from the way she stiffened that this had been a shock to her. She hoped that Alice was in so that she could leave Rachel with her and get back to Hal.

The door was ajar. Olivia called out in Malagasy but there was no reply. She leaned against the door and it opened. Sid, the chameleon, raised his head in greeting and then darted across the room. Rachel gasped.

'That is Sid. They aren't in. I'm sorry.'

'Get him out!' She cowered in the doorway.

'Sid lives here. I don't think that they will be long. Maybe if you wait outside in the shade? There is a nice big log out the back where Alice and William sit when they are cooking on the fire.'

'I can't.' Rachel's body shook. Olivia thought she was

laughing but then realised she was crying. 'My back hurts. I'm hot. Tired. I need water. A cup of tea. How can my mother live like this?'

'There is a doctor. Our village doctor lives close by. Would you like to wait with him? He could give you something to ease your pain and make a tea.'

'A doctor? Why didn't you say so before? Yes please.'

Olivia could have hugged Disney when she found him outside his cabin smoking a pipe. 'Disney, please could you look after Miss Wagstaff until Alice returns home? She has a bad back and would like some tea to make it better.'

Disney greeted Rachel as though she were a princess. He kissed her hand and led her into his consulting room.

'So, I can leave her with you?' Olivia was already making her getaway.

'Of course. It will be my pleasure. Disney will make all of your pain go away.'

44

Alice knew that it was William before she reached what she had thought was a bundle of clothing. He was lying on one side cradling his ankle.

'William! What have you done?'

His face lit up in relief when he saw her. 'Oh, thank God. I think I've sprained my ankle.'

'But what are you doing here, alone? I could have come with you.'

'It was meant to be a surprise. Ouch. I can't put any weight on it.'

Alice supported William to stand up but he could not walk. She wasn't strong enough to hold his weight. 'I'll go and get help. Disney will have something for the pain. You need a strong man to help you walk back to the ship.' She gave him her bottle of water and made sure he was comfortable. 'I'll be as quick as I can. What was the surprise?'

William gave a plaintive look that could have meant – just go and get help quickly, or I don't want to ruin it. Either way, she took the hint.

'Okay. Hang on in there.' She blew him a kiss and jogged back the way that she had come.

The door to Disney's cabin was closed which meant he was consulting and should not be disturbed. Alice bit her lip. It would take fifteen minutes or more to run down the hill and summon help from the village, longer to reach the ship. William was exposed to the sun and she didn't know how long he had been lying there before she found him. Her lips curled upward as she felt a smile within. The sweet man was planning a surprise for her. That was the reason for his subterfuge. She felt a tenderness for him that was different to the feelings she had towards Tom, her husband. William's gentleness, his innocent sometimes boyish demeanour made her feel protective towards him. He had a great capacity to love but until now, Alice suspected that he had little opportunity to demonstrate this. Maybe she should be the one to distance herself, to prepare him for her departure, but she couldn't. Every day they had together was precious.

Laughter came from within – Disney's rich belly laugh and another higher, girlish one. It continued, with the faint sounds of a person gasping for breath then more helpless laughter. The consultation could not be too serious, maybe now was a good time to interrupt. She knocked on the door and then edged it open to call in.

'Disney, could I have a quick word?'

The door flew open. 'Come in. Come in. We have been waiting for you.'

Alice frowned. Disney was high. 'I really need your help, Disney. William has sprained his ankle. I need help getting him back to the ship and a painkiller or something to bring down the inflammation.'

'Mummy?' Rachel appeared in the doorway behind Disney.

Alice gasped. It was like seeing an apparition. Rachel – here – in Disney's cabin. 'Rachel. What are you doing here?'

'Come and sit down, Alice. Would you like something to calm you?'

'You have to try Doctor Disney's tea. It's amazing.'

Alice definitely felt like she was in Wonderland – possibly at the Mad Hatter's tea party. She had so many questions but first William needed help. She closed her eyes and took deep breaths trying to ground herself. 'Disney. I have just come from the cliff edge, close to the spot you first took us. William can't walk. Can you help him? If not, I'll run on down to the village.'

Disney nodded and touched Alice's arm. He plucked some potions and herbs from the selection adorning his shelves and filled his tote bag. 'I'll see William gets safely back to the ship.'

Alice watched him move as quick and stealthily as a mountain lion covering the ground much faster than she ever could. Rachel was in the cabin, waiting and Alice didn't know what to say, how to greet her. Was this where her new life ended? The past coming up to meet her like a tidal wave, dragging her down, sweeping her away?

Rachel was kneeling, her bottom supported by a plump cushion, her knees splayed. 'Oh Mummy, you don't know how relieved I am to see you. But you look different.' Rachel peered at Alice, her eyes glassy.

There was a tin mug on the mat alongside Rachel. The remains of her tea. Alice picked it up and smelt the contents. Then she fished out a leaf. Cannabis. 'How much tea have you drunk?'

'Two, three, maybe four. I'm not sure. It's very good. It made all of the pain go away.' Rachel smiled her eyes dreamy.

'When did you get here? How?'

'On an aeroplane. And then I had to climb for miles. Did you know that there is a reptile in your house? A great big thing. Why are you living in an oil drum?'

'Let's get you back to the ship.' Alice heaved Rachel to her feet.

'Is it safe? Shouldn't we wait for a guide or someone to take us down?'

Alice laughed. 'You are safe with me.'

Rachel followed Alice's lead, happy to be manoeuvred by her as they wove their way down the hill.

'I've come to take you home, Mummy.'

'I guessed you had darling. Mind that tree root.'

'I missed you.' Rachel stopped and clung to Alice's arm. 'I mean, I *really* missed you.'

'Well, we didn't see much of each other when I was in Norfolk.'

'That's what I mean. I missed you when you moved to Norfolk. I wanted you to live near me so that we could spend time together. You are my mother!'

'Yes dear, and I love you. Why did Disney give you his special tea?'

'Because I put my back out lifting my luggage. It worked. I'll have to ask for that medicine on prescription when we get home.'

'You might have trouble finding a doctor in Bethnal Green willing to prescribe it. Nearly there. When we get on the ship you can freshen up in my cabin. I'll see if Chef or Frederic can rustle you up a meal. You must be tired and hungry, darling.'

They continued in this way, Alice supporting Rachel and cajoling her as she objected to the heat, the terrain, the lack of facilities, and the unfairness of her life. It was a relief when Halcyon Seas was in sight.

Rachel's passport was in her luggage, which, Olivia

explained on meeting them as they boarded, was now in Alice's cabin. The security guards were reluctant to allow Rachel to pass them without it, so Alice went ahead. She did a bit of a detour, checking the lounge, café, and theatre in the hope of finding Captain Moore or Gideon so that she could explain why Rachel was there and prepare them for her departure from the cruise. She owed it to Gideon, as he was responsible for persuading her to join him on Halcyon Seas. Neither of them were around. Gloria said that the captain was enjoying a rare day off. Alice was no fool, she guessed that Gideon would be with her. Good luck to him. They made an attractive couple and the chemistry between them had been obvious since day one. William still didn't know of her plans. As soon as she settled Rachel, she would go and look for him.

Rachel's luggage almost filled Alice's small cabin. Her passport was easy to find, tucked into a pocket of the rucksack. There were some pills too. Alice checked the label. Prozac. Her heart sank. Poor Rachel. She had been so caught up with her worries that she had forgotten to be a mother to her youngest. It didn't matter that Rachel was forty-two, she was still her little girl and she hadn't been there for her. Alice zipped up the pocket and hurried back to rescue Rachel from interrogation by security. She was in no fit state to answer questions and might give the wrong impression.

When they were alone, the cabin door locked so that they wouldn't be disturbed, Alice made Rachel drink a bottle of water. She gently removed Rachel's sandals, as though she were a toddler and swung her legs up onto her bed.

'Have a little sleep, darling. I'll wake you in an hour so that you can have a shower and something to eat.'

'He left me, Mummy. Greg left me for another woman.' Tears slid down the sides of her face.

'Hush. Everything's going to be alright.' She stroked

Rachel's hair until she fell asleep. And then she went to find William in his cabin.

45

As Olivia approached Halcyon Seas, Hal secured to her back with a shawl, she saw a group forming on the bank, children, mothers, and babies.

'What's going on?' she asked one of the mothers.

'We can't board. The men say no more school. We are not welcome.'

The women and children hung around, maybe hoping that the men were mistaken. Nobody could believe that Mrs Gloria and Patty did not want them to attend their classes. Olivia had been waiting for this, she knew that things would end badly.

'I will have to report for work,' Olivia said to Gracie. 'Can you take Hal back to Mammon? Then, you had better get back to your own work.'

'It's not fair! Why do I have to fetch the water and farm? I've just had my nails painted. Ask if I can have a job in the beauty salon. I know how to do a manicure.' Gracie tried to push past Olivia so that she could step onto the gangplank.

'Gracie, no! You can't board the ship anymore. We will be

setting sail. I'm sorry but it's time for us to go. Our stay here finished.' Olivia cut the air with her hands. Then she swung Hal from her back and bundled him into Gracie's arms. 'Look after your nephew. I'll say goodbye to everyone before the ship sails. Now go!'

Hotel staff were hoovering the gangways, polishing glass, and handrails. The lounge was being transformed from a community centre back into a smart reception room. Gloria was shouting directions, a clipboard in her hand.

'What would you like me to do?' Olivia asked.

'What would you have done before things changed?'

'Clean the cabins and corridor on my deck.'

'Then what are you waiting for?'

Olivia scurried off, disorientated by the change in her routine. She hadn't stepped foot in her cabin since the day Pascal and Luc came for Hal. It was strange to be back. Her bunk was covered in the belongings of the other three girls. Whilst she stayed in her family home, the girls had made good use of the space she had vacated. Olivia left everything where it was and changed into her uniform. Although she still had some baby weight, the trousers needed a safety pin and her pink tunic gaped.

She loaded up a cleaning trolley. First, she would visit Alice to find out what happened when she met up with her daughter. Olivia hesitated; they had been told not to socialise with the cruise guests. Would anyone notice if she sneaked in?

Olivia knocked on Alice's door, remembering the first time they had spoken – when Alice had been frightened by the ship's alarm. She had been in awe of the elegant English woman who was now one of her dearest friends. There was no reply and so Olivia pushed open the door and called out, 'Alice. May I come in?'

Olivia Rose report to Mrs Busby immediately. Olivia jumped.

Was she being spied on by a CCTV camera? Before leaving, she took a peek. Alice wasn't there.

'Captain Moore wants to see you,' Gloria said when Olivia found her in the lounge. 'This way.' She strode ahead silently and Olivia followed with trepidation.

There was a meeting room close to the bridge. Gloria knocked on the door and then signalled for Olivia to go in. Her legs felt like jelly as she crossed the carpet to stand in front of Captain Moore's desk.

'It has come to my attention that your father is responsible for the detainment of Halcyon Seas.'

Olivia wanted to argue that her father only spoke to a councillor in Malatanga and in doing so the captain received the loan of a generator. It wasn't fair to blame Pappa. But she couldn't say anything to Captain Moore, she was intimidating at any time but today her anger scorched Olivia, flaying her skin and curdling her stomach

'This is a serious matter and there will be consequences. The US navy and Head Office have been informed. We hold you personally responsible for this deceit. As such, Silver Seas can no longer employ you. You are dismissed with immediate effect. Mrs Busby will escort you off the ship.' Captain Moore pressed a key on her laptop and seconds later Gloria entered the room.

'I'm sorry,' Olivia managed to say. The captain did not reply; she exchanged a look with Gloria, who ushered Olivia out of the room where a security guard was waiting for them.

'I'm sorry it ended like this,' Gloria said squeezing Olivia's arm.

If she didn't get away quickly, everyone would witness her tears. Captain Moore had been so unlike herself – the captain Olivia had come to admire and respect for her kindness and fair treatment of staff. To have brought out this anger in her,

Olivia was ashamed. But the captain was right, all that had befallen Halcyon Seas had started with her trying to hide her pregnancy.

Nobody expected her at home, Hal was being taken care of and Olivia needed time alone to calm herself. She took a shady path and weaved her way through the trees following a steady incline. There must be other jobs. Maybe she could find work in Malatanga or Tana. There were some hotels in Tana, with her training and command of French and English she would make a competent maid, maybe even the front desk. It would mean leaving Hal with Mammon. The journey from Tana would make visiting difficult but not impossible. In some ways, it would be better than working on a cruise ship. It was the only way she could support Hal and help her family pay for the fishing boat.

Without realising it, Olivia had joined a path which led to the water spring. Even from her vantage point halfway up the hillside, Olivia could see that great progress had been made in digging the trench. If they had been able to continue the village might have had a tap with running water by Christmas. That would have been a miracle. A gift like none other. But miracles didn't happen – not even at Christmas, despite the mushy films Americans were so fond of.

'Hey,' she called, delighted to see Alice and her daughter a little ahead.

Rachel turned, and seeing Olivia, touched Alice's arm. They waited for Olivia to catch up.

'I hope you did not have to wait too long for Alice yesterday,' Olivia said.

'Doctor Disney took good care of me. Mummy is showing me what her friends have achieved here. I must say it's remarkable. Do you really not have any fresh running water in the village?'

Olivia shook her head. 'It's okay. We carry it down a couple of times a day.'

'It's not okay. Everyone should have access to clean water. I had no idea that the drought here was so severe. I blame climate change. You people are suffering as a result of the greed of western countries.'

Alice winced. 'Malagasies are incredibly resourceful. They are strong, courageous, and despite everything, the happiest, most hospitable people I've met.'

'All the more reason that they should not suffer like this. What's going to happen when Halcyon Seas leaves tomorrow or the day after? It's outrageous.'

Olivia didn't understand why Alice's daughter was so angry. They were no worse off than before the Westerners arrived. They had managed before and they would do so again.

'I agree, darling but we will be leaving soon and I don't know what else we can do.'

'I will be staying here, Alice. I am going to miss you.' Olivia could not stop the tears now.

Alice dropped the pots she was holding and hugged Olivia. 'Hush now. You are going to be with Hal and your lovely mammon.' She kissed Olivia's forehead and wiped away her tears. 'I've made a decision too.'

'Mummy is going to live with me in London. We're buying a flat together as soon as I've released Mummy's money from Silver Seas.'

Alice looked sad and Olivia wondered if she was thinking about William and how she would miss him. They had seemed so happy collecting orchids and making a home in the old shack. 'Is Mr Fellows staying here?'

'No. William injured his ankle and can't go anywhere until

it's healed. Maybe he will come back one day.' Her voice was wistful, as though she didn't believe he would.

'Do you know when the ship is leaving?' Olivia said.

'Maybe tomorrow. We are being kept updated. There are restrictions on the time we can spend on shore. Sorry, we won't be able to finish the trench. I wish we could do more for you all.'

Olivia nodded afraid that if she tried to speak there would be more tears. Malagasies did not believe in showing their emotions in public, she was becoming more and more like a Westerner. She picked up Alice's pots and signalled that she would collect the water.

'If you're sure. Goodbye, Olivia. Hopefully, we will see each other again before we leave but if not take care of that beautiful baby boy.'

Alice blew kisses and Olivia did the same before turning with a heavy heart to climb the last stretch.

46

When Olivia left the room, Marianne pressed her knuckles against her forehead. Her head ached. The way Gloria had looked at Marianne made her feel ashamed. She knew that she was taking out her anger on everyone but the person who deserved it. If Gideon had been trying to find her, she would not know as she had kept a low profile avoiding the places where they used to meet. His treachery was unbelievable – listening to her talk about her aspirations, how her dream had been stolen from her when he was responsible – it was as low as a person could go. The man that she thought she loved did not exist. It had all been a pretence to get her into bed. She was just another conquest. Well, damn him. Damn the whole of the male species.

There was a knock on the door. Marianne's stomach somersaulted. She should have asked security to prevent uninvited passengers from this part of the ship. Gloria inched the door open. 'Have you got a minute, Captain?'

Marianne let out her breath. 'Yes, come in, Gloria. Take a seat.'

'I need to brief you on a few things.'

Marianne nodded. 'Go on.'

'Alice Wagstaff's daughter has booked a room for the next week if that is okay. They are both planning to leave the ship when we reach Durban. I have told Mrs Wagstaff that she needs to apply to Silver Seas for reimbursement of her fees, as per the contract.'

Marianne nodded.

'We are picking up twenty-one of the passengers who chose to wait in Durban. Fourteen have returned home and are seeking compensation for the termination of their cruise.'

'It wasn't terminated.'

'I know. I'm in contact with HQ regarding the release from contracts.'

'Thank you, Gloria. You have taken on more than you signed up for as cruise director. I do appreciate all that you've done. A hotel director is joining the ship in Durban. Just a few more days.'

'There was one other thing.' Gloria looked uncertain as if afraid to deliver the news. There was nothing she could say that would make matters worse than they already were. 'Gideon Flynn isn't coming with us. He's making his way back to England from Madagascar.'

'Fine. I mean, thank you for telling me. I'm going to do one last check before we set sail. So much for Jamboree sending a replacement ship.'

It was a relief that he was going. She felt emotionally raw, bruised, and fragile. Her judgement had been flawed – her instincts unreliable. There was a reason that she wore a uniform, it was a barrier to protect her from emotional involvement. Marianne pulled on a boiler suit– nobody was getting close. Never again.

47

Since Rachel's arrival, Alice had barely seen William. He could hobble around on crutches but chose to remain in his cabin, writing notes and resting his ankle. That evening, Alice excused herself from dining with Rachel at their usual table, so that she could share a meal in his cabin.

'You missed Captain Moore's update this afternoon,' Alice said, as she arranged a candle and a single stem vase containing a little purple flower, on the balcony table.

William manoeuvred himself from his chair to the balcony. 'You can tell me all about it, and how you are getting on with your bossy daughter. This looks very grand. What's the occasion?'

Alice sighed. 'Our last night in Madagascar. Because you need spoiling. Because I've missed you.'

William lowered himself carefully into a chair. A few lights studded the dense black on the opposite bank. Water lapped gently against the hull. The night was still, the air warm.

'Is that what Captain Moore said? That we're leaving tomorrow?'

'We've been told to be back on board by 2 pm tomorrow.'

There was a knock on the door. Alice opened it to receive a trolley with their evening meal. A fish Alice didn't recognise in a sauce, cassava and sweetcorn from a can.

'I wonder when our meals will return to the five-star cuisine of a cruise ship,' she said placing their plates on the table.

'I would happily eat roasted cicadas if it meant sitting in front of our fire with you.'

'Sid is going to miss his fine dining too.'

They ate in silence, putting off what had to be said. A boy called out into the night. Somewhere, an oar hit the water. Then, a splash.

'A Perinet,' William said, nodding at the flower.

'Frederic gave it to me when I was asking for a vase.'

'You can tell me, Alice. I'm not a teenager anymore.' His lips curled up in something resembling a smile but his eyes said otherwise.

Alice lay down her fork. 'Rachel came here to take me back to England. If she was her usual bossy self then I would have stood up to her but she's not. Rachel is needier than I realised. Her partner has been having an affair and she has been asked to move out of the home that they shared. I thought they'd bought it together but apparently not. Rachel paid the bills and bought the groceries and her partner Greg paid the mortgage. The house is in his name. She wants to buy a flat with me, using what's left of my capital when we have negotiated with Silver Seas. I'll pay a lump sum and then Rachel will pay off the mortgage over time.'

'Hmm. I see.' He concentrated on boning his fish.

Alice poured them both some water. She was having trouble swallowing and gave up trying to eat. 'When I found you on the cliff edge, you said that you were planning a surprise for me.' She wanted to reach the version of him that lay on his back whilst Sid ran across his chest, the boyish man who tested how quickly different things burnt on the fire, who danced in delight when they discovered a new orchid. He was still there somewhere behind the thick spectacle lenses and armoured shell.

'Oh that. It doesn't matter now.'

'It matters to me. Please, William, tell me your surprise.'

He removed his glasses and wiped them with a handkerchief. When he had pushed them back up his nose, and cleared his throat, he said, 'I wanted to take a cutting from an orchid I discovered. I've been trying to find out if it's a new species and although I don't have any confirmation – yet, I've great hopes for this one. I'm almost certain.'

'Why didn't you tell me? I thought we were partners.' Alice's heart lifted as she saw her William start to re-emerge.

'Because I was planning to name it Alice. As a surprise. But now, we are leaving without it. I can't take a cutting and we will never know. Or, when we find out, it will be too late and someone else will claim the discovery.'

'That is the most beautiful gift anyone has ever given me.' Alice's heart hurt with love.

'But I didn't give it to you. I failed.'

'The thought. That is enough.'

'Do you want to live with your daughter in London?'

She knew he would ask and she had been rehearsing an answer in her head, one that was loyal to Rachel and made up for her lack of maternal care but she couldn't. 'No, I don't.'

'Then why are you agreeing to her proposal?'

'Because, when Tom and I moved to Norfolk I wasn't as available to my children as perhaps I ought to have been. I thought Rachel was a strong, independent woman and left her to get on with her life. If I had been more present, I might have realised that she was unhappy. Rachel is forty-two but she will always be my little girl.'

'What about you? What makes you happy, Alice?'

'You know what makes me happy. If we could have frozen time and stayed just as we were, say a week ago, it would have been perfect but life doesn't work like that. Halcyon Seas is picking up the cruise where we left off. I can stay on the ship travelling round and round the world until I'm dizzy or make a home back in London. It's not so bad, I have friends there. But I will miss you and Madagascar.'

'You could stay in Madagascar with me.'

'I wish we could but it's impossible. A fantasy. Where would we live? How would we survive?'

William shrugged. He looked as miserable as Alice felt. 'Are you getting off the ship tomorrow?'

'Yes. I'll say goodbye to Sid for you and ask Disney to care for our orchids. I did ask if we could take them with us but unless we smuggle them out, we need permission to remove them from the island.'

'Okay. Do you mind if I rest now? This ankle…'

Alice could hear the emotion in his voice. 'Of course. I'll pop in tomorrow before I leave and again when we get back. Do you need anything?' He shook his head and Alice kissed him on the cheek. 'Goodnight then.'

The next day, Rachel accompanied Alice as she climbed the path to their shack. It felt good being the braver one, reassuring Rachel when she saw a snake or gecko, explaining the sounds which made Rachel jump and cling to her mother.

'Did you and William sleep in that place?'

'No, we didn't. It was somewhere for us to work but we enjoyed spending our evenings there. It's peaceful up here.'

Rachel shivered. 'All those creepy crawlies and that horrible creature with bulging eyes. Not very hygienic. Ooh, what did you do when you needed the toilet?'

Alice didn't bother answering, Rachel would never understand, and she was too preoccupied squirting herself with insect repellent and batting the air to notice.

At the cabin, Rachel waited outside whilst Alice fussed with Sid, feeding him some beetles she found under a log. Then she gathered the potted orchids and carried them out in her arms.

'We need to drop these into Disney.'

'Oh good. I'll see if he has some more of that herbal tea. It worked wonders on my back.'

Disney was out and so Alice left the orchids at his door. She had been hoping that he would help her take a cutting from William's undiscovered orchid. If they couldn't do it today, she could at least ask him to look out for a more accessible one of the same species.

'There's one more thing I need to do. Are you happy to walk with me through the jungle up to the cliff edge? It's a lovely walk and you will be rewarded with a panoramic view.' Alice knew that Rachel would not object as the alternative was for her to walk back alone.

'What's the deal between you and William? I mean, are you having *a relationship*?'

'That depends on what you mean by a relationship. We've become close.'

'Oh, okay. Nothing serious then?'

Alice was hurt on behalf of William. He meant a great deal to her but she didn't want to expose what they had to Rachel's critical eye and risk her size six boots stamping all over the green shoots of their affection. 'I will be sad to leave him.'

Rachel gave her a sideways look as if trying to interpret

what this meant. They had come out of the dense trees onto the soft gorse where she, Disney, and William had once shared a joint. The expanse of sea and sky always lifted her spirits. She was about to try and put into words her conflicting feelings about leaving with Rachel for London when she spotted a fishing trailer on the horizon. Not just one boat but several. There were yachts, motor boats, and small ships, and they were all headed for the mouth of the Maloogy river where Halcyon Seas was moored.

Alice ran to the cliff edge. Frightened. Excited. Confused. 'What's going on? Have you got anything to do with this, Rachel?'

Rachel puffed as she jogged up behind her. 'No, why would I?'

'Your campaigning nonsense.'

The ship's horn sounded three times.

'We'd better get back quick. See what's going on.'

48

Olivia was on her way to collect water with Gracie when they saw the flotilla of ships and boats approaching. 'We are at war!' she declared. 'The USA has sent their navy. Pappa and his associates have started a war between Madagascar and the United States.'

'Really?' Gracie bounced on her toes, waving her hands. 'This is so exciting.'

'It's not exciting. It's a disaster. We'd better get down there and see what's going on.'

They scrambled down the hill, leaving their empty pots. Olivia's heart was thumping against her chest. As the boats got closer, she noticed banners and flags attached to masts. One of them had, *Choir of Angels,* in blue paint on a white sheet, another *The Climate is Changing so Should You.*

'I don't think it's the navy. But why are all these people here and how do they know about the choir?' Olivia slowed down, reluctant now to face a mob of strangers.

'I don't want to meet them,' Gracie said. 'Let's hide somewhere and watch what happens.'

'If you're not going to help here then you might as well go back up the hill to fetch the water. I'm going to find out what they want.'

Gracie stayed close to Olivia as she made her way to the jetty. The shoreline resembled an American holiday boat parade. Most of the ships had dropped anchor, a few boats lined up alongside the jetty and still more boats gathered on the horizon.

Splashes sounded one after another, as people jumped into the sea and then swam to the shore. A family had already settled on the beach with a picnic rug and a hamper.

Pascal, Luc and Jay Jim had been working alongside the jetty sorting the morning's catch. This was their territory. Nobody arrived here without their knowledge and approval and yet they stood back watching with open mouths as Westerners clambered over the jetty, helping one another off their boats. One of the men had taken charge of overseeing the process.

'What's going on?' Olivia asked Pascal, breathless from exertion and adrenalin.

'No idea. Maybe they've come to the wrong place.'

A group of young men and women were whooping as they opened cans of beer. It wasn't even midday.

'Please could you help me?' A woman with long hair tied in a ponytail asked Pascal.

He darted a look at Olivia and she responded on his behalf as her English was better. Besides, he looked terrified. 'We will if we can. Welcome to our village.' Olivia put her hands together and bowed her head.

The woman responded by copying Olivia and then she said, 'I am looking for my father, Gideon Flynn. He's a passenger on Halcyon Seas.'

'Of course. I am Olivia, these are my brothers Pascal and Jay Jim and that is Luc.'

The two men nodded awkwardly but Jay Jim gave a broad smile and shouted 'Hello.'

'Paige,' the woman said, putting a hand to her chest.

Olivia didn't have to find Gideon as he came bounding across the sand to meet them. 'Paige.' He hugged his daughter. 'I didn't expect this turnout. It's amazing, well done.'

'I didn't either. I've got Ricky with me, he's an influencer and a photographer. Can we have a look at the water trench and meet the choir? It's so good to see you, Dad.' They hugged again.

Alice and her daughter joined them. They too had questions. Everyone was talking at once but Olivia was still mystified. Nobody had explained to her what was going on.

Eventually, Gideon said, 'Olivia, please could you take my daughter Paige, and Ricky to meet your father? They are interested in the water project. Then, perhaps we could ask Gloria to get the choir together for a performance?'

'Why? You need to explain it to me first. Why are all these people here?'

Paige answered, instead of Gideon. 'My dad sent me a film of the Choir of Angels and told me about the trench you have been digging. The world has been following the story of Halcyon Seas and so when we posted about what had gone on here and how it would end when you all leave, it went viral. The choir captured everyone's hearts. It's a wonderful Christmas story. Now, everyone wants to help. They're all here to show their support.'

'Are they prepared to dig?' Alice asked.

'Absolutely! We have pledges for the supply of pipes, cement, and lots of willing workers.'

'In that case, I'll take you to Pappa straight away.'

49

'Is there a Madagascar regatta or a holiday event?' Marianne asked Gloria, as more boats joined the array, now blocking their exit from the Maloogy River.

'Not that I'm aware of.'

Marianne read one of the banners flapping in the breeze. 'It looks like a climate change protest but why here?'

They were interrupted by a junior officer. 'Captain, Libby Braithwaite is trying to reach you.'

'Thank you. I'll call her back.' Then, to Gloria, 'Maybe she will know what the hell is going on. They're blocking our exit and if we have to stay on this miserable island for one more day, I'm going to go insane.'

The officer was still there, hopping from one foot to the other. 'Sorry, Captain, Ms Braithwaite wants you to join a video conference. We've set you up in the meeting room.'

What was it now? It could only be bad news. Nothing had gone right for her. The whole fucking year had been a disaster. 'Okay, I'm coming,' she snapped.

. . .

Frederic had left a plate of cookies and a pot of coffee in the meeting room. Not the delicious pastries he was famous for but those disgusting things made with sorghum. At least they still had some coffee. Marianne poured herself a mug.

The young officer crept into the room as though afraid Marianne would bite his head off. She felt mean for being sharp with him. None of this was his fault. He fiddled with the laptop and then Libby Braithwaite, Stanley Arthur, who was one of the Jamboree directors, and Jonny, her old boyfriend from HR, came onto the screen. Marianne took a sip of coffee and spat it out. 'This is disgusting. Urgh. Too weak.'

'Sorry Captain. I'll tell Frederic. I think supplies are low.'

'No, I'm sorry. Please thank Frederic.' Marianne tried to compose herself to hear what the trio had to say. If she was about to be dismissed then she wanted to keep her dignity.

'Thank you for joining us at short notice, Captain Moore. Under the circumstances we were confident that you would not have any other demands on your time,' Libby said. 'I think that you know everyone, Stanley Arthur, and Jonny from HR.'

Marianne nodded. 'Yes, I do. Thank you.' She wished that they would cut to the chase. Maybe she should take control of the conversation – confirm the time of their departure but if she was about to be dismissed that could be humiliating.

'I'm sure *you do* have other things to attend to, Captain Moore,' Stanley Arthur said and Libby blushed. 'It has been a challenging time for you and I have to say that you have managed the situation admirably.'

Marianne felt a surge of adrenalin at this unexpected compliment. 'Thank you, Sir.'

'The Silver Seas initiative has not played out as we hoped.'

Thanks to Gideon Flynn and his conniving ways, Marianne thought, and she felt a stab of pain in her core. She took a deep breath. Must stay cool, calm, and positive. 'I'm sorry sir.'

'You have nothing to apologise for, Captain Moore. It was a bit of a gamble, an untried model combining cruising with the care of elders. The directors of Jamboree, and McIntyre Retirement Living met and a decision has been made. We are going to decommission Halcyon Seas and terminate the Silver Seas initiative.'

Marianne stole a look at Libby's face. She looked smaller – meek. It was Libby's first position as a director so she too could be facing redundancy.

'Mermaid of the Seas will be replacing Halcyon. There will be a full-staff establishment: a hotel director, cruise director, chief engineer, first officer, and of course a captain. Passengers from Halcyon Seas who would like to continue to live on a cruise ship will be offered the opportunity to transfer to Mermaid of the Seas at no extra cost. However, the ship will also take regular cruisers.'

'I see,' Marianne said. It made sense and was in her opinion a wise decision. The question was, what was to become of her?

'I asked Jonny from HR to join us as I have a proposal for you. We would like you to captain Mermaid of the Seas. I understand you previously expressed an interest. The leadership and courage that you have demonstrated in these difficult times have been noted. You will make an excellent captain.'

Marianne was overwhelmed. This was not what she had been expecting. 'Thank you. I don't know what to say. Yes. Yes, please.'

'Good. Then I'll leave you to discuss the details with Jonny. Thank you for all that you've done. The recent media attention has been a great asset to Jamboree. I just hope that forthcoming engagements for interviews do not interfere with your new job. The Wendy Williams Show, I hear.'

Marianne said her goodbyes and agreed to stay online to chat with Jonny but while she went through the motions her head was spinning – Wendy Williams? As soon as Libby and Stanley Arthur had disconnected, she pounced on Jonny. 'What's going on? I have no idea what Stanley was talking about – Wendy Williams?'

'A film of a choir – the Choir of Angels – has gone viral. The Guardian, a UK paper, want to write a story on what has been achieved by your passengers and crew since being stranded in Madagascar. The Wendy Williams Show wants to book you and the choir. It's big, Marianne. Climate change campaigners have jumped on this story and it's making news as a Christmas feel-good tale – The Angels of Madagascar. Amazing publicity for Jamboree and it seems good news for you too. I've maintained throughout that you should captain the Mermaid.'

It was too much to take in at once. 'I thought we had bad publicity. That the public was angry at our ship being detained in Madagascar. I was half expecting the US navy to come storming over the horizon not this. Have you seen the number of vessels surrounding us?'

Jonny laughed. 'Crazy, huh?'

'It makes no sense. How can I have gone from villain to hero in just a couple of weeks? And Wendy Williams? What's that about?'

'It's like I said, film of the choir and shots of the old folks digging a trench have gone viral. It's a good Christmas story. Now, we need to discuss your contract. If things go according to plan, the Mermaid will be with you tomorrow and we would like you to take on the role of captain with immediate effect.'

'What about the current captain? I saw you had appointed.'

'He's been moved to another ship. Your first officer is temporary captain until the Mermaid reaches Madagascar. This will be her maiden voyage. You will of course need to meet your new crew members and senior officers. Congratulations, Marianne. You deserve this. Don't forget you promised me a dinner date.'

When Jonny's smiling face froze on the screen and then disappeared Marianne sat still with her thoughts. This was what she had worked towards since announcing to her father that she would be the captain of a cruise ship. 'I've done it, Dad,' she whispered and felt his presence in the tingle of her skin. 'I've finally done it.' Had it been worth the cost? There was nobody who would care about this news as much as she did; nobody who would whoop with joy. The elation was balanced with despair. A tear trickled down her cheek. A pain in her heart – it was the loss of her father she was grieving – not him. Marianne swiped away the rogue tear. Her dream had come true. It was emotional exhaustion that was all. When the news had time to sink in then she would feel excited and happy. There would be a lot to do in the next couple of days. She just had to keep busy. A knock on the door.

'Captain? A Ms Flynn is asking to meet with you.'

Marianne heard the name Flynn and her disobedient heart leapt with excitement. If things had been different…

'If you are free now, shall I show her in?'

This time the words registered. A female Flynn. 'Who is she and what does she want?'

'Paige Flynn. She's visiting with the press. Ms Flynn has asked for a few minutes of your time if you are not too busy.'

Gideon had not tried to see her since she returned his phone via security. Gloria said he wasn't re-joining the ship – a coward. As much as it hurt, she had to accept that she had completely misread him. What did she expect? She had no experience of relationships, to think that she had fooled herself into believing she was in love.

'Captain?'

'Yes, show her in.'

The young woman who stepped into the meeting room was about forty. She stood tall, her shoulders back and chin jutting forward a little showing determination and perhaps some apprehension. Paige Flynn reminded Marianne of her younger self before she had experienced so many knockbacks and grown battle weary.

'Captain Moore, thank you for agreeing to meet with me.' She bit her lower lip. 'May I have some water?'

Marianne poured her a glass and slid it across the table. 'I can spare ten minutes. If you would like a longer interview then you must arrange it through Jamboree's communications team.'

'Yes, of course. I'm sorry.' Paige licked her lips. 'I've come to apologise and to explain.'

Marianne sat up. 'Who are you?'

'Gideon is my father.'

Marianne felt sick. She wanted to push the woman out of the room with force, releasing her pent-up rage. 'I don't want to hear an apology from you or your father.'

'Just let me explain.' When Marianne did not interrupt, she continued. 'I am a freelance journalist for the travel and leisure industry.'

'Get out!' Her heart hammered. 'I don't want to hear.'

'Please. My father wouldn't do anything to hurt you.'

But he did, Marianne thought. She wasn't going to lose her cool in front of this madam. She wanted to tell her again – *get out* but was afraid to speak in case she cried. So, she reached for a glass of water. They both watched as the water tipped in her shaking hand. Marianne lowered her glass and placed her hands firmly on the table.

'It's my fault. It's because he's a good father – the best. I desperately needed a good story. This was my last chance. Since I was a little girl, I wanted to be a journalist. I made my own newspapers and magazines. Sold them for twenty pence to the kids at school. Dad told me, "Follow your dream. Don't worry about what is going to earn you more money – do what you love and you will be good at it." He was right. I am a good journalist – but I couldn't get a break. It's so competitive. I'm not whining. I don't mind hard work. I'm prepared to struggle. But I'm forty-five and to be honest, until I started selling stories about Halcyon Seas I didn't earn enough to keep a hamster alive. I've been living off what I can earn dog walking and living in a flat owned by my dad rent-free. It's true. He came on this cruise to spy. It was my idea and being the kind of dad that he is, he agreed. But then he came to know you and the stories changed. What you are doing here is amazing.'

Marianne hadn't spoken for some time but this reminder of how Gideon had betrayed her triggered her fury once again.

'So, Gideon Flynn sabotaged the success of Halcyon Seas and destroyed my career to save yours?'

'At first, he did send information that resulted in bad publicity for Silver Seas but it wasn't meant to be personal.'

Marianne snorted. 'I don't care what his intentions were, he brought down the Silver Seas enterprise, costing more than one person their job. But he saved yours, so I'm meant to conclude that makes everything alright? Well, I'm sorry to disappoint you but it doesn't. I've given you enough of my time.'

'Please. Hear me out. The emails Dad sent changed sometime before the papers reported the hijacking. He didn't want to share any negative news and was full of praise for you. Then you stayed in Madagascar and these wonderful images and stories were sent to me. Dad wanted me to share them with the world so that everyone could see what you had achieved here. He's your biggest cheerleader.'

Marianne nodded. Gideon may have had his reasons but it didn't excuse what he had done. When she lay in his arms on that deserted beach telling him about her dreams and fears, he had kept quiet. He had deceived her. 'Thank you for telling me. Is that all?'

'Dad – Gideon, doesn't know that I'm meeting with you. He said that he doesn't deserve your forgiveness but I am asking you to understand so that you can find it in your heart to give him another chance. It hurts me to see him so unhappy. Dad is leaving the island with me by boat later today. Please say goodbye to him and let him know that he's been forgiven. If it wasn't for Dad, you wouldn't have all of this support.'

Marianne felt tears welling. She couldn't let Paige see her distress. 'I'm sorry but that's not possible. I have a busy schedule preparing to set sail tomorrow on another ship. Goodbye Ms Flynn.'

When Paige left, Marianne let the tears flow. They could have had something special if only … There was no, if only – Gideon Flynn had signed up for the forever cruise with the sole intention of sabotaging it. Everything about him had been a lie.

50

Alice, Patty, and Barbara met for breakfast in the dining room of Halcyon Seas. It was a rare event but today felt special as they were marking a significant moment. Today, Mermaid of the Seas would be arriving and with it some of the passengers who had opted to stay in Durban; others had returned home. The visitors to the island had taken over some of their jobs, and there would be no school on the ship today, so the three women were free to enjoy a lazy breakfast.

'Richard was up early, ready to direct his troops. He's in his element organising the volunteers. They'll dig that trench much faster than we ever could.'

'I know. Have you seen the muscles on those men?'

'I saw you ogling them when you were meant to be collecting water.' Alice laughed.

'Well – we're allowed to admire the scenery, aren't we?'

'What are you both planning to do when Mermaid of the Seas arrives?' Barbara said.

'Alice will be ordering a Pornstar Martini from the newly-stocked bar,' Patty quipped. But they both knew what Barbara meant and for a few seconds they sat in silence.

'Rachel expects me to go back to London with her. I had no idea she was so unhappy. I'm afraid that I may have failed as a parent.'

Patty covered Alice's hand with hers. 'We all fail as parents. It's in the job spec. If you think you are a perfect parent who got everything right then you are probably the worst. We do our best and have to accept that is good enough.'

Alice guessed it had taken Patty a lot of angst and therapy to come to terms with her daughter's behaviour and she felt bad for mentioning her relationship with Rachel. 'What about you, Patty? Are you staying on the island?'

'I am. When Captain Moore said that Halcyon Seas would remain here until she is taken away to be scrapped, I made up my mind. Jamboree is allowing us to continue using the ship to support the village. The mother and baby group will need me. Olivia is staying and so she will need help with Hal. I've plenty to keep me busy. Why would I leave?'

Rajesh, their waiter, arrived with a fresh pot of coffee and topped them all up. 'It is good to see my favourite ladies back in the dining room. I won't have guests who lay the tables for me on the new ship.'

Alice observed Patty and Barbara's contentment, they had found a place where they belonged and were needed, Rajesh was happy too – he would be joining a big new cruise ship doing a job that he loved.

'I will bring you a platter of fresh fruit to celebrate,' he said.

'Has that all been agreed – using Halcyon Seas?' Barbara spooned brown sugar into her coffee.

'So, Gloria told me. They will have to leave an officer in charge. It will cost Jamboree but according to Gloria, it's good publicity. I don't suppose it will be for long but if it gets us through the drought,' Patty said.

'Richard is confident there will be enough manpower to complete the trench by January, and that's assuming sixty per cent of the supporters leave before Christmas.'

'I wish you weren't leaving, Alice. We're going to miss you.' Patty took her hand again.

Alice reached for Barbara's and held on to both of her friends. 'Not as much as I will miss you. All of this. And William.'

Rachel seemed to have attached herself to Ricky and Paige, escorting them to wherever they wanted to visit. While Alice was having breakfast, they had been filming Gracie and other villagers carrying water down the hill and talking to Mr Rose about what access to fresh water would mean to the village. Rachel updated Alice when she rushed into her cabin looking for a couple of lambas she could borrow. 'One for me and one for Ricky. It will look better on film.'

Alice ought to be surprised that Rachel had muscled in on being filmed but it was typical of her daughter. She was now an expert on climate change and life in Madagascar. 'Have you seen Gideon, Paige's father?'

'No. He might be hanging out in that run-down old shop. Can I take this too?' She held up Alice's wide-brimmed hat, the one she liked to wear when searching for orchids.

'Yes. But please don't lose it.'

'Thanks, Mummy.' Rachel kissed her on the cheek. 'Ricky says you're awesome the way that you and William made up that oil drum place in the woods and trekking through the forest hunting orchids.'

Rachel hurried away, breathless and excited, reminding

Alice of how Rachel was as a child, organising the other kids in the street to carry out her latest mission – a yard sale or making rose petal perfume to sell. She was relieved to see her relaxed and happy. Thinking back, Rachel was more like her old self than she had been with Greg. With him, she had seemed subdued and anxious. Alice liked Ricky. He thought she was 'awesome'. She smiled to herself as she gathered together her laptop, drawing pad, and some watercolours. William was not yet able to walk to the shack but there was plenty of work to do cataloguing their specimens and doing some research on rare species that might be found on the island.

William was in his usual spot on the deck, sitting at a table in the shade, overlooking the river. His face lit up when Alice stepped through the door making her heart swell.

'Shall I get you some coffee,' Alice said when she had organised herself.

'No thank you. I don't want you disappearing again. Tell me about your morning.'

She had only been apart from him for three hours but loved that he missed her and was interested in her life. William had also heard that Halcyon Seas might be staying put when the Mermaid left.

'I'll stay on the ship until I've weatherproofed the shack and then I'll move in there.'

Alice wasn't surprised, she had guessed that this would be William's plan. If not for Rachel, it is what she would have proposed for them both. 'Maybe I can come back to visit you. We'll have to keep in touch if we're going to write this book together.'

William gave a hollow laugh. 'Indeed. Maybe not a book. I could write a couple of articles for the magazine.'

'Nonsense, William. You – we, will have enough material

to write a book on the orchids of Madagascar. Our little collection is just the start. There's so much more we can achieve.' She felt her heart quicken with excitement. The idea, like a baby in her womb, making itself known – new life. A sense of direction and purpose. 'We have to do this. Together.'

William grinned. 'We'd better make a start then.' He opened his notebook, filled with neat writing in closely packed lines. 'Did you have a go at drawing the species we've collected?'

'I did.' Alice hadn't yet shared her drawings with William and felt a little hesitant. She hadn't tried drawing anything for years but as soon as she started the accomplishment she had enjoyed as a young woman returned and she poured over her work, carefully matching shades by mixing watercolours she found in a store cupboard on the ship. It had kept her busy whilst William was immobile. Now, handing over her drawing pad, she held her breath and watched as he turned the pages.

'You have captured the tiny heads of the Cynorkis papillosa perfectly. These are wonderful. I had no idea you were a talented artist.'

'I wouldn't go that far but thank you.' Alice glowed with pride. 'I had forgotten how much I loved to paint. I hadn't picked up a paintbrush in decades.'

They worked companionably side by side. The sun moved and they were no longer in the shade. Alice had been using her laptop but looked up when the sun made it impossible to read the screen. 'Look, William.' She stood up and shielded her eyes. 'Mermaid of the Seas. It looks as though she's going to berth further out and use tenders.'

It was a huge ship, much bigger than the Halcyon. Alice felt both excited and sad. It was the end of an era. Whatever happened from here on, it would be a new chapter in all of their lives and for the village.

51

The arrival of Mermaid of the Seas had most of the villagers rushing to the shore. Craft stalls were laid out on flattened cardboard or rugs: woven baskets and bags in cerise, bright green, and yellow; wooden carvings of African masks, abstract women, turtles and toy boats; vibrant lambas made from local silk; and bundles of vanilla pods. Traders from miles around had seen or heard of the cruise ship's arrival and now the beach resembled a souk.

Olivia was carrying Hal on her back. Since losing her job she had not boarded Halcyon Seas. There had been plenty for her to do, harvesting crops, cooking and cleaning, but Olivia felt as though she had lost her sense of direction. She had always known exactly where she was headed, now her future was bleak. It was as though the past four years of achievement had been erased and she was fifteen again unsure what the future held, except then she had been full of hope and optimism.

Hal squirmed, kicking his legs against her waist. A discontented whimper. Olivia loosened the wrap and swung him into her arms. 'Hello, mon ange. Did you have a lovely sleep?' She nuzzled his neck and the whimper turned into a wail. 'Are you hungry?'

A tender boat was sailing away from the Mermaid, carrying people to the shore. Olivia didn't want to miss the arrival of what might be passengers or crew. She had heard from Patty that some of the cruisers who were previously on Halcyon Seas were returning with the Mermaid and she wanted to say hello.

Pascal, Luc, Jay-Jim, and Gracie were sitting on the jetty; four pairs of bare legs swung in order of size. 'You won't get much fishing done, with all of this commotion,' Olivia said looking up at them.

'S'okay. We went out early this morning. Jay-Jim, you should be selling the fish, man. These guys are loaded.' Luc nudged Jay-Jim and he had to hang on to stop himself from slipping off.

'They can't use fresh fish. If the chefs wanted some, it would have to be bigger proportions than we can supply. The cruise passengers are well fed,' Olivia said.

'Eight thousand kilos to feed two thousand passengers.' Jay-Jim showed off his newfound knowledge. Luc pushed him off the jetty and he landed like a cat on all fours.

'Here they come. Hop off Gracie, unless you want to help bring them in.' Pascal clambered to his feet as the first tender approached.

Pascal and Luc were waved away as the ship's officers assisted their passengers off the tender. It amused Olivia to see her brother and his friend dismissed from what they considered to be their jetty.

Luc and Pascal were scuffing the sand with their toes, and skimming stones whilst criticising the officers' boating skills when Olivia recognised the roll of his gait. At first, she didn't catch this recognition, it was as if she glimpsed it in the periphery of her consciousness, making her more alert. Then a shaved head made her heart contract with the memory of him. A voice. His voice. He was thanking the men who had brought him ashore his hand raised, as he strode off the jetty.

'Can you hold Hal for a moment?' she asked Luc, who was nearest to her. She didn't wait for him to reply as she thrust the now quiet babe into his arms. Olivia wandered across the beach her eyes following Raf, glimpsing him between the other newcomers strolling off the jetty, looking disorientated as if trying to fit this image of a colourful crowded beach with what they had seen in the news. What was Raf doing here in Madagascar? Her body tussled with the urge to run to him, to feel his arms around her and the need to restrain herself, to wait and plan her story. Olivia clenched her fists but failed to stop her wayward feet from taking her to him.

Raf saw her straight away and opened his arms, 'Olivia. Oh my god. Olivia. It's so good to see you.'

It would have been easy to throw herself into those arms. To imagine things had not changed between them. Her body ached to hold him.

'What are you doing here?' she asked, keeping her distance.

He dropped his arms and she saw the uncertainty in his eyes. 'I put myself forward for a job on The Mermaid when I heard what had happened …' He didn't add 'to you' but Olivia guessed his meaning. Raf had found out about her pregnancy and being Raf was here to do 'the right thing'.

'It's good to see you but there was no need. I heard that you got a job as a bar manager on New World.'

'I did. And then I asked to be moved to Mermaid of the Seas.' He narrowed his eyes.

'So, that's why you're here?'

He took a step closer and Olivia breathed in his scent before taking a step back.

'That's not the only reason. I wanted to see you.' He reached out his hands. 'Olivia?' A question furrowed his brow.

'Hey, Liv.' Luc called, holding Hal at arm's length.

'Is that your baby?' Raf said.

'Yes. Hal.' She wanted to tell him. She couldn't tell him. 'After Halcyon Seas. It was meant to be temporary but it kind of stuck.'

Luc was striding towards them cradling Hal on his shoulder.

'It was Luc who came to my rescue with my brother Pascal. They were going to take Hal home but as you know that didn't work out as planned.'

Luc was now by her side. Hal's eyes fixed on Raf.

'Can I hold him?'

The resemblance between father and son made her tummy flip. 'Maybe another time. He needs changing and a feed.' She tried to sound brisk but came over as flustered.

Luc whistled to Pascal to wait for him.

Olivia hissed to Luc in Malagasy, 'You are Hal's father. Don't forget you owe me after making me lose my job.'

He rolled his eyes and then kissed Hal before handing him back to Olivia. Then, as an after-thought, smacked her lightly on the bottom. If Luc thought that was what was required of him as a partner and a father then just as well, he wasn't either. Olivia laughed awkwardly as Luc nodded at Raf and then rushed off to tend to some project or other with her brothers.

They stood staring at one another. The unsaid words held them in a suspended world that neither wanted to break.

Raf said, 'Is he?'

'He needs feeding.'

'Sure.' He didn't move, just kept his eyes on her.

'I'm sorry.'

A few more seconds and she would have been in his arms. She turned and walked away from Raf for the second time in her life but this time it had to be the last.

52

It felt like the beginning of any cruise. All of the passengers had boarded. Mermaid of the Seas had a full crew. She was the captain of the ship and this time supported by an experienced chief engineer, first officer, hotel director, and cruise director. Alice Wagstaff, William Fellows, Richard and Barbara Lopez, and Patty Gray had decided not to sail with them. Jamboree had agreed to leave Halcyon Seas where it was under the supervision of a small team which included Gloria Busby. It would only be for a couple of months until it was ready to be towed away and scrapped but hopefully long enough for the volunteers to complete the freshwater project. It was less than three weeks until Christmas. They would inevitably lose some of the volunteers before then but Marianne was glad that the village would get a water supply. She hadn't been angry with Mr Rose and the local politicians for long. Maybe she was wrong to dismiss Olivia Rose but Marianne was confident that everything would work out for Olivia. There was nothing else that she could do here and yet she felt as though something had been left undone.

'He hasn't gone yet.' Gloria interrupted her thoughts.

'I don't know who you are talking about. Have you come to say goodbye?'

'Au revoir. If I don't join you on the Mermaid later, then maybe on another ship in the future.'

'Maybe. It's not too late for you to pursue your dream as a performer in your own right, Gloria. One thing I have learnt this past year is that we are never too old to make our dreams come true.'

'Or to discover a new passion, a different dream. I love coaching the choir even more than performing myself. Sometimes we have to open ourselves up to new possibilities and let something greater than what we envisioned find us. Are you sure that you're going to be okay? If you want to say goodbye to Paige Flynn and Ricky, they will be leaving with Gideon in a couple of hours.'

Marianne gave a weary smile. 'No, I hate goodbyes. Don't worry about me. I've got everything I ever wanted. Go and make music with your angels.'

~

Alice, pleased with her illustrations, was tidying away her watercolours when Rachel arrived breathless on the deck of Halcyon.

'Mummy. Could you look after my luggage for a few weeks?'

William pretended to be absorbed in writing his journal but Alice knew he would be as mystified as she was at Rachel's question. 'Whatever for, darling? We will be leaving for London in a few days.' William looked up at this comment and shot Alice a look. He must have been hoping that she had changed her mind. Alice wanted to hug him, to tell him that she didn't want to desert him.

'I'm going to join Ricky on a tour around Seychelles, once we drop Paige and Gideon off so that they can get a flight from Tana. Ricky can work from anywhere.'

'I don't understand, darling. What about your work? The enquiries you made about renting us a flat? Isn't this all a bit sudden?'

'Ricky says that I should be more spontaneous, like you. I arranged with work to have a month off anyway so that I could get you settled and celebrate Christmas with you. They were very understanding about your situation, with it all being on the news, and agreed that I needed to put you first.'

Alice waited for more, an explanation of how Rachel made the leap from supporting her and spending their first Christmas together in four years, to heading off on a month-long jaunt with what seemed to be a new boyfriend. When none was forthcoming, she probed just to make sure. 'Does that mean we won't be spending Christmas together?'

'Oh, Mummy! You don't need me, you've got William and all of your friends. So, is it okay to leave my suitcase in your cabin? I'll just take the rucksack. Oh, can I hang onto the lambas and your hat?'

Alice didn't want to lose her hat but the prospect of Rachel leaving without her more than compensated for the loss. 'Yes. Have you got everything else that you need?'

'I think so. My suitcase is under your bed. I'll pick it up around the new year. I'm not sure yet when we're coming back but I have to return to work by the 5th of January.' Rachel kissed Alice on both cheeks, a new affectation no doubt influenced by her current peers.

'Hold on. What about the flat in Bow? I thought you wanted me to pay the deposit so we didn't lose it.'

'Oh, you can go ahead if you like. I'm not sure of my plans.

Ricky says there's a great vibe around Brick Lane. He might even know some people who are looking for someone to share with them. Anyway, I've got to go now. They're all waiting for me.'

'We'll see you off.' William stood up and seemed to make himself taller. 'We don't want you missing your ride.'

Alice stifled the urge to laugh. This was typical of her daughter. Mum had to be one hundred per cent available when she felt needy but was discarded without a backward glance when her life was good. That was okay. Rachel was happy and that was a relief to Alice. It also meant that she was free to do what she wanted and that was to stay on the island with William, at least until Halcyon Seas was scrapped. Maybe by then, they would have made their shack habitable – or, be ready for another adventure. There were orchids all over the globe.

As they followed Rachel off the ship, William took Alice's hand and squeezed it. She slid him a knowing look, one that said. *I am so happy. We have the whole world before us.* Alice felt as though she were sixteen again.

A couple of photographers and other reporters were boarding the catamaran. Ricky waved to Rachel from the deck and she hitched up her rucksack before running to him. Alice wished that Rachel would hold back a little at least until she knew him better.

'Are you staying on Halcyon?' Gideon said, joining them on the jetty.

'We are now. William and I have work to do discovering new species of orchids and cataloguing them. We'll help with digging the trench and other duties of course. But it will be marvellous working in our shack again. How about you Gideon? Are you returning to London? I thought you would join Mermaid of the Seas. Isn't it fantastic that Captain Moore is going to transfer to the new ship?'

'It's great news.' He sounded sad and Alice wondered what had happened between the two of them. For a while, she had been convinced they were having an affair. 'I'm going back to London for a while. Not sure what my long-term plans are.'

'Well, say hi to Kate and tell her that we would love to see her if she fancies a trip to Madagascar.'

As they waved the boat off, William put his arm around Alice and she leaned into him. Their bodies fitted together perfectly as though they had always been a couple. She had found her home.

Marianne watched as the catamaran carrying Gideon, his daughter, and the reporters powered away from the jetty. It was not so long ago that she had jumped on board a fishing boat, knowing that Gideon was hiding in wait. She remembered the butterflies in her stomach as she took the boat out to sea, feeling but not seeing his presence. Sun on her skin. Salt on her lips. Full of expectation and longing. And then he had emerged from the cabin, tousle-haired, and freshly baked. His open shirt flapping in the wind. It had been torture keeping her hands off him. Waiting.

She could see Gideon on the deck now. He looked in her direction and she momentarily dropped the binoculars. Why hadn't he made more of an effort to say goodbye? To explain himself? If she had heard it from him, would it have made a difference?

'Are you okay?' It was Gloria again.

'Shouldn't you be on the Halcyon? If you're not careful we'll set sail with you on board. Yes, I'm okay. Thank you.' Marianne gave Gloria a hug. 'Thank you for being a friend as well as a dreadful hotel director.' She grinned. 'It was a big ask getting you to take on Hans's job as well as your own.'

'I never want to be a hotel director again, but I will *always* be your friend. Now I have my work cut out as our little choir of angels might be in demand. There are plans to release the song that has gone viral as a single to raise funds for the water project. One of the guys who arrived with Paige has been working with them. It's incredibly exciting.'

Marianne had said all of her goodbyes. Tonight, they would set sail and she would be greeting their passengers at the captain's welcome night.

53

Olivia had not seen Raf again, despite prowling around the jetty hoping to catch him arriving or leaving. That he had been so easily persuaded Hal was not his son, proved he was relieved. She had done the right thing and yet it felt wrong. Every ounce of her being ached to be with Raf, to tell him *this is your son*. She wanted them to be a family more than anything but it would never be.

'It's not fair that Kanto has a solo on our single. She's too young to be a pop star.' Gracie flounced around their hut, her over-excitement and frustration disturbing Hal, who let out a wail.

'For heaven's sake, haven't you got anything useful to do?'

'I'm going to join the choir and that is my point! Kanto is already there and everyone is treating her like some kind of superstar. I'm older than Kanto. It's not fair. I haven't even got a new dress to wear and we are going to be on the TV.'

'That is enough.' Mammon clapped her hands. 'All of this nonsense is going to your head. I will find you plenty of work

Gracie. For a start, you can empty the latrine. Pappa forgot to do it before he left for the shop.'

Gracie was up like a shot. 'Sorry, Mammon. I'm late for choir.'

Olivia could almost see the sand flying off Gracie's Cuban heels as she took off, a new plastic handbag slung over her shoulder.

'Seriously, I am worried about that child. Now that you are staying here you will have to try and reign her in, Olivia.'

'I can't stay here for long, Mammon. I need to find work in Malatanga or Tana. But I will try and help Gracie find her purpose.'

'That girl's purpose is to drive her mammon crazy. Are you taking Hal with you this morning?'

'Yes. I'll go and see what's happening on Halcyon now that Mermaid of the Seas has left. It will be strange not seeing Chef, Frederic, and the others.'

'So long as those young people keep digging our trench and helping with the harvest, I have no complaints. Just try and stop your sister from making a fool of herself. She is too young for boys and there are far too many of them around for my liking.'

It wasn't so bad, Olivia reassured herself, as she took the well-trodden path from their hut down to Halcyon Seas. The village was benefitting from the volunteers and use of the ship. Somehow, they had managed to keep up payments for the fishing boat and they had enough food and water to survive. If her heart wasn't breaking, she would be joyous. They were all healthy and she had a fine son. Olivia gave thanks to her ancestors as Halcyon Seas came into view.

Patty was helping the youngest children thread painted seeds into necklaces. She was assisted by three young Western women and Olivia felt a bit put out that she wasn't needed.

'Nonsense,' Patty said, patting the seat next to her. 'You are always needed. Settle Hal and then tell me the latest news.'

Olivia positioned Hal on her knee so that he could see what was going on. 'You are the one with news. Which staff have stayed on this ship apart from Gloria?'

'Haven't you met our manager? He's a darling. Good looking too.'

'No. Was he on Halcyon?' Olivia tried to think who it could be.

'Ah, here he is now.'

Olivia looked up to see Raf watching her from across the room. It was as though nobody else was there. If Patty was talking, she couldn't hear her. All she could hear was the beating of her heart as he crossed the room.

'May I?' Raf put out his arms to take Hal and Olivia's stomach cartwheeled.

She stood up and gently lowered Hal into his pappa's arms.

'When were you going to tell me?' Raf whispered as he offered a little finger to Hal who grasped it tight.

Olivia steered Raf away from the group. 'I thought you left on the Mermaid.'

'Did you want me to leave?'

'No. I mean yes. I didn't want you to compromise your future for us. I heard that you had met someone else.'

'I haven't been involved with anyone since you left me in Miami. If I hadn't been called to a meeting that day, I would have been there to wave you off. Every night I've been sending you my love on the North star, praying that I would find you again. When I heard about your pregnancy, I realised that Hal was my son but that wasn't why I came to find you. At least, it wasn't the only reason. I love you, Olivia. With or without Hal, I would have travelled across the world to be with you again. Maybe you don't feel the same way. I wondered at first if I had got it wrong – the way that you greeted me when I arrived.'

'I let you think that Luc was Hal's father.'

Raf laughed. 'I know enough Malagasy and can read body language to guess that you told Luc he was to pretend to be your partner. Not at all convincing. Especially when I asked one of the girls to come on to him and then ask him if he was single. I briefed her to ask Luc about you and the baby. Luc told her that he was just doing you a favour. So, your cover was blown. Sorry.'

'I'm not.' Olivia's heart felt as though it would burst with love for her two men. 'There has never been anyone else but you, Raf. I'm sorry to burden you with a baby before you are ready. That is the only reason I kept Hal from you. I would have told you in time – for Hal.'

'How can you be sorry for giving me this perfect little boy? Look, he has my nose and that expression is one hundred per cent you.'

'I think that face means he's done a poo.'

Raf laughed. 'I would change him but not a good idea when I'm wearing this white jacket.'

Olivia took Hal from him. 'Will you be returning to The Mermaid when Halcyon is scrapped?'

'I didn't tell you, because it would have sounded boastful but my family own a string of bars in California. My father wanted me to get my training in the cruise industry but I was always going to manage one of them. If you don't mind living in California?'

'You mean live with you and Hal? That you would give up working on a cruise ship? What would your parents say?' Olivia was afraid she would wake up and it would all be a dream.

'Are you kidding? Mom will love Hal. My parents are cool.

Dad will be pleased to have me managing one of the bars sooner than expected. But what about you? Won't you miss your family? Hal has two grammys – your mom will want to see him too.'

'Not just Mammon. Patty too. Come and meet her properly so I can introduce you as Hal's pappa. So long as I am with you and Hal I don't mind where we live.'

'Okay, but then, I want to meet your family.'

'My life here is a bit different to your family life in California.'

'Of course, it is. I've already visited your village and I've fallen in love with Madagascar.'

'I don't believe it. Olivia – everyone, look!'

Rain hammered against the windows. Whoops and cheers startled the babies who joined the cacophony with their own cries. Someone banged a tin mug with a spoon. Olivia jumped up and down. They had been sent rain. 'Come on.' She grabbed Raf's hand and pulled him through the lounge. Others were already on the stairs calling out to each other as they took them as quickly as they could – the young ones running and elders stopping to laugh and remark on the miracle of rain.

Raf stopped to remove his jacket and store it behind the security desk. Olivia didn't wait for him she ran across the gangplank and then the pier. She had to witness the riverbank receive this blessing, to watch the cracked earth fill with precious water, the ground baptised and replenished so that it glowed fiery red and burnished gold. Olivia opened her arms and spun round and round. She threw back her head to feel the rain on her face. It was a heavy downpour creating a silvery curtain so Olivia did not see Raf until he was up close. His shirt plastered to his chest was transparent.

'At home, we just put up an umbrella.' He laughed. Then he lifted Olivia up and spun her around.

The downpour was short and sharp. As the rain became a gentle cadence, a rainbow appeared. It was a sign from their ancestors – the promise of good things to come.

Patty joined them with Hal in her arms. 'Ain't it something? It smells so fresh. And the colours!'

Raf took Hal from Patty and held him up to his face. 'Did you see that, son? Your first experience of rain.'

Patty grinned. 'Son?'

'Patty this is Raf, Hal's pappa and my beloved. Raf this is my dearest friend and Hal's unpaid carer, Patty.'

Raf shook Patty's hand. 'Maybe we could steal Patty away with us to live in California as a paid nanny. You will need help with Hal.'

'You're going to California?' Patty hugged Olivia. 'I will miss you and Hal but maybe when I've finished my work here, I could take Raf up on that offer. Whatever happens, you're not getting rid of me. I consider myself Hal's honorary Grammy.'

54

TEN WEEKS LATER

'Live from New York City it's the Wendy Williams Show and here are our special hosts Kim Whitley and Finesse Mitchell.' Marianne watched from a monitor in her dressing room as the audience whooped and clapped. She practised cheering – waving her hands and jigging around, in the hope that she would release a bit of enthusiasm but the response was Meh.

'Marianne!' Gloria burst through the door and embraced her. 'It's so good to see you. Can you believe it – the UK Christmas number one and now we're topping the USA charts?'

'It's incredible. I knew you could do it. I'm so proud of you and your choir. What? Why are you looking at me like that?'

'Something's up. You got the job you wanted – the captain of Ionian's flagship no less, you are the darling of Cruise and Travel, a guest on the Wendy Williams Show and you've a face as long as a ladle.'

If Gloria had picked up on her mood, she had better up her energy before going out on stage. 'I'm great. Couldn't be better. Having the best time of my life – the job, all of this positive media attention – it's everything I wished for and more.'

'Then why am I not convinced?'

'Because you are a romantic looking for what you consider to be a happy ending. This is my happy.' Marianne faked a smile. 'Now go. You're on before me and we both know that choir are no angels.'

Gloria laughed. 'You're right there. They've been a handful I can tell you. Catch you after the show?'

'The choir will sing and then Kim and Finesse will chat with you and the men about your adventure,' a girl with a tablet explained whilst a make-up artist powdered Marianne's face.

'Men? Who's being interviewed with me?'

The girl consulted her tablet. 'A Richard Lopez and Gideon Flynn. Ready?'

No, she wasn't ready to see him. 'I didn't know. Perhaps you don't need me as well?'

'No, you are definitely expected. This way.'

Gideon and Richard were already on stage. Richard perched on the edge of a purple sofa; Gideon reclining, his feet stretched out in front of him. He looked good, she had to admit. His hair floppy as though freshly washed. He wore a soft denim shirt, neatly pressed. The man might be in his sixties but he looked like a rock star. As soon as Gideon saw Marianne, he sat up straight. For a moment she was afraid he would cross the stage to speak to her. Meeting him was hard enough without an attentive audience and a film crew.

'If you could sit on the sofa next to your friend.' The girl indicated a tight space next to Gideon. The sofas were way too small to accommodate two people comfortably. There was an empty sofa and Marianne was about to suggest she sit there when the audience started to cheer. It wasn't for her – their hosts had returned from interviewing Gloria and the choir on another set. The girl was waving frantically at Marianne so she took the hint and sunk onto the sofa next to Gideon. Her thigh pressed against his and she felt his muscles tighten.

The stage lights were making her hot. Her breath quickened. She focused on the faded black of Gideon's jeans. His hands hung loosely between his knees as though he were completely at ease. Kim Whitley was talking, introducing them all.

'I adore your shoes, Captain Moore. May I call you Marianne? Stand up, show us how tall you are.'

Marianne wished that she hadn't worn her five-inch heels. Getting off the low sofa was going to be a challenge. She would have stayed put but the audience was whooping like hyenas and so she had no choice. Gideon offered his arm for leverage and Marianne managed a graceful ascent.

'Isn't she gorgeous? A big hand for Captain Marianne Moore.'

Marianne hoped that the questions were not going to be about being a woman in a man's job or where she bought her shoes. She need not have worried because Kim moved quickly on to Gideon.

'We all heard about the pirate attack. Here is our hero of the day, Gideon Flynn.' More whooping.

Gideon was asked to relay the events which led to him falling overboard. He entertained the audience making them laugh and gasp. Throughout his interview, Gideon talked Marianne up – how she was an incredible captain, the excellence of the retirement cruise package, and his disappointment when it came to an end.

'But it didn't end there, did it? You and your daughter

Paige brought the work of your fellow passengers and Captain Marianne Moore to the attention of the world. You helped raise over thirty million dollars to bring fresh water to a remote village in Madagascar and other villages experiencing drought. I'm sorry Paige couldn't join us today. I understand that you were also instrumental in ensuring the future of a retirement cruise option.'

This was news to Marianne. She wriggled in her seat to try and get a view of his face but it was impossible.

'I felt responsible for Halcyon Seas getting a bad press. It's a great concept and I know many of my peers would have been disappointed if they could not live out their forever cruise.'

'And now I understand that they can alongside regular cruisers. I might sign up myself. Before we talk to Captain Moore about the future of retirement cruising let's move on to hear about developments in the Malagasy village that is home to the Choir of Angels. Richard Lopez ….'

Finesse, Kim's co-host, was talking over a sequence of shots that showed the water tap being turned on in the village. Marianne knew about the money raised, it was astounding that what started as an activity to keep the elders occupied and distracted from the interruption of their cruise had become a beacon of hope and inspiration to the world. It was true, if not for Gideon's intervention the trench would have been unfinished and forgotten. He had changed the lives of the people in Olivia's village and her own. She may have been appointed captain of the Mermaid or another cruise ship anyway, if not for the bad publicity, but she would not be in demand for chat show and magazine interviews. Marianne felt uncomfortable being in the spotlight but recognised the opportunities of having a public platform.

The audience was clapping and cheering. The topic had

changed and they were being directed off the set. Their eyes met. There was so much that needed to be said, Marianne could feel the words bunching up in her chest. But then he was gone. Led away in the opposite direction by one of the studio staff.

Gloria bounded over. 'Weren't they magnificent?'

Marianne could no longer see the blue of Gideon's shirt as people, props, and cameras came between them. 'Yes. Who?'

'The choir! Didn't you hear them?'

'Yes, they were amazing. Well done, Gloria. Do you know what that was all about – Gideon Flynn being "instrumental" in securing the retirement cruise option for Jamboree?'

'Ah that's what, or should I say who, is distracting you? Ask him.'

'Sure. Now tell me your news.' Marianne tried to give Gloria her full attention but part of her was still with Gideon, as though by holding him in her head and heart she would stop him from disappearing before they could talk.

Gloria paused and Marianne tried to remember what she had been talking about – an album? A show? 'That's fantastic,' she said.

'You haven't been listening to a word I said. Go and find him. It's what you should have done ten weeks ago.'

Richard and Barbara were in the guests' lounge drinking coffee. Marianne congratulated them on their success with one eye on the door. Gideon was bound to join them as soon as he had finished whatever it was that he had been whisked off to do.

'How are our fellow cruisers?' Barbara asked.

'Great. It's working well combining a retirement cruise

package with a regular cruise. Good of Gideon to support Jamboree.'

'Yes, he's a good man, Gideon.'

Marianne waited for more, hoping for an explanation. 'I thought I would find him here. I haven't had the opportunity to thank him personally.'

'Oh, Gideon left. He was in a hurry. I think he had a plane to catch.' Barbara barely paused before moving on to ask about news of Patty and Alice.

It was good to be reunited with her old friends but Marianne couldn't enjoy their company as she ached to put things right between her and Gideon. Gloria was right – everything may have been good in her world but without Gideon in her life it meant nothing. How could she have been so stupid to let him go? What more did he have to do to make up for his poor judgement?

Mermaid of the Seas was staying in New Jersey for a couple of nights. Guests welcomed the opportunity to see New York and Marianne's appearance on the Wendy Williams show had been scheduled to fit in with the cruise's itinerary. Back on the ship, Marianne made some enquiries and discovered Gideon Flynn invested in Jamboree's retirement package when McIntyre Retirement Living pulled out. Gideon must have assumed that she knew about his financial contribution. He must have thought her hard and unforgiving. If she had known he was going to be on the show then she might have done a bit of research first. Who was she kidding? Since becoming captain of the Mermaid she had tried to forget him.

'Will you be dining with the new guests this evening?' It was her cruise director, a handsome young man who would be causing a few hearts to flutter.

'Of course. My favourite night.'

It seemed that some of their guests chose Marianne's ship because they wanted to meet her. She had to pose for one selfie after another and sign anything from T-shirts to magazines with her face on the cover.

Marianne cast her eyes down the list of people who joined the cruise in New Jersey. *Gideon Flynn.* He had boarded the ship that afternoon. Gideon had left the studio in a hurry to board her ship. Her heart expanded, pressing against her rib cage. He was there – in the dining room, waiting for her. How was she going to keep her cool? To act professional?

'This passenger.' Marianne pointed to Gideon's name. 'Please could you locate him and ask him to meet me in private?'

'Now, Captain?'

'Yes, please. I will be late for the welcome dinner. There's some urgent business I need to attend to. I will be waiting for Mr Flynn in my private meeting room.'

He knocked on the door. Marianne steadied herself, leaning against the desk. 'Enter.'

He wore a silk patterned tuxedo in blues and purple with a black collar. A white shirt and groomed beard. 'Captain Moore.'

Marianne held his gaze. Words were not enough and she didn't know where to start. 'Gideon. I'm sorry to take you away from your table. I needed to speak to you alone. I don't think this will work.'

Gideon frowned.

'You being a passenger on this ship.'

'Sorry. I just thought with it being a five-day cruise that you would be okay with it. I wanted to talk to you and this seemed the only way. I'm sorry Marianne – for everything. If you want me to leave the cruise now I will, although I was looking forward to the lobster thermidor.'

Marianne crossed the room. His aftershave triggered memories she wanted to relive. 'I don't want you to leave but you can't be a paying passenger. It won't work having you this close and not being able to do this.' She kissed him.

Gideon wrapped his arms around her. 'Then what do you suggest, Captain?'

'You will be my personal guest. That's if you don't mind sharing my cabin?'

'I think I could rough it. Does that mean I'm forgiven?'

Marianne kissed him again. 'It does. Do you think it would be very unprofessional if I asked for our meal to be served in my suite?'

'Very.'

Marianne's suite and bedroom led off the private meeting room and that is where they stayed for the rest of the night. Tomorrow they were headed for Nova Scotia and that was as far ahead as Marianne wanted to think. She had spent her entire working life looking forward. It was time to take pleasure in the moment. Who knew what was over the horizon?

AUTHOR'S NOTE

I must confess that I have not yet visited Madagascar, although John Gimlette's wonderful book *The Gardens of Mars: Madagascar An island story,* and *Gone with the Wind in Madagascar: A cruise to an Indian Ocean paradise* by Avrill Sellars transported me to the island providing valuable information about the landscape and people.

I have travelled extensively across five continents and enjoyed many cruises. It was on a thirty-day cruise of Asia that I was inspired to write this story. A young woman working in the restaurant told me about her heartache in being parted from her infant son. Her story was similar to Charanya's and many of the staff who work on cruise ships sending money home to support their families.

Thirty days was a long time to be at sea enjoying a life of luxury and I questioned what if? What if we could end our days sailing around the world? Would this fulfil us or would we become restless looking for ways to make a meaningful and valued contribution to life?

In addition to the two books mentioned, and my own experience visiting impoverished homes and villages in Cambodia, and Africa, I found inspiration online. Below are just a few of the sites that informed this story. All of the links provided were last accessed on 8th August 2022.

https://www.cruisingworld.com/first-impressions-madagascar/

https://www.123rf.com/photo_18724042_malagasy-typical-village-in-nosy-be-north-of-madagascar.html

https://reliefweb.int/report/madagascar/don-t-look-other-way-madagascar-grip-drought-and-famine

I got the idea for the rainbow at the end of the story from this article:

https://www.wateraid.org/ca/stories/from-mountain-to-fountain-how-one-village-in-madagascar-got-clean-water

The idea for the Malagasy choir of angels came from this footage:

https://www.cbsnews.com/news/zaza-kanto-a-capella-group-young-boys-songs-of-joy-rise-from-the-slums-of-madagascar/

The village of Malatanga is fictional. I pinpointed a place on the map, South of Toliara, where there was an estuary from the Mozambique Channel. Although fictional, I checked the distance and travel times by sea and road from the location of this village to Antanarivo and Toliara.

Now that we can travel again, I am planning a trip to Madagascar. Researching and writing this story made me feel as though I was there so I hope it is every bit as wonderful as I imagine it to be.

ABOUT THE AUTHOR

Deborah has worked as an occupational therapist, a health service manager, a freelance journalist, and management consultant in health and social care.

In 2005 a national report she co-wrote and edited on behalf of health and social care regulatory bodies, *Living Well in Later Life,* was the UK's leading news story on publication day and resulted in a change of government policy improving services for older people.

Deborah writes page-turning, uplifting stories about friendship, community, and emotional courage. Her novels, *The Borrowed Boy,* and *Just Bea* have won multi-international awards.

Deborah lives on the Essex coast, where she loves to walk by the sea or the surrounding countryside filling her pockets with shells, and acorns, and her head with stories.

Visit me on my website at:

www.abrakdeborah.wordpress.com
Or follow me:
Twitter @DeborahKlee
Facebook: Deborah Klee Author
Instagram: deborahkleeauthor

If you enjoyed reading The Forever Cruise a review would be much appreciated as it will help other readers discover this story. A rating and/or just a few words would be great.

For behind-the-scenes information and other writing news subscribe to my newsletter:

www.abrakdeborah.wordpress.com

PRAISE FOR DEBORAH KLÉE

'What an amazing read I really didn't want this book to end… A heart-warming read with romance, mystery and a reminder that we're all human. Deborah's writing is a pleasure to read and I cannot wait to read her future releases.'

'Wow! this is a beautiful story, packed with emotional conundrums yet also tense and exciting. A lovely story told with heart and humour and one which will hold you rapt until the end.'

'Part mystery, part whimsy, and full of heart, this book will make you want to jump into your own life and live it!'

'Deborah Klée has again, created a story that draws you in immediately with fully rounded characters that you feel you really need to understand and want to get to know.'

'A lovely story, told with heart and humour and one which will hold you rapt until the end.'

'A heart-warming and emotional story that hits home a serious issue of today's society.'

'I am struggling to put into words how great this book is.'

'Such a clever, emotional read that entertains and informs.

I was really impressed by this author and will look forward to reading more.'

'The writing is stunning, with such clear description that I really felt I could be walking on the beach alongside Angie and Danny, following them on their journey. The characters are colourful and substantial.'

'An accomplished book that touches on a myriad of emotions whilst delivering an exciting plot that keeps you turning the pages.'

'I'm not quite sure where to begin with my review to do this book justice. I can honestly say that I've never come across a story like this with so many real-life twists and emotions. The characters were all wonderfully written, the scenery was brilliantly described and the plot was well-thought through. A combination of the mystery, my connection to the characters and the short chapters left me promising myself 'just one more chapter'. A thoroughly enjoyable book with unknown depths and a gritty real-life edge to it.'

ACKNOWLEDGMENTS

My husband and travel companion, named Mr Long Island by a waiter on a cruise ship because his favourite cocktail is Long Island Tea, for our shared memories of cruises and the many lands we have visited together.

A huge thank you to Ellie Holmes because without her encouragement this story idea would have been abandoned before it was written. To the Frinton Writer's group, many of whom were beta readers: Paula Guyver, Janet Bridger, Catherine Rendall, Anita Belli, Peter Best, Gerald Hornsby, Janine Swann, and Annika Dann. And to Sue Chotipong a beta reader and patient friend who listens to all of my writer talk.

To editors and proofreaders: Paula Guyver, and Laura-Jade Vaughan. And to Asya Blue for yet another beautiful cover design.

Here's a sneak preview of my next book: The Last Act

THE LAST ACT

PROLOGUE

The Victorian theatre was already ablaze. It illuminated the sky as if turning a spotlight on the pink, green, and lavender doves that swooped in circles, as bewildered as the onlookers.

Fifteen minutes earlier, Howdy! magazine's junior reporter had been sitting in the front row between an enthusiastic man from The Evening Standard, and a talkative lady from The Tatler, wondering at her fortune in being asked to cover the prestigious Golden Globe Easter Gala. The press had been invited to witness a new talent that would change the face of theatrical magic. Top producers had already offered contracts, there was talk of a TV series and film rights.

When flames leapt from the stage floor, she had sat on the edge of her seat intrigued. There had been a murmur of approval. The audience was gripped.

'Fire! Fire! Evacuate the building.' It took a few seconds for her to register – this wasn't an act. The theatre was on fire.

Outside a fuffle of bunny girls huddled together, men's jackets draped over their shoulders.

'Do we know how the fire started?' the Howdy! reporter asked as she edged her way into the circle of puff ball tails.

'We were in the bar. You probably know more than we do.'

In the distance, a siren wailed. The theatre was crackling now, reminding her of bonfires and fireworks when she was a child. A parrot's squawk pierced the night, another refugee from the burning building.

'You can't stand there. The assembly point is in The Strand.' A man in an orange tabard tried to shepherd them.

An explosion. Screams. People were running towards the theatre. Blue lights flashed.

'Keep away from the building. Make your way to the Strand.'

She watched the chaos and felt sick. If anyone was still in the theatre, they wouldn't have survived. The man from the Evening Standard was taking photos. Damn, she didn't have a camera – only a notebook and her ears. Listening, and observing were what she did best. Nobody seemed to notice her as she wove in and out of groups eavesdropping on conversations. This was how she came to discover a much bigger story than the fire which destroyed The Golden Globe Theatre.

Now, nearly a year on, she had interviewed everyone concerned. It was the perfect time for Howdy! to publish this compelling story. The scribbled notes blurred and danced before her tired eyes. She took a slug of strong coffee and turned the page.

. . .

'I don't care what anyone says, it was the curse of Molly May. It had been going on for years – unexplained accidents and the like. If you were alone in the theatre at night, you'd hear her, a horrible moaning and rattling. I only stayed once on my own, never again. There were mice too, and rats. They'd run over your feet when the lights went out. Well, I thought they were rats, now I'm not so sure.' Sly shivers, then lowers her voice leaning in, 'I reckon Molly May had something to do with that other girl's disappearance. It was only a matter of time before something really bad happened.' Sly Fitzgerald, Hocus Pocus dancer.

'The Globe was a beauty, that's for sure. Everything preserved just as it was in her day. They don't make them like that anymore: the mechanics, the pulley systems, the workings under the stage. Before Peter Walker took it on, there was talk of turning it into a museum of Victorian magic. It would have rivalled the set-up they have at The Magic Circle, by all accounts. But he had big ideas. Wouldn't be told about what needed doing to make it safe. I swear I tried. Maybe I should have tried harder. Don't write that down. It was an accident waiting to happen.' Pedro Lopez – Caretaker and Front of House.

'It started with a bit of kit falling from the gantry. That was no accident, someone or something must have meddled with it for that to happen. I'm not saying nothing like that happened before, it did. But that was when it got me thinking. I started watching out for things and when you do that, you see things that others don't.' Lenny points to his eyes. 'You know what I mean? Well, I saw, and I saw that things weren't right. I just wished I'd said something sooner. Before it was too late.' Lenny Charles – Stagehand.

She had read and reread the stack of notes. Circled and underlined. Now, the truth was clear. The story to be told. It had started when Nico walked into The Hawley Arms and on meeting the beautiful Jojo Evans, conjured three white doves to fly out of her handbag. Because from that moment on Jojo was under his spell.

CHAPTER 1

FEBRUARY 1980

The stage was partly lit casting a pearly blue mist around Jojo's feet. A spotlight shimmered centre stage, a ghost of the last performance. The seats now empty. Sometimes, she had to hug herself to affirm that she was really here. Everything about her life was different. She was a professional performer –paid a proper wage to do what she loved best. Magician's assistant was the first rung of a ladder – Jojo knew that she could be more. But this – everything, her life with Nico, the flat they shared... Where was Nico? She was meeting Annie in fifteen minutes. Jojo strode across the stage to stand in the spotlight. If he was in the auditorium, he would see her.

'Nico? You there?' Her voice loud, with no audience to absorb the noise, bounced off the walls. She held up a hand to shield her eyes. 'Nico, I'm going now. To meet Annie.'

Something moved. A scraping sound and then a squeak, like a lazy gate swinging on its hinges. Jojo shivered. The ancient mechanics that swung above the stage and turned noisily beneath, gave her the jitters.

'Nico?' There was something out there moving within the shadows.

'Watch out!' Nico seemed to come out of nowhere. He pushed her with force and before she could yell in protest there was a resounding thump on the stage behind her.

She tried to turn around to see what had happened but he held her tight. Too tight. 'I'm okay.' Still, he held her, his body rigid, unyielding, as though she were clamped in iron. Jojo could barely breathe. 'I'm okay. I'm okay.'

He relaxed and Jojo took a few seconds to steady herself. His arms were still around her but no longer trapping her movement. She turned to see a shaft of metal lying across the stage. It was in the spotlight where she had been standing. Jojo's knees wobbled and she grasped Nico for support.

'Oh my god. It could have killed me.'

Nico hugged her, gently now. 'Don't. I can't bear to think what might have happened.

Charlie joined them on the stage. 'I don't know how that came loose. I checked it myself. Are you okay Jojo?'

She felt Nico's body tense; his attention now on the stage-hand. Like a cat arching his back. 'I'm fine Charlie. I'm just glad Nico was there to save me.'

'Yes. What good luck.' Charlie said, with an attitude that did nothing to diffuse the growing tension.

Not this again. Not now. Why couldn't the two of them get along? Nico charmed every woman young or old; he was popular with the other magicians and stagehands. Likewise, Charlie was everyone's friend. A joker. One of the hardest working stagehands and a good friend to Jojo. When Nico had introduced her to The Golden Globe as his assistant, she had been overwhelmed. It was an enchanting place to work, but there was an undercurrent born from ambition, jealousy, and fragile egos. If Charlie hadn't come to her rescue in that first difficult week, when the showgirls were eyeing her with suspicion, and Nico was preoccupied talking prop design with the technicians, then Jojo may not have been accepted so quickly. She had been reading a DC comic in Cake Presto, the Globe's café when Charlie joined her table. They discovered a shared love of comic books, although Charlie favoured Marvel. From there on they adopted an easy banter and to the rest of the performers, it was as though Jojo had always been one of the troupe. Unassuming, funny, and down-to-earth, Charlie created calm in a storm. Nobody was threatened by him and so under his cloak of protection, Jojo had slipped into the life of the Globe without creating many waves. Nobody that was except for Nico. Charlie and Nico were facing one another now like a showdown at high noon.

Exasperated, Jojo broke away. 'I'm going to be late.'

'Surely, you're not still going to meet your friend? Not after a shock like that?' Nico said.

Charlie rolled his eyes before leaving them alone on the stage.

'It's fine. I'm over it now. Nothing happened. You saved me.'

'Let's have a quiet night in.' His warm breath tickled her ear. 'If you go home now and run a bath, I'll join you when I've finished here. A couple of sirloin steaks with salad. A bottle of Beaujolais.'

It was tempting. They had been rehearsing for ten or twelve hours, every day that week and she was exhausted. Jojo checked her watch behind his back. 'Mmm. But no. I can't. Annie will be waiting.'

Nico pressed against her and she felt him grow hard. 'If you're sure that's what you want to do.' He had mischief in his eyes.

Damn him, no wonder she couldn't concentrate on

anything else. Jojo backed away from 'essence of Nico,' the unique scent of his warm skin, a lingering scent of olives, and a delicious cedar aftershave. 'No. But it's what I have to do.'

Nico shrugged and raised his palms in defeat. 'Go then. Give Annabelle my regards.'

When Jojo glanced back at the stage, Nico had already left. The spotlight died. One stagehand called to another. Then all was quiet. And dark. Jojo stood still, waiting for her eyes to adjust. Someone else was there; she could feel their presence pressing against the darkness. A chair squeaked. Jojo scanned the balcony boxes. 'Who's there?'

It would be easy to let her imagination run away with her. There was bound to be creaking in a place that old. The rows of seats were visible now and she made her way towards the illuminated exit at the back of the theatre. A voice startled her.

'I saw what happened. Freaky.' It was Bobbi, one of the showgirls, who was sitting in the back row, her long legs slung over the seat in front. She blew out a plume of smoke. 'Don't tell.'

'Jiminy Jillikers. You scared the life out of me.' Jojo wasn't surprised that Bobbi was smoking in the theatre. Bobbi was the kind of girl who had probably been breaking rules all of her life just for the hell of it, but why was she lurking back there in the dark? 'Funny place to chill. Sitting here with the lights out.'

Bobbi laughed. 'It's perfect. Don't you love this old theatre when it's quiet? You can sense its magic. A place absorbs everything – good and bad. I bet this theatre holds a few secrets. Like who, or what pushed that lump of metal just now.'

Jojo shivered. 'It was an accident. Unless you saw something we didn't?'

Bobbi shrugged, 'I saw Nico save your life. Lucky, he knew it was about to fall.'

Jojo didn't have time to gossip. The story of the falling kit would be known by everyone in the Globe by the following morning, exaggerated beyond recognition. Theatre folk loved embellishing the truth. 'He did. My hero!'

'It's not the first time something like that has happened,' Bobbi said, flicking her ash onto the threadbare carpet.

'What do you mean?' She had to ask; Bobbi wasn't going to let her go until she had told her story.

'Unexplained accidents. Things falling from the gantry. Objects flying across the stage as though they had been thrown. Restless spirits. Ghosts.'

The hairs prickled on Jojo's neck. It was nonsense. She laughed under her breath. 'Spooky.'

Bobbi stood up and stretched, arching her back. 'A double scotch is what you need darling.

She did need something strong, but it would have to wait until she was with Annie. 'I can't I'm meeting a friend.' Jojo checked her watch; she was already fifteen minutes late.

As Jojo ran the best she could in her clumpy boots, it felt as though she was being pulled in opposite directions: Nico willing her to stay, Annie claiming the friendship of a lifetime – her neglected friend. Jojo stopped to catch her breath. Nico had seemed disappointed. Maybe he had forgotten she was going out. If he had planned a special meal perhaps, she should go home to be with him. Annie would understand. When Jojo imagined explaining to Annie, telling her about the near miss, she guessed her friend's reaction. She would be outraged on Jojo's behalf. Since they were little kids, she had taken on the role of her protector. Jojo smiled to herself, dear Annie. She set off again for Lee Changs. Somehow, between rehearsals and being with Nico, she would find more time to see her friend.

CHAPTER 2

Annie had ordered a bottle of Liebfraumilch and nearly finished her first glass of wine, when Jojo blew in like a colourful whirlwind, in a psychedelic mini dress of purples, pinks and green, her auburn hair in a high ponytail. Today it was a 1960's look, but it could have been any outfit from the 1920s through to the 1970s. Pleasure at seeing her dearest friend was tempered with annoyance. It was the first time they had met in weeks and Jojo was forty minutes late. Annie resolved not to ask about the theatre or Nico; that's all Jojo wanted to talk about. No, let Jojo ask about *her* life for a change. Annie poured Jojo a glass of wine.

'Oh, I need this!' She held up her glass and grinned. 'Annie Apple Cheeks. It is so-oo good to see you. Cheers!'

Annie smiled, at Jojo's irrepressible energy and joy for life. 'So, what kept you this time?' Her voice was playful, disguising any lingering resentment.

'Same old. Rehearsals. You know what Nico's like.'

Annie wanted to talk about something else, like her parents' announcement that they planned to sell up and move to Scotland, but this was a red flag. 'No, Jojo. I don't know what Nico is like. I've never met him.'

'You will, I promise. In fact, come to The Golden Globe on your day off and we'll meet for a cream tea in Cake Presto.'

Annie pursed her lips unwilling to let Jojo off that easily.

'A nice bit of Battenberg,' Jojo coaxed. 'I know! Mrs Brew does a fabulouser Black Forest gateau.'

'Okay. Okay. It's a date. But don't leave me sitting in there like one of your forgotten props. Tell me a time and I'll be there.'

'Promise.' Jojo said this softly and reached for her hand.

Annie wanted to cling tight. To beg Jojo to come back. To be the way they were a year ago, before she met Nico, instead she smiled. 'It's a date. Now let's order.'

The waiter had been hovering by their table, since Jojo's arrival. Lee Chang's was busier than usual, with it being a Friday night and still early enough for pre-theatre diners. Some office workers - men in suits and girls in heels - were a little raucous, celebrating the start of the weekend. They had probably been drinking since lunchtime.

Annie ordered more than she could eat because Jojo never ordered enough and always ended up eating everything in sight.

'When's your next public performance? It's about time I saw you in this act with the Amazing Nico.'

'The *Incredible* Nico.' Jojo did jazz hands. 'In four weeks, but it's a really important one. The Starlight show attracts some of the top talent scouts and decides who will be the last act at the Easter Gala.'

As dishes arrived at their table, Annie organised them. She topped up their glasses, emptying the bottle. 'Is it important, who does the finale?'

Jojo dropped a spring roll from her chopsticks. 'Jiminy

Jillikers! Of course, it's important. The press know that the last act is the one that's attracted the attention of the talent scouts. You've no idea how many famous magicians made it to the big time because of Easter Gala. Yes. It's important. It's a *really* big deal.'

'Okay,' Annie said with care. She did seem to have lost touch with Jojo, but she would visit her for tea at Cake Presto, and go to this important show. Envy? Jealousy? A little green worm had been eating at her soul and Annie was ashamed. 'Then I wish you success.' She raised her glass. 'To the Incredible Nico and his even more incredible assistant Jojo!'

'Are you going to eat the rest of those pork balls?'

'No, help yourself.' Annie smiled, as she watched Jojo checking with her before finishing up everything on the table, just as she had predicted.

'Jessica's getting married,' Annie said.

'Really? Your little sister. When did she get old enough to even have a boyfriend?'

'I know.' There must have been something in her voice because Jojo stopped eating and gave Annie her full attention.

'That's good, right?'

'I guess.' But it wasn't. Everyone was moving on in their life except her. 'He seems a nice bloke – Gary. They met at a bowling alley.'

Jojo scooped some rice from the bottom of her bowl. The meal was over. Soon, Jojo would leave, but Annie wasn't ready to say goodbye.

'Do you remember when you first started at our infant school – Brookfields? You would stand on your own in the playground and be so absorbed in your game, that I was afraid to talk to you. It was as though you were surrounded by imaginary friends.'

'I probably was. I got used to being on my own at home. I

remember you beating up Simon Pugh because he was calling me names.'

'I didn't beat him up. He was making fun of you. Simon wasn't known for *his* imagination.'

'Whatever you said, or did, it worked. With Annie Apple-cheeks as my friend, nobody messed with me again.'

They both laughed, although this was a story frequently told. It reaffirmed the bond between them, but that evening Annie sensed their ties weakening.

'How are your parents?' Jojo asked.

It felt as though Jojo was checking she had covered all that was expected of her before she returned to a world that Annie knew nothing about. 'They're talking about moving to Scotland.'

'Oh,' Jojo said, and Annie was pleased that she had saved this important news. 'Does that mean they will sell your house?'

'Yes. Once Jessica's married. Dad wants to return to his Highland roots and Mum's ready for a change.' Annie sighed.

'What about you? Where will you live?'

Annie wanted to wail, *I don't know. I'm lost. I'm scared. I'm lonely.* 'I'll find somewhere,' she said.

'Shall we get the bill then?'

So that was that. Annie had dropped her bombshell, but it barely made a ripple on the surface of Jojo's world. Annie knew that her friend had already disconnected and was mentally making her way home to the Incredible Nico.

Whilst Jojo was digging around in her bag, Annie said, 'What about Monday?'

'For what? I can never find anything in here.'

'Give it to me,' Annie reached out a hand and Jojo passed her the battered leather bag. 'I've not seen this before. Did you get it from Portobello Road or Camden market?'

'No. It belonged to a magician – a Gladstone bag. I found it in the props room and Charlie said I might as well take it because it would only get thrown away.'

'Well, it's ridiculous. You can't find anything in here.'

'It is a magic bag,' Jojo laughed. Annie rummaged and then held aloft Jojo's green purse.

'So, Monday? For afternoon tea?'

'Oh. Okay. I think that's alright, but we're really busy with rehearsals for the Starlight show.'

'Fine.'

'But I will be there. I promise. About four?'

They hugged each other goodbye. Jojo said she would get a taxi and offered Annie a lift, but they were going in opposite directions.

It was still light and the streets buzzed with anticipation for the weekend as girls with big hair, dressed in animal print and silks strode with meaning and young men with attitude gave them the eye. Everyone was going somewhere except for Annie. Before Jojo moved in with Nico they might have met up on a Saturday in Camden to scour the market stalls looking for old clothes for Jojo. *I'll spend the evening with Mum for a change. Buy her a box of orange Matchsticks, her favourite, and we'll watch Dallas together.* But Annie's heart was heavy. She knew that one day Jojo would meet someone, that their lives would take them in different directions. It was just that Jojo knew where she was going, and Annie had no idea. It was as though she had been waiting for the right bus to come along, watching everyone else leave. Then, when she was alone at the bus terminal, the news that there would be no more buses. Her bus had come and gone without her.

. . .

Annie only worked at the travel agents on Saturday mornings and so by mid-afternoon she was back home. When she popped her head around the kitchen door to say hello, Annie was greeted by the comforting smell of baking. 'I thought I'd stay in tonight Mum. Have a bit of a girls' night. We haven't done that in a long while.'

Janet Daley wiped her hands on her apron. 'What a good idea. We haven't seen Jojo for a long while.'

Jessica joined them. She leaned against the kitchen counter and eyed the warm fairy cakes. 'Isn't she shacked up with some Italian stud in the West End?'

How could Jessica be her sister? They were so different. Annie sighed. 'Jojo is living with her boyfriend, Nico, who also happens to be her stage partner.'

'That's what I said. And he's Italian, right?' Jessica reached for a cake and Mum swiped her hand with a tea towel.

'At least wait until they've cooled down. This batch is for the freezer and they're not for you. They're for the WI Spring fayre. Margaret did tell me that Jojo hadn't been home in a while, but I don't think she knows Jojo's living with an Italian.'

'We don't even know if he is Italian.' The sharp tone in Annie's voice caused her mum and Jessica to throw questioning looks. She softened it. 'Jojo's mum and dad don't know anything about him because he makes no effort to meet with her family or friends. *I've* not even met him.'

'But he is Italian,' Jessica said. Somehow, she had managed to sneak a cake unnoticed and was talking through a mouthful.

'So, he would have us believe, but as far as I can make out, he hasn't told Jojo anything about his life or upbringing. I tried to warn her about moving in with a man she knows nothing about, but you know what she's like. Anyway, Jojo's not coming over. I thought you and I could watch Dallas together Mum.'

'Hmm. Why don't you sit down, Annie love? I'll make a pot of tea and we'll sample this bake. There'll still be plenty for the Spring Fayre.'

'Why does she get offered one and not me?'

'Because you've already helped yourself.'

'Oh-ho. Sounds like you're in for a mother-daughter chat.' Jessica stole two more and scurried from the room before she was caught.

Annie unpacked a Radio Times and the Matchmakers from her bag. She flicked through to Saturday evening's entertainment. 'Perfect. Love Story is on straight after Dallas.'

Her mum fussed around with plates, and tea things then sat down heavily opposite her. 'That would be lovely, but your dad and I are having dinner with the McIntyres. I'm sure we told you.' She cocked her head. 'You've been a bit out of sorts. Is something troubling you?'

'No. Not really.' Annie sighed. She didn't know why she felt so lost. It wasn't Mum and Dad's plans to move to Scotland, or Jessica getting married. She missed spending time with Jojo, but it wasn't just that. 'I'm probably tired. A quiet night in is exactly what I need. It's been busy at work with everyone booking their summer holidays. It's okay, I'll watch Love Story and eat all of the Matchsticks.'

Her mum poured the tea. 'Meanie. Save a few for me. I know you miss Jojo. You've been a good friend to her. Poor kid had a hard time of it at home; just as well she had you.'

'And her imagination,' Annie added.

Her mum smiled. 'Yes, she has plenty of that. But what about you darling?'

A lump formed in Annie's throat. That was it. She had no imagination. If she had a smidgen of Jojo's creativity then she might be able to see a life beyond the family home in Fenwood and working as a travel agent. But she couldn't. Her horizon was bleak. Empty. 'I'll think of something,' Annie said.

'You're a born carer. Jojo doesn't need you to look after her now that she's a grown woman. What you need are children of your own.'

Jessica stomped into the kitchen hauling a bag containing her bowling ball and shoes. 'She'd have to find a man first, and that's not going to happen.'

Annie wanted to throw the ball at her sister. Knock her down like a bowling pin. 'There are plenty of men who are interested in me.'

'True. But none of them survives beyond a first date with the ice queen.'

Mum shook her head in exasperation and started to clear away the plates.

'Just because I'm discerning.'

'Nobody's good enough. You know that you're going to end up living on your own with a load of cats.'

'Fine. I'd rather share my life with cats than geting married for the sake of it. I don't need a man.'

Later that evening, when the house was quiet Annie relaxed in a warm bath sprinkled with Radox salts and breathed in the scent of pine. Finding a man of her own was not the answer to her problems, but maybe she should be a little more open-minded. Nobody was perfect, including herself. Perhaps she did set her expectations too high and was a little quick to judge. It was a big commitment to get involved with someone. If she was too cautious then Jojo was the opposite. Jojo was fearless. She took risks, trying out new things as though selecting an outfit from her dressing-up box.

Annie was happy to be led by Jojo: discovering Camden market together, helping Jojo set up her street performances – collecting the money thrown into a hat. One Saturday they had hired roller skates and taken them to Hyde Park. Life without Jojo was like champagne with no bubbles. Annie sighed and hauled herself out of the cooling water. The bath salts had almost completely relaxed her, but one worry would not be washed away. It niggled like a burr beneath her skin. She was afraid for Jojo and didn't understand why. Was she being overly suspicious or just a teeny bit jealous of Nico? Maybe, but there was something else. Jojo seemed distracted – entranced. It was as though she was watching her friend, but they were separated by an invisible screen. She couldn't reach her. On Monday, she would meet Jojo at Cake Presto with an open mind. She would reach into Jojo's world and reassure herself that all was as it should be.

CHAPTER 3

'Don't you have a leotard from your days as a dancer, bella?' Nico watched as Jojo tossed garments out of an old trunk, a pained expression on his face.

'Those horrid lycra things with legs cut up to the waist? No thank you. Ah, my polka dot 50s skirt. That'll do if I wear it without the petticoats.' Next, Jojo threw open the lid of a vintage hatbox which was stuffed full of ribbons, evening gloves, silk stockings, and other accessories to complete her outfits, and chose a matching red ribbon.

Nico groaned. 'We should have left by now.' He squatted alongside her and screwed up his nose as he peered into the trunk. 'There must be something more suitable for climbing in and out of props.'

A wing of black hair fell across one eye and Jojo gazed at him in wonder. He was so perfect. So beautiful. She let the ribbon slide from her fingers and draped herself across his back.

'What on earth is this?' Nico held up a fur stole with a fox's head.

'That's Freddy. He looks real but he's not. I found him in my granny's attic. He was all alone, curled up in the bottom of that very trunk. Which is *now* my dressing up box.'

Nico dropped Freddy and shivered. 'It's disgusting.'

'Don't be mean to Freddy.' Jojo rescued the faux fur from Nico. It was one of her most precious acquisitions, not just because of the family history, her grandfather had saved for months to buy it for her grandmother but because it was a collector's piece being in such good condition.

'Come on find something. Anything. We're late.'

'You don't mean *anything*, otherwise, you'd be okay with my polka dot skirt. But I'll find something else.' She sighed.

'Just something a bit more…'

'Debbie McGee? Nico, I don't want to look like every other magician's assistant. I want to look like *me*. The day you wear a high-cut satin leotard I will but until then…'

'Okay. Okay. Five minutes and then we've got to leave.'

They were greeted at The Golden Globe by three teenage girls and a gawky boy brandishing autograph books. Nico gave his pseudo-shy smile and Jojo witnessed the melting of at least two hearts. Always the showman he pretended to search for his fountain pen, flourishing silk handkerchiefs from a pocket, and then a bouquet of paper flowers which he presented to the prettiest girl, a tall blonde. Nobody was interested in Jojo. 'I'll go ahead then,' she said.

'Okay,' he said without looking up. 'Room three.'

The rehearsal and prop rooms were in an extension of the theatre. There was a back entrance, but Nico and Jojo always arrived at the front of house and walked through the theatre. Nico to please his fans; Jojo because she liked to stop at the altar of her dreams - the stage with its velvet curtains. One day she would be the star act. The audience would hold their breath in awe and disbelief as she performed an illusion that defied expectation.

'Miss Jojo?' Pedro, the caretaker, interrupted her daydream. 'Someone left this at the box office for you.' Her heart lifted; she had a fan. But no, it was addressed to Nico's Assistant. Not Jojo Evans. It was just another way for one of Nico's fans to get his attention. Jojo hoped it wasn't a pair of panties. The last ones, revolting pink kami knickers, she had thrown with a pincer grip into the bin. And to think Nico had the affront to turn up his nose at Freddy the Fox.

Hocus Pocus had just finished a workout and the changing room was fragrant with peach, apple, and cucumber gels melding in the steam of showers. Jojo unzipped her white boots - a buy from Oxfam. They went well with the bibbed 60s hotpants that she had chosen to wear that day as a compromise, as well as the psychedelic dress she had worn the previous day. Besides, Nico couldn't resist them. She remembered his passion last night when she returned from dinner with Annie.

'A good night?' Bobbi smirked, interpreting Jojo's expression correctly.

'I'd better learn to be less transparent if I'm to become a magician,' Jojo laughed.

Bobbi finished wiping her face with a cotton wool ball - the almond scent of Anne French cleansing milk, familiar and comforting. She paused, watching Jojo's reflection. 'Is that what you want? To be a magician in your own right?'

Why had she said that out loud? Jojo felt her cheeks flush. 'No. I mean, I don't know. Maybe.' Was she greedy wanting more when she had all this? 'I just think I could contribute more to our act.' Now she felt disloyal.

Bobbi released her hair and it fell about her shoulders. She swivelled around to face Jojo. 'Even if Nico's ego allowed it, I doubt Peter Walker would. This place is stuck in the 50s. Haven't you noticed all of the women performers are either dancers or assistants? It's fine when you're starting out, but when you get to my age you need a bit more security. This face and these,' she pushed up her breasts, 'aren't going to be enough when I turn forty.'

Apart from the trickle of a shower, they were alone in the changing room. It was a rare moment for Bobbi to share something so personal with her and Jojo was both surprised and honoured. 'That's a long way off.'

'Unfortunately, not. I wanted to star in West End shows and look at me now.'

Jojo did and she saw the Globe's most talented and successful dancer, a woman who possessed effortless grace and worldly sophistication. To say this would give away her inferiority and Jojo wanted to hang on to the feeling of being Bobbi's equal for just a little bit longer. 'What about the classes you teach at The Mango? Couldn't you set up your own dance school?'

Bobbi gave a half-hearted chuckle and stood up. Dressed in a luxurious velour leisure suit she was on her way out. 'Saturday Night Fever started something of a craze, but how long will that last? Anyway, we were talking about you. What is it that you think you could introduce to Nico's act? And I warn you, for all of his sexy charm, our Nico is a bit of a chauvinist.'

Jojo didn't like to hear Bobbi speak badly of Nico, but she suspected Bobbi was right. 'I don't know. Ariel acrobatics. Juggling. I can do more than contort my body. I trained as a dancer too.'

'Wow. You can do ariel acrobatics?' Bobbi seemed genuinely impressed. 'Could you teach me? Nothing complicated. It would be perfect if I added that to the Hocus Pocus routine. Just something simple for the matinee which starts in three weeks. I've put Adele Pearson, owner of Mango, on the guest list. I doubt she'll show up for any of the shows but if she does, she'll be so impressed. We have a harness and the wires.' Bobbi was almost jumping up and down in her excitement.

Jojo glowed with pride. Bobbi wanted her, Jojo, to teach her something. 'Of course, I can.' She hoped that Nico would release her from their gruelling routine to work with Bobbi.

'And you know the world is changing? Peter Walker might be a bit behind the times, but he can't hold back the revolution in entertainment.' In response to Jojo's frown, she continued, 'Monty Python transformed the comedy scene, The Sex Pistols, music. Maybe it's time Jojo Evans transformed the world of magic.' Bobbi winked, and Jojo felt as though she had been accepted into Bobbi's exclusive club. An outsider at school, she had just become the confidante of the most popular girl at The Golden Globe.

'I'll start work on Nico. Try and persuade him to let me improvise.' Already her mind was racing ahead with possibilities. There wouldn't be time to change their act before the Starlight show, but there was no reason why they couldn't work together to create something unique. Bobbi was right – everything was changing in the world of entertainment. Traditional cabaret acts would soon be passe. They could be at the leading edge of change. New wave magic.

'Late afternoons are good for me if you could find some time this week,' Bobbi said, slinging a pink leather duffel bag over her shoulder.

Jojo nodded eagerly. Nico wouldn't like it, but she would just have to make up the time by starting rehearsals earlier.

It wasn't until she was alone that Jojo remembered the letter passed to her by Pedro. There was just one typed line.

If you value your life keep away from him.

She turned the paper over looking for an explanation. Nothing. Then, she searched for the envelope, but it was empty. Was it a warning or a threat? A deranged fan? Surely, it wasn't a threat to her life. Jojo's instinct was to tell Nico but she knew what he was like. He would become obsessed with the note when in reality it was probably nothing. There was no point winding him up, especially with the Starlight show fast approaching. He was already on edge, driving them both relentlessly, and over-reacting to any imagined threat. Take the falling gantry, for example. Jojo was tired of hearing about Charlie's incompetence and how she could have been killed. Nico would be unbearable if he saw this note and it would affect his performance. She didn't want him throwing knives at her if his mind was elsewhere. She pushed the note deep into her bag, thankful that it would get lost in there.

Printed in Great Britain
by Amazon

25591564R00240